Glorified
Nine~Patch

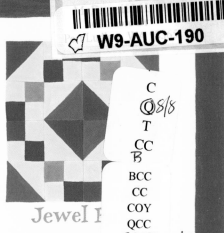

Jewel B

Jack
in the Pulpit

Rosebud

Sawtooth Star

Castle Wall

The Winding Ways Quilt

An Elm Creek Quilts Novel

Jennifer Chiaverini

DOUBLEDAY LARGE PRINT HOME LIBRARY EDITION

Simon & Schuster

New York   London   Toronto   Sydney

This Large Print Edition, prepared especially for Doubleday Large Print Home Library, contains the complete, unabridged text of the original Publisher's Edition.

Simon & Schuster
1230 Avenue of the Americas
New York, NY 10020

First Simon & Schuster hardcover edition April 2008

SIMON & SCHUSTER and colophon are registered trademarks of Simon & Schuster, Inc.

Manufactured in the United States of America

ISBN-13: 978-0-7394-9236-9

This Large Print Book carries the
Seal of Approval of N.A.V.H.

In loving memory of
Mark W. Schnorbus

Acknowledgments

Readers often write to thank me for writing the Elm Creek Quilts novels, and in turn I thank Denise Roy, Maria Massie, Rebecca Davis, David Rosenthal, Aileen Boyle, Kate Ankofski, Molly Lindley, Mara Lurie, Honi Werner, Melanie Parks, Tara Shaughnessy, Geraldine Neidenbach, Heather Neidenbach, Nic Neidenbach, Virginia Riechman, Leonard Chiaverini, Marlene Chiaverini, Laurie Chittenden, teachers who told me I could write, librarians who urge their patrons to read my books, booksellers who keep my books on their shelves, longtime readers who place copies of my novels in their friends' hands and insist they open the covers, and every reader who has ever sent an e-mail or come to a book signing to urge me to "keep writing."

Without you, and without the love and encouragement of Marty, Nicholas, and Michael Chiaverini, I would have followed a very different winding way and the Elm Creek Quilts novels would not be.

Sylvia

Sylvia woke to a gentle breeze and bird-song beyond the open window. Sitting up in bed and stretching, she saw clouds in the eastern sky, pink with the new light of dawn. Andrew had risen earlier, without waking her, but she knew there was only one place her husband could be at that hour on a Sunday morning.

She dressed in a light sweater and slacks and went to join her husband, pausing at the top of the grand oak staircase to savor the brief, reverential stillness that descended upon Elm Creek Manor on Sunday mornings. In a few hours, the gray stone artists' retreat would bustle and hum with the sounds of dozens of eager quilters arriving for a week of quilting, friendship, and fun, but for the moment, Sylvia, Andrew, and the manor's other three permanent residents had the estate all to themselves.

After descending the staircase, grasping a banister worn smooth from the hands of generations, Sylvia crossed the black marble floor of the front foyer and turned to walk down the older west wing of the manor, built by her great-grandfather in 1858. She brushed the wall lightly with her fingertips, wondering what her great-grandparents would think of the changes their descendants had brought to the farm they had founded, nestled in the fertile Elm Creek Valley in central Pennsylvania.

Voices and the smell of frying sausages drifted to her from the kitchen at the end of the hall. Sarah would be at the stove, no doubt, preparing breakfast for five, but who kept her company? Her husband, Matt, most likely, although usually he was too busy with his caretaker's duties to linger in the kitchen. Perhaps Sarah's best friend and fellow Elm Creek Quilter, Summer, had finished her daily yoga routine early and had decided to lend a hand, taking advantage of the opportunity to contribute more vegetarian options to the meal.

"Good morning," Sylvia sang out as she entered the kitchen, but she stopped short at the sight of Sarah sitting on a bench and resting her head in her arms on the kitchen table. Her husband tended the stove, a pink calico apron tied around his waist.

"Morning," Matt said, throwing her a grin over his shoulder and raising a spatula in salute. Sarah managed to lift her head long enough to give Sylvia a pale smile. Then she groaned and let her head drop onto her arms again, her long, reddish-brown ponytail falling onto an open package of saltine crackers beside her on the table.

"Goodness, Sarah. Are you ill?" Sylvia sat down on the opposite bench, brushed Sarah's ponytail away from the food, and felt her forehead. Sylvia detected no trace of fever, thank goodness, but the younger woman clearly was not well.

"I'll be all right." Sarah's voice wavered feebly, belying her words. "I think I finally understand why Summer won't eat meat. I never realized how awful it smells."

Sylvia thought breakfast smelled delicious, but she knew better than to discuss food with someone suffering from a stomach bug. "Perhaps you should go back to bed, dear. Matthew seems to have everything well in hand, and you wouldn't want to pass on whatever you have to our guests during registration."

At the stove, Matt choked back a laugh. "I don't think we have to worry about any of them taking home this particular souvenir."

"We can't be too careful."

"I'll be all right in a moment." Sarah pushed herself to her feet. "It's my turn to fix breakfast and I'm not going to shirk my duty."

"Shirk away, honey," said Matt. "I have everything under control."

"Beginning today, we'll have a professional chef on staff again," Sylvia reminded her. "Anna's planning a cold buffet for lunch, but supper will be a gourmet feast. She phoned me with the menu. Mushroom and rosemary soup, salmon filets, an eggplant ratatouille that Summer is sure to love, and chocolate mousse for dessert. Best of all, no more kitchen duty for the rest of us!"

"I can't wait," Sarah croaked, then pressed her lips together and hurried from the room.

"She'll be fine," said Matt when Sylvia rose to go after her. "Don't worry. Just give her a minute, and she'll be back here scrambling eggs."

Sylvia wasn't so sure, but she put on a pot of coffee and offered to mix up a batch of biscuits. Just as she was about to dust her hands with flour to knead the dough, Sarah returned, looking remarkably better. She insisted on taking over, and when the younger couple overruled Sylvia's protests, she left them to their work. She filled two travel mugs with coffee—cream and sugar for her, sugar only for Andrew—and carried them out the back door and down four steps to the rear parking lot.

Outside the air was cool from the night and misty, dew fresh on the grass. Insects chirped and buzzed and darted in the sunlight shafting through the forest canopy, the elms barely stirring in the still air. Sylvia knew the day ahead would be warm and humid, but the gray stone walls of Elm Creek Manor would keep their arriving guests cool and comfortable—as long as she reminded Sarah to open all the windows and keep plenty of lemonade on ice.

With a mug in each hand, Sylvia crossed the bridge over Elm Creek without spilling a single drop. Andrew's favorite fishing spot, a large, round, flat rock on the creek bank beneath a willow tree, had been her favorite secluded hideaway as a child. Whenever she had needed time alone to think or to cool her temper after an argument with her sister, she had stolen away to the willow and the rock. The musical burbling of the creek never failed to soothe her, and sometimes even now, a woman grown, she favored the private spot for quiet contemplation.

But she was happy to share it with her dear Andrew.

She knew better than to scare away the fish by calling out to him when she spied him through the willow branches, that faded, worn fishing cap on his head, a tackle box on the rock by his side. She approached quietly, but her footfalls alerted him when she was still several yards away. He glanced over his shoulder, and his face lit up at the sight of her. "There's my girl," he said, his voice low. Shifting his fishing rod to one hand, he patted the rock beside him.

Sylvia gladly took the offered seat, handed him his coffee, and rested her head upon his shoulder as he drew her closer. "Anything biting?"

"No keepers. Not like you." He sipped his coffee and nodded to show it was just the way he liked it. "You're definitely a keeper."

"I'm glad to know you don't plan to throw me back."

"Not on your life."

She smiled, and they sat in companionable silence, watching minnows draw close to the hook and dart away into the shadows. "Sarah and Matt have breakfast cooking," Sylvia remarked. "Sarah seems to be under the weather."

Andrew grinned. "She's not sick. She's just sick of cooking."

"No, that's not it. I urged her to return to bed, but she flatly refused." Sarah wasn't a shirker. If anything, she worked herself too hard. "But I think we'll all be happy when Anna Del Maso joins our staff today. We've been without a real chef for too long."

"If those cookies she brought to her job interview are any indication, she's going to be a great addition to the staff."

"I couldn't agree more. If she can make a simple sugar cookie taste that delicious, I can't wait to see what she'll do for Judy's going-away party." Sylvia sighed and sipped her coffee. "I only wish it weren't necessary."

"Judy couldn't turn down such a great offer from an Ivy League school."

"Of course not. I wouldn't expect her to. But I'll miss her very much."

"That's only natural. She'll miss you Elm Creek Quilters, too."

"She's one of our founding members," said Sylvia, steadying a quaver in her voice. "It's difficult to believe this is her last week." The Elm Creek Quilters were fortunate that one of their new hires, Gretchen Hartley, was willing to start right away. Although Gretchen and Judy had very different quilting styles, adjusting the course offerings was a minor inconvenience compared to the upheaval of canceling classes altogether. At least the rest of their staff would remain through the rest of the season, but then . . . "We won't have Summer for much longer, either."

"I thought she was staying through the end of September."

"That's what she says now, but I'm sure once camp wraps up for the season, she'll be eager to move to Chicago before the fall quarter begins."

"What about her boyfriend? Won't she want to stick around Waterford for him?"

"I'm not so sure about that. She's more likely to delay her departure for her mother than for Jeremy."

Andrew chuckled. "Gwen's so proud of her, I wouldn't be surprised if she drove Summer to Chicago and walked her to class on the first day."

Sylvia smiled at the image of Gwen in

a brightly colored gypsy skirt and beaded necklaces escorting her red-faced, twenty-eight-year-old daughter to her first graduate school symposium. "Gwen might do exactly that, if she didn't have her own students to worry about. And if Summer wouldn't faint away from embarrassment."

"Summer doesn't seem the fainting type."

"No, I suppose you're right." It was far more likely that the spirited young woman would welcome her mother's companionship. Gwen and Summer were very close, and Sylvia was so happy for them both, so proud of Summer's accomplishments and her prospects, that Sylvia could almost forget to regret her leaving them.

Almost.

Andrew finished his coffee, drew in his fishing line, and began packing his gear. "Do you think you'll finish your quilt in time?" he asked.

"Unfortunately, no. The grand unveiling I had planned for Judy's going-away party will have to wait."

"Think of it this way." Andrew

squeezed her hand in sympathy and helped her to her feet. "Now we'll have an excuse to visit Judy in Philadelphia. A quilt that special ought to be delivered in person."

Sylvia nodded, but the thought of a future visit was small consolation. She had worked on the quilts all summer in secret, tracing the templates on the back of her favorite fabrics, carefully cutting the pieces, pinning and sewing each curve by hand.

Winding Ways. The pattern's name was as evocative as the design was lovely. A mosaic of overlapping circles and intertwining curves, the circles would appear only if the quiltmaker created a careful balance of dark and light hues, if she harmonized the colors and gave contrast its pride of place. Such was the harmony and balance of the Elm Creek Quilters, whose friendship had been tested by time and conflict. In the years ahead, it would face the test of distance, as well. The quilt—or quilts, rather—that Sylvia was making would capture the spirit of that friendship, the necessary journeys that sometimes led one woman far from the embrace of her beloved friends.

"When I think of all the winding ways the path of my life has followed," Sylvia said as she and Andrew strolled arm-in-arm back to the manor, "I believe it's a miracle that I ended up back in this beautiful place, surrounded by so much love and friendship. I could have followed my winding ways anywhere, and yet here I am, exactly where I am meant to be."

She would have to trust that Judy's and Summer's own winding ways would lead them to joy and fulfillment. They both deserved happiness in abundance.

"My favorite winding path is the Pennsylvania Toll Road," remarked Andrew.

Sylvia laughed, her melancholy momentarily forgotten. "Why is that?"

"Because it brought me back to Elm Creek Manor, and to you."

Judy

Judy turned off the main highway and onto the narrow gravel road that wound through the leafy wood encircling the Bergstrom estate, trying not to think about how she would follow this shaded route only seven more times. When autumn came, she would miss the leaves turning on the stately trees that lined Elm Creek; a few months later, she would not see them raise their bare branches to a steel gray winter sky. Seasons would come and go, campers would come and go, Elm Creek Quilts would endure, all without Judy.

As tears welled up, she quickly reminded herself that the narrow gravel road was murder on her car's shocks.

She would not miss having to pull over halfway into the underbrush, tree branches scraping the length of the car, to make way for an oncoming vehicle. And really, the demands of two full-time jobs and a family were too much for one woman. Once they moved to Philadelphia, she could concentrate on one career, quilt only for pleasure, and have a few moments left over simply to relax.

And every time she picked up a needle, her thoughts would carry her to Elm Creek Manor and the circle of quilters it broke her heart to leave.

She could not have parted from them for anything less than the opportunity of a lifetime. When a colleague from her graduate school days at Princeton had encouraged her to apply for a tenure-track associate professor position in his department at Penn, she had known that hundreds of other professors at far more prestigious universities would be vying for the post. If Judy sent in her CV, the hiring committee would certainly wonder why someone with a doctorate in computer engineering had spent her career in the computer sciences department of a small, private, rural college better known for its humanities and liberal arts scholarship than the hard sciences. Waterford College didn't even have an engineering program. Judy could hardly tell them that she had become pregnant while finishing her dissertation, and since she and her husband, Steve, knew they couldn't afford a baby on her graduate student stipend and his freelance writing income, she had been obliged to take the first attractive offer that she had received. So Waterford College it was.

Judy had never regretted their decision. It had been the right choice at the time, and if she had not brought her family to Waterford, she would not have become one of the founding members of Elm Creek Quilts. But as the years passed, she eventually reached the limit of what she could accomplish in her research with Waterford College's limited facilities. When Rick tempted her with photographs of Penn's state-of-the-art facilities, and when she reflected upon how much easier it would be to care for her aging mother if she didn't have to drive halfway across the state every weekend, she could, for the first time, imagine herself leaving the small rural hamlet. When Steve was offered a job writing for the *Philadelphia Inquirer,* it was clear that the path their lives had followed up to that point curved suddenly to the east just ahead of them. For weeks, Judy and Steve debated whether they should accept their job offers, but even as they weighed the pros and cons, Judy knew there was only one logical choice.

Even with the hassles of packing and moving and finding a new home and enrolling Emily in her new school, Judy couldn't wait to follow their new path, and yet she couldn't bear to leave.

Late morning sunlight broke through the leafy wood as the road forked just ahead. By longtime habit Judy took the left branch, which led to the rear parking lot. The narrow road wound through the trees and emerged beside a sunlit apple orchard, then curved around past a red barn, climbed a low hill, and crossed the bridge over Elm Creek. All at once the manor came into view—three stories of

gray stone and dark wood, its unexpected elegance enhanced by the ram-
bling natural beauty of its surroundings.

She had passed those fond, familiar
landmarks a hundred times each summer, but already they seemed to belong
to someone else.

On the other side of the creek, the
road broadened and became a parking
lot circling two towering elms. Judy
pulled to a stop next to Andrew's enormous motorhome and climbed the
stone steps to the back door. She
smelled eggs, sausage, and biscuits as
soon as she set foot inside the manor,
but when a glance through the kitchen
door revealed only stacks of dirty dishes
in the sink, a cluttered countertop, and
an unswept floor, she continued down
the hall to the front foyer, where she
found Sarah, Sylvia, and Summer setting up for camper registration. As the
three members of the faculty who lived
in the manor, they were usually the first
to arrive at any Elm Creek Quilters'
gathering at the manor, but not always.
Some evenings Summer rushed in late
for evening programs after a dinner date

with her boyfriend, Jeremy, and for the past few weeks, the usually punctual Sarah had dragged herself downstairs for morning meetings, barely on time and looking a little green. If Judy didn't know her friend so well, she'd worry that Sarah was hung over, the way she clutched her stomach and nibbled on only a few dry crackers for breakfast. She had apparently given up coffee, too, but surely the effects of caffeine withdrawal would have faded by now and couldn't account for her rough mornings.

This morning Sarah seemed her usual, cheerful self as she glanced up from her work and threw Judy a grin. "Thank goodness, another pair of hands."

"Where do you need me?" Judy asked. "Should I start in the kitchen?"

"Absolutely not," said Sarah. "Let the delinquents clean up the mess. That's their job."

"Delinquents" was a harsher term than Judy would have used for the three young men who had worked for them all summer, but she couldn't deny that they deserved it. Earlier that spring, in an act of bewildering cruelty, the three seniors from Waterford High School had broken into, robbed, and vandalized Bonnie Markham's quilt shop. So thorough were they in their destruction that Bonnie was forced to close the shop for weeks. When she reopened for a going-out-of-business sale, she barely earned enough to pay off her outstanding debts. After Bonnie lost her lease, Sylvia proposed opening a new quilt shop in Elm Creek Manor, but Bonnie had yet to act on the proposal. At first Judy thought her friend was merely waiting for the insurance check, but the funds had sat untouched in her savings account for several weeks now, collecting interest. Perhaps Bonnie realized any other shop would be a poor imitation of the business she had built from the ground up. Perhaps she was saving the insurance money for another, yet undiscovered dream.

After the boys had been caught and forced to face up to their crime, Bonnie—dear, compassionate, forgiving Bonnie—had asked the judge for leniency. The boys had never been in trouble before, and all three had intended to start college in the fall. She couldn't bear to think that their future prospects were ruined because of one very bad mistake.

"They threw those futures away when they broke into your shop," said the judge, who had expected Bonnie to demand justice and restitution. Impressed by her pleas, he relented and sentenced the boys to probation and community service, which they would serve at Elm Creek Manor. He would consider the terms fulfilled after the boys earned back every cent they had cost Bonnie.

"But that will take years," burst out Mary Beth, mother to one of the offenders. "Anyway, her insurance will pay for everything."

The judge regarded Mary Beth over the rims of his glasses. "What an astonishing sense of entitlement given the circumstances. I'm beginning to see why your son is here today. If it takes years, so be it. They can come back every summer and every school holiday until the debt is paid."

Mary Beth had had the good sense to look chagrined and she uttered not another word of protest. Bonnie was satisfied with the decision, and Sylvia had readily agreed to her part in seeing to it that the young men fulfilled their sentences, but most of the Elm Creek Quilters thought they had not been sufficiently punished. "If they showed one sign of remorse, just one," Sarah had grumbled to Judy earlier that summer as she ordered her reluctant new employees outside to scrub out garbage cans. "Working instead of enjoying a carefree, three-month-long summer vacation isn't a punishment. It's normal life for most of us."

Judy agreed, and she, too, had saved the worst, dirtiest, and most tedious jobs for the vandals without a single twinge of conscience. And she had to admit that all three had worked hard that summer, probably harder than they had ever worked in their lives. She couldn't say whether they were genuinely remorseful or just sorry that they had been caught, but she knew that few young men had ever had more reason to welcome the approach of autumn.

Leaving the kitchen to the young men, Judy joined in helping her friends prepare for registration. They arranged the long tables on the black marble floor and set up the usual stacks of forms, chatting companionably, occasionally glancing at the tall double doors in case an early arrival surprised them. Invariably, some eager quilter wouldn't be able to wait for the first day of camp to begin at noon. Once a camper had entered through the back door at nine o'clock in the morning and had sat alone in the kitchen, sewing a quilt block and helping herself to the coffee still in the pot from Sarah and Matt's breakfast. The Elm Creek Quilters didn't discover her there until it was time to prepare lunch.

A few veteran quilt campers preferred to drive around back, park their own cars, and enter through the back door as that early arrival had done, but most preferred to use the front entrance and have Matt or Andrew valet park for them on the first day. Judy understood that, especially for new campers, it was the approach that mattered, the sense that they had arrived at another, separate, sheltered, and sheltering place, a haven from the chaos and disappointments of ordinary life. As their vehicles emerged from the leafy wood, the gray stone manor suddenly appeared, steadfast and welcoming, surrounded by a lush green lawn. Then the newcomers would spy the wide, covered veranda whose columns spanned the front of the manor. As they drew closer, they would see the twin arcs of the stone staircases descending to the driveway, which encircled a fountain in the shape of a rearing horse, the symbol of the Bergstrom family. Judy enjoyed watching campers take in the scene for the first time, awestruck and thrilled that they would be able to spend a week in such a grand place. Judy still experienced that same thrill, even though Elm Creek Manor had become as familiar to her as her own home. Sometimes it felt like her true home, the home of her heart.

One by one the other Elm Creek Quilters arrived. Gwen, her gray-streaked auburn hair rippling in thick waves down her back, made a dramatic entrance in a swirl of long batik skirts and the clinking of beaded necklaces. Diane appeared soon after, tall and blonde and enviably slender, clutching a coffee cup and scowling as if she had been dragged unwillingly out of bed only moments before, although Judy was certain she had already done Pilates, prepared breakfast for her husband and two sons, and shepherded the whole family to nine o'clock Mass. With Diane came Agnes, Sylvia's sister-in-law, her snowy curls as neatly arranged as if she had left the hairdresser only moments before. Her blue eyes were bright and guileless behind oversize pink-tinted glasses as she surveyed the preparations and immediately took charge of room assignments, a task everyone agreed she handled better than anyone. Although Sarah did her best to accommodate every camper's special requests as soon as their registration forms arrived in the mail, sometimes mistakes occurred. Other times the campers did not make their preferences known until they stood in the foyer. A quilter might need a first-floor room, only to discover that she had been given the key to a third-floor suite and that all first-floor rooms were booked. Two campers might decide on the way over from the airport that they wanted to room together, and roommate assignments would have to be shifted quickly and delicately, without hurting anyone's feelings. Agnes, with her perfect combination of diplomacy and amiable resolve, deftly spun solutions that made everyone feel as if they had received the best part of the compromise.

Bonnie arrived last, and with only moments to spare, breathless and red-cheeked from her sprint from the rear parking lot. The other Elm Creek Quilters would have forgiven her no matter how late she came, and not only because she had the longest commute. After her soon-to-be-ex-husband changed the locks to their condo and badgered her into selling it, Bonnie had lived with Agnes for a while before finding an apartment of her own in Grangerville, ten miles from Waterford. Agnes had enjoyed Bonnie's company and had urged her to stay on at her home near the Waterford College campus, and Sylvia had offered her one of the manor's coziest suites for as long as she liked, but Bonnie insisted on proving that she could survive on her own.

"Prove it to yourself or to Craig?" Diane had asked.

"A bit of both," Bonnie had replied. She and Craig had had their difficulties through the years, but Judy knew Bonnie had never expected to find herself spiraling into divorce at her age, her business in ruins. She deserved better.

The Elm Creek Quilters fell into their usual roles, the anticipation that heralded every new week of camp rising as the hour approached. Judy collated maps of the estate with class schedules and descriptions of their evening programs, Agnes and Diane arranged fresh flowers from the cutting garden in each suite, and Gwen paired room keys with quilters' names. Bonnie and Summer inspected the classrooms to be sure that sewing machines, lights, and audiovisual equipment were in working order, while Sarah and Sylvia supervised and helped out wherever needed. Matt and Andrew stood ready to park cars and assist arriving guests with their luggage.

"I bet you won't miss this chaos," Diane remarked in passing as their deadline approached.

Judy managed a smile, but fortunately Diane hurried off without waiting for a reply. Judy *would* miss it, every frazzled, haphazard, crazy bit of it. How many people had the chance to create a thriving business from scratch with her best friends? Every bit of effort, every drop of sweat, every moment of worry had been worth it. She knew that as an empirical fact when she heard Sarah recite her financial reports at their board meetings, but she felt it as a certain truth when she saw women transformed by a week at quilt camp. They arrived stressed, tentative, uncertain; they departed refreshed and happy, with a new confidence in themselves and their ability to create beauty, comfort, and warmth for themselves and those they loved. Sylvia often remarked that the Elm Creek Quilters performed minor miracles every day. To Judy, the real miracle was how a former Vietnamese refugee, forced to flee Saigon as a child after her American serviceman father abandoned her and her mother, had traveled the long and winding way that led her to this place, to these beloved, wonderful people.

On the opposite side of the table stood her best friend among them, Gwen Sullivan. Like Judy, Gwen was a professor at Waterford College, but since the American Studies faculty kept offices in the liberal arts building on the other side of campus, their paths rarely crossed during the course of an ordinary day. When school was in session, they met every Tuesday for lunch at a small café across the street from the main campus gate. Judy wondered who would occupy the seat across from Gwen at their favorite corner table when the new semester began.

Gwen must have sensed Judy's gaze upon her, for she glanced up from her work and smiled. "Are you all packed?"

"Far from it." The family had so much work left to do before the moving van pulled out of their driveway that Judy became lightheaded just thinking about it. "Are you offering to help?"

"Sure. I'll gladly take charge of packing your fabric stash."

Judy laughed. "I bet you would, and all of my best batiks would mysteriously end up in your car instead of the moving van."

"Good morning, everybody," someone called out behind her. Judy turned, expecting to see their first camper of the day, and instead discovered Anna Del Maso standing at the entrance to the west wing hallway. Behind her stood Summer's boyfriend, Jeremy, tall, dark-haired, scholarly, and, Judy remembered, Anna's across-the-hall neighbor in their downtown apartment building.

Judy had completely forgotten Anna was due to start today.

"Jeremy was kind enough to drive me so I didn't have to carry grocery sacks on the bus," Anna said, still lingering on the edge of the foyer. "We let ourselves in through the back door. Was that all right? Maybe we should have knocked first, but Jeremy said no one would hear us and I wanted to get the groceries put away."

"Of course you didn't need to knock." Sylvia crossed the foyer and greeted the newcomer with a fond hug. "We're not so formal here, as you'll soon discover. Elm Creek Quilters come and go as they please."

"That's what I told her," said Jeremy. "Is Summer around?" When several Elm Creek Quilters pointed to the classroom, he gave Anna an encouraging smile and went in search of his girlfriend.

As Anna thanked Sylvia for the welcome, Gwen seized her by the shoulders and kissed her dramatically on both cheeks. "You are now an official Elm Creek Quilter. Use your powers only for good."

Startled, Anna burst out laughing. "I will. Thanks. I'm glad to be here." She glanced around the circle of welcoming faces, and Judy suddenly realized that she alone had held back, standing on the bottom step of the grand oak staircase and clutching the banister as if she would bar entry to the secret realms upstairs. She forced a smile, but it was too late. Anna had already looked away.

"I thought I would set up the lunch buffet." Anna deferred equally to Sylvia and Sarah, as if she were not exactly sure who was in charge. She had the tall, robust, dark-haired beauty and passionate gaze of an opera singer. Ever since Judy had met her at her job interview earlier that summer, she had half-expected Anna to burst into a Puccini aria at any moment.

"You want to get right to work, don't you?" said Sarah, beaming with relief.

"I thought I should allow enough time to find all the dishes and correct my mistakes," Anna continued, with an apologetic laugh that suggested she didn't expect to make any. "Were you thinking inside or outside? That north patio would be a lovely spot, and the weather's perfect for an *al fresco* lunch."

Judy felt a thrill of alarm and indignation. The campers weren't supposed to set foot on the cornerstone patio until the Candlelight ceremony that evening after the Welcome Banquet. Anna was only ten minutes into her first day, and already she wanted to jettison their beloved traditions.

"We'll have lunch inside," Sarah said, taking her arm. "I'll come to the kitchen with you to show you where everything is."

As they disappeared down the west wing hallway, Gwen remarked, "Thank the goddess our macaroni and cheese days are over."

Diane glowered, but remarkably did not retort. She was convinced Gwen's references to a female deity were only meant to annoy her, but Judy had discussed religion, politics, and every other conceivable subject with Gwen so often that she knew Gwen spoke from true feeling. Still, Gwen did refer to "the goddess" more often when Diane was around, although Judy wasn't sure Gwen was aware of it.

At five minutes to noon, one of the tall double doors opened and three quilt campers in matching fuchsia T-shirts entered, chattering happily and pulling their luggage along behind them. Bonnie and Summer hurried forward to help them carry their suitcases up the four

marble stairs, designed in the days before anyone gave a thought to wheel-
chair accessibility. Judy took her seat at
the registration table and assigned their
first guests of the week to their rooms—
two of them together, the third in a single next door. As she placed the keys in
their hands, the door opened to more
campers, and then, for the next two
hours, they came at such a steady pace
that Judy hardly had a moment to reflect
upon her last registration day. Which
was all for the better, she thought, rising
as Diane offered to take her place so
Judy could break for lunch. If she
marked every last this and that of her final week as an Elm Creek Quilter, she
might not be able to go through with the
move.

From the registration table, Judy had
overheard campers exiting the banquet
hall in absolute raptures about the
lunch. Anna had promised a simple,
cold buffet, so Judy had naturally expected cold cuts, rolls, and pasta salad.
What she saw arranged on the linen-
draped table by the windows made her
gasp in amazement. There were fixings

for sandwiches, to be sure, but also six different tantalizing salads; a beautiful fruit tray with two sauces, yogurt and ginger; and a several-tiered arrangement of whimsically frosted cupcakes for dessert. The meal put Judy's wedding buffet to shame.

Attending to the buffet in a white chef's coat, her long, dark brown hair twisted up beneath a tall white toque, Anna spotted Judy rooted in place and bit her lip in worry. Judy roused herself and forced a smile as she gathered up a plate and silverware.

"Is everything all right?" Anna asked. "I could have done some chicken satays or California rolls—"

"It's perfect just the way it is," Judy interrupted. "It couldn't be nicer."

But I could be, she thought as Anna breathed a sigh of relief and went to answer a camper's question about the gluten-free vermicelli. She couldn't blame Anna, who wasn't even Judy's official replacement. Judy was wrong, wrong, wrong to envy Anna for what awaited her, the friendships, the discovery of the beauties of the Elm Creek estate, the sense of belonging and accomplishment. Judy had enjoyed it all, and now it was Anna's turn.

She filled her plate with a small portion of each salad, unable to choose among them, then made her way across the room to a table of quilters who were waving frantically for her to join them. Although they were first-timers, they recognized Judy from her photo on the Elm Creek Quilts website, and three of them planned to attend her borders and bindings workshop the following day. They peppered her with questions about the class—and about the mysterious initiation ceremony they had heard other campers whispering about in the foyer.

"You'll just have to wait and see for yourselves," Judy said. "There's nothing to be afraid of."

"I didn't think there was until you said that," said one of the women, alarmed.

Judy's only reply was to raise her eyebrows significantly and take another bite of one of Anna's flavorful salads—couscous, corn, and black beans with a southwestern kick. She would miss teasing the newbies every summer Sunday. It had become a sport for Elm Creek Quilters and veteran campers alike, but it was all in good fun. If these newbies returned next year, they would find out that second-year campers were the most enthusiastic teasers of all.

The registration rush subsided for a time after Judy returned from lunch, then surged in the late afternoon as long-distance travelers completed their journeys. Matt made several trips to the airport, bus, and train stations in the Elm Creek Quilts minivan, dropping off car-loads of weary travelers whose fatigue seemed to fall away as soon as they entered the manor. Far-flung friends cried out in delight and rushed to reunite with campers they had not seen since the summer before, while some who had come alone, knowing no one, hung back, a bit overwhelmed by the bursts of laughter and emotional scenes going on all around them.

"You'll get to know everyone soon," Judy promised a tentative brown-haired woman, offering her a room key and an encouraging smile. "I know it can seem that everyone knows everyone but you, especially your first time staying with us."

"I really hope you're right," the woman said timorously. She grasped the handle of her suitcase, rolled it across the foyer, and lugged it upstairs to the second floor. As far as Judy could tell, she didn't pause to exchange a word or a glance with anyone.

"Name badges," said Sarah, who had observed the scene. "We should really start using name badges, like at the national quilt shows, with the campers' names and hometowns on them. When people see where you're from, they ask questions and you almost always find something in common."

"I don't think in this case a name badge would have helped," said Judy with misgivings. She wished she had thought to accompany the newcomer upstairs and introduce her to some especially friendly campers she remembered from previous years. Or she could have previewed the class rosters and helped the woman meet a soon-to-be classmate.

As the number of room keys on the

table in front of Judy dwindled, the other Elm Creek Quilters began closing down their stations and making ready for the evening's events. The last straggler finally arrived shortly before six, looking rather frazzled and windblown, and muttering about construction on the turnpike. Judy signed her in, gave her the last room key, and hurried off to call her husband, Steve, before the Welcome Banquet. Delicious aromas drifted down the hallway from the kitchen. Judy's mouth watered when she considered what Anna might do to top her amazing inaugural lunch.

Steve answered on the first ring; he and Emily were on their way out the door to fetch pizza, DVDs, and Emily's best friend, Courtney, as Steve had agreed to let Emily invite her friend to spend the night.

"That's a great idea," said Judy. She wanted Emily to enjoy as much time as possible with her best friend before they had to part ways. Steve knew this, too, although he hadn't said so. They had been married so long and so well that most of their communication took place in the silences between their words, in their own subliminal shorthand.

After promising Steve she would return home soon to help him supervise the sleepover, Judy slipped away to Summer's room to freshen up before the Welcome Banquet. By the time she returned downstairs to the banquet hall off the front foyer, nearly all of their guests had seated themselves. The room had been transformed from its more casual lunchtime atmosphere by white tablecloths, centerpieces of flower petals sprinkled amid candles, and Sylvia's fine heirloom china, nearly translucent, with the Bergstrom rearing stallion in the center. Voices were hushed yet full of anticipation. Judy had only just found herself a place at the nearest table when the delinquents emerged from the servants' door, neatly attired in black slacks, white shirts, black ties, and white aprons. They looked so professional that one would hardly know they had once destroyed an entire quilt shop just for fun.

With them were Diane's two sons, legitimate seasonal employees rather than part of the chain gang. The eldest, Michael, directed the others as they carried in the first course, but by this time, so late in the summer, they knew the choreography so well that they needed little guidance. With practiced nonchalance, they set the steaming bowls of mushroom and rosemary soup before the campers and their hosts, and Judy knew even before dipping her spoon into the bowl that this was going to be the best soup she had ever tasted. The organic baby green salad that followed was perfection itself, as were the salmon filets and eggplant ratatouille, which required all her willpower not to devour entire. It was a good thing she was leaving, or she would have to take up marathon running to fend off the pounds.

She did manage to set down her dessert spoon after one bite of the chocolate mousse—not because it wasn't delicious, but because she honestly couldn't eat another bite. "You probably get tired of eating like this every day," said one of her dinner companions enviously, licking the last rich chocolate morsel from her spoon.

Judy would have explained that until recently, their campers had to make do with brownies from a box mix and ice cream, unless one of the Elm Creek Quilters had remembered to stop by the German bakery in downtown Waterford, but a sudden hush in the room distracted her. Evening had fallen; the floor-to-ceiling windows on the western wall opened onto a violet and rose sky in the distance beyond Elm Creek. Sylvia stood near the door, and in a clear voice that carried the length of the banquet hall, she invited everyone to follow her outside.

It was time for every Elm Creek Quilter's favorite part of quilt camp, when the week still lay before them promising friendship and fun, and their eventual parting could be forgotten for a while.

Sylvia led the campers from the banquet hall through the west wing of the manor and outside to the cornerstone patio. When their voices rose above a murmur, Sylvia smiled and gestured for silence, adding to the aura of mystery.

Earlier Matt and Sarah had arranged chairs in one large circle on the patio, and now Sarah beckoned the campers to sit. Murmuring, questioning, the campers took their places, and occasionally a nervous laugh broke the stillness. The quilters' voices fell silent as Sylvia lit a candle, placed it in a crystal votive holder, and took her place in the center of the circle. As the dancing flame in her hands cast light and shadow on her features, Judy felt a tremor of excitement and nervousness run through those gathered around her.

Slowly Sylvia turned around, gazing into the faces of her guests. "One of our traditions is to conclude the first evening of quilt camp with a ceremony we call Candlelight," she told them. "It began as a way for our guests to introduce themselves to us and to one another. Since we're going to be living and working together closely this week, we should feel as if we are among friends. But our ceremony has a secondary purpose. At its best, it helps you to know yourselves better, too. It encourages you to focus on your goals and wishes, and it helps prepare you for the challenges of the future and the unexpected paths upon which you might set forth."

Sylvia allowed the expectant silence to swell before she explained the ceremony. The campers would pass the candle around the circle, and as each woman took her turn to hold the flickering light, she would explain why she had come to Elm Creek Quilt Camp and what she hoped to gain that week. There was a pause after Sylvia asked for a volunteer to speak first.

"Not me," someone whispered so tremulously that a ripple of laughter went up from the circle.

A woman with a blue cashmere sweater thrown over her shoulders raised a hand. "I'll volunteer, although this honor ought to go to someone with a grander vision." She took the crystal candleholder from Sylvia and studied the small yellow light for a moment. "Where to begin . . . With my name, I suppose. I'm Nancy, and as the newly elected president of the Waterford Quilt Guild, I've come as an ambassador. Under our previous administration, relations with Elm Creek Quilts have been strained, to say the least. While some of our guild members have attended camp sessions on their own, our official guild policy was not to communicate with Elm Creek Quilts. You sent us invitations to free classes and special lectures, and our officers didn't pass the information along to the rest of the guild. You asked us to participate in making a wedding quilt for your founder, and your request was returned to you in very rude fashion."

"I'll say," muttered Diane, who had been present.

"I'm here to make amends," said Nancy. "A personal disagreement between our longtime former president and an Elm Creek Quilter was the root cause of our estrangement. Our former president is no longer affiliated with our guild, and I hope whatever quarrel she had with your staff member can be put in the past. I believe that the Waterford Quilt Guild and Elm Creek Quilts have similar goals and interests, and we ought to work together to promote the art and heritage of quilting in the Elm

Creek Valley. So I decided to see for myself what Elm Creek Quilts is all about, and I hope that in getting to know me, the Elm Creek Quilters will decide to give the Waterford Quilt Guild a second chance."

"You may be sure of it," said Sylvia, with a sidelong glance at Diane, the Elm Creek Quilter involved in the long-standing battle of wills. "I would like nothing more than to work together. I'm sure we have much to offer one another, but I must disagree with you on one point."

Nancy's eyebrows rose. "And that is?"

"That someone with a grander vision should speak first. What grander vision than peace and reconciliation, and what better way to begin our Candlelight?"

Nancy smiled, and as the other quilters murmured their approval, she passed the candleholder to the next woman in the circle. The shy, brown-haired woman Judy had assisted at registration accepted it with a faint squeak of alarm. Judy wished that Nancy had passed the candle around the circle in the other direction, so that the brown-haired woman could have gone last instead of second.

"My name is Marcia, and I'm from Illinois," the brown-haired woman said in a voice little more than a whisper.

"Speak up," someone boomed from the other side of the circle.

Marcia cleared her throat and raised her voice, but not by much. "My name is Marcia, and I'm from Illinois. This is my first visit to Elm Creek Manor, and I was almost too scared to come." When a few giggles of surprise interrupted her, Marcia hunched in her chair so that her shoulders almost touched her ears. "I know how silly it sounds, but it's true. I've never even been brave enough to join my church's quilting guild. Usually I quilt alone, or with a few of my friends at work. Every Tuesday we sew together in the office lunchroom and once a month we spend our lunch hour at a quilt shop. Last spring, my friend Dana found the Elm Creek Quilts website and convinced us to sign up for a week of camp. Ordinarily I would have been petrified at the thought of coming so far to spend a week with so many strangers, but I thought with my three friends around, it wouldn't be too bad." She took a deep breath. "You might have noticed that I'm a little shy."

No one said anything. Perhaps they feared frightening her into silence, or like Judy, they were wondering what had become of her three friends.

"We were all looking forward to the trip. Even me. Then our boss noticed that we had all scheduled the same week off and insisted that one of us stay. I volunteered, but he chose my friend because she's more experienced. Then my other friend got hit by a boy on one of those motorized scooters and had to have knee replacement surgery, so a long plane trip was out of the question. We were down to two, but I still thought that would be okay. Then yesterday my third friend called me and said she couldn't come because she had chicken pox."

An exclamation of astonishment went up from the group.

"Oh, don't worry," said Marcia, misunderstanding. "I had it in first grade. I didn't bring it with me to infect everyone. Well, after all that, you can see why I wanted to cancel my trip."

"Not me," Judy overheard one camper whisper to another. "I'd get the heck out of there before the next calamity struck."

"When I told my husband I couldn't possibly go without my friends, he insisted that I come anyway. He packed my suitcase, drove me to the airport, dropped me off at the curb, and told me he'd see me in a week. It was all I could do to get on the plane. I'm so worried that it's going to be like high school all over again—no one to sit with at lunch, no one to chat with before class, and watching all the fun from the outside of the circle. So. Why am I here?" Marcia fell silent. "To improve my quilting, of course. My friends are counting on me to share everything I learn with them. But I'm also hoping to make some new friends. I've joined a few Internet quilt lists, and the ladies are always talking about how much fun they have with their quilting friends when they finally meet in person, and how quilters are such wonderful, welcoming people. I decided to be brave and find out for my-self. Honestly, if I can't make friends among quilters, then I must really be a hopeless case."

A few murmurs of protest went up from the circle, but they quickly fell si-lent.

"I'm going to try my best, but I have a favor to ask of all of you." Marcia's voice had fallen to a near whisper again. "I know it's easy to forget us outsiders when you're having so much fun with your old friends, but please try to be more aware of the people who sit out-side your usual circle of quilters, and consider stretching that circle a bit to let in someone new."

Quickly Marcia passed the candle to the next quilter, her face flushed and eyes downcast. Judy doubted she had ever said anything so confrontational in her life. As confrontations went, it was fairly mild, but Judy knew that some of the women were bound to take Marcia's plea the wrong way, as criticism instead of a cry for acceptance. Sure enough, Judy saw one woman roll her eyes and whisper in the ear of a friend, whose shoulders shook with silent laughter. Disappointed, Judy looked away, but then she was heartened to see the three women who had arrived in matching fuchsia T-shirts whispering and nodding together as they cast smiles in Marcia's direction. The shy woman completely missed their friendly glances, so intently was she staring at the gray patio stones beneath her brown sandals. Judy hoped the fuchsia-clad women planned to invite Marcia to sit with them at breakfast the next morning. Time would tell.

The woman seated at Marcia's right was at least twenty years her senior, with short, wild curls and bifocals. She regarded Marcia with maternal fondness as she took the candle. "Thank you, Marcia, for reminding us that circles can exclude as well as include. I hope we will all resolve not to be miserly with our friendships." She looked around the circle of shadowed faces in a way that reminded Judy of her fairminded but firm seventh-grade teacher. "My name is Doris and I'm from Lincoln, Nebraska. Three summers ago, I could barely sew on a button—unlike my four best girlfriends, who had quilted for years and were always going on quilt re- treats and shop hops. Whenever the four of us got together, they would talk about their adventures and I would feel terribly left out and, I admit, the tiniest bit jealous. I decided to learn to quilt just to keep up with them, so I signed up for a week of Elm Creek Quilt Camp, and I was hooked. Now, not only do I get to join in my friends' quilting adventures back home, but I've also made more wonderful friends here." She smiled and looked around the circle of faces, warmly illuminated by candlelight. "Sometimes it's hard for me to remem- ber which came first, the quilting or the friendships, they're so closely inter- twined in my memory. This week I hope to rekindle old friendships, make new ones, and return home with some new sewing tricks to impress my friends."

As she passed on the candle, approv- ing murmurs rose into the night sky, har- mony restored after the discordant note of Marcia's shy confession. Doris had spoken of quilters the way they wanted to see themselves, Judy thought, and not the way they could sometimes be when they forgot to look beyond their own familiar circle. She hoped Marcia's humble plea for acceptance would not be too quickly forgotten.

The next quilter eagerly seized the candleholder. "I'm Sue Anne, and I came because I'm sick of getting third-place ribbons in my quilt guild's annual show." Her declaration met with a burst of laughter. "Every year the judges' comments are the same: borders are crooked, borders are wavy. Binding isn't full enough. Binding should be cut on the bias. Binding should not fall off the quilt." More laughter. "Those nitpickers take off points for everything. So I asked my sister-in-law for advice, and she should know, because she's forever throwing extra scallops into her borders just to show off. I thought she would give me a few pointers, but instead she urged me to sign up for Judy DiNardo's seminar at Elm Creek Quilt Camp. I called the next day, and it's a good thing, too. The girl who answered the phone told me that this is my last chance to take Judy's class because she's leaving!"

Judy's heart fluttered nervously as all eyes suddenly went to her. She smiled weakly and managed an apologetic shrug.

"You're leaving?" another woman gasped. "How could you?"

"I have a new job—"

"What new job could be better than this? I'd sweep the floors for room and board if they'd let me."

As others chimed in their agreement, Sylvia quickly stepped in. "That's a story for another time, if Judy chooses to share it." With a gracious smile, she gestured for Sue Anne to pass the candle on to the next quilter, one of the three wearing fuchsia T-shirts. As soon as Sue Anne handed off the candle, she frowned as if suddenly remembering that she had not finished her story.

"I'm Connie, and I'm one of the Flying Saucer Sisters," the next camper began, indicating the other fuchsia-clad women. "We aren't related by blood or marriage, but by our one sad affliction: Our closets are stuffed full of UFOs.

Those are Unfinished Fabric Objects,"
she added for the beginners' benefit.
"Since we rarely finish anything we start,
our beds have store-bought quilts on
them and our walls are bare. This must
stop." She jabbed her finger in the air for
emphasis. "We've made a pact. Before
we're allowed to start a new project, we
have to cut our UFO backlogs in half.
We're a support group and we also keep
one another from cheating. Some of us
are more honest than others." She cast
a sidelong look upon one of her friends,
who covered her eyes and shook her
head in shame. "My goal is to finish five
UFOs this week, and at that pace, I'll be
able to start a new quilt when I return to
camp next year."

Around the circle the candle went,
passed from hand to hand as the violet
sky deepened and the stars came out.
Women who could barely sew had
come for their first lessons; accomplished quilters had come for the opportunity to learn new skills or to work un-
interrupted on masterpieces they could
as yet only envision. They had come to
sew quilts for brides and for babies, to

cover beds or to display on walls, for warmth, for beauty, for joy. Through the years Judy had heard similar tales from other women, every summer Sunday as night fell, and yet each story was unique. One common thread joined all the women who came to Elm Creek Manor. Those who had given so much of themselves and their lives caring for others—children, husbands, aging parents—were now taking time to care for themselves, to nourish their own souls. As the night darkened around them, the cornerstone patio was silent but for the murmuring of quiet voices and the song of crickets, the only illumination the flickering candle and the light of stars glowing high above them as their voices rose into the sky.

Occasionally a camper would steal a curious glance at Judy as if unable to fathom her decision. What, they surely wondered, could compel an Elm Creek Quilter to leave the manor? It was, for that brief time they lived within its gray stone walls, the world as it should be: women of all ages, from widely varied backgrounds, coming together in harmony to create objects of beauty and comfort. Differences were not merely tolerated but accepted and even admired. For one week the world was not so much with them, the stress and monotony of daily routines could be forgotten, and they could quilt—or read, or wander through the garden, or take a nap, or stay up all night laughing with friends—as their own hearts desired. Patient teachers stood by willing to pass on their knowledge; friends offered companionship and encouragement. Confidences were shared at mealtime and in late-night chats in cozy suites or on the moonlit veranda. Resolutions were made, promises kept. Quilters took artistic and emotional risks because they knew they were safe, unconditionally accepted.

If only the same could be said of the world they would return to when the idyll was broken.

The darkness hid Judy's wistful smile as she gazed out upon the campers, drinking in their fellow quilters' stories, blissfully unaware of all the effort it took behind the scenes to create their serene oasis. They thought the Elm Creek Quilters were on vacation, too. For an Elm Creek Quilter to choose to leave the manor put cracks in the illusion, tarnish on the magic of Elm Creek Quilt Camp. Judy wished her eager student had not announced her impending departure, not then, not there.

Marcia's fears that she would not find friendship at Elm Creek Manor had also cast shadows of doubt on the sunny summer week that lay ahead. As confident as Judy was that Marcia would not spend the days isolated and lonely, she could not guarantee it. Marcia had to be willing to venture out of her room and cast off some of her shyness, and the other campers had to meet her halfway. For all the vaunted generosity and kindness of quilters, Judy knew that the admirable qualities of the group did not always manifest in certain members, at least not every day. Quilters were individuals with their own quirks and foibles. Although she hoped Marcia would find herself embraced by friends soon, Judy knew all too well that be-

coming a quilter did not guarantee acceptance into a loving circle, no matter
how much one deserved to belong.

Judy had fallen in love with quilts long
before she had learned to sew them.
Perhaps it was more accurate to say
that she fell in love with one quilt, and
later learned to love others, though each
one fell short of the faded heirloom that
first captured her imagination and became her heart's longing.

Judy was in second grade when her
mother, Tuyet, met John DiNardo. Judy
adored him, and in her mind he became
the father she and her mother had come
to America to find, for his kindness and
gentle manner made the American serviceman and his cruel rejections fade
from her memories. When Tuyet married
him, she disobeyed Judy's birth father's
orders and contacted him one final time,
crisply asking him to relinquish his parental rights so John could adopt Judy.
He did so without hesitation, apparently

forgetting that he had once insisted those rights were not his to give.

Judy was eight when she saw her new grandmother's quilt for the first time. Her parents had been married for less than a year, and the newly formed family had traveled to her father's childhood home for Easter. As they drove across Pennsylvania, her father reminisced about the hundred-year-old red-brick colonial house in Ohio, the warren of rooms, the attic full of toys and old treasures, the woods with the pond and the treehouse, and the dozens of aunts, uncles, and cousins eager to welcome Judy into the family. She had met her new grandparents and some of her father's other relatives at the wedding in Philadelphia, but not everyone had been able to attend. She couldn't wait to see everyone at the same time, in the place where her new daddy had been a little boy.

Her grandparents' home was everything her father had promised, and after some curious stares and questions about her hair and eyes, her new cousins accepted her as naturally as if she had been born into the family. They ran through the house, shouting and laughing, until the adults shooed them outside, where they played hide-and-seek in the woods and kickball on the grassy lawn. At night they unrolled sleeping bags on the family room floor and stayed up late giggling and whispering until one of the uncles came downstairs to hush them. Grandma and the aunts cooked marvelous meals, and while the adults lingered over coffee and talked of old times, the children were free to do as they pleased within the bounds of Grandma's rules.

Sunday morning, the children were scrubbed and brushed and put into their Easter suits and dresses. Judy felt like a princess in her white gloves and sky blue dress trimmed in white lace. She held hands with her two favorite cousins throughout the church services, and when the children returned to their grandparents' house, each discovered an Easter basket full of jellybeans and chocolates. After brunch, while their parents looked on from the back porch, the children ran through the yard searching for colorful Easter eggs hid-

den in thick tufts of grass, balanced on
fence posts, or nestled into the nooks of
trees. Judy found only two eggs, the
least of anyone, but two of her cousins
each gave her one of theirs and consoled her with promises that she would
do better next year, when she knew the
best hiding places as well as they did.

Later, when the children went inside
to take inventory of their baskets and
swap treats, Grandma called all the girls
aside and invited them to accompany
her to her bedroom. Judy's cousin Susan, who was only two months her
elder, whispered that Easter was the
only time the girls were allowed into her
room to see her most cherished possessions, and that messy boys were *never*
permitted. Mystified, Judy obediently
trailed after her grandmother and cousins, wondering what this treasure could
be, so precious that it could only be displayed once a year.

The six little girls fell silent as their
grandmother led them into her bedroom, which smelled of furniture polish
and rosewater. The carved dark walnut
bedposts stood taller than Grandma,

and the mattress covered by an ivory candlewick bedspread was so high that a small four-step stool stood beside it to ease the climb into bed. Two plump pillows lay near the gleaming headboard, and at the foot, a tapestry-covered chest. Grandma motioned for Miranda, the eldest granddaughter, to help her lift the curved lid. With the creak of hinges and a whiff of mothballs, the lid fell open and instinctively the girls stepped closer to peer within.

From her seat on the floor, Grandma looked up at them, an amused smile playing on her lips. "Patience, girls," she rebuked them mildly over the rims of her glasses. She had a long, thin nose with the slightest hook to it, large gray-blue eyes, and a small mouth. Judy had never seen her without her long graying blonde hair in a French twist or the delicate pearls around her neck.

"You know what's inside," she continued, reaching into the chest. As she withdrew a soft bundle wrapped in a white sheet, she gave Judy a quick, appraising glance. "Except for you, of course, dear. Why don't you let her in the front, girls, so she can see better? She's such a tiny little thing."

When her cousins made room, Judy eagerly came forward and knelt beside the chest, tucking in her skirt in what she hoped was a ladylike fashion. Grandma appeared not to notice, which told Judy she had done the right thing. A mistake would have sent those arched eyebrows soaring.

Grandma unwrapped the bundle and unfolded a quilt like none Judy had ever seen—sixteen bouquets of daisies arranged in four rows of four, surrounded by three concentric square borders of yellow, white, and green, and a wider border of single daisy blossoms. The colors were as soft and clear as a spring morning, the tiny stitches graceful and swirling in crosshatches and spirals.

Judy drew in a breath and pressed her hands firmly to her sides lest they reach for the quilt unbidden.

"It's all right. You may touch it," said Grandma, but first inspected Judy's hands to be sure she had washed them after brunch. Carefully Judy ran her small hands over one corner of the beautiful quilt, traced a daisy with a fingertip, and measured the bouquets with the span of her hands. The stitches were so tiny it was as if a fairy had made them with a piece of dandelion fluff, but she knew better than to say something so silly in front of Grandma.

"It's beautiful," she said instead, inching out of the way as her cousins pressed forward for their turns. "Did you make it?"

Grandma let out a small laugh at the very thought. "Oh, no. Not I. My mother made it for me as a wedding gift. This is my bridal quilt."

"She used to keep it on the bed," piped up Susan, "but not anymore, because the sunlight fades the colors."

"And also because your grandfather has a terrible habit of tossing his shoes on the bed," Grandma remarked.

The granddaughters giggled, and, following Grandma's instructions, they spread the quilt open between them, tucking their legs beneath. Each girl picked out her favorite daisy, although privately Judy thought that they were so nearly identical that she could hardly choose one over another. They listened as Grandma told them about her wedding day, about how the bridal party and guests had made a mad dash from the church to the hall in a torrential downpour, but that no one had cared about the weather. Who minded a little rain while the band played so merrily for two young people so well suited for each other and so obviously in love? "We still are," remarked Grandma, folding up the quilt after her granddaughters reluctantly let go. "We've been married forty-five years, and not one anniversary passes that your grandfather doesn't thank the good Lord for me."

Her airy disregard startled Judy, but her cousins giggled as if this was a familiar joke.

Grandma set her bridal quilt aside and withdrew a second bundle from the chest. It was thinner than the first, and after Grandma unwrapped it, Judy saw that it was just a quilt top, not a finished quilt with a backing, a fluffy middle, and tiny stitches holding the three layers together. The six little girls carefully spread it open between them and rested it on their laps as they had the first quilt. Gazing upon it, Judy let out a tiny sigh of amazement. Even unfinished, this quilt was lovelier than the first, although the two were so similar that Judy was certain it had been made by Grandma's mother, too. Instead of daisies, pink tulips with green stems and leaves were arranged in sixteen circular bouquets. Pink, white, and green concentric square borders framed the bouquets, and surrounding those was a wider border of pink tulips in clusters of three flowers on a white background. The outermost green border had been embellished with a gentle scallop on the inside edge.

"After my wedding," said Grandma, "my mother began this tulip quilt for my younger sister. It would have been her bridal quilt."

"Why didn't your mother finish it?" asked Judy.

"My sister never married. She drowned in a boating accident when she was only sixteen." Grandma inspected the quilt top, frowned slightly, and picked off a stray thread. "After that, my mother quite understandably didn't have the heart to complete it."

Judy was sorry she had prompted such an unhappy memory. "It's still a beautiful quilt," she said softly.

Grandma allowed a brief smile. "I think so, too. It's very precious to me. It reminds me of my sister, even though she never used it."

The granddaughters admired the quilt top until Grandma told them it was time to put the quilts away until next Easter. Judy watched regretfully as the pretty tulips and daisies disappeared into their cotton covers and were shut away in the trunk. It seemed like such a waste to enjoy their beauty only once a year. If they were hers, she would bring them out often—maybe not every day, she conceded, remembering the warning about colors fading in the sunlight, but at least once a month.

Grandma beckoned to Miranda, who hurried over to help her to her feet. Grandma thanked her, patted her shoulder, and said, "One day, my daisy quilt will belong to you, my dear. You're my oldest granddaughter and it's only fitting that my wedding quilt should be yours."

When none of her cousins protested, Judy realized that this was old news to them. She couldn't really feel disappointed. She had not considered until that moment that Grandma might give away her quilt, and she couldn't think of a reasonable argument against her grandmother's choice. There was only one daisy quilt and there were six granddaughters—so far—and Miranda was, after all, the oldest. It was only fair. Judy also knew that when Grandma said "one day," she meant when she died, and wishing for the quilt to be hers felt too much like wishing for Grandma to die.

"What about the tulip quilt?" piped up one of the younger girls.

Grandma's eyebrows rose. "You asked the same question last year."

The little girl, not much older than four, squirmed and hung her head. "I don't remember what you said."

"Will you give it to your oldest grandson?" asked Judy. That seemed fair.

"Heavens, no," said Grandma. "Boys

can't properly appreciate a quilt. The tulip quilt will go to the most deserving of my granddaughters, the one who learns how to finish it."

"Why not just give it to the second-oldest granddaughter?" another cousin asked.

Grandma regarded her with dry amusement. "If you want it, Carrie, you're going to have to learn to quilt first. Something as beautiful and as precious as my mother's last quilt could only go to someone who wants it so much she will learn how to quilt as beautifully as my mother did. Not only that, she must give me her solemn vow that she will finish the quilt. Many people who are capable of completing a task lack the will and perseverance to do so."

With that, Grandma ushered the girls from the room, her private audience concluded. They went downstairs to join the rest of the family, but as soon as she could, Judy took Susan aside. "Maybe we can learn to quilt and finish the tulip top together."

Susan nodded eagerly, but then hesitated. "Which of us gets the quilt afterward?"

"We can take turns. You can have it on odd-numbered years, and I can have it on even-numbered years."

Susan agreed that this was a marvelous plan, adding that when they grew up, they ought to live next door to each other so that each could visit the quilt whenever she liked. Judy happily agreed.

On the trip home to Philadelphia, Judy described the beautiful quilts with such enthusiasm that her mother teased her father for not telling her the family home contained such treasures. "I'd forgotten she had them," Judy's father replied. "I think she showed them to me and my brothers once as children, and she showed them to my brothers' wives after they married."

"She didn't offer to show them to me," Judy's mother said mildly.

"That was before they had kids. Now it's become this secret annual rite between my mother and her granddaughters. She probably wanted to continue that tradition."

"Ma," Judy broke in, "when we get home, would you teach me how to quilt?"

"I don't know how to quilt, but I could teach you to sew, and that would give you a very fine start."

In the weeks that followed, Judy took to her mother's lessons eagerly. She learned how to sew on buttons, to hem a handkerchief, and to embroider silk. The last was Judy's favorite, and after months of practice she learned to create pretty pictures with the slender threads. For her grandmother's Christmas gift, she stitched a cozy winter scene of a red-brick house surrounded by snow-covered trees and framed it, with her father's help. Her grandmother praised her and hung the embroidered picture on the family room wall. Susan studied the gift with wide eyes and whispered in Judy's ear that the tulip quilt top would surely be hers one day.

"But we're supposed to finish the quilt together," Judy whispered back. "Haven't you been learning how to sew, too?"

"Not like that," said Susan, nodding

to the embroidered picture in its place of honor on the wall. "I don't know if I could ever make something like that."

"You could if you tried," Judy said, wishing she could teach her cousin, but she had left her sewing basket and silk threads in Philadelphia.

When Easter came, Judy almost danced with excitement as Grandma led her granddaughters upstairs to her bedroom. As before, Miranda helped her lift the lid to the tapestry-covered trunk, and once more Grandma reminisced about her wedding day and told the much briefer story of the loss of her sister. Judy hung on every word, drinking in the quilts with her eyes. They seemed even more beautiful than she remembered.

Even the youngest of the cousins recalled what Grandma had said the year before about the tulip quilt top, so no one asked who would receive it one day. Judy did not expect Grandma to choose anyone so soon, so she was caught off guard when, as they were returning the quilts to the trunk, loyal Susan piped up that Judy had already learned how to sew very well.

Grandma's eyebrows rose. "Sewing and embroidery are not the same as quilting," she said, fastening the latch firmly. "Still, I must wonder how Judy managed to find time to do what you other girls did not."

Judy felt her cheeks grow hot. For a moment she feared her new cousins would resent her, and she almost regretted the sewing lessons she had begged from her mother. But instead of glaring angrily at her, the other girls nodded meekly up at their grandmother. Judy's relief was short-lived, however, for she knew that next Easter, she would not be the only one of them who knew how to sew.

Sure enough, next year all of the cousins except for the youngest had mastered basic sewing skills, even Miranda, who didn't have to. Carrie had sewn a small doll quilt from squares of calico and glowed proudly to Grandma's praise, although Grandma still made no promises regarding the fate of the quilt. Twelve months later, Carrie had made a second, larger quilt for her newborn brother and Susan showed off a Nine-Patch lap quilt she had made with her mother. "I'm sure one day you'll be able to make a quilt all by yourself," Grandma said, inspecting the stitches. "This is a fine beginning."

Her granddaughters exchanged looks of silent understanding: Grandma intended to keep them in suspense until one of them possessed the skills, and not just the potential, to complete their great-grandmother's beautiful tulip quilt. They had time, years perhaps, before she would choose.

Quilting, the cousins believed, could wait. Judy reminded them that quilting was like ballet or piano: Practice made perfect, and not one of them doubted that Grandma demanded perfection. They couldn't put off beginning to learn skills that might take a lifetime to master, not if they wanted to call the beautiful tulip quilt their own someday.

As the years passed, four new cousins joined their annual Easter viewings of the quilts, while the granddaughters' interest in learning to quilt waxed and waned. Some years several cousins brought small sewing projects to demonstrate their improving skills; other times no one, not even Judy, had anything to show for the previous twelve months. Once, when Judy was thirteen, her cousin Carrie ventured a question the girls had only whispered to one another: What would Grandma do with the tulip quilt if none of her granddaughters learned how to finish it?

As if she could not believe her ears, Grandma drew herself up, her mouth tightening. "I certainly hope it won't come to that. I do hope at least one of you cares enough to preserve your great-grandmother's legacy and my sister's memory."

Stinging from the rebuke and reminded anew how much she longed to call the tulip quilt her own, Judy resolved to learn to quilt before another Easter came.

Back home, having learned all she could from library books and craft kits, she asked her mother to help her find a quilting class. Within a week, Tuyet enrolled Judy in a beginner's course at a quilt shop a half-hour drive from their home. At first the instructor was reluctant to accept a much younger student, but at Tuyet's insistence, she allowed Judy to sit in on the first day, after which she agreed that Judy could remain in the course. When Judy proved herself an apt pupil, willing to hear criticism and never failing to participate diligently, the teacher forgot her earlier resistance and often stayed after class to help Judy master a challenging skill. By the end of the summer, Judy had completed her first bed-size sampler top, and with the help of her fellow students, she spent the last day of class layering and basting it. Her teacher showed her how to adjust the lap hoop to hold the layers snugly but not too taut, how to pop the thread through the back of the quilt and conceal the knot within the batting, and how to take small rocking stitches with her right hand while feeling beneath the quilt for the tip of the needle with her left.

As autumn passed into winter, Judy developed a callus on her fingertip and noted with increasing delight that the stitches, which had become smaller and more precise with practice, gave her sampler new dimension, grace, and depth. After spring rains had melted the winter snows, Judy's mother drove her to the quilt shop so her former teacher could demonstrate how to finish the quilt with a narrow, double-fold bias strip that concealed the raw edges of the quilted top. Judy stitched the last few inches of binding to the back of her quilt on the long drive to her grand-mother's house on Good Friday, tying the last knot just as they crossed the border into Ohio.

Judy could not wait until Easter morn-ing to unveil her masterpiece. As soon as she had hung up her jacket and properly greeted everyone, she lugged her tote bag into the living room and brought out her sampler quilt—made entirely by hand, twelve different blocks, some pieced, some appliquéd, some a little bit of both. As Grandma put on her glasses to inspect her stitches, Judy told everyone about her quilting class, how many months she had spent and spools of thread she had used up, and how she was going to put the quilt on her bed back home and sleep beneath it every night. Everyone wanted a closer look at her quilt; everyone complimented her handiwork, even the boys, even Carrie, the second most accomplished quilter of the cousins.

Grandma was the last to speak. "Very well done," she proclaimed, and that meant it was so. Judy had never known a prouder moment.

That night, Judy and Susan slept on top of their sleeping bags and shared Judy's pretty new quilt as a cover. "You've won the tulip quilt for sure," said Susan.

"I don't think it's a contest we can win or lose," said Judy, afraid of letting her hopes rise too much. "Grandma never said she'd automatically give the quilt to the first granddaughter who made a full-size quilt."

Susan squeezed her arm fondly. "Maybe not, but you deserve it."

Secretly, Judy thought so, too, but she didn't dare say so aloud. Grandma was very particular, and Judy still might not have done enough to prove herself.

On the afternoon of Easter Sunday, the ten granddaughters followed Grandma upstairs to her bedroom. She didn't sit on the floor anymore, but in her chair by the window and instructed Miranda and Carrie to open the chest and carefully unfold the daisy quilt. Judy savored the story of Grandma's wedding day. Though new details emerged with each retelling, the stories had become so familiar that Judy could close her eyes and envision the celebration as clearly as if she had been among the wedding party. Then the tulip quilt came out, and as they all admired it, Judy, with a practiced quilter's eye, imagined the crosshatches and feathered plumes that would best enhance her great-grandmother's graceful appliqué.

"We might as well just tuck this in Judy's suitcase today," said Miranda, eighteen years old and full of plans for her upcoming high school graduation. The other cousins offered teasing sighs and laments of agreement, except for Carrie. Although each of the cousins would have gladly taken the tulip quilt top home had Grandma offered it, all but Judy, Carrie, and ten-year-old Beth had long ago abandoned any hope that they would ever quilt well enough to meet their grandmother's exacting standards. Even Carrie had brought nothing new to show how her skills had improved over the past year, and although Beth proudly showed off the Seamstress badge she had earned in Girl Scouts, she had only two crib quilts to her credit.

"That's unkind," snapped Grandma, gesturing to Miranda to gather up the quilt top. Startled, Miranda roused herself and put the pretty tulips away for another year while her cousins exchanged looks of astonishment. Never had their special time with Grandma ended so abruptly.

Miranda fastened the latch, then turned to face her grandmother, clasping and unclasping her hands. "I'm sorry. I didn't mean that I'm in any hurry—I mean, I know you're going to leave the quilts in your will—"

"Oh, my dear girl, that's not it at all." Grandma held out an arm to Miranda, who gratefully hurried forward to accept one of her brisk hugs. "I meant that it's unkind to tease Judy so, after all she's done to try to motivate the rest of you girls."

Susan shot Judy a look of utter bewilderment. "But Miranda wasn't teasing. Judy's the best quilter of all of us."

"I know I'm not good enough to finish your mother's quilt yet," said Judy, "but I'm working hard to improve, and I know I could be good enough someday."

"Oh, Judy." Grandma sank back in her chair, shaking her head in dismay. "Surely you understand that my mother's quilt has to go to one of my real granddaughters, so it can stay in the family."

The room went abruptly silent. From elsewhere in the house came the sound of distant laughter and the squall of a cranky baby.

Judy's breath constricted. Somehow she managed to push herself to her feet and leave the room.

She couldn't go downstairs and face the questions her unexpected appearance alone would prompt, so she flung herself on the bed in her father's old room and stared up at the ceiling. She took deep, slow breaths and blinked away tears the moment they threatened to form. After a few minutes, she heard her cousins descending the stairs and Grandma's slower tread following after. She waited another five minutes before sitting up and smoothing the wrinkles in her new Easter skirt.

Determined to avoid the other granddaughters, Judy went outside to the back porch where the younger children played, but Susan sought her out. "She has a mean streak," Susan said, her blue eyes narrowed in anger. "I don't want her stupid quilt anymore. None of us do."

"Don't. You're making it worse."

Susan held out her arms and Judy let herself be embraced, resting her head on Susan's shoulder, sick at heart. The giddy shouts and laughter of the younger children seemed suddenly remote, a pageant she could only watch and not join in, and not because she was too grown up for play.

Susan whispered in her ear, just as when they were children with secrets to share: "I don't care what she says. I know you're a real cousin."

None of the other granddaughters said a word to Judy about their grandmother's remark, her cool assessment of Judy's place in the family, but Judy heard their disbelieving whispers, saw the glances of stricken sympathy. She hoped her mother did not. Tuyet knew something was wrong; she kept feeling Judy's forehead and watched her sharply when she picked at her dinner. Judy longed to confide in her, but she could imagine how her proud, protective mother might react. In defense of her daughter, she might do or say something that would get Judy and her parents banished from the family home forever, just as she had so many years ago in Saigon.

Judy kept silent, but she could not force her cousins to do so, and eventually word got around to her parents. Judy didn't think anything of her aunt's phone call until her mother and father knocked on the door to her bedroom, where she had been finishing her algebra homework. Their expressions told her that they knew everything, but still they asked for the story. Her breezy account and assurances that she had known all along that the quilt wouldn't go to her and that it was no big deal did not convince them, but to her surprise, it was her gentle father and not her fiery mother who confronted Grandma. Tuyet held Judy wordlessly, stroking her hair, while downstairs, her father smoldered and raged on the phone.

"A 'real granddaughter,' Mother? What's that supposed to mean?" Silence. "She's not 'just a stepdaughter.' I adopted her. She's mine. I'm her father and that makes her your granddaughter, no different from the other girls." An icy pause. "Would the adoption be more real if Judy looked more like you?" Another silence. "Oh, how very generous of you, Mother. I'm thrilled to know that if Tuyet and I have our 'own' daughter, she'll be eligible." A brief pause. "No, *you* listen. She's your granddaughter as much as I am your son, and if she isn't good enough for you, than neither am I."

He slammed down the phone.

After that, Judy feared that they

would never go back to Grandma and Grandpa's house, but they did. When Christmas came, they made the long drive through the snow and everyone welcomed Judy and her mother as they always had. Judy's father kissed his mother on the cheek in greeting as if they had never argued. Judy looked on and marveled at the adults' capacity for pretense.

Grandma never said a word about that Easter afternoon, not to apologize, not to explain, not to assure Judy that she was as much a member of the family as Susan and Miranda and the other cousins. It was as if they had all agreed to pretend the whole ugly scene had never happened, but Judy sensed that nothing had been resolved. Grandma still did not consider her a real and true grandchild, and her father still resented it.

Forever after, when Easter came, Judy found ways to be too preoccupied to follow Grandma upstairs to her bedroom to see the quilts. She would be busy helping Aunt Grace prepare a special dessert, or helping Uncle Peter change a diaper. Susan was the next to drop out of the annual audience, and then, as the grandchildren grew up, formed families of their own, and began dividing their holidays between new families and old, the tradition passed into history. Emily was only a few months old when Judy's grandmother died, having never met her newest great-grandchild. Miranda inherited the daisy quilt, as everyone had expected, and the tulip quilt went to Carrie, who sent Judy a long e-mail confessing that she had given up quilting long ago, and that she preferred to give the top to Judy, the only one of the grandchildren capable of finishing it properly. Judy was touched by the gesture but told Carrie to keep her inheritance, adding that it was fine to leave the top as it was, as they all remembered it. Leaving it un-quilted was, in fact, what quilt restorers recommended for antique tops.

Judy looked around the cornerstone patio at the women passing the candle from hand to hand, some sharing amus-ing tales, others confiding their most closely guarded secrets. She could imagine their disbelief and indignation if she confessed her own secret, that for most of her life, a quilt symbolized love and acceptance denied, a circle closed against her. Not until coming to Waterford and joining the local guild had she learned about the abiding friendships nurtured around the quilting frame. Only after knowing Sylvia, Gwen, and the others did understanding come like a revelation: Judy's grandmother had never learned to quilt, or she would have finished the tulip top herself. Perhaps if she had been a quilter, she would have found it unthinkable to use a quilt as a tool of division, setting her granddaughters against one another and setting Judy apart. Perhaps if Grandma had quilted, she would have understood the necessity of contrast and value, of joining together what seemed too dissimilar to fit, and thereby creating strength and beauty and enduring bonds.

The time to leave the protective circle at Elm Creek Manor was too quickly approaching. Nothing could replace these dear friends, their presence in her life or their place in her heart, but Judy had learned that wherever quilters were, friendship abided. Though miles would soon separate Judy from the other Elm Creek Quilters, their friendship would endure, and wherever the winding ways of her life's path led her, there she would weave new ties, forge new bonds, and she would help her daughter to do the same.

The Elm Creek Quilters had shown her how.

Sylvia cut the last four pieces for Judy's quilt, four triangular shapes with flat bases and concave sides, curving and narrowing until they met at a point. She had searched her stash for the perfect fabrics for her departing friend, silky prints with images of tortoises and cranes, symbols of the land of Judy's birth. She chose reds and golds, Vietnamese colors of celebration, but mixed in reds and blues, the school colors for the University of Pennsylvania. The shifting hues marked the winding ways

Judy had followed from Saigon to Elm Creek Manor to her new life in Philadelphia. For the lighter pieces, Sylvia plucked from her stash a half yard of a whimsical fabric—navy images that resembled computer circuits and diodes on a white background. For the life of her Sylvia could not remember purchasing such an odd print, but it had found its way into her stash somehow, and at last she had the perfect use for it. She smiled as she traced around her template on the wrong side of the fabric, imagining Judy's laugh of delight when she held her quilt—or rather, her portion of a larger quilt—and interpreted the different symbols Sylvia had hidden within the scraps.

When that day would come, Sylvia did not know, but winding paths often curved back upon themselves, and Sylvia hoped Judy would not delay her return journey too long. Though Judy must leave them, she would always have a place at Elm Creek Manor. When she returned, Sylvia would present her with her gift of friendship and show her how it fit into the greater whole.

Sarah

"They know," Sarah told her husband, blinking up at the ceiling in the early morning sunlight.

Matt, already showered and almost dressed, sat on the edge of the bed to pull on his socks. "Are you sure? They're acting perfectly normal. Normal for Elm Creek Quilters, anyway."

"That's only because they don't know that I know they know. When they're able to show that they know, that's when the uproar will begin."

Matt took a moment to puzzle out who knew what when. "We were going to tell them soon anyway."

"Yes, but I wanted it to be on my

terms, so I could keep the chaos under control."

Matt grinned and bent over to kiss her on the cheek. "Hon, I think your days of keeping chaos under control are numbered. Better get used to it."

Groaning, Sarah snatched up his pillow and covered her face—and then, abruptly, she realized that for the first time in weeks, she didn't feel sick upon waking. Her nausea had vanished so completely that she had almost forgotten it. "Matt, what day is it?"

"Tuesday, August fifth. Why?" Suddenly Matt's eyes widened in alarm. "Oh, no. Sarah, I'm sorry. I completely forgot."

"Forgot what?"

"It's our anniversary."

"Oh, right. Don't worry about it. I forgot, too."

"I didn't even get you a card."

"That's okay. I didn't get you anything, either." As Matt sighed with relief, Sarah quickly counted the weeks, then bounded upright in bed, triumphant. "I am now officially in my second trimester, and look! No morning sickness, right on time. Don't tell me chaos can't be managed. This is one fetus who knows how to keep a schedule."

She shrieked and ducked out of the way before he could swat her with a pillow.

Her friends hid it well, Sarah thought as she went downstairs, but surely they had already figured it out. How else did they account for her morning bouts with nausea, a prolonged stomach virus only prenatal vitamins could cure? She had experienced every typical symptom exactly when *What to Expect When You're Expecting* warned her it might appear, and since all of the Elm Creek Quilters except for Summer had been pregnant at least once, they knew what to look for.

They were very good actresses, Sarah decided. They knew her so well that they couldn't possibly have overlooked such a profound change in her life. Gracious friends that they were, they were waiting for Sarah and Matt to share their big news on their own schedule. That time had come.

She'd break the news at lunchtime,

and it would be a relief to finally have everything out in the open. Sarah and Matt had so much to do to prepare, and only six more months to do it. They had to transform their suite's sitting room into a nursery, purchase the layette, arrange for a diaper service, take baby CPR lessons—so many important tasks that Sarah could barely fit the spreadsheet on her computer screen unless she shrank the font. But less organized people than Sarah had babies every day, and if they could manage, she certainly could.

Breakfast was a pleasure for the first time in weeks, and not only because Anna's orange-ginger waffles were sublime. If only she could have indulged in a cup of coffee—but medical research conflicted on this point, and Sarah had decided to err on the side of caution and eschew caffeine for the duration. Sylvia's favorite mint tea didn't pack the same wallop as Sarah's favorite French roast, but she carried a steaming mug up to the office anyway, to sip as she plowed through the usual pile of daily paperwork. Judy's impending departure had thrown her regular course schedule into disarray, but the replacement instructor, Gretchen Hartley, had assured Sarah that she had taught classes similar to Judy's specialties and could step in at a moment's notice.

Gretchen and her husband were moving into the manor on Wednesday, so Gretchen would have a few days to observe the daily camp routine before anyone thrust her unprepared into a classroom. Sarah breathed a sigh of relief and leaned back in the tall leather chair, closing her eyes and resting her hands on the cool oak desk. She loved her office in the manor's stately library, which spanned the entire width of the manor's south wing. Light spilled in through tall diamond-paned windows on the east and west walls, and between the windows stood tall bookcases, shelves bowing slightly under the weight of hundreds of volumes. Gentle cross breezes cooled the room in summer, and in winter, a fire burning in the large stone fireplace on the south wall kept the library warm and snug. Two armchairs and footstools sat before it, while more chairs and sofas were arranged in a square in the center of the room, awaiting other Elm Creek Quilters who might stop by to discuss camp business or to relax during breaks from the busy classrooms downstairs. Sylvia and Summer worked in the office, too, but everyone saw it as primarily Sarah's domain, since she spent most of her work days there, handling the camp's finances, marketing, and operations. Come September, when Summer left for graduate school, Sarah would also take over her curriculum, personnel management, and Internet duties. Sarah doubted she would teach classes anymore, but she didn't mind that her contribution to Elm Creek Quilts took place mostly behind the scenes. Not teaching gave her a certain flexibility that she knew she would need once the baby came.

They would have to set up a little play area in the library, with a bouncy seat, a little swing, toys, and a cradle so Sarah could work while the baby slept. She would make a crib quilt for the baby, of course, something cute and simple like a Nine-Patch or Sawtooth Star, in cheerful rainbow colors suitable for either a girl or a boy. If she started in September, after the last week of camp, she would be able to put the last stitch in the binding well before the baby arrived.

At noon, the hour she had chosen to make the big announcement, it was no small task to get all the Elm Creek Quilters together before they dispersed throughout the banquet hall. On days like this, Sarah regretted Sylvia's decree that the faculty should dine with a different group of campers every day instead of clustering at their own table. By stationing herself in the foyer and taking her friends aside as they exited the ballroom, she was able to herd them together, although Gwen kept eyeing the buffet table longingly through the open doorway. Summer was the last to arrive; she always lingered until every student's questions were answered. It was little wonder the campers' evaluations never failed to list her as a favorite teacher.

"I'm sure you know what I'm going to say, so I'll make it quick," said Sarah when she had gathered her friends around her. "Matt and I are going to have a baby."

Sylvia nodded sagely and Agnes clasped her hands together and exclaimed with delight, but the others just stared at her.

"You're having a baby?" Gwen echoed. "Now?"

"Not now, as in today, but yes. I'm having a baby."

Summer peered at her. "And . . . this is good news, right?"

"Of course it's good news. It's great news." Or at least Sarah had thought so, until that moment.

Something in her expression must have told her friends that she had expected an entirely different reaction, for they suddenly roused themselves and offered the fond hugs and joyful congratulations more befitting the occasion. "You knew all along," Sarah teased, hugging each of her friends in turn. "You can drop the act."

"I did have my suspicions," Sylvia admitted, but the others declared that her announcement had come as a complete surprise. Sarah wasn't sure she believed them.

"You're going to make a wonderful mother," said Judy.

Tears sprang into Sarah's eyes. "Thank you." Until then, she had not realized how much she had wanted someone to reassure her of that.

"What did your mother say when you told her?" asked Bonnie. "How many years ago was it that she started that crib quilt here at camp? She must be thrilled that you're making her a grandmother at last."

"I'm sure she will be," said Sarah, "when I tell her."

Her friends groaned and exclaimed in dismay.

"You should have told her first," Sylvia admonished. "She's your mother."

"And she's been praying for this news for years," added Diane. "She probably gave up all hope long ago."

"I'm going to tell her," Sarah protested. "I have my first prenatal appointment tomorrow morning. I promise I'll call my mother afterward."

"Your first appointment?" asked Gwen. "How far along are you?"

When Sarah told them she had just entered her second trimester, there were more exclamations. "Why didn't you tell us sooner?" cried Bonnie.

"I thought you had already guessed." Honestly, didn't they pay any attention to her at all? "Besides, the later you hear the news, the less time you have to worry."

"And the less time we have to work on quilts for the baby," said Diane accusingly.

"You should have seen your ob-gyn before now," said Judy.

"When would I have had time?" Sarah said, somewhat defensively, for she knew her friend was right. "If I'd had any unusual symptoms, I would have called urgent care, but I wanted a particular doctor and she was fully booked. To be taken on as a new patient, I had to wait until she had an opening. My research indicated that she would be worth it."

Diane rolled her eyes. "We wouldn't want to contest your research."

"Your baby's due in February," said

Summer, thinking ahead, and then her face fell. "And I won't be here to welcome her. Or him."

Judy reached over and patted Summer on the shoulder consolingly.

"You can meet the baby when you come home for spring break," said Sarah. "I'll send lots of pictures, too. I promise."

"What are you going to do about work?" asked Agnes, her blue eyes large and inquisitive behind her pink-tinted glasses. "I must say, I always considered you one of those career girls who never really wanted to start a family."

"I won't have to take any time off of work," Sarah promised. When her friends regarded her skeptically, she added, "At least, not much. The baby's due in February, which should give me plenty of time to recover before the start of the new camp season at the end of March. I'll work ahead and get most of the summer's marketing, scheduling, and registration out of the way. Things should run as smoothly as ever."

Diane burst into laughter. "Are you trying to convince us, or yourself?"

"You, I suppose. I'm not worried." Sarah noticed the other Elm Creek Quilters struggling unsuccessfully to hide their grins. "Why, do you think I should be?"

"A baby changes everything," said Bonnie. "From this point on, you should expect the unexpected."

"Nothing's completely unexpected if you plan ahead."

This time, Diane was not the only one to laugh.

Sarah looked around the circle, shaking her head. "Thanks for your support, oh ye of little faith."

"Sarah, if anyone can have a by-the-book pregnancy, it's you," said Gwen. "We won't hold you to it, that's all."

"You shouldn't hold yourself to it, either," added Agnes. "If you need to take some time off, we'll cover for you. If you need extra help now and then, don't be afraid to ask for it. This would be an excellent time for you to learn to delegate more, and to be more flexible."

As her friends chimed in with promises of help, it was Sarah's turn to laugh. "That's what you say now, but we'll see how many of you volunteer when it's time to change diapers."

Everyone laughed, and as the circle broke up to enter the banquet hall, Gwen caught Sarah's eye. "You are going to use cloth diapers rather than poison the environment with disposables, right?"

"That's an excellent idea." Sarah decided to practice delegating. "You're just the person to help me find an affordable, environmentally sensitive diaper service. Still eager to help?"

Gwen accepted the assignment, but she warned, "Not all wrinkles will be ironed out so easily. Some, you just have to learn to live with."

"I know," said Sarah cheerfully, although as a quilter, she had yet to encounter a wrinkle she couldn't smooth out with the right iron and sufficient time.

The next morning, Sarah and Matt drove the pickup into downtown Waterford, a college town of about 35,000 permanent residents and 15,000 young adults, who swelled the population when Waterford College was in session. The downtown bordered the campus, and aside from a few city government offices, it consisted mainly of bars, trendy restaurants, and shops catering to the students and faculty. The local residents knew they owed their livelihoods to the transient student population, and although they were grateful for the income, many resented the dependence. Sometimes the town's collective annoyance erupted in a flurry of housing and noise ordinances, and the students would strike back with boycotts and sarcastic editorials in the school newspaper. Since Sarah had friends on both sides of the fray, she stayed out of it and enjoyed Waterford's small-town appeal as well as the cultural amenities the college offered.

They passed the square, a popular park near Waterford's busiest intersection, and ascended Hill Street on their way to the medical office. Sarah was relieved they would avoid Main Street bordering the college campus because she still found it difficult to drive past the empty storefront where Bonnie's quilt shop had once been. Not long after moving to Waterford, lonely and miserable in her unsuccessful job search, Sarah had passed the shop while running errands and had paused to admire a beautiful Lone Star quilt in the window. Its bright colors and intricate design charmed her inside, where she met Bonnie, Summer, and several other future friends—and learned that the reclusive owner of Elm Creek Manor had made the Lone Star quilt in the window. Sarah often wondered how different her life would have been had she not wandered past the shop that day. Now the thought of seeing an empty space where the red-and-gold GRANDMA'S ATTIC sign had once so proudly hung pained her. She could only imagine how much worse Bonnie felt.

Inside the clinic, Sarah left a urine specimen and stepped gingerly on the scale, steeling herself that those numbers wouldn't be coming down for quite some time. After leading Sarah and Matt to a private room that smelled of antiseptic soap and tongue depressors, the nurse asked Sarah to climb onto the examination table so she could take her vitals. "Your blood pressure is slightly elevated," said the nurse, a woman with short, tight red curls and a wild abundance of freckles on her face and forearms. On her scrubs, penguins in red scarves skied down snowy mountains in defiance of the hot August sunshine outside.

"That's normal," said Sarah, remembering to add deferentially, "right?"

"We'll want to keep an eye on it." The nurse unfastened the pressure cuff and offered Sarah a brisk nod that was probably meant to be reassuring. "As I said, it's only slightly elevated. Running in from the parking lot or hurrying up the stairs could have been enough to raise your numbers. We'll take your blood pressure again at the end of your appointment just to be sure."

"You don't think I have preeclampsia, do you?"

"Ah." The nurse made a few notes on Sarah's chart. "I see we've been reading the Internet."

"I can't afford to go on bed rest,"

Sarah explained. "I'm going to work until my due date."

The nurse rested one freckled hand on her hip. "It's much too early for preeclampsia, but I'm sure that in the unlikely event you come down with it, you'll follow the doctor's instructions and do whatever is necessary for your health and the health of your baby."

"Of course," said Sarah, and Matt nodded as if he would see to it personally. If bed rest was the worst-case scenario, she could still make it work. She could invest in a laptop computer and work from bed, and keep the phone within reach. But it would not come to that, she told herself firmly. There was no reason to fear that she couldn't get an additional six months of work in before the baby came, just as she had planned.

As if she had spoken aloud, the nurse said, "You should also keep in mind that babies rarely arrive precisely on their due dates."

"This baby has explicit instructions," said Matt solemnly. From the look the nurse gave him as she left them alone in the examination room, Sarah knew she didn't understand his sense of humor.

Waiting for the doctor, Sarah lay back and rested her hands on her abdomen while Matt perused the brochures about prenatal classes. "We should take this one, Childbirth Preparation 101," he said. "This one sounds good, too: Yoga for the Expectant Mother."

"I don't think you're qualified for that one, honey."

"I meant for you—" Matt broke off as the door opened and the doctor entered. Sarah sat up and tugged the hospital gown over her knees, sizing up Dr. Jamison as they exchanged greetings. She was of medium height, with a solid build and very short gray hair, although Sarah guessed she was only in her mid-fifties. While she didn't seem particularly maternal, she possessed an aura of reassuring competence that only years of experience could give.

Dr. Jamison read over the nurse's notes, asked a few questions about Sarah's general health, and proceeded through the checkup with brisk efficiency. Matt stayed in the room the entire time, offering Sarah reassuring glances whenever she looked his way.

Dr. Jamison pressed down on her abdomen, feeling for the height of her uterus. "When did you say you last had your period?"

"June."

"Not May? Are you sure?"

"Pretty sure." Summer months were so packed full of camp activities that she sometimes forgot to mark her calendar.

"The height of your uterus suggests that you're closer to fourteen weeks into your pregnancy. The level of hormones in your urine specimen will help confirm that, but I'll schedule an ultrasound just to be sure."

"I'm sure I just entered my second trimester," said Sarah, although she was feeling less sure with each passing moment. She lay on the table with her feet in the stirrups, running through the dates in her mind. The date of conception should have been . . . but on the other hand, there was that one night . . . They had been trying for a baby for so long that she couldn't remember the dates properly, especially not while lying there in that awkward position, being poked and prodded in places she preferred to keep to herself.

Just as Sarah thought the examination was nearing its end, Dr. Jamison said, "Why don't we see if we can detect the heartbeat on the fetal Doppler?"

"Oh, yes, please," said Sarah eagerly.

"Doppler," mused Matt. "I thought that was for the weather forecast."

"Same principle, different device." Dr. Jamison squirted a cool gel on Sarah's bare abdomen and pressed a handheld monitor against her skin. A low, steady thudding sounded over the speaker. "That's your heartbeat," she said, sliding the monitor lower, listening, moving the monitor again. Suddenly the speaker emitted a soft, rapid pulsing noise, and the doctor smiled. "And that's your baby."

Tears sprang into Sarah's eyes. "Is it all right? Is it supposed to sound like that?"

"I hear a good, strong, steady heartbeat," the doctor assured her. "At one hundred fifty beats per minute, it's just right for fourteen weeks."

"But I'm only twelve weeks pregnant," Sarah reminded her, but stopped short at the doctor's sudden, thoughtful frown. "What is it? What's wrong?"

Matt reached over and took Sarah's hand as the doctor slid the monitor around to the other side of her abdomen, pursing her lips slightly, frown lines deepening. Sarah shivered, but not from the cold. She knew something was wrong, but she dared not speak, not while the doctor was listening so intently. She wanted to know, and she didn't want to know. She wanted to prolong the moment before the doctor announced that something was dreadfully wrong with her child, because the moment she heard those words, her world would come crashing down.

Then a different sound filled the room, the same quick wooshing of the baby's heartbeat, overlying a faint echo of the same pulse.

"Holy crap," said Matt. The doctor glanced up and nodded, with a faint, knowing smile.

"What? What is it?" said Sarah with rising panic.

"I'm detecting two heartbeats."

"Right," said Sarah, puzzling it out. "Mine and the baby's."

"No, yours is that slow, deep one, remember?" Dr. Jamison repositioned the monitor. "Do you hear them now?"

Sarah felt dizzy. "You mean . . . twins? You can't mean twins."

"I do indeed mean twins."

Matt let out a whoop of delight. "Twins! That's awesome! Can you tell if they're girls or boys? Or one of each? That would be so cool."

"I can't determine that from the heartbeat, contrary to folk wisdom. I'll definitely want to schedule an ultrasound under these circumstances, and if the babies cooperate, we might be able to get an answer for you then." Dr. Jamison set the monitor aside, wiped most of the gooey gel from Sarah's abdomen, and handed her a towel so she could finish. "You can sit up now. I'll step out for a moment so you can dress."

Distantly, it occurred to Sarah that it was rather silly to be concerned for her modesty now, after all the doctor had just seen of her. She nodded, unable to speak.

"Twins," Matt kept repeating, shaking his head in disbelieving joy. "Twins!"

"Let's hope it's only twins," said Sarah shakily, buttoning her blouse. She was fourteen weeks pregnant, apparently, not twelve, and with two babies, not one.

"Hey. It's okay." Matt embraced her gently. "I know this isn't what we expected, but it's going to be fine. Better than fine. It's going to be wonderful."

"Matt—" She desperately did not want to disappoint him. "I was worried enough about taking care of one baby, but two?"

He kissed her. "You're not going to be alone. I'll be there right beside you every step of the way, and so will a manor full of surrogate grandmas. Everything's going to work out. Have a little faith."

She buried her face in his chest. She did have faith—in everyone but herself. None of her plans included two babies, two cradles, two of everything, and everything divided in two.

She had not expected to trip over Gwen's unsmoothable wrinkle so soon.

As they left the medical center, Matt beamed proudly as he escorted her across the parking lot. "Twins run in my family, you know."

"Now you tell me," she muttered. The August heat rippled in waves off the blacktop, and she felt her morning sickness threatening. It would be hotter in the truck, even with the windows rolled down. For the hundredth time, she wished Matt would arrange for a mechanic to fix the air conditioner. He kept insisting he could do it himself for a fraction of the price, but he never found the time.

"Come on, you remember," said Matt, lacing his fingers through hers. "My dad has a twin brother and my mom had a twin sister."

Matt had adopted the past tense whenever speaking of his mother, although she was probably still very much alive, somewhere. She had abandoned her husband and son when Matt was only five years old, and as the years passed, she had stopped keeping in touch with Matt's father. Sarah could never be sure how much Matt truly remembered of her and how much his imagination had been reconstructed from photographs.

"Uncle Carl is your dad's twin?" asked Sarah, as if he had not mentioned his mother. She wondered how Matt could still speak of her so fondly. "They don't look anything alike."

"Fraternal. My mom and her sister, though, they were identical twins."

"You never told me any of this. I would have remembered." They approached the red pickup and, as Matt reached for the car keys, Sarah stopped short. "Oh, this won't work. This is no good at all."

"What?"

"This." Sarah gestured at the truck, suddenly tearful. "How are we going to fit an infant car seat—two car seats—in a pickup? What are we supposed to do, strap them in back with the cargo?"

Matt shot her a look of utter bewilderment. "It's no big deal. When we take the babies out, we'll use the Elm Creek Quilts minivan."

"What if one of the Elm Creek Quilters needs it for camp business?" cried Sarah, bursting into sobs. "What if Sylvia and Andrew are traveling? They always take the minivan in winter."

Matt stared at her. "I hope this is hormonal, and I hope it passes. Sarah, honey, we'll figure it out. We'll buy another car if we have to."

Sarah nodded and climbed into the truck, wiping away tears. Part of her wanted to snap at him for tossing the word *hormonal* around, while another part hoped he was right. Six more months of weeping at the sight of an unsuitable car would be unbearable.

Five and a half more months, she reminded herself. Not six. In her mind's eye she ripped up her calendar, spreadsheet, and plans and scattered the pieces on the medical center sidewalk behind them.

The other Elm Creek Quilters were busy with their classes when Sarah and Matt returned to the manor, so Sarah stopped by the kitchen for a glass of water before heading upstairs to the library. Anna stood at the counter chopping vegetables and directing Diane's eldest son as he stirred something on the stovetop. It smelled wonderful, rich and fragrant, and all thoughts of morning sickness melted away. She suddenly realized she was starving.

"How did your appointment go?" asked Anna as Sarah dug into the refrigerator.

Sarah snatched up cheese, sliced turkey breast wrapped in deli paper, whole-grain organic bread, and spicy mustard. "Twins."

A knife clattered on the counter. "Did you say twins?"

"Yep."

Sarah barely had time to set down her sandwich fixings before Anna cried out in joy and embraced her. "How wonderful! Congratulations times two. Twice the cuteness, twice the joy."

"Twice the diapers," said Michael.

Anna waved that off as a minor detail. "Just think how nice it will be for your kids to always have a playmate near while they're growing up. They'll never be lonely."

Sarah felt tears welling up again, but

this time they were infused with happiness. "I hadn't thought of it that way. I guess you're right."

"You're assuming they'll get along," said Michael. "Sometimes siblings hate each other."

"These two won't," said Anna so decisively that Sarah never thought to question how she could possibly know that. As Sarah reached into the cupboard for a plate, Anna added, "Here, let me make that for you. You should get off your feet."

Sarah had to laugh. "Thanks, but I'm not an invalid. I'm going to keep my usual routine until I can't anymore. Then you're welcome to wait on me hand and foot."

Anna insisted on making her a glass of decaf ginger iced tea, an offer Sarah gratefully accepted. It was so refreshing that Sarah almost wished she had let Anna make the sandwich as well. Their new chef had a gift for bringing out the flavor of the most ordinary ingredients, much like a master quilter transformed the most humble scraps of cotton fabric into a work of art.

Later, up in the office, Sarah dived into her work with a new vigor, knowing that next week's ultrasound was likely to prove Dr. Jamison right and move up her due date by two weeks. She fervently hoped it would be no more than that.

She shuffled papers and balanced accounts for most of the afternoon, enjoying the muffled, familiar sounds of quilt camp—voices and footsteps in the halls, laughter and birdsong through the open window, a delivery truck pulling into the parking lot, a lawn mower, the back door swinging open and banging shut. It was a happy, industrious sound, the background music of Sarah's days. She appreciated it most in those last weeks of summer as the end of the camp season approached. Next year would be so different with a baby—two babies—around. The melody of camp life would change key, taking on the sweet notes of babies' coos and music boxes, rattles and cries. By the end of summer, the twins would be crawling, and what a job of baby-proofing she and Matt would face before then! That oak staircase was an accident waiting to happen, and all the outlets would need covers—

A quick rap on the library door startled Sarah from her reverie. "Come in," she called, tapping keys to save the open document on her computer.

One of the double doors opened, and a slight, gray-haired woman in a floral skirt, lavender blouse, and sensible shoes entered. "Hello, Sarah," she said. "Anna said I might find you here. Joe and I just arrived. I'm sure you heard the truck out back. I hope the racket didn't disturb you."

"Gretchen," exclaimed Sarah, rising. In all the excitement, she had completely forgotten that their newest faculty member was moving in that afternoon—and she had done nothing to prepare the second-floor suite Gretchen and her husband would share. "How was the drive from Ambridge?"

"Oh, treacherous, just as I expected," said Gretchen with a laugh. "Neither of us has ever driven a panel truck before. Fortunately we sold most of our large pieces of furniture ahead of time, so we were able to rent a smaller truck than if we hadn't downsized first."

"I'll round up some strong, young guys to unload your things," said Sarah, thinking frantically as she retrieved the keys to Gretchen's rooms from her desk drawer. Where would the delinquents be at that time of the day? "Let me show you to your suite. I have you in the west wing. It's older, but you have a great view of the cornerstone patio and the north gardens."

"I'm sure we'll be very comfortable," said Gretchen, a smile lighting up her weary face. "It's good to be here."

"It's wonderful to have you," said Sarah, ashamed that Gretchen seemed unaware of the poor welcome she was receiving. Yesterday Sarah had planned to keep an ear tuned to the back parking lot so that she would know immediately when Gretchen arrived, and could race downstairs to meet her at the back door. She had intended to offer Gretchen and Joe refreshments before leading them upstairs to their immaculate, cozy suite. Now she wasn't sure if anyone had even remembered to sweep their bedroom floor.

"The other Elm Creek Quilters are teaching right now, but you'll see everyone at supper." Sarah led Gretchen from the library past the oak staircase with the view of the grand front foyer below. Gretchen basked in the elegance of her new home, smiling, greeting campers they passed on the way. They turned left at the end of the hall, passed a few doors, and came to Gretchen's suite. "I hope you don't mind staying among all the campers. I considered putting you on the third floor for privacy, but you said Joe has a bad back, and I didn't want to inflict that extra flight of stairs on him."

"I'd prefer to be among the campers," Gretchen assured her. "That's where the action is."

"We can always move you later." Sarah unlocked the door and gestured for Gretchen to proceed her, hoping against hope that someone had remembered to clean it.

Gretchen let out a sigh of delight as she stepped into her new sitting room.

"It's perfect." She went to the window to admire the view, tested the sofa, and spun around to take it all in.

"Thanks," said Sarah, glancing through the bedroom door and, to her horror, spotting the price tags dangling from the new mattress, the new pillows still wrapped in plastic, and a vase of brown, wilted flowers on the bedside table. If she moved quickly—but it was already too late, as Gretchen's explorations had led her to the bedroom.

"About the flowers . . ." said Sarah weakly.

Gretchen burst into laughter. "I hope they're left over from last week's campers and not a welcome bouquet. I'd have to wonder what you're trying to tell me."

"I'm so sorry," said Sarah. "I meant to change those and set everything up for you, but it's been a crazy day, and I'm more pregnant than I thought I was, and it completely slipped my mind—"

"Don't give it a second thought," said Gretchen. "I'm not one to fuss over such a little thing. It's a lovely suite, and I feel quite at home already. You go ahead and get back to your work. Joe and I can take care of settling ourselves in."

Relieved, Sarah insisted upon removing the dead flowers and drafting Michael and the other young men to unload the truck and carry the Hartleys' belongings upstairs. Only after she had welcomed Joe and sat the couple down in the kitchen for iced tea and cookies did she excuse herself and search the manor for Sylvia, the only other Elm Creek Quilter who was not teaching that day. Someone ought to remain with the newcomers, not just to make up for Sarah's shabby welcome, but to offer the assistance only someone familiar with the manor could give.

On a day with so many camp activities to enjoy and dozens of quilters eager to spend time with her, the last place Sarah expected to find Sylvia was inside her suite with the door shut, but the whirring of her Featherweight gave her away. "Sylvia," Sarah called, rapping on the door, "are you busy?"

The sewing machine stopped and Sarah heard a mad scrambling on the other side of the door. "Just a minute,"

Sylvia called back, her voice muffled. When she opened the door moments later, the table around her Featherweight was scrupulously clean, but Sylvia looked a bit distracted, tucking a loose lock of silvery hair behind one ear and brushing stray sewing threads from her lap and sleeves.

"Working on a top-secret project?" asked Sarah.

"Don't be silly," replied Sylvia. "Tell me, what's the word from the doctor? You're in tip-top shape, I presume."

"Oh, yes. All three of us seem to be."

Sylvia peered at her over the rims of her glasses. "She examined Matt, too?"

"No. By the three of us, I meant me, the baby, and the other baby."

Sylvia drew in a slow breath, her hand flying to her heart. "Oh, my heavens. Twins."

"Twins," Sarah confirmed, smiling.

Sylvia embraced her. "My dear girl, how wonderful. Congratulations. What did your mother say? She'll have to make another crib quilt to match the first, won't she?"

"I wouldn't expect her to do that. My

mother makes one quilt every two years. She'd never finish in time."

Sylvia held her at arm's length. "You still haven't told her," she scolded, easily guessing the truth. "You've been home for hours and you couldn't find a moment to pick up the phone?"

Sarah couldn't explain that she needed to recover from her own shock first. "I'll call her today, I promise, but first, I need your help." She explained about Gretchen's arrival and the haphazard welcome she had received.

"I meant to greet her at the door, too," said Sylvia, already heading into the hall on her way to Gretchen's suite. "I must have lost track of time, and I suppose I didn't hear the truck over the sewing machine."

"I thought you said you weren't working on anything."

"Not at all. You asked if I was working on a top-secret project and I asked you not to be silly." She held up a finger before Sarah could complain about the evasive reply. "I must say it troubles me to think that we've lost sight of the simple rules of hospitality. Gretchen is an

Elm Creek Quilter now and she deserved a proper greeting."

"We'll make it up to her. Tonight before the evening program, I can bring her onstage and introduce her to the whole camp. There's nothing like a round of applause to make a person feel welcome."

"I hope you're right. Honestly. Dead flowers at her bedside." Shaking her head, Sylvia continued down the hall. "You go back to the library, put your feet up, and write your little speech. I'll see to Gretchen."

"I don't need to put my feet up," Sarah said as Sylvia hastened away. Still, she did as instructed, crafting a warm, generous introduction from Gretchen's resume and the notes Sarah had taken during her interview earlier that summer. Gretchen's career as a quilter spanned four decades and gave Sarah ample material to draw upon. She had taken her first quilting lesson from none other than Sylvia herself, as a high school student in Ambridge, Pennsylvania, just down the river from Pittsburgh. After working many years as a substi-

tute home economics teacher, Gretchen
had helped keep the traditions of quilting alive in the years before the "quilting
renaissance" of the 1970s by sharing
her knowledge with friends. Eventually
that small circle of quilters grew into a
thriving guild, and Gretchen became so
renowned as a teacher that guilds from
hundreds of miles away invited her to
lecture and teach. Gretchen and a
friend—with whom Sarah gathered
she'd had a falling out, a detail she
would omit from her introduction—had
founded the most successful quilt shop
in western Pennsylvania. Sarah had
seen for herself that their newest
teacher possessed flawless technical
skills, and if she was a bit reluctant to in-
novate or to adopt the latest trends, her
devotion to traditional quilting compen-
sated for that. Gretchen was a marvelous addition to the circle of quilters at
Elm Creek Manor, and after Sarah introduced her to their campers, everyone
there would know it.

That ought to make up for the vase of
wilted daylilies.

While her document printed, Sarah

turned her attention to the second assignment Sylvia had given her. She took a deep breath and dialed her mother's number.

Carol answered on the fourth ring, just when Sarah had begun to hope for the answering machine. Not that she would have given her mother the big news on a recording, but an excuse to hang up and call back later would have been nice.

"Sarah?" her mother said when she picked up, breathless. "What's wrong?"

"Nothing's wrong. Is something wrong there? You sound winded."

"I'm in the backyard working in the garden. Gardening is a relaxing hobby, you know."

Early in their relationship, Carol had referred to Matt as "that gardener" too often for Sarah to miss her underlying meaning: Gardening was meant to be a hobby, not a career, certainly not a respectable way for a man to support a family. Carol could not or would not understand that Matt, with his college degree in Landscape Architecture and responsibility for the entire Bergstrom estate, did not spend his days merely digging aimlessly in the dirt.

"You don't sound relaxed," Sarah said, ignoring the barb, wondering if she should call back later. Then she imagined Sylvia's disapproving frown and realized she'd never be able to invent an acceptable excuse for not sharing the news now that she finally had her mother on the phone.

"Oh, I'm fine. I'm on the cordless, and you know how that is. I can hear it ring, but I can only answer if I'm within ten feet of the base station. I saw your name in the caller ID and made a run for it."

Sarah, who often didn't pick up when she saw her mother's number in her own caller ID, felt a twinge of guilt, likely the first of many depending on the length of their conversation. "Sit down and catch your breath," said Sarah. "I have some news."

"Why should I sit down? People only tell you to sit down when they have bad news." Sarah heard the metallic scraping sound of a patio chair being dragged across concrete. "Is Sylvia all right? She didn't have another stroke, did she?"

Sarah held back the instinctive retort that any other worried mother would have asked first about her son-in-law, not her daughter's friend and business partner, even one as dear as Sylvia. "Sylvia's fine and so is Matt," she said. "We're all fine. In fact, Matt and I have great news."

"Really? What's that?"

"I'm pregnant!"

There was a pause. "Huh."

Sarah waited for more, but her mother was silent. "I tell you I'm pregnant and all you can say is 'Huh'?"

"Did the doctor tell you this or did you just take a home test?"

"Mom, you're a nurse. You know the home tests are as accurate as the ones the doctor offers."

"Yes, technically, but there's always user error to consider."

"I think I know how to pee on a stick. Even if I could mess that up, the doctor confirmed it today. I'm definitely pregnant." And her friends wondered why she had put off this call. "Honestly,

Mom, I expected a much more enthusiastic response considering you've been warning me about my ticking biological clock for years."

"I have not." Her mother inhaled deeply as if the news were an aroma of suspicious origin. "If I seem restrained, it's just that I've been waiting for this news for so long that I don't want to get my hopes up."

"Should I have waited to tell you until I was on my way to the hospital to deliver them?"

"Of course not. I just need time for it to sink in." She paused. "Did you say 'to deliver *them*'?"

"That's why I thought you should sit down."

"Twins?"

"We heard two heartbeats."

"Oh, no, Sarah. I'm so sorry."

"Why?" said Sarah, incredulous. "Matt and I are thrilled." Maybe that was overstating it, but she was compelled to make up for her mother's lack of enthusiasm, as if the babies had overheard their grandmother's lament. "If one grandchild is wonderful, aren't two even better?"

"Certainly, if they're spaced a few years apart. Twins will be so much harder, and the potential for complications is so much greater. I hope you won't have to have a C-section."

Sarah winced. "Thanks for planting that worry in my head."

"It's a very real possibility with multiple births. Surely your doctor mentioned it. Maybe I should call him and speak to him myself."

"He's a she, and no, Mom, you are not speaking to my doctor."

"At least give me her name so I can check her out."

"Absolutely not."

"There aren't that many ob-gyns in that little town. I'm sure I could figure it out."

"I'm begging you not to try." Sarah held the phone at arm's length, closed her eyes, and counted to five before returning it to her ear. "This is how it's supposed to go: I call you, I give you the happy news, you jump up and down for joy, you declare how happy you are, and you tell me everything's going to be fine and not to worry."

"Everything *is* going to be fine," her mother said. "And I'm very happy. I don't know why you think I'm not."

"The 'huh' remark was something of a clue."

"Sarah, I know you're hormonal but there's no need to be snippy. I already explained that I was surprised. It's such good news that I can hardly believe it."

"Great. I'm glad."

"You don't sound like you mean it."

She didn't. "I'll call you this weekend after we have the ultrasound, okay? Maybe I'll know if you'll have grand-daughters or grandsons or one of each."

"I'm rooting for two granddaughters," her mother said, "and I hope they're exactly like you were when you were a child."

"Yeah, that'll show me. Thanks, Mom," said Sarah, and hung up the phone.

Sarah had suspected her mother would find a way to sour her good news, and sure enough, she had. She hadn't even wished Sarah and Matt a happy anniversary, not that Sarah could complain after forgetting the date herself. The only good to come of the phone call was that at supper Sarah was able to tell Sylvia that she had fulfilled her filial duty. "What did your mother say?" Sylvia asked, passing Sarah the basket of warm, flaky rolls seasoned with rosemary. "I imagine she was speechless with delight."

If Carol had been speechless, that would indeed have been a delight. Sarah didn't want to spoil her appetite for Anna's marvelous cooking, so she told Sylvia that her mother had been surprised but happy, and that as a medical professional she was mindful of potential complications with multiple births.

"Of course she's going to worry," said Sylvia, nodding thoughtfully. "Be sure to tell her you're receiving excellent prenatal care, regular checkups, and all the rest. That will put her mind at ease."

"I'll do that," Sarah agreed, but since the six campers seated at that table were listening in with eager curiosity, she quickly changed the subject. She didn't mind talking about her pregnancy, but she had no desire whatsoever to bore everyone with an anti-Carol tirade. Sarah knew she always came off looking like an ungrateful daughter who should be more tolerant and forgiving of a concerned mother who, though perhaps somewhat overbearing, was actually quite harmless.

No one would find fault with Sarah if they knew the real Carol, or if they knew of her unfathomable dislike for Matt. Carol never failed to be on her best behavior on her rare visits to Elm Creek Manor. As far as the other Elm Creek Quilters knew, she had grown to respect her son-in-law, and she and Sarah could enjoy a warm relationship if only Sarah would stop dredging up slights and mistakes from years long past. They didn't understand that after all these years, Carol still disapproved of Matt, but she had learned to hide it from people whom she wanted to think well of her. The only real change was that she had come to tolerate Matt as a permanent part of Sarah's life that no complaining on her part would excise. Although this was a welcome improvement, Sarah longed for her complete, wholehearted acceptance. Matt had done nothing to earn his mother-in-law's enmity. He was a good man and a faithful husband, and Sarah knew he would be a wonderful father. He was everything Sarah wanted in a husband and a friend. What more could Carol ask of him?

Although the aromas of Anna's delicious chicken cordon bleu enticed her to take another bite, Sarah suddenly found herself without an appetite. What if Carol criticized Matt in front of the children? Or worse yet, what if her disapproval of Matt extended to her grandchildren? It was painful enough to have to defend her husband from her mother's slights. Sarah couldn't bear it if her mother disparaged the babies.

Carol's restrained reaction to the news of Sarah's pregnancy did not bode well.

Sarah set down her fork and took a quick drink of ice water, hoping no one would notice her hand trembling as she grasped the glass. Children deserved doting grandparents, but Sarah's father had died when she was in high school and Matt's mother had made herself scarce. Matt's father had raised him on his own, and his sense of humor and patience would make him a wonderful grandpa—but rarely could he take time off from his contracting business, so visits would be few and precious. Of the twins' two grandparents, Carol lived closer and had the most time to spend with the babies, but would she want to? And if she did, could Sarah trust her to have sense enough not to criticize Matt when they could overhear?

Surely Carol would muster up the same self-control in front of her grandchildren that she did for the Elm Creek Quilters. She had to know that the twins would only end up resenting her for speaking ill of their father. Then again, Carol did not seem to care how she angered Sarah with her unreasonable hostility toward Matt—or the many other friends and loved ones Sarah had unwittingly subjected to her mother's scathing criticism through the years. Even Sylvia had not escaped Carol's withering judgment, although Sylvia did not know it. In the early years of Elm Creek Quilt Camp, Carol had offered dire, unsolicited predictions about the likelihood that the fledgling business would fail, and she had warned Sarah about the imprudence of trusting her future to the whims of an elderly eccentric. To Sarah's relief, Carol had changed her mind entirely after coming to Elm Creek Manor and meeting Sylvia and the others, her worries no match for the Elm Creek Quilters' generous welcome and unconditional acceptance.

If only that force of good had been in place on her eighth birthday, when her grandparents made the long drive to Pennsylvania to spend the weekend. Sarah much preferred to visit them in their small, cozy home in Michigan's Upper Peninsula, especially in winter, at Christmastime. While her parents stayed indoors, Sarah and her grandparents would ice-skate on the pond, sled down a long, steep hill precariously dotted with pines, and build snowmen until they could bear the cold no longer. Inside, while Grandpa stoked the fireplace, Sarah would bundle up on the sofa under two or three of Grandma's old quilts, munch cookies, sip hot chocolate, and watch through the window as snow blanketed the yard and the surrounding trees. But in May, Sarah had school and her parents had to work, so Grandma and Grandpa had come to them.

On the morning of Sarah's birthday, Grandma couldn't wait for the afternoon birthday party for her to open her gift, so while Sarah's mother was busy in the kitchen frosting the cake, Grandma presented Sarah with a large, ribbon-tied box. When Sarah lifted the lid and saw a beautiful pink-and-white Sawtooth Star quilt nestled in tissue paper, she was almost afraid to touch it. "Is this for me?"

Grandma laughed. "Of course, darling. Do you see any other birthday girls here?"

Speechless with delight, Sarah flung her arms around her grandma, still holding fast to the beautiful quilt. It was warm and soft, just like its maker, and it smelled faintly of Grandma's talcum powder.

"You didn't need to do that," Sarah's mother said from the doorway, spatula in hand, the white rubber end covered in pink frosting. "I just bought her a new bedspread two months ago."

"A granddaughter deserves a hand-made quilt," said Grandma. "It was a joy to make."

"She'll just spill something on it and ruin it."

"No, I won't," Sarah piped up. "I promise."

"Don't you like the bedspread we picked out together?"

Her mother's warning tone signaled that she was thinking back to their shopping trip, how her mother had pa-tiently taken her from store to store in the shopping mall until Sarah decided on a pretty pastel-striped bedspread. Then her mother had agreed to back-track to the far end of the shopping mall, where they remembered seeing pretty flower-shaped pillows that matched the bedspread perfectly. Afterward, they had enjoyed lunch at a fancy restaurant instead of grabbing fast food in the food court. It had been a rare, good day, just the two of them, with no disagreements or bickering to spoil everything.

Yet over her grandma's murmured protests, her mother urged Sarah to say which she preferred, her grandmother's quilt or the bedspread they had chosen together. Sarah hemmed and hawed, reluctant to hurt either of their feelings, unwilling to lie. When her mother would not relent, Sarah finally confessed that she liked the Sawtooth Star quilt best.

Sarah's heart sank as her mother snatched up the quilt and returned it to the box. In a voice as taut as a wire, her mother promised Grandma that Sarah would take very good care of the quilt, and then she carried it from the room.

Sarah fervently willed another outcome, one in which her mother admired the quilt and prompted Sarah to thank her grandma for the lovely gift. It was her birthday, a day for wishes to be fulfilled, but the day passed without another glimpse of the quilt.

On the following evening, Sarah found the quilt folded at the foot of her bed. She yanked the comforter to the floor, spread the quilt in its place, and slept beneath it for the remaining nights of her grandparents' visit. Upon their departure, her mother returned the quilt to the box and stored it, out of Sarah's reach, on the floor of the master bedroom closet.

After that, Sarah was permitted to use the quilt only when her grandparents visited. They traveled to Pennsylvania less frequently as they aged, and often months passed without a glimpse of the pink-and-white patchwork. Now, with her grandparents long deceased and her mother's house no longer her own, Sarah had not seen the quilt for years. For all she knew it remained wrapped in tissue paper in the box on the floor of her mother's closet.

On those rare occasions when a certain shade of pink or a Sawtooth Star block in a camper's quilt reminded her of her grandma's gift, Sarah was tempted to ask her mother for it. The quilt was rightfully hers, a precious memento of her grandma's love. Knowing how devoted Sarah was to the art of quilting, her mother should have voluntarily returned the quilt to her long ago. Perhaps she had given the quilt away or had discarded it. Perhaps she hoped that Sarah had forgotten it, because returning the quilt to Sarah now would prompt a deluge of questions Carol would certainly rather not answer: Why had she kept the quilt from Sarah for so long? Why had she twisted Grandma's generous gift into a test of Sarah's loyalty? At the time, Sarah had assumed that she had hurt her mother's feelings by admitting that she preferred the quilt, and that her mother had withheld the quilt as punishment. Now she knew that nothing between mothers and daughters was ever so simple. And what was her grandmother's role in the drama? Was she the innocent, generous gift-giver Sarah had always assumed her to be, or had Sarah missed some darker undercurrent, some conflict between the two older women? Did Carol scorn her mother's handiwork, or had she always longed for a quilt of her own only to be refused? Had Sarah received the gift Carol had been denied? Had Grandma worked on the Sawtooth Star quilt for months, or had she begun to sew it only after Carol told her about their successful shopping trip? What had prompted Carol to leave the quilt on Sarah's bed the next day without a word of explanation—a rebuke from Grandma, or something else?

The more Sarah mulled over those questions, the less certain she was that her mother had been solely in the wrong, and that was a difficult admission for her to make. She did not want to doubt her grandma, who had always showered her with kindness and affection, and she was reluctant to concede anything to Matt and Sylvia and others who were too quick to forgive her mother's thoughtless malice. But her mother must have learned her coolly critical ways somewhere, from someone. Perhaps Sarah's grandma had hidden a darker side from Sarah the way Carol hid hers from the Elm Creek Quilters.

Sarah rested her hand on her abdomen and hoped that she would be different, that she would teach her children another way.

Determined to enjoy the evening program, Sarah put aside her mother's cautionary words as well as thoughts of the pink-and-white Sawtooth Star quilt and the uncomfortable questions it raised. The sun was just beginning to set when she joined the other Elm Creek Quilters in the ballroom to prepare for the scavenger hunt. Diane had insisted upon making a last-minute change to the list of items, so as they waited for her to return with new printouts, the Elm Creek Quilters entertained the campers with anecdotes about camp life behind the scenes. Gwen had cleverly implied that details in their stories would help the campers as they searched the estate—which very well could turn out to be true and sounded much better than confessing that they were merely filling time. At last Diane rushed in and distributed the lists to the campers, who had already divided themselves into teams of four. Sarah searched the crowd for shy Marcia and was pleased to find her standing with the Flying Saucer Sisters. The three original ladies had exchanged their fuchsia T-shirts for butter yellow and Marcia had donned a polo top in a slightly lighter shade. Even though Sarah had done nothing to help Marcia find her way into a welcoming circle of quilters, she felt vindicated, as if the celebrated hospitality of Elm Creek Manor had won the day.

When Sylvia announced the hunt was on, the campers raced off laughing and shouting to search Elm Creek Manor and the estate grounds. Diane's list included twenty items the campers might find anywhere on the estate, but they were strictly forbidden to take anything from their own stashes, suitcases, or sewing baskets. They *were* permitted to borrow things from campers on other teams, however, so teams often formed tentative alliances with competitors, swapping a particular square of fabric for an unusual notion or trading a spool of thread for a newly pieced quilt block.

The first team to meet the Elm Creek Quilters on the verandah with as many of the twenty unusual items they could find would win Elm Creek Quilts pins, the most coveted prize at camp.

As the campers dispersed through the estate, Sarah and Summer went to the kitchen to help Anna carry refreshments outdoors. "I remember that recipe," said Sarah, spying two platters of sugar cookies decorated to resemble quilt blocks. Anna had brought a batch to her interview earlier that summer, and although she had not known the head chef job was available and had applied for a teaching position, after sampling her tasty treats, the Elm Creek Quilters were eager to welcome her to their staff. "I hope you made enough for your hungry coworkers, too."

Summer hefted a pitcher of lemonade in one hand and iced tea in the other. "Help yourself. You're eating for two now."

"Three," said Sarah, shaking her head in disbelief as she stacked napkins and plates in a basket.

"Three," echoed Anna with a laugh as

she followed Sarah and Summer out of the kitchen, balancing a cookie platter on each palm without dropping a single crumb. "Let me know if you have any special cravings. When the babies are old enough, I'll show you how to make your own baby food from organic fruits and vegetables."

"You do understand that you can't ever leave, don't you?" Sarah asked her. Then she glanced at Summer and wished she could make the same teasing demand of her.

Teams of campers hurried past as Sarah, Summer, and Anna carried the treats back through the manor and outside to the front veranda. The other Elm Creek Quilters and the three husbands living in the manor—Matt, Andrew, and now Gretchen's husband, Joe—had settled into Adirondack chairs and were observing the scavenger hunt with speculative amusement, pretending to place bets on favorites and calling out encouragement to teams that had fallen behind. Only then did Sarah learn that Diane had played a naughty trick on Andrew: Item number 14 on the list read "A kiss from Andrew." After the first quilt camper planted a smooch on his cheek and demanded one in return, Andrew looked only mildly surprised. Three kisses later, his expression had changed to baffled alarm. When a half-dozen determined quilters charged the veranda, he scrambled from his chair, snatched Matt's familiar baseball cap from his blond curls, planted it on his own thinning gray hair, and pulled the brim low over his eyes in a vain attempt at disguise. When Andrew's cheeks were as red from lipstick smudges as from embarrassment, Diane took pity on him and handed him a bag of chocolate kisses. Relieved but still wary, Andrew tossed the foil-wrapped candies to any quilter who approached the veranda long before they came within arm's reach. "I'm a happily married man," he reproached Diane, lofting a chocolate over the balcony railing as his friends laughed. As his happily married wife, Sylvia laughed as merrily as anyone.

"Watch out for him," Gretchen warned Diane, leaning back in her Adirondack lounge chair and crossing her ankles. "From the look in his eye, I suspect he's plotting revenge."

"He's too busy dodging quilters to plot anything," said Diane.

Sure enough, as the Flying Saucer Sisters plus Marcia climbed the curved stone staircase, Andrew tossed chocolates their way and ducked behind Matt.

"You must be Andrew," teased one of the ladies as the four scooped up their kisses.

"We're completely mystified by number twenty," said another. "The description seems open to interpretation. How do we know if we've chosen correctly?"

"I'll accept any answer you can make a persuasive case for," said Diane. The Flying Saucer Sisters and Marcia mulled over her reply as they walked off toward the north gardens, disappearing into the deepening twilight.

"Please tell me you didn't ask them to find a unicorn or a four-leaf clover," said Gwen. "They'll be out there all night."

"Of course not," retorted Diane. "I know better than that. They'd just turn in drawings or figurines."

Curious, Sarah wondered what the

twentieth item was, but Diane had given all copies of the list to the campers and waved off Sarah's questions with unconvincing protests that campers might overhear and gain an advantage. Sarah suspected Diane had other surprises in store for her friends, and she eyed Andrew's bag of kisses to see whether he had enough for the campers who had not yet found him.

"Smile, Sarah," a voice rang out just as a camera flash blinded her.

Startled, Sarah blinked away the spots dancing before her eyes. "What was that about?" she asked the other Elm Creek Quilters as a team of campers dashed off into the darkness, flashlight beams darting over the lawn.

"I have no idea," said Diane innocently. Too innocently. Sarah studied her, eyes narrowed, but Diane avoided her gaze.

Sure enough, in the minutes that followed, four other teams approached the veranda and turned their digital cameras or camera phones on Sarah. Sometimes the teams posed with her, other times they asked her to stand up and point to her tummy. "I assume from all this that a photo of me is item number twenty?" she asked Diane.

"Something like that," she replied.

As the night deepened, the song of crickets filled the air and fireflies glowed and faded in a silent dance over the lawn. More teams snapped photos of Sarah, while others plopped themselves down on benches and chairs and declared that they had found everything they could. They helped themselves to refreshments as Diane checked off the items on their lists.

". . . A spool of orange thread; a state quarter from Pennsylvania; a swatch of fabric with an insect on it—oh, I see, a ladybug on a leaf, that'll do; a kiss from Andrew—hey, this is just a wrapper," Diane protested.

"All that running around made me hungry," the camper explained, reaching for one of Anna's cookies.

"A wrapper doesn't count—" Diane broke off as Andrew handed the camper a new kiss, which she added to her team's pile. "Okay, then. With that, you have a total of twelve out of twenty items. You're our new leader."

A team who had been lingering on the stairs waiting for the results to be tallied whooped with joy. "We can beat that," one of their members declared, emptying a tote bag on the table in front of Diane.

She checked off items one by one. ". . . a Jonathan apple from the estate's orchard; a six-inch Friendship Star block—this is still warm from the iron. Did you just now make it?"

"That was easier than trying to find one," the camper said, quickly adding, "all the fabric and supplies came from the classroom scrap bag, so we didn't break the Forbidden S rule."

"She has an honest face," said Sylvia. "I'd trust her."

Diane nodded and made a check mark on the team's list. "Then you have sixteen out of twenty items, and you've moved into first place. Can anyone do better?"

By that time, two hours after the scavenger hunt had begun, all of the teams had returned to the veranda. One by one Diane went through their lists, occasionally listening skeptically as teammates pled their case for a particular object that did not seem to qualify. She accepted a cone of orange thread instead of a spool, but she rejected a swatch of black fabric with a silver spiderweb design on the grounds that the spider that had made the web was not shown, and spiders were arachnids, not insects. A few campers showed Diane images saved on their digital cameras or cell phones, and after a whispered conversation, she would nod and check off the twentieth item on their lists.

Only two teams found all twenty of the items, so the one who had returned to the veranda earliest won the game. The winners and first-runners-up were invited to take a bow, and Diane, in an unusual act of spontaneous generosity, bent the rules and declared that all eight would win Elm Creek Quilts pins.

The other quilters applauded, none too disappointed, for they knew other chances to win pins would come their way. As the quilters chatted and enjoyed refreshments, Sarah caught up to the winning team, one of the first to snap her photo. She asked to see their scavenger hunt list for a moment, and quickly read through the array of quirky trinkets until she came to the last: "A photo of a twice-blessed quilter."

"A few people submitted photos of themselves, if this was their second trip to camp," said Diane, coming up behind her. "I also accepted photos of a camper with two grandchildren, or with two new friends, and one who won the lottery twice. I had to draw the line at the woman with two divorces, though, since at best that's only a mixed blessing."

"Depends who's involved in the divorce," Sarah replied in an undertone, nodding to Bonnie, happily engrossed in conversation with some of her students.

"I couldn't agree more."

Sarah returned the scavenger hunt list to its owner with her thanks and watched her hurry off to join her teammates. "Some people might argue that twins are a mixed blessing, too."

"Those people don't know what they're talking about," said Diane. "I'm not saying you don't have difficult days and sleepless nights ahead of you, but you already know that. In the months ahead, you're going to hear from everyone how difficult parenting is, how you can kiss your social life good-bye, how you'll stumble through the days in a fog of sleep deprivation, how it's impossible to do everything correctly, how you'll feel plagued by guilt half of the time and want to run away the other half."

"But that's not true?" Sarah finished for her.

"Don't you wish. It's true, all right, but it's not the complete truth." Diane took her by the elbow and steered her to the far end of the veranda, where they would not be overheard. "What people won't tell you, because they can't put it into words, is that children will bring you more joy than you ever suspected existed in the universe. Even when they're driving you crazy, you'll fall in love with them again and again. I've never laughed so hard or found so much beauty in simple things since becoming a mother. It's an impossible contradiction. They're frustrating and glorious.

They throw your life into uproar and they teach you contentment. You'll remember every mistake you make as a parent and yet your children will love you anyway. I'll tell you something: Nothing on this earth can compare to a spontaneous, heartfelt hug from a toddler." Tears filled Diane's eyes. "I'm so happy for you, and I envy you. You have it all ahead of you, all those years with your children at home. In a few weeks, my youngest baby is going off to college. Now I have all the time in the world to myself, and I'd trade a year of my life now for one more day of finger paints and nursery rhymes. Enjoy them while they're completely yours. Even when you think you'll collapse if you have to change one more diaper or sing one more round of 'Old McDonald'—enjoy them. The days are long, but the years are short. They pass much too quickly."

Sarah stared at her, breath catching in her throat. "Diane, in all the years I've known you, I don't think I've ever heard you string together so many sentences without a single word of sarcasm to hold them together."

"Why do you think I brought you all the way over here?" Diane blotted tears from her eyes and checked her fingertips for smears of mascara. "Don't you tell anyone I got all sentimental. Especially not Gwen."

"Your secret is safe with me," Sarah promised, embracing her friend.

But Sylvia's ears were sharper than they suspected, and she caught every word. She hid a smile, amused by Diane's reluctance to reveal her vulnerability to anyone but a friend apprehensive of what she might face in the months and years ahead. Although Diane's sons had grown into fine young men, they had given her quite a time of it through the years, especially her eldest. Diane was not one to idealize the difficult road a mother walked. When a pragmatic realist like Diane spoke with such passionate longing about motherhood, Sarah would do well to take heed.

Sylvia only wished she had personal

experience of her own to share with Sarah, words of sound advice that might guide her young friend, but her own dreams of motherhood had been thwarted long ago. But perhaps Sarah would have more than enough advice from the experienced mothers among the Elm Creek Quilters. Sylvia could assume a different role, that of listener, helper, and friend.

Later, when only crumbs remained on the cookie platters and every trace of the twilight hunt through the estate had been cleared away, Sylvia joined Andrew in the manor's master suite, which they had shared since their wedding night. Before retiring, Sylvia lingered in her sitting room, resting her hand on the back of a chair as she studied the nine Winding Ways quilt blocks she had sewn for Sarah. Somehow she must have sensed the secret her young friend had been keeping, for she had chosen deep roses and clear blues for the narrow, arcing triangles and whimsical prints for the concave wedges. The light and dark hues created a secondary pattern of circles winding outward and back to the center, gathering in, protective.

Sarah, too, worked upon a masterpiece, Sylvia thought as she turned out the light and climbed beneath the covers beside her dear Andrew. The pieces would lie just as Sarah placed them, sewed neat and fast, the blocks in orderly rows. But only when Sarah stepped back and gazed upon her handiwork in a moment of quiet contemplation would she discover the secondary patterns, circles upon circles, overlapping and unending. Only then would she marvel at the unexpected beauty her years of labor had brought forth and know that it sprang from a source much greater than herself.

Bonnie

Bonnie slowed the car as she turned onto Main Street, but all of the metered spaces were full and the surging traffic did not permit her to stop in the middle of the street. That was reason enough to continue straight ahead, but her hand automatically went to the turn signal, her gaze to the rearview mirror. With a sigh, she changed lanes, drove around the block, and came to a stop in an alley where the view through the windshield was only partially obstructed. She shut down the engine without glancing at the clock, annoyed at herself but unable to drive on without taking measure of her former home.

The construction company had filled

another whole Dumpster since the previous day. A few water-stained ceiling panels stuck out through the rubble at awkward angles, and with a painful flash of recognition, Bonnie spotted a broken plane of oak wainscoting that had once adorned her dining room. At this rate, in a few weeks her former building would be an empty shell, with no sign of the cozy quilt shop that had once occupied the first-floor storefront or the condo above it where she and Craig had raised their three children, built a life, and watched their marriage fall apart.

In retrospect, Bonnie wished she had thrown Craig out after discovering his first betrayal, the "cyberaffair" he had carried out with a woman he had met in a Penn State football chat room. Bonnie had thwarted their attempt to meet and bring their romance from the virtual world into the physical, and when Craig begged for a second chance, Bonnie had forgiven him—until he tried to sell their home and Grandma's Attic without her consent after a real estate developer made plans to turn their building into student housing.

She held out as long as she could, but she gave up the fight when she knew she couldn't win. She agreed to sell the condo and allowed the shop's lease to lapse, signing away her home, her livelihood, and her marriage with a few strokes of the pen. She wasn't sure which of them she missed most. Craig's transformation into a belligerent stranger colored all of her memories of their married life, so it was impossible to remember even the happy, early years without finding signs of its inevitable demise. As for the condo, though her children had learned to walk and had blown out candles on birthday cakes there, it was also the place where Craig had spent hours at the computer, sending passionate e-mails to another woman. Only her beloved quilt shop had remained a haven for her throughout the upheaval of the past few months, until the day she unlocked the front door, discovered it in a shambles, and realized that she was gazing upon the beginning of the end.

The simultaneous loss of her home, her business, and her marriage had nearly broken her. Preparing for the divorce proceedings, struggling to avoid financial ruin, and wrestling with her children's varied responses to the collapse of their parents' marriage had piled on more stress and confusion than she had known she could bear. If not for Elm Creek Quilts and her friends, Bonnie wouldn't have endured the summer.

She sighed and turned the key in the ignition. The Elm Creek Quilters had always been there for her, and this was how she repaid them. Glancing at the dashboard clock, she pictured campers finishing breakfast, or coming in from morning strolls through the apple orchard, or gathering their supplies for the first classes of the day. Once again Bonnie would be late for work, but her friends would not rebuke her. If they knew that her ritual observations of her former home and not the commute from her Grangerville apartment were to blame for her tardiness, they would worry. They would be even more concerned if they saw the state of her apartment, if they knew she had unpacked only the necessities. Most of her belongings remained stored in cartons from the move, lined up against the wall of her living room as if she didn't intend to stay in the apartment long enough to justify unpacking.

She wasn't sure what her intentions were anymore, but she did know that putting dishes in cupboards and clothes in closets wouldn't transform that apartment into a home.

She pulled back onto Main Street, sparing a glance for the empty storefront in passing. Her heart cinched at the sight of the faint discoloration of the stone above the door where the red-and-gold GRANDMA'S ATTIC sign had proudly hung for so many years. She had kept the sign, of course; it lay under her bed wrapped in an old tablecloth, treasure salvaged from a happier epoch. Bonnie had not laid eyes upon it since moving from Agnes's house to the apartment in Grangerville, and she was not sure why she had saved it. As a souvenir of past success, a talisman promising the return of prosperity in better days? As a symbol of her failure, cautioning her not to risk too much or dream too grand a dream too soon? Or in a place so deep in her heart that she could avoid subjecting it to reasoned scrutiny, did Bonnie believe that as long as she kept the sign, someday it would once again beckon quilters into a cozy shop full of delights and marvels?

It hurt unbearably to acknowledge that Grandma's Attic was truly gone, but holding out hope that she might one day reopen the shop kept the wounds of her loss fresh. Her friends meant well when they asked her when she planned to take Sylvia up on her offer to open a shop within Elm Creek Manor; they could not suspect how much their innocent encouragement pained her. A small shop in the parlor might make a modest profit supplying notions and fat quarters to campers who had forgotten to pack all they needed, especially since Sylvia was unlikely to charge Bonnie any rent, but Bonnie recognized the offer for what it was: charity. All of the Elm Creek Quilters knew how Craig had left her in dire financial straits after draining their joint bank accounts, changing the locks to the condo, and bullying her into selling their home. Bonnie half expected them to pass around a collection plate with her name on it after every business meeting. Though Sylvia's generosity moved her, still she balked at accepting the handout. Perhaps this was because of what came to mind every time she remembered her days at Grandma's Attic—unpacking new stock while customers browsed, ringing up purchases and wrapping parcels, changing window displays to entice passersby indoors, chatting with new friends and old as they contemplated new projects. She knew it could never compare to what a small shop in the manor's parlor could provide. She recoiled from visions of herself hovering hopefully nearby while campers with a break in their schedules looked over a few tables offering a limited number of goods. After knowing the pride of ownership and the joy of fulfilling a dream, managing a small room in the manor was too far to fall.

Bonnie turned on the radio to crowd out the timorous voices whispering of loss and failure. Somehow they all sounded like Craig.

She left the campus and downtown Waterford behind, driving quickly to make up for lost time, slowing her pace only when she turned off from the main highway and onto the narrow dirt road that wound along the forested southern border of the Bergstrom estate. Sunlight danced in the leafy boughs overhead and sparkled on the rushing waters of Elm Creek as it tumbled alongside her route until it split off and disappeared into the deeper forest. When her car emerged from the trees, Bonnie's heart gladdened at the sight of the apple orchard, familiar and yet ever changeable. All through that most difficult part of her life, she had watched buds form on the bare branches, faint green leaves deepen and grow lush, blossoms burst forth and sweeten the air with their perfume, apples ripen under the sun. Every day as she drove past the orchard on her way to the manor, she had found comfort in the orchard's promise that patience and endurance would be rewarded. One day, the breeze whispered as it moved through the heavily laden branches, she would taste sweetness again.

As she passed the barn, she spotted Matt shoving the tall doors open, his worn, sun-faded baseball cap tugged low over his wild blond curls. Nearby stood Gretchen's husband, Joe, but the men were too engaged in conversation to notice Bonnie's wave. Was Joe planning to join Matt's staff, or was he simply keeping the younger man company? Gretchen had mentioned that her husband had worked in a Pittsburgh steel plant until a serious injury left him bedridden for more than a year. Thanks to his union, Joe had received disability payments and a modest pension, which Gretchen had supplemented by working as a substitute teacher until she became part-owner of a quilt shop. From the scant, uncomplaining details Gretchen had let fall, Bonnie guessed that the Hartleys had struggled all their lives to make ends meet. They must have welcomed Sylvia's job offer with great joy, especially considering that it included a generous salary plus room and board at Elm Creek Manor. Joe certainly seemed pleased with their new surroundings, and Bonnie often caught him watching his wife with proud affection.

It never ceased to amaze her how adversity drew some couples closer together, while ordinary, uneventful times doomed others to drift apart. Was it boredom that had driven Craig from her? Had he grown impatient with her predictable, pleasant faithfulness? There was nothing dangerous or exciting or mysterious about her, nothing to intrigue him anew each day. She was just a good, ordinary woman who kept her marriage vows and raised her children to be decent members of society. That was the bargain: Be true, work hard, and retire contentedly. Or so she had believed. She had kept her part of the deal only to discover that somewhere along the way her husband had changed the rules.

Bonnie shoved the thoughts away. She couldn't dwell on where she had gone wrong or what she might have done differently. Retracing her steps to find that place where her path had diverged from Craig's wouldn't bring back the sweet, charming man she had married. Time had replaced him with a stranger, a man who was unkind to her, who could not love her. Her only option now was to stoke her courage and continue upon this new, unknown, winding way, though she had no idea where it might lead.

The engine shuddered and coughed to a halt as she parked the station wagon behind the manor. "Hang in there," she said grimly as she hurried up the stairs to the back door, her purse slung over one shoulder, her tote bag stuffed full of class samples over the other. She was speaking to the car, which she could not afford to replace, but also to herself. If she stayed in motion, if she did not pause too long to think about how her life was in shambles, she would be able to persevere until she figured out what to do next.

As she passed the kitchen, Anna darted into the hallway, a long wooden spoon in her hand. "Bonnie," she exclaimed, "do you have a minute?"

"Not really. My class starts—" She glanced at her watch. "In thirty seconds."

"I'll talk fast. Do you have any menu suggestions for Judy's farewell party?"

"Maybe you should ask Gwen." Bonnie wanted to help, but she had run out of time. "All I know is that if you want Judy to eat it, make sure it's low-fat and low-cal."

"Maybe some Asian-Venezuelan fusion cuisine," Anna mused, tapping her palm with the spoon. "What do you think?"

"Sounds perfect," Bonnie called over her shoulder as she dashed off, though she had no idea what Anna was talking about.

She made it to her classroom with seconds to spare, smiled brightly at her students, and unpacked her tote bag, smoothing out wrinkles in the reversible quilted jacket that was the subject of their weeklong workshop. Earlier that week, each student had completed the large, patchwork rectangles from which they cut their jackets' pieces. Now came the difficult part, sewing them together. When Bonnie asked for a volunteer, a woman from the back row came forward to try on the jacket so everyone

could see how the darts fit in back. Her
students listened, leaning forward eagerly in their chairs or jotting notes, as
relaxed and content as Bonnie was
windblown and harried. Maybe Bonnie
needed to follow their example and escape for a week at quilt camp as a
guest, not a teacher. Maybe any vacation would do. After the last day of the
camp season, she ought to plan a little
getaway—except, of course, that she
couldn't afford one. She also couldn't
miss the divorce hearings, which her
lawyer warned her would switch into
high gear at the end of the month.

Someday, she promised herself.
When things settled down, when she
had a little money set aside, she would
treat herself to a day at a spa, dinner at
a fine restaurant, and an evening with a
good book and fine chocolates. In the
meantime, she would enjoy simple plea-
sures wherever she found them—in her
students' flattering admiration of the
quilted jacket she had designed and
sewn, for one. In the late-summer
beauty of the Bergstrom estate. In imagining the mouthwatering delicacies

Anna would create as the apple harvest came in. In her belief, part determination and part hope, that things had to get better soon, because they couldn't possibly get any worse.

After lunch, Sylvia met Bonnie at the foot of the grand oak staircase where she had sat down to change into her walking shoes. "Going out for your daily constitutional through the orchard?" Sylvia asked, falling in step beside her as she crossed the foyer's marble floor.

"Am I that predictable?" said Bonnie lightly.

"Daily exercise is good for body and soul. We would all do well to follow your example." But rather than accompany Bonnie outside, Sylvia placed a hand on her arm to bring her to a halt. "Before you dash off, may we chat for a moment?"

With a sinking heart, Bonnie realized that Sylvia had not been following along, but rather guiding her to this precise spot. They stood just beyond the foyer where the original west wing of Elm Creek Manor intersected the south wing—right beside the doorway to the formal parlor. "I have a class at one-thirty," Bonnie excused herself, but Sylvia firmly steered her into the room, a veritable tableau of Victoriana. The overstuffed sofas, embroidered armchairs, beaded lampshades, and ornate cabinets might have seemed stuffy if they were not so comfortably worn. Sylvia had once remarked that every antique piece of furniture remained in the exact spot where her grandmother had placed it when she married into the Bergstrom family. Aside from the electric lights, the only sign of the modern era was the large television in the corner, but even that was concealed by a late-nineteenth-century Grandmother's Fan quilt unless someone was watching a program.

"Perhaps you've been much too busy this summer to think about setting up shop here," said Sylvia, scrutinizing the room, hands on her hips, "but as soon as camp wraps up for the season, I believe we should begin planning in earnest."

"Do you think so?" asked Bonnie weakly.

"If we want to be ready for the first day of camp next season, indeed I do. Gretchen tells me that her husband is quite a woodworker. Perhaps he can help you design some custom-made shelving to make the most of this small space."

Bonnie seized her opening. "It *is* a very small space, isn't it? Quilters hate browsing in cramped shops. Maybe we should give it some more thought before we make any permanent changes to your parlor."

Sylvia laughed and patted her arm, a gesture of reassurance that made Bonnie feel worse. "We'll have all winter to think and plan, and I'm sure Joe will contrive something so your customers won't feel crowded."

"But what about your grandmother's furniture? I couldn't ask you to displace your family heirlooms."

"Nonsense! We can find another place in the manor for these pieces, and once we do, the room will seem much larger. You'll see." Sylvia gestured to the wall adjacent to the doorway. "In my opinion, this would be the best place to set up the cash register, and perhaps Joe could build a cutting table for the center of the room." She indicated the other walls in turn. "Fabric bolts there, wall racks for notions there, and bookshelves here." Nodding to a narrow wall right beside the door frame, she added, "And this would be the perfect spot to hang that framed photograph you used to keep on your desk in your office. The woman in the portrait is your grandmother, and the inspiration for your first store, if I'm not mistaken?"

Bonnie nodded and tried to smile. "I can see you've given this a lot of thought." She forced a laugh. "Much more than I have."

"Perhaps too much thought." Sylvia peered at Bonnie over the rims of her glasses. "Perhaps I've overstepped my bounds, telling you how to arrange your shop when I don't have a single day's experience to compare to yours."

"Oh, no, no, that's not it," Bonnie hastened to explain. "It's not that I have to do it my way. I just don't know if I should do it at all."

Sylvia studied her, the fine lines of her face gathering in a worried frown. "Surely you're not worried that Grandma's Parlor will suffer the same fate as your first shop. You needn't fear any vandals here."

"Grandma's Parlor." Bonnie's laugh, though soft, was genuine. "You've even chosen a name."

"You don't have to keep it," said Sylvia. "You'll be in charge, of course, so the choice should be yours. I hope you won't think me presumptuous, but Grandma's Parlor seemed fitting to me. It acknowledges the new location while calling to mind its origins, both the place and the person who inspired it."

"It's a good name," Bonnie assured her. "I'll think about everything you've said. We'll talk more soon."

Then Bonnie hurried off, crossing the distance between the parlor and the back door as quickly as she could without breaking into a run, leaving more than one camper speculating that in all the time they had known her, Bonnie had never seemed so eager for exercise.

Grandma's Parlor. Bonnie mulled over the name as she strode through the orchard, pumping her fists, feeling the first beads of perspiration forming on the nape of her neck. Sylvia had no idea how perfectly it suited, or how much it would have delighted the woman in the photograph Bonnie had once kept on her office desk.

Grandma Lucy, her first quilt teacher, her tutor, her most steadfast champion. Sometimes the peal of a camper's laugh, a glimpse of a brunette flip, or a carefree woman dancing onstage at the campers' talent show reminded Bonnie of her grandmother. How Grandma Lucy would have enjoyed quilt camp, and how proud she would have been to know that her granddaughter was one of its founders.

Grandma Lucy had always told Bonnie that she could accomplish anything if she set her mind to it. "The world is full of possibilities," she liked to exclaim, throwing her arms open in the backyard and twirling around as if to embrace the sunlight, the warm breezes, the grass, and the open sky.

Bonnie and her younger sister, Ellie, adored their grandmother. They didn't mind that their mother worked as a secretary instead of staying home like their friends' mothers, because it meant they could spend a few hours after school and every long summer day at Grandma Lucy's house. When the weather was fair, they would explore Erie, Pennsylvania, on bicycles, go hiking along the lakeshore, or play marathon games of croquet on the front lawn. On rainy days, Grandma Lucy would take them for a "machine ride" to the library, where they would check out armloads of books and pass the day reading on the shaded screen porch, safe and dry while thunder rolled overhead. But what Bonnie and Ellie liked best of all was when Grandma Lucy beckoned them up the creaking attic stairs, where they would throw open old trunks and play dress-up with clothes from the olden days, when Grandma was a young lady. Feather boas, high-heeled shoes, fringed dresses, and white satin gloves that reached almost to the girls' shoulders—such lovely, beautiful things. "If I had such pretty clothes, I would wear them every day," Bonnie had often declared. When Ellie chimed in her agreement, Grandma would merely throw her head back and laugh.

Dressed in their grandmother's finery, they would play marvelous games of make-believe. They were glamorous movie stars traveling to exotic locales to shoot a new feature; they were secret agents posing as a singing group in order to outwit a gang of notorious bank robbers; they were princesses and queen battling an evil sorcerer intent on destroying their kingdom. While rain pattered on the sloped roof or winter winds swirled icy snow crystals against the windowpane, their grandmother's attic transformed into a place where anything they imagined could come to pass.

Their mother's voice calling up the narrow staircase would break the spell, and Bonnie and Ellie would scamper downstairs and watch as their glamorous ensembles worked their own magic upon their mother's face, as laughter erased the weariness around her eyes. Sometimes, as they changed back into their ordinary clothes, the girls begged to stay and have dinner with Grandma Lucy and Grandpa Al, but usually their mother scooted them outside to the car, to race home and prepare their own supper before their father came home from work.

Grandma knew how to tap dance, and she had saved every dance costume she had worn since she was eight years old. She taught Bonnie and Ellie the jitterbug and the fox-trot, and sometimes she and Grandpa Al would waltz around the living room while the radio played. They had met at a dance at the Lakeside Pavilion when she was seventeen and he was nineteen. Grandma was very popular and danced with many young men, unaware that Grandpa, who attended a different school, had taken notice of her. When the bandleader announced a contest, Grandpa strode across the dance floor and took her hand just as she was about to take a classmate's brother's arm. "You're the best dancer here," he told her, leading his astonished partner to the middle of the dance floor. "Whoever has you for a partner is going to win, and I need to win."

"The prize was a new pair of shoes," Grandma would explain. "He might not have been so bold except he really needed those shoes."

"How did Grandpa know the shoes would fit him?" Ellie always interrupted at that point of the story.

"The prize was a gift certificate to a shoe store, dearie. The winner would get to pick out whatever he liked."

Grandma helped Grandpa win first prize, and they danced every dance together for the rest of the evening. "We've been partners ever since," Grandma would conclude the tale, and if Grandpa was in the room, she would throw him a teasing glance and add, "I think he kept me around in case he ever needed to add to his wardrobe."

As the years passed, marriage and family did not change Grandma's popularity. Her circle of friends evolved as their husbands' jobs took them to distant towns and as their common interests waxed and waned, but she was never without companions. By the time Bonnie and Ellie came along, Grandma Lucy's favored circle was her quilting bee, the Stitch Witches. Ever since she was a young bride, Grandma Lucy and nine friends had met once a week to sew and chat. They had seen one another through marriages and births, illnesses and disappointments, and there were very few secrets they did not share around the sewing circle. "They've got the goods on me, all right," Grandma Lucy told Bonnie once as she mixed batter for a pineapple upside-down cake to serve at a Stitch Witches' bee. "If we ever had a falling out, and they told the world my secrets . . ." Grandma Lucy shook her head, imagining the disastrous result. But of course, the Stitch Witches would never betray her, and not only because Grandma Lucy knew their secrets, too. The years of shared confidences had forged a bond between them that nothing would ever shatter. Bonnie knew that Grandma Lucy's secrets, whatever they were, were safe.

When Bonnie was old enough, Grandma Lucy occasionally allowed her to attend when the Stitch Witches met at her house. Bonnie's interest in learning to quilt charmed the older ladies, and as she struggled to sew together squares for her first top, a Trip Around the World, each offered her advice, some of it contradictory.

Sometimes, if one of their circle needed to finish a quilt quickly, the Stitch Witches would put aside their individual projects and set up a quilt frame in Grandma Lucy's living room. Pulling up chairs around it, they would sew the three layers together—patchwork top, batting, and backing—with deft and meticulous stitches. Bonnie would sit on the floor beneath the frame, the quilt a canopy over her head, and watch the darting needles pierce the layers and wrinkled, blue-veined hands push them back through to the top. Bonnie was responsible for picking up dropped thimbles and spools of thread, but her duties were so light that sometimes the Stitch Witches forgot she was there and their talk turned to matters usually not discussed in front of children. Holding very still, barely breathing lest she remind them of her presence, Bonnie listened wide-eyed to laments about husbands straying, daughters dating unsuitable men, sons struggling to find work or finish school, or siblings arguing over inheritances. In later years, the details of the individual dramas faded from her memory, but she never forgot how each woman seemed to feel her burden lightened when shared with her friends.

The Stitch Witches relied upon that unconditional acceptance and support even more as the years passed. Time, which initially allowed their friendship to ripen and mellow, eventually began to exact its toll upon them. One of Grandma's girlhood chums was the first of the Stitch Witches to pass away, unexpectedly and far too soon, from a heart attack when she was only sixty. The shock of their loss cast a shadow over the circle of quilters, and although no one said so in Bonnie's hearing, she sensed beneath their visible grief their reluctant acceptance that this would be only the first of many partings.

Then Grandpa Al died, and the Stitch Witches were there to console Grandma Lucy, as she later consoled those who followed her into widowhood. Gradually, sadly, their numbers diminished as old friends retired and moved away, or succumbed to illnesses, or became homebound. Even though Bonnie was too involved with her own circle of friends in her teenage years to attend quilting bees, she often looked back wistfully upon those days, her heart aching for her grandmother, who grieved deeply for every lost friend. She resolved to do all she could to fill the void when the last of Grandma Lucy's circle of friends left her. For it was inconceivable that vibrant, clever, indomitable Grandma Lucy would not somehow, miraculously, escape the fate that awaited her aging friends. It was true that she wore bifocals now and did not bound up the attic stairs the way she used to, but Bonnie could not imagine a world where her grandmother was not holding court in her two-bedroom brick bungalow with the attic full of marvels.

The first signs were easy to ignore. Everyone misplaced car keys sometimes or forgot what errand had compelled them to enter a room. Bonnie misplaced her dorm room key so often that her freshman-year roommate resigned herself to leaving their door unlocked for most of the fall semester. Bonnie's own parents sometimes called her by her sister's name, so it was no big deal when Grandma Lucy called her by her mother's name when Bonnie phoned to chat.

Then, on a rare weekday visit home from Penn State, Bonnie and her family had just finished dinner at Grandma Lucy's house when the remaining Stitch Witches arrived for their weekly meeting. Flustered, Grandma Lucy invited them to sit and offered them dessert, and she teasingly scolded them for changing the date without telling her.

Her friends apologized and departed, reluctant to interrupt a family dinner even though everyone assured them they were welcome. Later, as she helped clear the table, Bonnie surreptitiously studied the calendar hanging inside the pantry door. The Stitch Witches' meeting was clearly marked for seven o'clock that evening.

From that day forward, her grandmother's lapses in memory became more frequent and bewildering. Grandma Lucy sounded puzzled when Bonnie called her on Sunday afternoons, and Bonnie often had to remind her that she couldn't come to dinner because she was more than two hundred miles away at school. "Of course," her grandmother said one afternoon in early February. "And how are your classes?"

"They're fine," Bonnie replied. "My lowest grade is in calculus, but that's no surprise. I'm supposed to declare a major by the end of the year, but I still can't decide between business and the liberal arts. History and art are much more compelling, but I'll have an easier time finding a job after graduation if I take a business degree. What do you think I should do?"

"Heavens, Bonnie, you're at college, not trade school. Seize the opportunity to expand your horizons. Education isn't just a means to an end; the journey itself is what truly matters. A liberal arts degree will show employers that you're intelligent, hardworking, and an able learner. Let them worry about job training after they've hired you."

Bonnie laughed. "You sound just like my resident assistant. She's a philosophy major."

"Obviously a person of great wisdom. While we're on the subject, how are your classes going?"

"They're fine," said Bonnie, surprised. Apparently she hadn't provided enough detail to satisfy her grandmother. "Like I said, my calculus grade isn't that great, but I'm still passing, and I should be able to bring it up with a good score on the final."

"I'm sure you'll do fine, dearie. Are those bureaucrats in the administration pressuring you to choose a major yet?"

Bonnie hesitated, wrapping the phone

cord around her finger. "I have to decide by the end of the semester."

"Are you leaning toward anything in particular? You have to follow where your heart leads, you know. Study something you enjoy. Education shouldn't just be a means to an end."

Bonnie felt a sudden, deep chill in the pit of her stomach. "The journey itself is what matters."

"Precisely," declared Grandma Lucy, triumphant. A long pause followed. "Are you coming to dinner Sunday? I thought I'd make pork roast. That's your favorite."

Pork roast was Bonnie's mother's favorite; Bonnie didn't care for it. "No," said Bonnie, with a catch in her throat. "I can't make it."

As soon as Bonnie got off the phone with Grandma Lucy, she phoned her mother. After telling her about the unsettling conversation, she listened, numb, as her mother's confession spilled forth: her own repetitive conversations with Grandma Lucy, lost items discovered later in bizarre places, unexpected outbursts of anger, and one frightening occasion when Grandma Lucy had driven to meet a friend for lunch only to show up more than two hours later at the public library, confused and asking for Grandpa Al.

"Why didn't you tell me?" was all Bonnie could say as her mother choked out sobs on the other end of the line.

No one wanted Bonnie to worry, came the reply. She was doing so well at school and they were so proud of her. They didn't want to upset her so much that her grades would suffer. They meant to tell her everything when she came home for summer vacation. Not that she had any reason to worry, even now. Grandma Lucy was under a doctor's care and Bonnie's parents were hopeful that she would be on the mend soon.

But by the time spring semester ended and Bonnie returned to Erie, Grandma Lucy had taken a drastic turn for the worse. Instead of providing cures or treatments, her doctor warned Bonnie's parents that Grandma Lucy's symptoms were likely to worsen over time. Instead of remedies, he offered brochures for nursing homes where she could be looked after properly so that she did not hurt herself or someone else.

"I won't put my mother in a home," Bonnie's mother said, voice trembling, as she recounted the events of Grandma Lucy's most recent examination. Bonnie's father reached across the dinner table and took her hand, while Bonnie and Ellie looked on, helpless.

Bonnie had just begun her junior year when her parents decided the time had come to sell Grandma Lucy's house and have her move in with them. Although Grandma Lucy was adamantly against the plan, Bonnie's parents moved Bonnie's twin bed into Ellie's room and arranged Grandma's furniture in Bonnie's old room. When Bonnie heard how her grandmother had cried and argued on her last night in her beloved home, she felt guiltily, horribly relieved to have missed the ordeal and to have played no part in Grandma Lucy's traumatic loss.

The closing date for the brick bungalow was scheduled for the first Thursday of December, so Bonnie, Ellie, and their mother spent Thanksgiving vacation clearing Grandma Lucy's attic of its treasures. They kept all of Grandma Lucy's quilts as well as her old sewing machine, which she asked for almost daily, and which would fit between the bed and the window in her new room. Their mother could not part with the family photographs, including the large, hand-colored portrait of Grandma Lucy's mother in its ornate frame and convex glass. After those obvious items were carried downstairs to be loaded into the car at the end of the day, Bonnie, Ellie, and her mother gazed around the cluttered attic, hardly knowing where to continue.

The girls wanted to save everything. Every vintage garment, every worn wooden toy, every faded quilt preserved a priceless childhood memory. Their mother, determined to prune ruthlessly, reminded them that they simply did not have room for anything but the most important family heirlooms. "I can't decide what's most important today," Ellie protested. "I don't even remember everything that's up here."

"Once we give something away, it's gone," Bonnie added, feeling tears threatening. "It's better to keep everything and sort it out later, just in case."

"When is 'later'?" their mother replied. "This attic has to be cleared out before our closing date, and you girls are going back to school on Monday." But when her daughters pleaded, she relented, saying, "If you can find a place for it in your own room, you may keep it."

Even though the sisters' things were divided between home and school, they had little space in their shared bedroom for anything but their own clothes and belongings. After careful consideration, they packed a steamer trunk with their favorite vintage garments, occasionally pausing to try on a dress or a pair of shoes and reminisce about playing dress-up and make-believe. Their mother rewarded them with laughter, which too soon dissolved into tears. In a moment the three women were embracing, weeping, mourning the vibrant woman they loved who was lost but not yet gone.

Bonnie and Ellie were safely back at school the day their parents removed the last of Grandma Lucy's possessions from the small brick bungalow where she had lived since marrying Grandpa Al. Bonnie could not have borne seeing the empty house, hollow and lonely, with every trace of her grandparents swept away. Bonnie did not care what curtains the new owners hung in the windows or what furniture they set out on the porch, but she hoped they would tend Grandpa Al's prize roses as attentively as Grandma Lucy had. The bungalow was just another house now, the attic just another attic. Its magic had left with Grandma Lucy.

After the exhausting whirlwind of finals, Bonnie returned home to a family transformed. The twin burdens of work and caregiving had drained her mother of her liveliness, adding lines to her face and gray to her hair. Bonnie's father, frustrated and powerless, did his best to comfort his wife and manage the family finances, stretched thin by the demands of two college tuitions and medical bills. When Bonnie offered to look out for

Grandma Lucy while she was home from school to give her mother a break, the sheer relief and gratitude in her mother's eyes dismayed her. Her parents never complained over the phone, but offered the straightforward facts about Grandma Lucy's deteriorating condition with no embellishments, such as how they felt or what they feared. Bonnie had had no idea things were so bad at home.

The truth she admitted only to herself was that part of her had not wanted to know. She did not want to believe that anything at home had changed, that the Grandma Lucy she had adored all her life would not be waiting for her, ready to beckon her upstairs to explore the attic for an as yet undiscovered treasure. Bonnie was happy at Penn State, enjoying her classes and campus life, going out with her steady boyfriend, and working part-time at the Creamery. It was a relief to know that that life was waiting for her back at school. But until she returned for the start of the spring semester, she was determined to alleviate her parents' burdens as best she could.

Bonnie soon learned that Grandma Lucy had to be cajoled into leaving her bedroom, where the familiar furniture seemed to comfort her. Even so, when Bonnie was able to convince her grandmother to come downstairs to the kitchen for a game of cards or a cup of tea, she brightened and resumed some of her old spirit. Bonnie listened to each retold story, laughing anew at Grandma Lucy's witticisms even if she had told the same joke only moments before. She dutifully answered her grandmother's repeated questions about school and about her friends. The Grandma Lucy she had always adored was still in there somewhere, she told herself, hidden in a fog of confusion. If Bonnie were patient, the air would clear and Grandma Lucy would appear again. This was what she privately believed, though sometimes her grandmother would look about in confusion and ask for Grandpa Al, or slam her fist on the table and insist that Bonnie take her home right that minute, or stare gloomily out the windows and shake her head vehemently when Bonnie or Ellie offered to drive her to the library or to pay a call on one of the Stitch Witches.

The four other remaining members of the quilters' circle still met regularly, though now only monthly. They never failed to invite Grandma Lucy, but to Bonnie's astonishment, her grandmother had apparently lost all interest in attending. Occasionally a Stitch Witch would drop by with a pie or a loaf of banana bread and sit with Grandma Lucy for a while, but when Bonnie listened in, she knew from her grandmother's voice that she believed she was merely chatting pleasantly with a friendly stranger. If even those cherished old friendships had faded from her memory, how much longer could Bonnie hope to remain?

Though Grandma Lucy had drifted away from her circle of quilters, she still pieced blocks by hand. On a particularly good day, she described for Bonnie the lovely Glorified Nine-Patch quilt she intended to make as Bonnie's bridal quilt. "I know I'm starting early but I don't want to rush at the end," Grandma Lucy explained, grinning mischievously. "Do you have a boyfriend yet?"

"Yes," said Bonnie, taking from her purse the photo her grandmother had seen dozens of times. "His name is Craig Markham. Here we are at Beaver Stadium during the homecoming game last year."

As she always did, Grandma Lucy studied the photo, frowning slightly. "Well, he's handsome enough, but when you finally settle down, choose someone with kind eyes, like your grandfather."

Bonnie promised to do so. She excused her grandmother's implied criticism because she wasn't exactly sure what "kind eyes" looked like and why her grandmother apparently thought Craig lacked them. Besides, on both occasions when Grandma Lucy had met Craig, she had found him charming. He could be when he wanted to. Craig always knew what other people wanted to hear, and if he was in a good mood, he said it. Sometimes he said the exact opposite of what people wanted and expected, but he had never been contrary with Bonnie. For her, he never failed to be sweet and generous with compliments, which proved how much he loved her.

"I'll have this quilt done before you meet Mr. Right," teased Grandma Lucy, pinning together two pieces of fabric along the line Bonnie had traced around a template on the wrong side of the fabric. Bonnie threaded her needles for her, too, but Grandma Lucy did all the sewing on her own, as if her fingers had preserved the memory of the stitches when so much else had been forgotten.

In January, Bonnie returned to college feeling as if she had given her overworked parents a respite and her grandmother solace, despite her confusion and increasing isolation.

The months passed, given over to lectures, papers, and exams, to dances and dates, to study breaks with her roommates, and long, idle musings about their futures in the real world after graduation, now little more than a year away. Classes, Craig, and her part-time job kept Bonnie on campus except for a spring break trip to Daytona Beach, so she did not return home until the second week in May. Time had worn smooth the edges of her worry, so she failed to consider how much more of her grandmother might be gone when they next met.

At the end of the semester, Bonnie and Ellie's father drove to State College to bring them home. Though they already missed their college friends and freedom, the prospect of three months with no classes had the sisters planning beach trips and get-togethers with high school friends—until the sleep deprivation of finals week caught up with them a half hour into the long drive. For the rest of the trip home they did little more than doze, fiddle with the radio, or chat drowsily about taking a week or two off before looking for summer jobs. They had almost reached the exit to Erie when Bonnie thought to ask their father what awaited them at home. When he sighed and flexed his hands around the steering wheel, Bonnie knew that he had dreaded the question. Even before he spoke, she knew that Grandma Lucy would not recognize them when they walked through the front door.

Bonnie knew her grandmother couldn't

help it. She knew that. And yet it wrenched her heart anew each time Grandma Lucy called her by a long-lost friend's name or, worse yet, eyed her suspiciously and demanded to know what Bonnie was doing in her room. She had to be watched almost continuously now. In April she had set a kitchen towel on fire while making herself a cup of tea—a detail Bonnie's parents had omitted from their phone conversations, once again to avoid worrying her. Bonnie's mother had cut back her work hours and enlisted a neighbor to check in on Grandma Lucy during the day. "Mr. Carew made it very clear that he expects me to come back full-time soon," Bonnie's mother told her daughters over dinner on their first evening home. "I know it's a lot to ask, but I hoped you girls would look out for your grandmother while you're home for the summer. I need to go back to work before I lose my job and I hate imposing on the neighbors. It's not fair to you girls, but . . ." Their mother gestured helplessly. "I'll pay you whatever you would have earned taking a summer job."

"Don't be silly," said Bonnie. "You don't have to pay us to look after our own grandmother."

"But you'll want spending money at school next year."

"We can still get jobs," said Ellie. "I didn't want to work full-time all summer long, anyway. I'll work mornings and Bonnie will work afternoons."

"Or we can alternate days," Bonnie quickly chimed in. Their mother looked dubious, but she agreed to let them try.

Within a week, Ellie found a job as a lifeguard, watching over early-morning swimmers in the lap pool and kids taking their first swimming lessons. Bonnie went back to her old waitressing job at Eat'n Park, earning more in tips from the dinner and late-night crowd than she would have made at a full-time office job. Soon the hot summer days fell into a routine: In the morning, Ellie biked to the pool while Bonnie made breakfast for Grandma Lucy. They would pass the day reading, working in the garden, playing cards, or going for walks, the summer air fragrant with marigolds and freshly cut grass. On bad days, Grandma Lucy only wanted to sit in the living room and look out the window; on very bad days, she would unnerve Bonnie with tears or temper. Sometimes Grandma Lucy insisted that she wanted to be left alone in her room—"I'm a grown woman and I need my privacy"—so Bonnie would write letters to Craig, read a library book, do housework, and keep one ear sharply tuned to her grandmother's bedroom. When Grandma Lucy was in those solitary moods, Bonnie knew she was working on her Glorified Nine-Patch quilt. She doubted her grandmother remembered that it was supposed to have been Bonnie's wedding quilt.

Ellie would arrive home from the pool about a half hour before Bonnie had to put on her uniform and head off to the restaurant, and in that interval, Bonnie would quickly brief her sister on the day's events, their grandmother's mood, and what their mother wanted Ellie to put on for dinner. Then she would hurry off to Eat'n Park, where she was thankfully too busy to think about anything at home. Upon her return home, often near midnight, Ellie and their father would already be in bed, but Bonnie usually found her mother with Grandma Lucy, looking at photograph albums or chatting, or sometimes merely sitting.

On one hot, sticky night in late July as she trudged up the driveway, Bonnie heard her grandmother shouting. She hurried inside and upstairs to find Grandma Lucy clad in a nightgown and resting one hand upon the sewing machine cabinet to steady herself as she thrust a fistful of quilt blocks in her mother's face. "You did this," Grandma Lucy shouted. "All of my hard work, ruined!"

Bonnie's mother ducked out of the way and held up her palms to calm her. "No one touched your quilt blocks, Mom. No one ruined your quilt."

"Look at these stitches. Just look at them!" Grandma Lucy turned the blocks over and jabbed a gnarled finger at the seams. "Terrible, terrible!"

"Those are your stitches, Mom. You sewed those blocks."

Grandma Lucy recoiled as if she had been struck. "How dare you," she muttered, shuffling backward to the bed and sinking down upon it. The quilt blocks fell from her hands. Bonnie watched helplessly from the doorway as her mother fluffed the pillow and eased Grandma Lucy down upon it and tucked her in, strangely, suddenly docile.

When Bonnie's mother stooped over to pick up the scattered quilt blocks, she spotted Bonnie frozen in the doorway. Bonnie began to speak, but her mother held a finger in front of her lips and motioned for her to turn off the light. She obeyed and waited in the hallway until her mother emerged carrying the quilt blocks and softly closed the door.

"Mom—"

"It's late. You should go to bed." Her mother's voice was heavy with resignation as she turned the blocks over in her hands. "I remember how beautifully she once sewed. Now she doesn't even recognize her own work."

"She did yesterday morning." Grandma Lucy had sewed nearly all day. Bonnie was barely able to trace templates and cut pieces quickly enough to keep up with her.

"Maybe she will tomorrow, then."

Bonnie knew her mother didn't believe it.

The next day, after her parents and sister left for work, Bonnie sat with her grandmother on the front porch watching the passersby—mothers pushing baby carriages, neighbors visiting friends. Grandma Lucy called out a cheerful greeting to everyone, her mood so sunny it was as if her outburst of the night before had never happened. She even asked for her sewing basket, and after a moment's hesitation, Bonnie brought it to her. They spent the morning working on the Glorified Nine-Patch quilt, Bonnie pinning together pieces for her grandmother to sew. For the first time in ages, Grandma Lucy chatted about the Stitch Witches, but she spoke of them as if they were newlyweds and young mothers. Bonnie knew her mother wanted her to gently correct her grandmother when she went on in that way, but Bonnie was too tired, too unwilling to spoil Grandma Lucy's rare good mood. Instead she went along with her fantasy, murmuring vague agreement and nodding at appropriate times. If it contented her grandmother to believe her friends were still near, still full of life, Bonnie could not bring herself to distress her with the truth.

"It's almost August," Ellie reminded Bonnie when she returned home, sun-tanned and smelling of cocoa butter and chlorine. "In less than a month, we'll be back at school."

Her sister's words lingered with her as Bonnie raced off to the restaurant, ashamed by the comfort they offered. Soon she and Ellie would escape back into their carefree college lives, but what about their mother? What about Grandma Lucy?

When Bonnie returned home at half past eleven, she heard Grandma's harsh shouts over the chirping of crickets as she unlocked the front door. Drawing a long, slow breath, she debated whether to rush upstairs, wondering how her father and sister could sleep through the noise. They probably were lying awake in bed, she decided, too weary to rush into the melee.

It was tempting to follow their example.

Bonnie left her purse on the hall table and trudged upstairs. She found her mother in her grandmother's bedroom, tearfully explaining that Grandma Lucy herself was to blame for the large, crooked stitches that barely held the quilt blocks together. Her grandmother denied it again and again, and suddenly Bonnie couldn't bear it any longer. "You're right," she said, striding into the room. "Valerie made those blocks. She should stick to Four-Patches."

It was a teasing remark Grandma Lucy had often made about her friend before her death. "Valerie?" Grandma Lucy echoed, her gaze shifting to her granddaughter, her eyes narrowed in doubt.

"Yes." Bonnie gently freed the quilt blocks from her grandmother's grasp. "Should I tell her to pick out the stitches and do them over?"

Grandma Lucy bobbed her head, satisfied, and as Bonnie's mother helped her into bed, Bonnie retrieved the red-handled seam ripper from her grandmother's sewing basket and left the room. When her mother joined her at the kitchen table a few minutes later, Bonnie had already picked out one seam and had started in on another.

Her mother stood watching her for a moment, then sighed and sank into a chair. "I don't know whether to scold you or thank you."

"Then I'll pick door number two."

Her mother almost laughed. "Very well, but what's going to happen tomorrow when Valerie hasn't redone her quilt block?"

Bonnie didn't bother to respond. They both knew Grandma Lucy wouldn't remember.

The next day, when Grandma Lucy wanted to work on her quilt, Bonnie pinned the pieces she had taken apart the night before, threaded the needle, and gave them to her grandmother to sew back together. With a vague, nagging sense of dishonesty, Bonnie traced templates and cut new pieces, chatting idly with her grandmother as she struggled, slowly and carefully, to master the once-familiar motions of quilting.

For two weeks, she prepared blocks for Grandma Lucy to sew by day and

undid all her painstaking work by night.
Eventually, she was sure, her deception
would catch up with her, even though
her grandmother's fragile memory made
that unlikely. She dreaded the scene
that might ensue if Grandma Lucy ever
decided she had accumulated enough
Glorified Nine-Patch blocks for a top.
Bonnie knew she must have something
to hand over if that day ever came, so
she began sewing together the block
pieces herself after picking out her
grandmother's shaky stitches. She had
not quilted since piecing that Trip
Around the World top as a child, but
with patience and practice, her handiwork gradually improved. One August
morning, she slipped her completed
blocks into Grandma Lucy's sewing
basket, and was both proud and dis-
heartened when her grandmother could
not distinguish Bonnie's sewing from
her own. A few years earlier, Grandma
Lucy would have inspected her blocks,
pointed out her mistakes with affectionate humor to smooth over the critical
sting, and encouraged her to do them
over. Bonnie would have gladly picked

out every stitch for one glimpse of the old Grandma Lucy. But without her grandmother to spur her on to work harder and imagine greater possibilities, Bonnie had to become her own coach, her own teacher. By the time she returned to Penn State for her senior year, her skills had improved so much that they were almost as good as her grandmother's had once been, making Grandma Lucy's acceptance of Bonnie's duplicity easier to bear.

That fall, Bonnie's mother persuaded her boss to let her return to part-time hours and the helpful neighbor resumed checking in on Grandma Lucy while she was away. Grandma Lucy continued piecing quilt blocks, and when her outbursts began again, with Bonnie no longer around to pick out the stitches, Bonnie's mother took over. On her next visit home, Bonnie traced templates, cut pieces, and borrowed needle and thread from her grandmother's sewing basket to take back to school to work on during study breaks. She mailed the finished blocks home from time to time so that Grandma Lucy could observe the pile steadily growing. When Grandma Lucy suddenly announced that she was ready to assemble the quilt top, Bonnie's mother sewed the blocks into rows with the sewing machine, set up the old quilt frame in the family room, and taught herself how to quilt by following the instructions in a Girl Scout manual checked out from the library. Facing each other across the quilt frame, Bonnie's mother and grandmother spent the winter joining the three layers, adding dimension and warmth to the colorful pieced top infused with so much hope and disappointment.

Grandma Lucy died before the quilt was finished. Grief-stricken, Bonnie's mother abandoned the quilt as a painful reminder of the last months she had spent with her mother, who left them long before her death. It fell to Bonnie to learn how to bind and finish the quilt, which she completed three months before her marriage to Craig. She followed him to Waterford, where he had accepted an administrative job at a small college, and devoted herself to raising their three children. Longing for a circle of friends like the one her grandmother had once known, Bonnie joined the Waterford Quilting Guild and soon befriended Gwen, a professor at the college whose career achievements far outshone her own, and Agnes, an older woman who loved appliqué and antiques. As the years passed, the circle of quilters grew, the bonds tightened, until Bonnie realized that she had been blessed with a group of friends equal to her grandmother's Stitch Witches. That, too, she believed, was her grandmother's gift—and not her only legacy.

In those days, a frequent lament at meetings of the Waterford Quilting Guild was the lack of a decent quilt shop within a reasonable driving distance. In winter, especially, it was annoying to have to drive over the pass through the Four Brothers Mountains for a simple spool of thread or a new sewing machine needle. Then one day two signs went up in the window of the shoe store on the first floor of the Markhams' building: GOING OUT OF BUSINESS! 75% OFF! read one, and FOR LEASE, the other.

At first Craig opposed the idea. Bonnie had last held a paying job between college and marriage, years before, and she had never run a business. The kids were still young, although he grudgingly acknowledged that they were in school most of the day and could do their homework in the store's office while she worked. As a last-ditch attempt to dissuade her, he pointed out that they simply could not afford such a risky business venture.

"We can afford it," Bonnie replied, and reminded him of her inheritance. In one of her last lucid decisions about her estate, Grandma Lucy had left her house to her granddaughters. When Bonnie's parents sold it, they divided the proceeds and invested them into two mutual fund accounts, one for Bonnie and one for Ellie. When Craig balked, protesting that he assumed that money was intended for their children's educations and their own retirement, Bonnie threw herself into persuading him that her business would succeed so well as the only quilt shop in an underserved market that they would come out ahead, much better than if they simply let the money earn interest.

"I can see there's no talking you out of it," Craig finally said, resigned, when weeks passed and her enthusiasm for the quilt shop did not waver. The very next day, she signed a long-term lease for the shop and began ordering stock. Then she commissioned a sign to hang above the door, eagerly anticipating the day the red-and-gold letters would proudly beckon quilters inside to the haven she would create for them.

There was no question what she would call her quilt shop; no other name ever entered her thoughts. Her quilt shop would be cozy and welcoming, full of surprises, marvels, necessities, and endless delights. Upon entering, aspiring quilters who had never touched a needle would believe that anything they imagined could be realized if they worked hard and trusted that the world was full of possibilities. Thus Grandma's Attic became her grandmother's last gift to Bonnie, the destination their winding ways had been leading to as they walked along together.

Bonnie had hoped to pass this legacy on to her children, but they had dreams of their own, other roads to follow. And now the time had come for Bonnie to continue on, to steel her courage and set out on a new path, though she could not see beyond the first bend. She did not know where it would lead, but as much as she wanted to please Sylvia, she could not believe that her path ended at the parlor of Elm Creek Manor. It must lead to something greater than the place she had departed. She had to believe that, though she could not imagine where a place greater than Grandma's Attic might be.

But she knew Grandma Lucy would have wanted her to dance along the entire length of this unknown winding way, flinging her arms wide to embrace the possibilities.

Sylvia waited on the back steps for Bonnie to return from her walk through the orchard, but although many other quilters came and went, her friend was not among them. Glancing at her watch, Sylvia realized the time for the start of Bonnie's afternoon workshop had passed. Either Bonnie had failed to return, which was unlikely, or she had circled the manor and returned inside through the front door. Sighing, Sylvia rose and absently brushed fragments of dried leaves from her skirt. She did not like to think that Bonnie was deliberately avoiding her, but she clearly was not interested in continuing their conversation.

As eager as Sylvia was to see her friend happily bustling about her new quilt shop, she would drop the subject of Grandma's Parlor for now and wait for Bonnie to approach her with her own ideas, her own plans. Perhaps she needed time. She had only recently closed the doors to Grandma's Attic. Perhaps it was too soon to contemplate a new venture, especially with the distraction of that louse of a husband of hers and their impending divorce.

Sylvia returned inside and decided to stop by Bonnie's classroom just to make sure her friend had not twisted her ankle or tumbled into the creek on her walk. As she suspected, Bonnie stood at the front of the classroom demonstrating English paper piecing to several curious campers. She threw Sylvia a weak smile without missing a beat in her presentation, which confirmed Sylvia's suspicions. Honestly. Had Bonnie waded across the creek and snuck through the north gardens to avoid her? Such subterfuge was unnecessary among friends.

But a little secrecy was perfectly acceptable, for the right reasons.

After looking in on a few of the other Elm Creek Quilters' classes and satisfying herself that all was well, Sylvia returned upstairs to her suite and the Winding Ways quilt she kept hidden away from her friends' inquisitive eyes. Bonnie's portion of the quilt had been one of the first she had completed, but now she wondered if she had chosen the right fabrics, the right combination of lights and darks. Bonnie had always preferred country colors—barn reds, forest greens, midnight blues—but perhaps her tastes had changed. Perhaps Sylvia had assumed too much and listened too little.

Sylvia studied the Winding Ways blocks, her gaze following the smooth flow of the overlapping circles that touched and merged like ripples cast off by a stone thrown into a pond. Bonnie would love the gift even if her preferences had turned to pastels or brights, Sylvia decided. The homespun prints captured Bonnie's favorite colors at the time they had first become friends. Even if Bonnie found something new more appealing, the Winding Ways quilt preserved the memory of their friendship, which would endure in the midst of change, wherever life took them.

Gwen

Gwen longed to dig in her heels and drag the week to a screeching halt, but the days sped past, blithely indifferent to her misery. Judy was her best friend, and Gwen had no idea how she was going to get through her farewell party without weeping or, worse yet, flinging her arms around Judy's petite shoulders, sobbing into her long black hair, and begging her to stay. "You couldn't pass up an opportunity like this, either, so don't ask me to!" Judy would say, laughing as she pried herself free from Gwen's desperate grasp. And of course she would be right, but that didn't make Gwen dread their Saturday leave-taking any less.

A good friend would send Judy off with good wishes, fond reminiscences, and encouragement as she set forth on her challenging new path. A reasonable friend would note that Philadelphia was well within a half day's drive of the Elm Creek Valley, making occasional visits quite likely. Unfortunately, as the farewell party approached, Gwen found herself devolving into a sad, clingy, needy friend who could almost—but not quite—wish that Judy had not been offered the dream job that was taking her away.

Worse yet, she knew this was only a warm-up for the swirl of emotions that was sure to strike her when Summer left for graduate school a few weeks later. She couldn't be prouder of her daughter, or more certain that Summer had made the right decision when she chose the University of Chicago, but she'd had her daughter so near for so long that it was impossible to imagine her blazing a solitary trail almost six hundred miles away.

At least Gwen would have the other

Elm Creek Quilters to console her in her loneliness.

"Drama queen," she muttered, shifting in her chair and focusing her attention on the books and papers spread out on the kitchen table before her. With the fall semester approaching, she intended to make as much progress as possible on her research before classes resumed, when grading papers and preparing lectures would consume most of her work hours. Every summer began with her good intentions firmly in hand: She would teach no more than one class each week at Elm Creek Quilt Camp, direct only two evening programs a month, and devote at least four hours a day to research and writing. This summer, she had lowered her expectations earlier than usual. She had not expected the hiring of two replacement teachers to take up so much of the summer, nor had she anticipated the battering ram of office politics that had forced her to spend more time and energy defending her choice of subject— quilt history—than actually conducting her research.

After a chance conversation with Sylvia, she had discovered a new research subject perfectly suited to prove to her unenlightened department chair how socially, historically, and politically relevant traditional women's arts truly were. Sylvia told Gwen how she and her sister had entered the Sears National Quilt Competition held at the 1933 Chicago World's Fair, themed "A Century of Progress." The Bergstrom sisters joined 25,000 quilters—which translated to roughly one of every two thousand women in the United States—in pursuit of the one-thousand-dollar prize, an enormous sum for the time. A mystery surrounded the fate of the grand-prize-winning quilt, which was presented to First Lady Eleanor Roosevelt after the World's Fair and kept at the White House until it somehow disappeared. Its whereabouts were still unknown, perhaps befitting a history of the mood and values of a nation during one of its most difficult periods. If Gwen had chosen as a lens any other art form but quilting, her department chair, Bill, would have been all for it. Instead he encouraged her to forget about quilts and study architecture of the period instead.

Gwen had tenure, so she was free to disregard his advice. But word rapidly spread around the College of Liberal Arts that she cared more for her pet projects than for her status in the department. Then came the vandalism of Bonnie's quilt shop, and Gwen's deduction that the department chair's son was one of the perpetrators. Now William Jr. swept floors and washed dishes at Elm Creek Quilt Camp, and Gwen was the social pariah of Kuehner Hall.

Until the furor subsided, it would not help her situation if she turned out shoddy research—and that meant squeezing every minute of work out of the day, including fitting in some reading and note-taking between the campers' Farewell Breakfast and Judy's farewell party. Gwen pored over her books and scrawled notes on a legal pad, occasionally glancing at the clock. No one would care if she showed up fashionably late—Bonnie had taken to doing so almost every day—but the party would be her last chance to see Judy before her departure early the next morning. Gwen also didn't want to miss the presentation of Judy's farewell gift, a Rose of Sharon wall hanging that Agnes had sewn, devoting months to hand appliquéing the beautiful blocks with tiny, virtually invisible stitches. Judy had seen Agnes sewing upon it all summer long, but she had no idea that the finished quilt was intended for her, nor did she know that the other Elm Creek Quilters had signed the border with heartfelt messages and wistful good-byes. Gwen rarely found herself at a loss for words, but when the time came to add her note to the quilt, she hesitated, unable to capture everything that Judy's friendship meant to her in a few handwritten sentences. Instead she scrawled a cheerful, almost breezy phrase or two that left everything unsaid. Judy's new friends in Philadelphia would assume she and Gwen had been only casual acquaintances, but Judy would understand.

Sighing, Gwen set her work aside and dressed for the party, but on her way back downstairs, she remembered to mark her place in her book so that she could pick up her work where she had left off. Book in hand, an intriguing phrase caught her eye, and she stood reading for a few moments, tapping the bookmark idly against the back of the chair. A footnote mentioned a book she had not come across earlier, so she uncapped her pen and added the reference to her working bibliography. Would the Waterford College Library have a copy? Gwen sat down and switched on her computer, drumming her fingers on the desk as her browser opened and connected to the Internet. After linking to the library catalog, Gwen was delighted to discover not only that the library had a copy but that it was on the shelf and the author had two other relevant works elsewhere in the stacks.

Gwen needed only a moment to decide that she could swing by the library on her way to the party and still arrive before the grill cooled. Rumor had it that Anna was preparing a sumptuous barbecue feast to be served outdoors on the veranda, so Gwen's tardiness would hardly be as conspicuous as if they were dining indoors with white table-cloths and crystal. With all the spouses and kids milling around, no one would notice if Gwen turned up at the end of the meal.

The Waterford College campus was sparsely populated during the interim between the end of the summer session and the beginning of the fall semester, especially on weekends, so Gwen easily found a prime parking spot on Main Street, then hurried up the grassy hill crisscrossed by sidewalks to the main library entrance. Inside, a security guard nodded pleasantly when Gwen flashed her faculty ID. "We close at five today," he said. "Summer hours."

Gwen thanked him for the reminder, though she knew she would be en route to Elm Creek Manor long before then. She hurried past a set of glass double doors leading into a long, spacious gallery. On one wall hung several portraits of library benefactors, just opposite the exterior southern wall, composed of tinted glass windows looking out upon the grassy main quadrangle. Above, four skylights patterned squares of light on the gleaming parquet floor. The Waterford Quilting Guild held its annual quilt show in the gallery every summer, but none of the Elm Creek Quilters had submitted a quilt for the contest since Elm Creek Quilts was founded. For her part, Gwen had been too busy to make anything worthy of a competition, and she knew Summer was concerned about exposing her pieces to so much sunlight, but she didn't know why her other friends had not participated. Years before, they had planned their show quilts a year in advance, speculated for months ahead of time about what their strongest rivals might submit, and hardly slept the night before ribbons were awarded. Could their recent indifference be yet another example of the ridiculous enmity between themselves and the local guild? It was far too easy to place the blame solely upon Diane and the former guild president, neighbors and worst enemies. The Elm Creek Quilters had been disappointed each time the guild had turned down their invitations to quilting events at the manor, but how long had it been since the Elm

Creek Quilters had supported a guild activity?

As she passed the gallery on her way to the stacks, Gwen resolved to encourage her friends to enter quilts in next year's show. The new guild president had taken a risk in coming to quilt camp to broach the idea of greater unity between their two estranged groups. Participating in their quilt show would send a clear message that the Elm Creek Quilters were eager to mend the rift.

As Gwen searched the shelves for the book she needed, she reflected upon the courage it took to admit to wrongdoings and propose reconciliation. Someone had to take that initial step, to be the first to make amends, risking rejection and failure in the hope of achieving a greater good. Sometimes that meant entering new, unknown, and possibly unfriendly territory, as the Waterford Quilting Guild's new president had done in coming to Elm Creek Quilt Camp. Sometimes it meant returning home.

Perhaps even greater courage was needed if home was Brown Deer, Kentucky, a small town no one but its citizens had ever heard of, where nothing ever happened but everybody knew everyone's business.

A lifetime ago, in Gwen's first few weeks as an elementary education major at the University of Kentucky, she had quickly fallen into the habit of telling new acquaintances that she was from Louisville. She had grown tired of admitting she was from Brown Deer, population 1,200, west of Lovely, about halfway between Kermit and Pilgrim, home to three churches and no movie theaters. Gwen had been a brainy oddball who had earned a reputation as a troublemaking nonconformist by being the only girl in school to enroll in auto shop instead of home ec and to refuse to join the Future Homemakers of America. Until coming to college, a decadent weekend meant pretending to have cramps on Sunday morning so she could sleep in instead of going to Mass with her parents. For as long as she could remember, Gwen had longed to escape that dull, stifling, provincial backwater, and pretending that she was from a city on the opposite side of the state was the first step in putting it behind her.

Exultant with her newfound freedom, she threw herself into college life, eager to try everything, anything. Passionate professors shook her slumbering social conscience awake, fellow students taught her about fighting for justice and making her voice heard, and more worldly friends invited her to expand her consciousness in ways that she never would have imagined back in Brown Deer, where sneaking nips from parents' liquor cabinets was the dizzying height of audacity.

For her first two semesters, Gwen worked feverishly to make up for the unexpected deficiencies in her education. Although she was regarded in her hometown as the most brilliant student Brown Deer High had ever matriculated, within her first few days on campus she had made the jarring observation that she trailed behind her peers from better school districts. Her sharp intellect, quick wit, and competitive streak soon helped her to gain an equal footing, and once securely there, she was eager to cast off her reputation as a grind interested in nothing more than top grades. When her friends teased her about being an uptight, square, small-town girl, she became less particular about attending classes and completing assignments on time. Everyone said that a person's education took place outside of the classroom as well as in it, and it was difficult to care about, say, Elizabeth Barrett Browning when kids her age were dying in an illegal war on the other side of the planet. Classes became a drag; visits home to Brown Deer, unbearable. Her parents looked at her with increasing helplessness as if she had become a stranger. Gwen didn't think she had changed so much; she had merely stopped pretending to be what other people wanted her to be.

At the end of her sophomore year, Gwen decided to leave school and find herself. She had been stuck in a square little town for too long, chafing against her parents' and neighbors' expectations. She had no idea who Gwen Sullivan was or what she was meant to do with her life. College would always be there, if and when she decided to return. She only had a brief moment in the sun to be young, to love freely, to live as she pleased, and to discover who she really was.

She set out with two friends, hitchhiking across the country, crashing wherever they were offered a bed, sampling whatever was passed to her, watching the days slowly unfold as if through a rosy, warm haze. She parted with her friends in Denver and hooked up with another group headed out to California; she left them in Los Angeles and made her way north alone, hitchhiking up the coast. A casual invitation led to a lengthy stay in a commune in Berkeley, where she cooked for a changeable group of twelve perpetual students in exchange for a fold-out sofa and access to their collective library, shelved on wooden planks stacked on milk crates in a converted detached garage. She wandered the campus, joining in antiwar protests and occasionally sitting in on lectures. Knowledge was meant to be free, and her attendance wasn't preventing a tuition-paying student from occupying an otherwise empty chair. On one such day, she met Dennis, yelling epithets as he burned an effigy of the president outside of Sproul Hall. Her mother would have said Gwen was instantly smitten—that is, if her mother would not have fainted dead away at the sight of the long-haired, strung out, unwashed, pale young man with his arms around her daughter. Gwen was certain she had discovered her soul mate.

After their barefoot wedding ceremony on the beach—it was too cold to go barefoot in February, but Dennis insisted they have unencumbered contact with the earth—they traveled the country with two other couples in a van plastered with peace signs and antiwar slogans. They bartered for gas money and worked occasional odd jobs for food. They went where they chose, with nothing to hold them down, nothing to bear them up but each other.

The carefree times ended when Gwen realized she was pregnant.

She considered, for about half a

minute, ending the pregnancy, but even if she could have found a safe way to do it, she couldn't make herself think of the baby as anything less than a human being. How could she denounce sending American boys to die in Vietnam and yet condone killing her own child? She was careless, but she was no hypocrite. Her long-dormant pragmatism forcibly reasserted itself. Suddenly it mattered where their next meal would come from, where they would live, what kind of mother she would be. When she gave up pot—which she had only pretended to enjoy since it gave her migraines—Dennis's drug use, once a minor irritant, began to worry her. When she tried to persuade him to quit, he told her she was jealous, uptight, and square—that same old label he knew she hated. "Relax, baby," he said, blowing smoke in her face. Then he bent over to speak to her abdomen, still as flat as the day she had left Brown Deer. "That goes for you, too, baby."

Watching him, his head thrown back in a fit of helpless giggling, Gwen felt nothing for him but shame and disgust.

How could she have ever thought she loved him? How could she bring a child into the world and expect him to help her raise it? Dennis could barely remember to look after himself. Where would they get diapers and toys and clothes? She couldn't raise a child in the back-seat of a van, with a constantly shifting cast of characters filling the front seats.

The next time they stopped for gas, Gwen left her wedding ring on the dash-board, stuffed her few possessions into her backpack, announced that she had to take a leak, and left without saying good-bye. She walked along the high-way in the opposite direction the van was traveling, hoping to get a good head start before Dennis and the others realized she wasn't coming back. She considering returning to the commune in Berkeley, where the kind, gentle residents might welcome her, newborn infant and all. But after an hour of trudging along on the shoulder of the road, the only driver who pulled over was heading east. After a moment's hesitation, she accepted the ride.

A week later, she walked the last mile

into Brown Deer, filthy, hungry, and fervently hoping that no one would recognize her. A boy with baseball cards in the spokes of his bicycle wheels stopped on the sidewalk and stared as she climbed the stairs to her parents' front door and rang the bell. She gave him a pointed look over her shoulder until he sped off, but her stomach gave a sudden lurch at the sound of the door opening, and she spun back around.

Her mother stood with her hand on the doorknob, staring at her.

"Hi, Mom," Gwen said, shifting her backpack and attempting a grin.

Her mother promptly burst into tears.

Immediately Gwen let her backpack fall to the ground and reached forward to comfort her, but her mother had stepped away from the door to hurry into the other room. "Harry, Harry," Gwen heard her mother cry, "she's home!"

Gwen swallowed hard and entered the house as her mother disappeared into the kitchen. She caught a glimpse of herself in the three gilt-framed mirrors hanging above the sofa and saw that long wisps of auburn hair had come free from her braid and that her face was sunburned and streaked with dirt. Through it all shone that unmistakable knocked-up girl's glow. She wished she had thought to stop at a gas station and clean herself up first. She shouldn't have feared being recognized.

Her mother reappeared, knotting her hands in the white apron she wore over her flowered dress. Behind her trailed Gwen's father, his dark hair neatly parted on the side and slicked down, his eyes brimming with tears behind his black-framed glasses. "Gwen," he said, his voice shaking. "Where have you been? We were so worried."

Shame flooded her. She had never thought of them back home wondering about her, worrying, contemplating all the dangers a young woman might face in the world beyond Brown Deer. "California, mostly," she said, trying to remember the last time she had called or written. She let her backpack slide to the floor and tucked a loose strand of hair behind her ear. "I'm sorry I didn't keep in touch better. It's hard on the road. You know." Although of course, they had no idea.

"Never mind that now." Her mother came forward to embrace her, and her father reached out to pat her on the shoulder. "You're home now. Welcome home."

Gwen clung to her, filled with sudden anguish and relief.

While her mother fixed her something to eat, Gwen showered and slipped into some of her old clothes, which hung loosely upon her now, even around her middle. She studied herself in her vanity mirror, pressing her palm against her abdomen, while reflected behind her, her twin bed lay draped with the candy-colored Jewel Box quilt her mother had made. It was a little girl's room, pre-served as a shrine as if her parents still mourned a daughter they had lost in childhood. Perhaps they did.

A chicken salad sandwich with sweet dill pickles awaited her on the table when she went downstairs to the kitchen. Her mother looked up from washing dishes, turned off the tap, and dried her hands on her apron. "Do you want some milk?" her mother asked. "Lemonade? Iced tea?"

"Milk would be great." Good for the baby, Gwen added silently as she sat down and began to eat. The familiar flavors brought tears to her eyes, but she quickly blinked them away as her mother set a glass of milk on the table and seated herself across from Gwen. "This is delicious. Thanks, Mom."

"It's nothing." Idly, Gwen's mother brushed crumbs from the table into her open palm and scooted her chair over to reach the trash can beneath the sink, the chair legs squeaking on the linoleum. "How's Dennis?"

"Stoned, probably," Gwen said without thinking, and immediately regretted it when her mother recoiled. "I—I don't know. I left him in Kansas City."

Gwen's mother mulled this over. "Left him? You mean he'll be joining us later?"

"No, I mean I divorced him."

Gwen's mother looked horrified, for all that she had never met Dennis and had little reason to think well of him. "Oh, Gwen, no. Not a divorce."

Gwen picked the last crumbs from her plate, still ravenous. "We didn't marry in the church."

"That doesn't matter."

"To you? Since when?"

"A marriage is a marriage." Gwen's mother rose and took bread from the bread box and a covered bowl of chicken salad from the refrigerator. "Was it a Protestant service? What denomination?"

"A friend who had spent a year in a Buddhist monastery heard our vows on the beach." Gwen inhaled deeply and sighed, remembering the waves crashing on her ankles, numb from cold, the sunlight making the water sparkle, her friends' voices raised in song, Dennis's kiss. "It was a beautiful day."

Her mother fixed her with an inscrutable look, but her hands kept deftly working, making Gwen another sandwich. "Then it wasn't really a true, legal marriage."

"It was real to us."

"Well." Her mother passed the plate to Gwen and sat down again. "I think it's fair to say that you aren't really divorced.

You've just stopped living in sin. That at least makes matters less complicated."

Gwen bit into her sandwich and washed it down with a gulp of milk. "I'm having a baby." When her mother showed no response, she added, "In June, I think."

Her mother's eyes slowly filled with tears. "Well," she said again, her smile trembling. "Isn't that lovely."

"So you might want to tell your friends that I was really married after all. I'll go along with whatever story you want."

Her mother took a deep, shaky breath and dabbed at her eyes with the corner of her apron. "So you're planning to stay?"

Gwen's heart turned over. It had never occurred to her that her parents wouldn't want her to. But of course, this was Brown Deer. A daughter who left town with so much promise and potential, dragging herself home as a college dropout, divorced or never married depending upon your point of view, pregnant—of course they would want her well on her way out of town before she began to show. "I—just for a while," she stammered. "I know people will talk. I'll figure something out and leave before I give anyone anything more to gossip about."

"No." Her mother reached across the table and seized her hands. "You're staying here. Your vagabond lifestyle was bad enough when you had only yourself to think of. A baby needs a home and a family."

She spoke so fiercely that Gwen could only manage, "But the neighbors—"

"They'll have a lot to say, I'm sure. I don't care and neither should you. I'm not letting you disappear again, not with my only grandchild. I'm putting my foot down, as I should have done years ago. You're staying, so you might as well get used to the idea." Gwen's mother released her daughter's hands and gestured to the sandwich. "Go on. Finish your lunch. You're skin and bones."

For the first time in ages, Gwen found herself without a witty rejoinder.

She spent most of that first week home sleeping and rereading all of her old books. When her mother scheduled

Gwen a long-overdue checkup with their family doctor, she insisted so adamantly upon driving her that Gwen knew her mother feared that if on her own she would hop in the car and disappear forever. When she ran out of things to read and began to grow restless, her mother suggested that she invite some of her school friends over.

"Who did you have in mind?" Gwen asked, sitting at the kitchen table and toying with a bread wrapper twist tie while her mother unpacked groceries. She'd had only two good friends in Brown Deer: Kelly, an aspiring poet and editor of the school paper, and Angela, who could play any instrument she touched but could barely spell. Kelly was pursuing a law degree somewhere in New England, and Angela had left town the day after graduation to become a session musician in Nashville.

"I saw Vicky in the Piggly Wiggly this morning. She said she's thrilled to hear you're back in town and you should come over for coffee sometime."

"Vicky invited me to Chateau Sinclair?" jeered Gwen. "I don't believe it."

"She's Vicky Hixton now. I know you girls weren't real friendly, but you've both grown up and people change. She's married and has a baby, too, so she knows what you're going through."

"She has no idea what I'm going through," Gwen retorted. So Vicky had married Pete after all. How cliché—the cheerleader marrying the captain of the football team. She doubted either of them had ever left Kentucky, except perhaps for their honeymoon. Apparently Pete could read a map better than he could read a book, or they never would have found their way back to Brown Deer. Of course, Vicky had probably told him what the multisyllabic words meant, just as she had always done to keep his grades up so he could keep his academic eligibility. At least he could add money and make change; that and his winning personality would serve him well at his father's used-car dealership—

Abruptly Gwen abandoned her silent, scathing appraisal. Pete was dim, but he didn't smoke grass and he was probably a devoted husband and father. As much as she hated to admit it, Vicky had chosen a better father for her children than Gwen had—but that didn't mean Gwen admired her and wanted her for a friend.

Her mother pursed her lips, put a gallon of milk and a carton of orange juice in the refrigerator, and picked up the phone. "Think of something polite to say fast, because I'm calling her."

Against her better judgment, Gwen found herself two days later carrying a plate of her mother's best sour-cream cookies down the tree-lined streets of Brown Deer on her way to Vicky's house. Vicky greeted Gwen at the door wearing a cashmere twin set, lipstick, and pearls, her honey-blonde hair swept back in a headband. "Well, if it isn't the long-lost Gwen Sullivan," said Vicky, unsuccessfully masking her shock with a cheery smile. The towheaded baby in Vicky's arms stuffed a chubby fist in his mouth and stared at the visitor. "What a surprise to see you back in Brown Deer. I know your folks have missed you terribly."

"It's nice to be back," said Gwen as

Vicky ushered her inside, although at the moment she didn't believe it. She forced a smile and held out the plate of cookies. "These are from my mother."

"Isn't she sweet. That must be the secret recipe my mother says the bridge club raves about." Vicky showed Gwen to the living room, her smile never faltering as her gaze flicked over Gwen's worn sandals, patched jeans, and fringed vest. "Why don't you set that plate on the coffee table and take a seat?" She excused herself and hurried off to the kitchen, the baby riding her hip, and soon returned carrying a coffee service on a silver tray. "It's so good to see you," she said, pouring them each a steaming cup. "Are you home for the holidays?"

It was an odd question considering that Thanksgiving was still two weeks away. Either Vicky already knew the whole sordid story and was playing dumb, or she was so disconcerted by Gwen's sudden reappearance in Brown Deer that a holiday visit was the only possible explanation that came to mind. "No, I'm home for a while." Gwen leaned forward to stir cream and sugar into her coffee, praying she wouldn't spill anything on the plush white sofa or the shag carpeting, both strangely pristine for a home with a baby in it. "Your son is adorable. How old is he?"

"Six months. Pete Jr. is his given name, but we all call him PJ." Vicky shifted her son to her lap and took one of his feet in each of her hands. "My boobs have gotten so huge from nursing that his daddy can hardly keep his hands off me. I bet it won't be long before I'm in a family way again."

So this is the discourse of popular girls, Gwen thought as she forced herself to join in Vicky's laughter. This was what Gwen, Kelly, and Angela had missed out on while observing the cheerleaders with equal parts envy and disdain from the worst table in the school cafeteria, the one with the short fourth leg. If a newcomer set down a tray too suddenly, those already seated would find their food catapulted through the air. It had been one of the more humiliating occupational hazards of their exile. Pete, especially, had found it very entertaining, for slapstick was just about the only humor he understood.

"How is Pete, anyway?" Gwen heard herself ask. "How did he manage to avoid getting sent to 'Nam? I can't picture him burning his draft card."

"Oh, Gwen, you sure haven't changed. The cream hasn't even cooled your coffee and you're already talking politics." Vicky gazed heavenward as she untangled a long strand of honey-blonde hair from PJ's fist. "He tried to enlist, but he's stone-cold deaf in his right ear. Too many tackles, the doctor said, so he obviously doesn't follow sports because he'd know Pete hardly ever got sacked. It wasn't how many times he got hit, but how hard. You remember that game junior year against Greenup County?" She waved a hand dismissively. "No, of course you wouldn't. You never cared about the team. Anyway, I think that's the tackle that did it. And all that time I thought he was just ignoring me, when it turned out he couldn't hear a word I said if he was facing the wrong way. Isn't that funny?"

"Very," said Gwen, determined to be agreeable. "Who would have guessed?"

"Not me, that's for sure. But how about *you*? How have you been? I heard you got married."

"I was married. I'm not anymore."

"Oh, my. What a shame." Vicky tsked her tongue as she carefully selected one of Gwen's mother's cookies from the plate. "At least you're still young enough to find someone else, and since your ex isn't from around here you won't, you know, run into him at the post office or something. Thank goodness you don't have any kids."

"I will in about seven months."

Vicky's eyebrows formed perfectly plucked arches. "Oh." She sank back against the white velour. "I see." She held PJ a little closer, then fixed Gwen with a bright smile. "If you need to know the best places to get diapers on sale, or which girls you can trust to be reliable baby-sitters, all you have to do is ask."

It was the kindest gesture anyone from Vicky's crowd had ever shown her. "Thank you."

"Isn't it funny how things turn out?"

Vicky stroked her son's downy hair. "You were always so smart, getting that college scholarship and thinking you were too good for everyone. You couldn't wait to shake the dust of this town off your feet and never look back. Now here you are, right back in Brown Deer with the rest of us—knocked up, no husband, no job, no fancy college degree. I can't imagine what you're going to do next."

"Neither can I," said Gwen, although her inclination was to turn the coffee pot over Vicky's shining blonde head.

During the next two weeks, Gwen left home only to drive an hour away to the nearest library—escorted by her mother, of course—or to pick up necessities at the grocery store, or to attend church services with her parents. She didn't want to go; she believed less than half of what the priest droned, although she was drawn to the idea of Mary as an iconic mother goddess figure. Still, she went because she appreciated what it meant for her father and mother—who were head usher and leader of the Altar Society, respectively—to sit beside her in all her shame. She was their daughter, and despite her mistakes they intended to stand by her, dragging her out in public if necessary to prove that she had no need to cower inside ashamed. Touched by their faithfulness and impressed by their determination, Gwen resolved to give the neighbors nothing else to gossip about. After all, there was only so much they could say about a divorced pregnant former valedictorian, and Vicky had already said most of it.

Since Gwen was obviously making no effort to build her own circle of friends, her mother cajoled her to join her quilting club, the Brown Does. Gwen laughed off her invitations until she realized her mother was sincere—and resolved. Gwen had absolutely no interest in quilting, growing flowers for the Altar Society, or planning bake sales to support the volunteer fire department, and she was not about to pretend that she cared. She also didn't need all those matrons, including Vicky's mother, carrying home cautionary tales about Gwen's rapidly expanding waistline.

Then her father took her aside and offered his stern opinion. "These are your mother's friends," he told her. "They stood by her all those long years when you were gone. They held her when she cried. They prayed for your safe return home. The least you can do—the very least you can do—is show up for one meeting, put on a pleasant smile, and show them that you were worth it. It's nothing to you, but it would mean the world to your mother."

Chagrined, Gwen agreed to join the Brown Does for one weekly meeting in the church basement, but only after promising her father that she would keep her opinions about quilting to herself. It wouldn't be easy. She couldn't stand to see otherwise intelligent women waste their time on pointless busywork, trivial distractions that prevented them from devoting their time and energy to work that might actually make a difference. Registering women to vote, for example. Speaking out against injustice. Pursuing an education—not that Gwen had much credibility in that regard anymore.

She vowed to keep silent for her

mother's sake as she pulled up a metal folding chair and joined fourteen of her mother's quilter friends around a long table usually reserved for potluck dinners, wedding receptions, and yard sales. To her surprise, she was not the youngest present. Two of the Brown Does had brought their daughters, who were affectionately referred to as Fawns. Everyone seemed surprised to find Gwen among them, but when an older lady inquired if she was their newest Fawn, Gwen shook her head vehemently.

While the others worked on their own projects, Gwen sat idle, listening. To her relief, after asking how she felt and clucking sympathetically when she admitted to lingering morning sickness, they steered the conversation away from her pregnancy and left her blissfully alone to join in, or not, as she saw fit. The chat wasn't as dull as she had expected it to be, which shouldn't have surprised her, considering that she had known them and the people they discussed all her life, and she had a lot of catching up to do. She took a bit of guilty comfort in discovering that she was not the only resident of Brown Deer whose life had taken an unexpected and embarrassing turn; it wasn't schadenfreude so much as a dawning comprehension that others had recovered from worse downturns in fortune, and in time she might, too.

The next week, she told her mother she was willing to give the Does another try, almost regretting it when her mother greeted the news with unconcealed delight. Gwen had no intention of making the visits a habit, but she had finished her last library book and had nothing better to do. Upon her return to the church basement, the eldest Doe, a mother of twelve, greeted her with a box of gingersnaps, which she promised could cure even the worst morning sickness. Another Doe sought her opinion regarding a selection of fabrics for a new quilt, since, as she said, Gwen had such an "iconoclastic style." The women included her in their circle as if she belonged there. It was only later that Gwen learned that daughters were considered Fawns from birth regardless of their own inclinations.

As the weeks passed, Gwen grew tired of sitting around while the others pinned and sewed, so she began assisting the others on tasks that required little technical skill—tracing templates for one Doe, cutting pieces for another. When asked when she planned to start a quilt of her own, Gwen laughed and said she didn't have time.

"Seems to me you have little else but time," a Doe remarked.

"What are you afraid of?" teased the youngest Fawn, a senior at the high school. "That you'll make a quilt so ugly that you'll have to dump it in the lost and found?"

The others laughed so heartily that Gwen looked around the circle in surprise. Were they referring to her notorious refusal to take home ec? Why would they assume her quilts would be ugly? Just because she didn't *want* to learn to quilt didn't mean that she *couldn't*.

Sensing her bewilderment, her mother patted her arm reassuringly. "It's an inside joke," she explained. "There's been a Pineapple quilt sitting in the church lost-and-found box for ages. Whenever we're dissatisfied with one of our projects, we threaten to abandon it there."

"But we always let the other Does talk us out of it," another chimed in.

"That Pineapple quilt is perfectly nice, or it would be if it weren't wadded up and stuffed in a cardboard carton," said Mrs. Moore, Gwen's former fifth-grade teacher. "So our joke doesn't really suit."

"Why hasn't someone returned the quilt to its rightful owner?" asked Gwen, still perplexed. "Maybe she thought she misplaced it somewhere else, and she doesn't know to look for it here. You know all the quilters in Brown Deer. Don't you recognize the handiwork?"

"If we knew who made the quilt, we wouldn't have left it to gather dust in the lost and found, now, would we?" said Vicky's mother.

"Honey, when I said the quilt has been in that box for ages, I meant *ages,*" said Gwen's mother. "It was there when

I rummaged through the box looking for the glove I lost at my First Communion."

"For crying out loud, even a person can be declared dead after seven years," said Gwen. "If it's such a nice quilt, why would you leave it in the lost and found instead of taking it home?"

The Brown Does stared at her, shocked. "Because it isn't ours," the eldest said, fixing a sharp, accusatory stare upon Gwen as if she had suggested pilfering from the collection baskets.

"Whoever made that quilt, after all this time, she probably isn't coming back for it," Gwen pointed out, pushing back her chair. Behind her, the Brown Does broke into astonished murmurs that faded as Gwen climbed the stairs and made her way to the ushers' closet, where the water-stained carton sat where it always had, on the floor beneath the ushers' coat hooks. She knelt beside the box and dug through the assorted single mittens, Sunday school art projects, eyeglass cases, and hand-knit scarves, wrinkling her nose at the musty smell of rotten cardboard and wet wool,

until her fingers brushed soft patchwork. Unearthing the quilt, Gwen shook
it free of dirt and crushed bits of brown
autumn leaves and held it up for inspec-
tion. It seemed as well sewn as any quilt
that her mother had made, as far as
Gwen could tell, with narrow strips of
cotton prints sewn in an alternating dark
and light diagonal pattern around a central square. The navy blue, brick red,
and forest green color scheme was old-
fashioned, but not unattractive. Gwen
counted twelve rows of eight blocks
each, and, measuring with her hand,
she estimated that the blocks were six
inches square. The quilt felt oddly stiff to
the touch—not the top and the backing,
which were soft cotton, but something
within the layers that gave it a strange
crispness. When Gwen gave the folds
an experimental squeeze, they made a
muffled crinkling sound.

Gwen brushed off as much of the
dust and dirt as she could and carried
the quilt back downstairs to the basement. Brown Does were busily quilting
in silence, which told Gwen they had

broken off talking about her when they heard her footsteps on the stairs.

"Oh, so you found it," said Vicky's mother, her voice ringing with false brightness.

"Listen to this." When Gwen shook the quilt, several of the Does nodded knowingly at the rustling sound.

"It's foundation paper pieced," said Mrs. Moore. "She left the papers in."

"That might explain why she got rid of it," remarked Vicky's mother. "She was embarrassed by her mistake, or it was too stiff and uncomfortable to sleep beneath."

Gwen draped the quilt over the table and looked to her mother to decipher the quilt terminology. "This sort of quilt doesn't use templates," Gwen's mother explained as the Does and Fawns leaned forward to inspect the quilt, so eagerly Gwen surmised that most of them had never before seen the subject of their long-standing inside joke. "The block design is drawn in reverse on a foundation, a piece of paper or thin fabric. The quilter sews the block's pieces directly to the foundation, usually working from the center outward and sewing over previous seams. It's a useful technique for patterns like the Pineapple that are constructed Log Cabin style."

"The paper foundations are carefully removed afterward," added another Doe. "It's a tedious process, and it's easy to rip out stitches as you tear off the paper."

"Which is why some quilters prefer using muslin instead of paper," said Mrs. Moore. "Muslin foundations don't have to be removed. They make the top slightly thicker and more difficult to quilt through, but also a bit warmer."

"Not so you'd notice," said Vicky's mother dismissively. "If you leave paper foundations in, well, as you can see, you end up with a quilt that's noisy and uncomfortable."

The eldest quilter sniffed. "Whoever left those paper foundations in either didn't know what she was doing or she was lazy."

Several Does nodded their agreement, but Gwen shook her head, unconvinced. "She knew enough to piece all these tiny little blocks, and she wasn't lazy when it came to matching up all of these seams."

"Said the girl who doesn't quilt," teased one of the Fawns.

"I live with a quilter. One picks things up," said Gwen defensively. "Maybe she left the foundations in intentionally."

"Yes, to cut corners," said the eldest quilter. "Lazybones."

Before Gwen could rush to the unknown quiltmaker's defense, her mother spoke up. "It's a mystery, isn't it, one we're not likely to solve if we stuff the quilt back in that old carton and never give it another thought except in jokes. Gwen's taken an interest in it, so why not let her keep it? Maybe she'll find some clue to the quilter's identity that the rest of us missed."

Before Gwen could object that she was only mildly curious, the other Brown Does chimed in their agreement and Gwen found herself the owner of a long-abandoned, cryptic quilt that may or may not have been stitched by the laziest woman in Brown Deer, circa 1900.

Back home, Gwen draped the quilt

over her vanity and pondered it for a few days before deciding how to proceed. Her mother recommended searching the quilt for a signature or a bit of embroidery that might offer a clue to the quiltmaker's identity, but although Gwen examined every inch of each of the ninety-six blocks as well as the backing, she found nothing. When she asked her mother if the Pineapple pattern had any special significance, her mother mused that the pineapple was a traditional symbol of hospitality, but the quilt block pattern didn't have any symbolic meaning as far as she knew.

On her next trip to the library, Gwen searched for books on the history of quilts, but found only three academic texts among the many instructional booklets and pattern collections. Nibbling gingersnaps in front of the fireplace as she read, she found herself intrigued by the black-and-white photographs of antique American quilts from the eighteenth and nineteenth centuries, as well as quilted clothing and other artifacts that were older still. One of the books included reproductions of old quilt block patterns, occasionally with captions noting the origin of the pattern, its name, or both. A certain Revolutionary War battle inspired one block's name, the author noted in an aside, and resistance to an unpopular law another. The tantalizing glimpse into history alternately intrigued and frustrated Gwen. It seemed the author had expected her audience to be so familiar with her subject that only passing references to a common store of knowledge were needed. Apparently she had not anticipated an era when her book might be all that remained of traditions lost to history.

That same book included pictures of Pineapple quilts that closely resembled the one Gwen had rescued from the lost and found, as well as other Pineapple patterns completely different in design. To her disappointment, none of the books included that telling detail limiting the use of the Pineapple block to a specific social situation, era, or geographic region. The quilt could have been made anywhere during the last century for any reason. Undaunted, Gwen copied the books' bibliographies. Though she had exhausted the resources of the closest public library, someday, perhaps, she might be able to continue the search elsewhere.

At the next meeting of the Brown Does, Gwen reluctantly reported that her search had stalled. "At least you tried," said one well-meaning Doe. "We never expected you to find out who made the quilt."

"Only because it's been a mystery so long," Gwen's mother hastened to add. But Gwen, former valedictorian, failed academic prodigy, heard only that they had expected her to disappoint them. For all that she claimed not to care what the people of Brown Deer thought, their diminished expectations wounded her.

Late that night, lying on her childhood bed, hands on her rounding abdomen, Gwen thought about the quilt and about the eldest Brown Doe's certainty that the unknown quilter must have been either lazy or incompetent, all because of the paper foundations left within the layers. How unfair it was to assume the worst of her based upon that single factor, that one mistake, if it was a mistake, when everything else about the quilt suggested that it was the work of a talented craftswoman! Perhaps she had left the papers intact by choice. Perhaps it was not a choice any other quilter would agree with, but perhaps to her, it had seemed the best artistic path to follow.

If only Gwen could ask her.

Gwen propped herself up on her elbows and studied the quilt, still draped over her vanity next to the library books. Perhaps there was a way, but if she set out upon that road, she could not turn back.

She crept through the darkened house, finding her way by touch and moonlight, stepping over the squeaky third stair by a longtime habit she had forgotten until then. Her mother's sewing basket sat on the end table beside her favorite chair. Gwen risked switching on the lamp long enough to find her mother's seam ripper, which she quietly carried back to her room.

Spreading the Pineapple quilt facedown over her bed, Gwen knelt on the floor and peered closely at the quilting stitches that held the layers together. For the first time, she realized that the quilting had been completed by machine. Of course. The paper foundations would have been very difficult to sew through by hand, a problem the quilter would have discovered within the first few stitches. At that point, she still could have removed the foundations and proceeded without the impediment, or she could have abandoned the quilt top altogether. Her choice to continue on by machine offered more proof that she had wanted the papers intact.

Gwen thought she heard the Brown Does gasp in horror as she slipped the sharp tip of the seam ripper through one of the stitches fastening the binding to the back of the quilt and severed it.

Once begun, it was easy to proceed. Gwen picked out the binding stitches along two perpendicular sides of the quilt, then began the more painstaking process of removing the stitches sewn through a single block in the corner. In case her hunch had led her down a false trail, she wanted to limit the damage to one small portion of the quilt.

When she had removed enough stitches to separate the layers, she peeled back the backing, wrinkling her nose at the scent of mildew. More carefully, she lifted the fragile inner layer of cotton, a dull white flecked with what seemed to be bits of twigs or hulls. Some of the white fluff clung to the paper foundations, so Gwen gently brushed off the remnants, her heart quickening when she spied not plain paper, but a printed page, yellowed with time.

Eagerly she scanned the faded lines, but as she read, her puzzlement grew.

It seemed, as far as she could discern, to be a page torn from an outdated legal text, a few annotated paragraphs about some obscure matter of property law.

In other words, scrap paper.

Disappointment flooded her. She left the seam ripper on the vanity, turned out the light, and climbed into bed. Another dead end, another failure. And now she would have to explain to the Brown

Does that she had ruined the quilt in pursuit of a whim.

The next morning Gwen awoke hungry and cold. She had kicked off the bedcovers in the night, and as she rose shivering from bed, she saw that the room was filled with a familiar, diffuse light. Drawing on her robe, she went to the window to find the world outside blanketed in snow.

Without sparing a glance for the ruined Pineapple quilt, Gwen joined her mother and father downstairs for breakfast. Mulling over the previous night's disappointment, she barely heard her mother's cheery offer to drive her to the library.

"We'll have to wait for your dad to clear the driveway," her mother said. "Gwen? Are you listening?"

Gwen slapped the table, rattling the dishes. "It's outdated now, but it wasn't then," she exclaimed, bolting from her chair as quickly as her ample belly allowed. She hurried upstairs, seized the seam ripper, and swiftly picked out stitches holding a second Pineapple block to the batting and backing. After long minutes, she worked enough thread free to peel back the layers, enough to see that this second foundation was different in color and texture from the first—coarser, less brittle, with broad ink strokes instead of printed text. Peering closer, Gwen realized that it was a page torn from a composition book, with a nursery rhyme written in a child's careful, studied penmanship.

"Gwen," her mother gasped from the doorway. "What have you done?"

Gwen whirled around, instinctively blocking the quilt from her mother's view. "I had to," she said. "It was the only way to know. But it was worth it. See? I was right! Whoever made this quilt didn't choose pages from a single, outdated book ready to be pulped. She took them deliberately from several sources, and I'm sure she left the foundations intact just as purposefully."

She draped the quilt on the bed and waved her mother over. Her mother's alarm faded into puzzlement as she saw the page from the legal text sewn firmly to the child's penmanship homework. With a knowing frown, she held out her palm until Gwen sheepishly passed her the seam ripper she had taken without permission. Gwen's mother tentatively picked out more of the adjacent stitches until the two foundations directly below the first pair were revealed.

"It's a recipe," Gwen's mother said in wonder, reading the faint, penciled words. "A yeast bread with anise, egg, and . . . I can't make out the rest."

"Does it continue on the next foundation?" Gwen peered at the adjacent paper. "No, it's a shopping list, and the handwriting isn't the same."

"I have another seam ripper," Gwen's mother said, already hurrying from the room. Before long she returned with the tool and, starting from opposite ends of the quilt and working toward the center, she and Gwen worked together to carefully, swiftly pick out the quilting stitches. They uncovered more pages torn from legal books, though they were not numbered sequentially and did not seem to be from the same volume. They uncovered childish drawings, homework papers, a sentimental poem composed for Mother's Day, a report card boasting straight As—all, apparently, the work of the same boy, at different ages. Nothing remained of at least twenty of the foundations, the paper long ago having disintegrated, with only brittle scraps clinging to the threads to prove that they had once existed. Newspaper clippings, envelopes—more than seventy squares torn from unlikely sources, a bizarre, frenzied scrapbook of one quiltmaker's world.

"Could she have chosen them at random?" Gwen's mother suggested as they interrupted their work hours later for supper. "Perhaps they were the only papers she had, and they only seem odd to us because we're blessed with so many more suitable choices."

Gwen had studied the pages for hours without discerning a clear pattern, but she couldn't believe that the pages had not been chosen deliberately. "If she had one law book that someone had thrown out, why not take all the foundations from the same book? Or, since she obviously had access to many different law books, why didn't she take one blank page from each? There are always one or two extra blank pages at the end of bound books. She could have taken those, but instead she tore pages from the middle."

"And ruined lots of books in the process," Gwen's father said. "I wouldn't have wanted to be her when the lawyer, whoever he was, tried to look up some legal ruling and discovered that the page he needed was missing."

"He wouldn't discover it, not right away," Gwen mused. "The quilter wanted to hurt him, but for some reason she couldn't do it to his face. It had to be done secretly, so that she would be satisfied but he couldn't discover what she had done until she was beyond his reach. The lawyer must have held some kind of power over her."

Gwen's mother attempted to conceal a shudder with a laugh. "I think you might be reading too much into this. Maybe she had already used all the extra blank pages for other quilts. Maybe she knew the lawyer well, and asked him which pages he could spare."

Gwen read in her mother's face her reluctance to accept the picture of the quilter that was emerging—a woman spiteful, destructive, and full of rage. Gwen found it unsettling, too, but the unknown quilter's anger was the only constant in the wild assemblage of patchwork clues.

After helping her mother wash the dishes, Gwen returned upstairs, offering vague replies when her mother urged her to put the quilt away for the night and get some rest. Her thoughts whirled, making sleep impossible. Quietly, knowing her mother would wake at the slightest sound, Gwen spread out the quilt, studying one significant foundation near the center of the quilt: an envelope with a partial address.

The stamp was entirely gone, but part of the postmark remained: "November 13," no year visible, from a town in Kentucky that began with "Hen." Water must have soaked into the quilt while it languished in the lost-and-found box, for the blue ink had blurred and bled into the paper's fibers, obscuring most of the mailing address. The first line read only "Mr. and Mrs. Jo," and the second read "714 Junip." The third line offered the most promising detail: "Richar." Surely that meant Richardsport, a town about thirty miles west of Brown Deer. But what had been more important to the quilter: the letter's destination, or its origin? The return address was lost in a smear of fading blue ink, revealing nothing.

But at least she had a partial address, a place to start in the morning. Gwen turned out the light and drifted off to sleep.

She dreamed of a woman in turn-of-the-century dress, sitting on the floor, fuming, tearing page after page from fine leather-bound volumes. Then something pulled her from her sleep, slowly, an unsettling sensation in her abdomen, unfamiliar and strange. She woke gradually and lay still, her hands resting on her tummy, almost afraid to breathe. She had felt the baby move before, a wriggling, tickling motion that came and went, but this rhythmic spasm felt entirely different. In the thin February moonlight, she could see the taut drum of her stomach twitching, almost like a pulse—her own heartbeat? Her fingers flew to the base of her neck, but the baby's strange jerking movements kept a rhythm of their own out of step with the quickening beat of her own heart.

"Mom," she screamed. "Mom! Something's wrong with the baby!"

Within moments her mother was at her side. "What is it?" she gasped. "Contractions? Are you in pain? Are you bleeding?"

"No, no. I'm okay. But the baby—I think the baby's having a seizure!"

"What on earth—" As her mother placed her hands on her abdomen, Gwen tried to hold perfectly still but couldn't stop shaking. Then she watched the fear drain from her mother's face. "Is that what you're talking about, honey? That movement?"

"Yes, yes. That—" Gwen choked out, stricken. "What's wrong with my baby?"

"Oh, honey." Gwen's mother smiled through her tears. "It's nothing. Your baby has the hiccups. That's all."

"The hiccups?" Gwen stroked the top of her belly, where she imagined the baby's head was. "They can get the hiccups in there?"

"Of course they can. You used to get them all the time."

The hiccups. Gwen almost laughed, and yet— "Should we call the doctor just to be sure?"

"No, we shouldn't," her mother replied firmly, drawing up the covers and pulling the quilt over her. "It's four o'clock in the morning. The doctor is sleeping and you should be, too."

"I'll try." Gwen took a deep breath and willed her pulse to stop racing. "I'm sorry I woke you."

"It's all right. This isn't the first time a baby's woken me in the middle of the night, and I'm sure it won't be the last."

Gwen's mother smoothed back her hair and kissed her on the forehead, then quietly left the room, leaving the door ajar. Gwen drifted back into dreams, lulled to sleep by the rhythm of her baby's hiccups.

In the morning, Gwen endured some good-natured teasing served with her breakfast, but she could see that her parents were as relieved as she was that her nighttime fears had been unfounded. She could not find the words to tell them how grateful she was that she had been at home, that her mother had raced to her side. If she had still been on the road with Dennis, she doubted she would have been able to rouse him from his drugged stupor; even if she had, he would have offered her no help or comfort. As humiliating as it was to be the Hester Prynne of Brown Deer, Kentucky, for the moment there was no place Gwen would rather be.

Gwen spread the quilt on the living room floor where the light was better and spent the morning studying the quilt's foundations, struggling to piece together the quiltmaker's story, certain that the very clues she needed must have been written plainly on the twenty foundations that had disintegrated long ago. She felt as if she were trying to write a thesis with the letters H through P missing from her typewriter: Try though she might to compensate for the absences, no matter what she wrote, it would inevitably be incomplete.

Her mother, quilting nearby, said, "Think of what you have rather than

what you've lost. Seventy-six foundations, each with something to tell us
about our mysterious quiltmaker. Surely
there's enough here to identify her, even
if we never learn the whole story behind
her quilt."

"We should start in Richardsport,"
said Gwen, indicating the envelope with
a partial address. "Are you up for a road
trip?"

"I'd love to go, honey, but I have to
finish this block before the next Brown
Does' meeting." Without looking up
from her sewing, Gwen's mother added,
"You may borrow the car. I won't need it
today."

For a moment Gwen did not know
what to say. "I'll be back in time for supper."

Her mother smiled. "I know you will."

With a road map spread open on the
front passenger seat, Gwen drove alone
to Richardsport, the Pineapple quilt
carefully folded and tucked into a pil-
lowcase in the back seat. "Seems a little late to start treating it well," her father
had remarked as she departed, but

Gwen disagreed. It was never too late to offer something the respect it deserved.

Gwen had often passed road signs to Richardsport but had never visited, so upon her arrival, she drove along the main streets, sizing up the town. It was considerably larger than Brown Deer but much smaller than Lexington, so she easily found city hall and a library, on opposite sides of the street near a small park on the river. Gwen stopped by city hall first and asked a clerk for directions to Juniper.

"Juniper Street or Juniper Lane?" the clerk asked, reaching for a pen and paper. Her tone was frosty, and her glance lingered on Gwen's naked ring finger.

Gwen resisted the urge to slip her left hand into her pocket. "Both, please."

The clerk scrawled a few lines and slid the paper across the counter. "They're within walking distance from here, even for someone in your condition."

"Thanks." Gwen had other questions, but she gave the clerk a tight smile and left, pulling on her mittens, drawing her mother's winter coat over her belly, the loop closures straining.

The sidewalks had been cleared of snow, so Gwen headed east on foot until she came to Juniper Street. She walked its length—only four blocks—but there was no house numbered 714. Retracing her steps, Gwen passed the city hall and turned south, making her winding way past shops and businesses into a neighborhood of stately homes with broad, snow-covered lawns. Juniper Lane, lined with bare-limbed trees, climbed a hill and ended in a cul-de-sac, where Gwen halted in front of an impressive white stone Georgian home with black shutters and three chimneys. Two stone gateposts flanked the long driveway. One was engraved with the number "714," and both were topped by identical stone pineapples.

Gwen needed no other inducement. She pushed open the wrought-iron gate and made her way up a cobblestone footpath to the front door. A woman who looked to be a few years older than her parents answered the bell, and she did not seem the least bit surprised to have a stranger at her front door asking questions about her home.

"I assume you missed the walking tour last month," Mrs. Eldridge remarked as she led Gwen into the parlor, and Gwen did not correct her. "I do wish that blizzard hadn't forced us to cancel. The houses looked so lovely and festive decorated for the holidays, and oh, the hospital would have benefited so much from the auction. Fortunately, most people considered their tickets to be charitable donations and they were content to let the hospital foundation keep the money. The Historical Society would like to reschedule for the spring, but it's not easy for the Society Hill families to coordinate schedules."

"Society Hill?" Gwen echoed, taking the seat in a high-backed, tapestry covered armchair her hostess offered.

"The unofficial name for our neighborhood. Back in its day, Richardsport's most prominent citizens built their homes here, where they could enjoy the view of the river." Mrs. Eldridge gazed around her parlor fondly. "Joseph Wainwright built this home in 1890 as an anniversary gift for his beloved wife. Martha designed every room down to the last piece of crown molding, and Joseph spared no expense in fulfilling her dream. He had built a fortune as a successful lawyer and circuit court judge, and he became quite a philan-thropist in his retirement. He donated the land for the Wainwright Library downtown, and his wife was one of the founding members of the St. Luke's Hospital board."

"Do any of their descendants still live in Richardsport?"

"They had only one son, Thomas. They adopted him late in life, and by all accounts he was their pride and joy. Joseph hoped Thomas would follow in his footsteps, but Thomas became a doctor instead. He set up a practice in Louisville, and some of his descendants still reside thereabouts. You don't have to track down the Wainwrights' descen-dants if you have more questions about the family, however. The Wainwright Li-brary has quite a nice selection of books on local history." Mrs. Eldridge glanced at the mantel clock and smiled apologetically. "I wish I had more time to chat, but I was just on my way out when you rang the bell."

Gwen rose and thanked her for her time, eager to be on her way. The wind had picked up, and she buried her chin into her scarf as she made her way back downtown. Could Mrs. Wainwright be the anonymous quilter, her husband the owner of the law books? That did not fit with the tale of marital bliss Mrs. Eldridge had woven, but every marriage held its secrets. Surely their adopted son, Thomas, was responsible for the child's papers and drawings, and perhaps he had sent the envelope that had led Gwen to Richardsport. So many tantalizing details had emerged, and yet so many unanswered questions remained

As if the baby sensed her excitement, Gwen felt a strong kick. She laughed and rubbed her tummy. "Settle down, kiddo," she said. "You'll give yourself the hiccups."

The library was warm and well lit, with dark oak desks and shelves that smelled of lemon furniture polish. The librarian either didn't notice Gwen's lack of a wedding ring or she had a more generous heart than the clerk at city hall, for she cheerfully led Gwen to a small room devoted to local history. "This book contains a lengthy biography of Joseph Wainwright, and this history of the county describes many of his most important legal decisions," she said, pulling two weighty tomes from their shelves. "This book is a more recent history of the Society Hill families, assembled from documents preserved by the Richardsport Historical Society." The librarian placed a thinner, folio-size book on top of the pile. "It doesn't explore any single family in great depth, but the period photographs are wonderful, and they give you a real sense of the era."

Gwen thanked her and carried the books to a nearby table. Then she was struck by a sudden thought. "I understand that Joseph Wainwright provided the land for the library, but did his family donate anything such as personal papers or books?"

"We do have some of his legal papers in special collections. I could pull those for you, but you'd have to fill out a request form and give me a day's notice."

That wouldn't help Gwen today, but perhaps she could make a return visit. "How about other artifacts, household items like quilts? Do you think your historical society might have preserved anything of that sort?"

The librarian considered. "It's possible. I can give you the name of the Historical Society president, and perhaps he could help you. I don't believe Mrs. Wainwright would have been a quilter, however. For a lady of leisure, she was very busy promoting her philanthropic efforts, supporting her husband's career, and raising her son. She might have made a crazy quilt to be fashionable, but she employed domestic help to take care of all the household chores such as sewing."

Gwen thought of the Brown Does and almost pointed out that quilting was often more than a simple household chore, but the librarian seemed certain. Perhaps in Mrs. Wainwright's day, few wealthy women quilted for pleasure. Her mother might know.

Gwen thanked the librarian and settled down to read. She wasn't sure how accurate a picture of Joseph Wainwright would emerge from the dry legalese, so she read the biography carefully but only skimmed references to his legal decisions. Both accounts appeared to concur that as a judge, Wainwright had scrupulously followed precedents and was inclined to rule on the side of justice rather than mercy. He had been considered a pillar of the community, a regular churchgoer and philanthropist. Gwen could not find even the faintest hint of scandal about him—no suggestion that he had ever given preferential treatment to his wealthy friends, that he had ever given his wife any reason not to adore him, that he had not been a doting father. The only tragedy spoken of was his wife's barrenness, but even that sorrow had ended happily upon their adoption of an infant boy.

"Thomas," murmured Gwen, and she reached for the historical society's photographic history of Society Hill. She paged through the book until she came to a sepia-toned photograph of the

Wainwright family. A well-dressed couple who looked to be in their late forties sat in the lavishly furnished parlor Gwen recognized from her visit with Mrs. Eldridge earlier that day. A fair-haired toddler sat on the woman's lap, while the man stood beside them, his hand resting on the back of the chair. There were no other references to Thomas in the book, and only two additional photographs of his adoptive parents: one of Joseph Wainwright in a judge's black robe standing solemnly in a courtroom, and one of Mrs. Wainwright at a garden party with seven other women clad in summer gowns and wide-brimmed hats. Gwen found only a single quilt pictured in all three books, and that was barely visible, tucked over a young couple seated in a horse-drawn sleigh.

Gwen browsed the shelves and skimmed other sources the librarian had not pulled, but none contained as much direct information about the Wainwrights as those first three books. As the afternoon waned, she filled out a request form for the material in special collections and arranged to return to read them the following week.

Over supper, she told her parents what she had uncovered in Richardsport. Her father remarked that she looked rather downcast for someone who had had such a successful outing.

"I guess it was partially successful," Gwen replied. "I did learn a lot, but I wish I'd found some corroborating evidence that the Pineapple quilt was connected to the Wainwright family. Mrs. Wainwright apparently loved her husband and didn't quilt. It doesn't seem logical that she would have ruined his law books to make foundation patterns."

"But she must have made the quilt," said Gwen's mother. "I can't explain the law book pages, but speaking as a mother, I can say with absolute certainty that no one would be interested in saving a child's penmanship practice and Mother's Day verses except for that child's mother. Or, I suppose, a father, but I think it's even more unlikely that Judge Wainwright was the quilter of the family rather than his society wife."

"Thomas's mother," Gwen gasped. "Of course. She could have been the quilter."

"But you believed that Mrs. Wainwright . . ." Then Gwen's mother nodded, her thoughts leaping ahead to catch up with her daughter's. "You mean the woman who gave birth to Thomas. But how in the world would she have had access to Mr. Wainwright's law books and Thomas's school papers?"

"Maybe she lived in the house with the family. The librarian said that the Wainwrights had servants. Maybe Thomas's birth mother was one."

Gwen could imagine how it might have unfolded: A young, unmarried domestic had found herself pregnant and had gratefully accepted her childless employers' offer to conceal her secret shame and adopt her child. It might have sounded like a blessed arrangement, at first, but as the years passed and she watched her son grow, unable to hold him or kiss him or confess the truth that she was his mother—how her rage and despair must have grown. Perhaps she threatened to reveal the carefully guarded secret and was fired, or perhaps she left the household after her son grew up and moved away. The quilt had grown out of her grief and anger, piece by piece, an expression of the secret she dared not confess.

"It could be so, I suppose," her father said slowly after Gwen wove her fantastical tale. "But you don't have any proof that those pages came from Wainwright's law books—"

"But the envelope with his address . . ." Gwen sighed. "Could mean nothing. Maybe Mr. Wainwright was the quilter's lawyer. Or a cousin. Or maybe it really was the return address that she had intended to preserve in the quilt."

"Could be." Her father took Gwen's hand and gave her a kindly look. "What's more, if the Wainwrights' housemaid did make this quilt, how did it end up in the lost and found of a church in Brown Deer?"

Gwen had no answer for him, but she was determined to return to Richardsport and search Joseph Wainwright's papers for the answers.

But her hopes were swiftly dashed when she returned to the library the next week and learned that the archive of personal papers fit inside a single file carton. Most of the documents concerned Judge Wainwright's storied legal career and his role as a civic leader. She found blueprints of the house on Society Hill and a newspaper account of Thomas's wedding, but very little about Mrs. Wainwright, despite her prominence in the town, and nothing at all about their domestic help. If the carton had contained a receipt for fabrics purchased, Gwen might have been able to conclude whether Mrs. Wainwright had been a quilter. If it had included a record of wages paid to a servant, the list of names might have offered possibilities for the identity of Thomas's birth mother. But the archive preserved Judge Wainwright's life and accomplishments and all but ignored everyone else within his household. The absences spoke with unmistakable clarity of what—and whom—was considered an important part of the historical record and what was not.

Resigned, she returned the documents to the carton and carried it back to the reference desk, where the librarian who had helped her the week before waited, smiling expectantly. "Did you find what you needed?"

"Almost," said Gwen, unwilling to lie, reluctant to reveal her disappointment to the one person in Richardsport who had done the most to help her. "I was hoping to find an adoption record for Thomas Wainwright, but I didn't see anything like that."

"Have you checked at city hall?" the librarian asked. "The records might be sealed, but it wouldn't hurt to try. While you're there, you might want to stop by the glass case near the courtroom entrance. Judge Wainwright's law library and some photographs from his time on the bench are on display there."

With renewed hope, Gwen thanked her and hurried across the street to city hall, hand pressed to her belly in a silent apology for the sudden jostling. To her dismay, the same sour-faced clerk sat behind the desk. Though Gwen wore mittens, the clerk obviously remembered her, for her mouth pinched in dis-approval as her gaze flicked from Gwen's hand to her belly to her face.

Gwen quickly explained her errand, but even as the words left her lips, the clerk began shaking her head. "All adoption records are sealed," she said. "I'm not saying that we have any papers about the Wainwright case here, but if we did, you couldn't see them." She lowered her voice. "You of all people should understand why the people in-volved would want to keep such affairs secret."

Gwen felt a flicker of anger, but she knew she couldn't speak her mind to this woman and still obtain the answers she sought. "I'm doing a historical re-search project on the Wainwrights. Is there some protocol I can follow to have the records opened?"

The clerk shook her head. "You can try to get the law changed, but that'll take a while and you probably won't have much luck."

"Thanks anyway," said Gwen tightly. "I appreciate your help."

She turned away too soon to see if

the clerk picked up on her sarcasm. Following signs posted near the front door, she left the lobby and made her way down a short hallway to the courtroom entrance. Just as the librarian had promised, a locked glass display case held several shelves of leather-bound law books, the titles embossed in gold on the spines. Framed photographs of Judge Wainwright sat here and there on other shelves, but although Gwen studied them eagerly, she discovered nothing new. Most of the pictures were reprints of photos she had seen before in the library books, and none offered any glimpses of his family or household.

Steeling herself, Gwen returned to the clerk's desk. "Would you be willing to unlock the display case outside the courtroom so I could get a better look at Judge Wainwright's law books?"

"Why would you want to do that?"

Gwen shrugged, fighting to conceal her exasperation. "Maybe he added some notations. Maybe some of the volumes were gifts, inscribed by the giver. Would you please help me out here? It's important for my research."

The clerk sat back in her chair, eyeing Gwen skeptically. "Those books are very old and fragile, not to mention valuable. They're from Judge Wainwright's personal library."

"That's exactly why I need to examine them."

The clerk jerked her head in the opposite direction from the courthouse. "If you need to read up on adoption laws, there are legal references available for the public in the reading room. Judge Wainwright's books are out of date."

"That's not why I want to—"

"Anyway, they wouldn't do you any good." The clerk raised her voice to drown out Gwen's. "Some idiot went through and ripped out pages from them, long before the collection ever came to us. They're near worthless as law books, but as a memorial to one of our most prominent citizens, they're invaluable. You'll have to find some other way to do your research."

"That's all right," said Gwen, a slow smile spreading across her face. "You've answered my questions. Thank you."

There was still so much she didn't know—the quiltmaker's name, whether she was truly Thomas's mother, how the quilt came to Brown Deer—but the scant details she had crafted into a story still offered a glimpse into one family's past. She knew it was an incomplete account that hinted at more than it proved, but it was enough to convince her that the Pineapple quilt was an invaluable work of art and passion, a silent, unhappy woman's voice.

What other stories had women's quilts told through the generations? Denied a voice, how many other anonymous quilters had expressed their grief, their rage, their joy, their hope with needle and thread?

Gwen had never imagined that fabric could convey so much meaning.

At the next gathering of the Brown Does, Gwen held the quilters spellbound with her story of the Pineapple quilt's secrets and her search for answers in Richardsport. A few smiled indulgently and praised her for a job well done, but she could tell from their expressions that they doubted her theory about the quilt's origins had any merit. Most of the Does, while they found Gwen's reasoning credible, longed for completion—the quilter's name, some proof of Thomas's parentage, a plausible explanation for how the quilt found its winding way to Brown Deer. Gwen wished she could give them those answers, but she suspected she might search forever without finding the historical evidence to fill in the gaps of her story.

Back home, Gwen spread the quilt facedown on the living room floor and studied the foundations, though she had almost memorized them after so much careful scrutiny. She knew she had gleaned the last grain of information from the fragile papers, and yet she did not want to consider them spent, finished.

"After uncovering so much of this quilt's story," she told her mother, "I hate to cover up those foundations again, but I can't leave the quilt in this condition. I'm afraid the papers will deteriorate even faster exposed like this, and the batting definitely won't hold together."

"If you want to repair the quilt someday, you'll need to know how to do it," her mother responded. "You could practice by making a Pineapple quilt of your own. I could teach you. By the time you finish, you'll have the skills necessary to restore the quilt and the time you need to decide if that's really what you want to do."

Gwen smiled. "I'd like that."

As she awaited the birth of her child, Gwen prepared a layette, read books on childbirth and child care, and learned to quilt. On June 21, her daughter was born, a healthy, beautiful girl with a thick shock of auburn hair the same color as her own. Gwen named her Summer Solstice Sullivan, and although her parents grimaced at the middle name and the alliteration, they did not try to talk her into something more conventional.

Gwen finished her own Pineapple quilt when Summer was six months old. By then she had decided not to repair the one she had rescued from the lost and found, for even disassembled the quilt top was in perfect condition, and she could not bear to conceal the foundations. She was certain they confessed a long-held secret, and she would not silence the anonymous quilter as others had done.

When Summer was fifteen months old, Gwen returned to college. In the three years it took Gwen to complete her degree after switching her major to history, Summer lived in Brown Deer with her grandparents, and Gwen drove home to be with her on weekends and school breaks. It grieved Gwen to spend so much time away from her precious daughter, but she knew she would make a better life for them both if she completed her education. Summer was a happy, affectionate child, the light of her grandparents' lives, and Gwen often found herself overcome with gratitude for the way they had welcomed her home, cared for Summer so lovingly, and made it possible for Gwen to seize her second chance.

Her mother cried tears of joy at Gwen's graduation, and even her father's eyes shone to see her in her cap and gown. A few months later, they tried to conceal their sadness for her sake when she and Summer left for Cornell, more than six hundred miles away, where Gwen had been accepted into the graduate program. Before Summer's eleventh birthday, Gwen completed her PhD and accepted a job as an assistant professor in the American Studies department of Waterford College, in a small town that in some ways reminded her of Brown Deer.

Throughout her career, Gwen often reflected back upon her discovery of the mysterious Pineapple quilt rescued from the lost and found as the moment when she first became fascinated with women's history. She had made it her business as a scholar and a teacher to uncover as many of those tales as possible, before they were completely lost to time. Sometimes women's voices spoke in diaries; other times, domestic arts had been their media of choice. Inevitably, Gwen found herself in that same old tired confrontation with crusty academics who still did not offer pride of place to so-called "women's work," who considered it inferior not because of any intrinsic deficiencies it possessed but because it belonged to the traditional province of women. Most frustrating of all, Gwen's detractors included many who ought to have been her allies, who should have known better, who would never allow sexism or classism to creep into any of their other most strongly held philosophies but made a hypocritical exception where women's arts were concerned.

Sometimes Gwen felt as if she was the only standard bearer for women's arts—or at least the only one on the faculty of Waterford College. For that reason alone she could not abandon her research even if it meant jeopardizing her career. She had to persist in pursuing women's untold stories and hope that eventually her academic colleagues would come around.

A security guard on his rounds passed the table where she was engrossed in her work to remind her that the checkout desk would close in fifteen minutes. Gwen gathered up her things and checked out her newfound books, which had turned out to be even more promising resources than she had hoped for when she found them in the online catalog. Still, books could only tell her so much. A research trip to Chicago was in order. Their historical society would surely be a rich source of information about the 1933 World's Fair. Summer would want to come along, for she hadn't even found a place to live near the university, and the fall quarter would begin in a few short weeks. Gwen now understood how her parents had felt, watching her secondhand car pull out of the driveway and disappear around the corner. She would miss Summer desperately, but she was so proud of her daughter, so proud that she was breaking a new path for herself, a winding way that would surely lead to wonderful places.

Gwen was crossing Main Street with her armload of books when she stopped short in the crosswalk at the sight of her own car parked at the curb. "Lazybones," she chided herself, unlocking the door and setting her books on the passenger seat. Her home was within easy walking distance of the library, even toting heavy books. What was she thinking, taking the car instead of getting some much-needed exercise?

At home, Gwen fixed herself a cup of tea, muted the ringer on the phone, shut off her cell so anxious students wouldn't disturb her work, and settled down to her books and notes. Her thoughts drifted so often to the Pineapple quilt that before long she set her work aside, went upstairs to her bedroom, and removed the quilt from its protective storage. Studying the foundations, she hoped as she always did for some overlooked clue to leap out at her and answer her lingering questions, but she had learned that historical discoveries rarely traveled a straight and smooth road. She had learned to be content with a more winding way, one that curved in unforeseen directions, skirted unexpected obstacles, and often forced her to backtrack at dead ends. She had learned to persevere despite the uncertain destination, despite her own doubts, despite her critics' gloomy predictions that none of the answers she pursued ultimately mattered.

She would not give up before her journey was complete, for herself and for all of the forgotten women whose stories had yet to be told.

Sylvia held Andrew's hand and watched from the veranda as the Elm Creek Quilters and their husbands mingled and talked, seating themselves on Adirondack chairs, the stone steps, or old quilts spread on the lawn. Everyone, including Sylvia, made at least two trips to fill their plates at Anna's marvelous, irresistible buffet. It was a true banquet, with dishes bursting with fresh summer flavors finished off by decadent desserts. The children played games on the lawn or skateboarded in circles around the rearing horse fountain while their parents reminisced about the early days of Elm Creek Quilts and marveled at how far their ambitions had taken them. Laughter rose in bursts to the darkening sky, despite the wistful mood lingering over the party. Each woman said a silent prayer that this would not be the last time they gathered together—for even now their circle was not complete, although none of them drew attention to the conspicuous gap Gwen's absence created.

Agnes delayed the presentation of Judy's gift as long as possible, occasionally strolling to the edge of the veranda and leaning over the railing to try to see into the back parking lot. The stars came out, Emily sat yawning on her mother's lap, and still Gwen did not appear. Soon, Sylvia knew, Judy would hand off her sleepy daughter to her husband and announce that it was time to go. Sighing, Sylvia caught Agnes's eye and gestured to indicate that they had run out of time. They must bid Judy one last farewell, with or without Gwen.

Judy, who had remained calmly dry-eyed all evening, lost her composure when Agnes made a brief, tearful speech about friendship and farewells and presented her with the quilt that they had all signed. Blinking away tears,

she read each heartfelt message, sometimes smiling, sometimes pressing a
hand to her heart. "Thank you," Judy
said, folding the quilt lovingly and hugging it to herself. "I'll cherish this always. Wherever life takes me, this quilt
will bring me right back here to you in
my heart."

One last embrace, and then Judy left,
the quilt in her arms, her husband at her
side carrying a drowsy Emily. Judy did
not look back as she walked around the
side of the manor to the parking lot, but
Sylvia kept her in sight until the last.

Headlights shone and disappeared
around the red barn, and Judy was
gone.

A hush fell over the remaining Elm
Creek Quilters as if none of them could
believe Judy would not suddenly reap-
pear, laughing, and tell them she had
changed her mind, that she was staying
after all. Quietly, Anna began clearing
away the dishes, and Sarah rose to help
her.

Diane broke the silence. "Gwen better
be on her deathbed, or I'll put her
there."

"I'm sure she's fine," said Summer crisply, and Diane said nothing more.

After the mess was cleared away and her friends had departed, Sylvia wearily climbed the grand oak staircase to bed, her hand in Andrew's. She had only Summer's assurances that nothing terrible had prevented Gwen from attending the party. "I'm her emergency contact," Summer had told Sylvia as they carried dishes into the manor, "and my cell phone didn't ring all evening, so she wasn't injured on the way. She would have called me herself if she were sick. She probably just . . . forgot."

Sylvia had no idea how Gwen could have forgotten to say good-bye to her best friend.

Sylvia had chosen colorful, tie-dyed cottons and stylized florals reminiscent of 1960s patterns for Gwen's quilt, as a nod to her free-spirited nature—tolerant, daring, compassionate. But now Sylvia realized she must mix in some deeper, more tempered hues to reflect a side of her friend that she did not often reveal. Despite the confident face she showed the world, Gwen was no stranger to disappointment and loneliness, and the weeks ahead without Judy and Summer would surely test her. She would miss Judy all the more because she had been unable to bring herself to say good-bye.

Sylvia hoped the gift of her quilt would remind Gwen that the sad partings, however painful, had not left her alone in the world.

Agnes

As soon as Diane dropped her off in front of her white Cape Cod house a short walk from downtown Waterford, Agnes hurried inside, snatched up the phone, and dialed Gwen's number. It rang and rang, without even an answering machine to take the call, and eventually ended in an annoying beeping tone that meant the phone company wanted her to hang up. Exasperated, Agnes did, but she tried the number twice more before reaching the inevitable conclusion that Gwen had turned off the ringer as she often did when she needed to work undisturbed. What conference paper or lesson plan could possibly have been more important than Judy's party?

First thing in the morning, Agnes called back to ask Gwen precisely that. She called from her bedroom phone before climbing out of bed—no response. She called before going outside to pick up the newspaper from the end of the driveway—the phone rang and rang. Her exasperation rising, she fixed herself her usual breakfast of oatmeal and coffee and resolved to call one last time after breakfast, and if Gwen did not pick up, she would march over to her house and pound on her front door.

But this time, Gwen answered on the third ring. "Hello?"

Flabbergasted by her good cheer, Agnes cried, "Where were you last night?"

"I was here, working. Why, did you think I was out on Fraternity Row partying or—" Gwen gasped. "Oh, no."

"Oh, yes. You missed the farewell party, giving Judy her quilt, everything." Such careless irresponsibility was so unlike Gwen that Agnes did not have the heart to reprimand her further. "The moving van was supposed to arrive at seven o'clock sharp, but they'll need time to load it. You might be able to catch her if you hurry."

"I'll run right over," Gwen said, and hung up.

Agnes sighed and poured herself another cup of coffee, but the morning paper could not keep her attention. Honestly. Gwen's work was absorbing, but this was ridiculous. Even with the new semester only a week away, Gwen ought to have been able to take off one Saturday evening. What poor Judy must have thought when her closest friend among the Elm Creek Quilters did not show up to say good-bye!

After church, Agnes worked in the garden, leaving the windows open in case Gwen called back. The phone didn't ring, not once, so Agnes resigned herself to suspense until she saw Gwen later at Elm Creek Manor. She put away her spade and wheelbarrow, washed up, and was waiting on the front porch swing when Diane's white BMW pulled into the driveway. Agnes hurried over and buckled herself in before Diane even had a chance to shut off the engine.

"What's the rush?" Diane asked, glancing at the clock to confirm that she was right on time.

"I want to be sure that all's well with Gwen."

"Nothing's wrong with her that a vacation wouldn't cure." Diane backed out of the driveway and headed toward the main road out of Waterford. "She's a workaholic. She should cut out all academic work cold turkey for at least a weekend. That'll help her straighten out her priorities."

"She loves her work, and you know what they say about academia, 'publish or perish.'"

"One evening off with her friends wouldn't kill her or her career," retorted Diane. "Anyone who would put grading papers ahead of a good friend's farewell party is obsessed with work. It's unhealthy."

"She has so much on her mind," Agnes reminded her. "Elm Creek Quilts, that trouble with her department chair, Summer leaving for graduate school in less than a month—"

"My youngest is leaving for college in

a week, and you don't see me forgetting my friends."

Agnes muffled a sigh and dropped the subject, reluctant to spoil such a beautiful summer morning with an argument, especially when she didn't have enough information to properly defend Gwen's behavior. Until she spoke to Gwen herself, Agnes couldn't be sure if she deserved a defense.

They pulled into the rear parking lot, nearly empty as it usually was on a Sunday morning. Gwen's car sat in the spot farthest from the back door, for she liked to leave the choice spots for the campers. Diane used Agnes as an excuse to park closer, no matter how often Agnes protested that she could out-walk most women half her age. Bonnie had not yet arrived, of course; the commute from Grangerville was strangely busy every day of the week, not only during weekday rush hours.

Bonnie could have hitched a ride with Diane every day just like Agnes did if she had accepted Agnes's invitation to move in with her. Bonnie had shown up on Agnes's doorstep the night Craig had

locked her out of their condo and had
settled into a spare bedroom while she
sorted out the messy details of her col-
lapsing marriage. At first Bonnie had
hoped to move back into the condo after the dust settled, but that conniving,
deceitful Craig made sure that couldn't
happen. Agnes assured Bonnie she was
welcome to stay as long as she wished,
but halfway through the summer, Bonnie happily announced that she had
found a charming apartment in Grangerville on a quiet street near a nature preserve. Agnes worried that she had
somehow made Bonnie feel unwel-
come, but Bonnie assured her she only
wanted to assert her independence and
see how much she enjoyed the novelty
of living by herself. On moving day, Agnes helped her load her belongings into
the old station wagon and said, a little
sadly, "The invitation stands." Bonnie
promised to remember that and waved
cheerfully as she drove off.

Agnes had not yet seen her new
apartment, for Bonnie hadn't invited any
of the Elm Creek Quilters over, despite
their curiosity and their repeated hints

that they wanted to throw her a house-warming party. Agnes wanted to believe that Bonnie had simply been too busy to unpack and that she wanted to wait until she was settled before entertaining friends, but she couldn't help worrying that Bonnie's standard of living had taken a nosedive too embarrassing to allow her friends to witness.

If that was the case, the insurance settlement ought to help. Agnes was doing her part to help, too. It was she who had discovered that Craig had hidden his assets by decorating his office with valuable antiques whose true worth only an expert would recognize. Fortunately, a good friend of Agnes's late husband's had been just such an expert, and even now he was appraising the collection and preparing it for sale. Agnes didn't know what Craig had been using for office furniture ever since the court order obliged him to turn over the collection, and she didn't care. Let him sit on the floor and balance his computer on an old milk crate. It was more than that wretched man deserved after how he had treated Bonnie.

The final sale was supposed to go through any day, and the money would be split evenly between Craig and Bonnie. Agnes had made her friend promise to call her as soon as the sale was final so that she could be the one to break the good news. Her husband's friend had assured her it would be good news; the only question was how good.

It was a pity any of the money had to go to Craig.

At the sound of a car approaching, Agnes glanced over her shoulder, hoping to see Bonnie arriving right on time. Diane misread her line of sight and jerked her head toward Gwen's car. "She's here, all right. Better late than never."

Agnes placed a hand on her arm. "Diane, dear, I've known you since you were a little girl, and I've learned to accept that sometimes you speak without thinking. Today, however, I must insist that you mind your words. If Gwen didn't get to say good-bye to Judy, she's going to feel bad enough without you heaping criticism upon her. This is not the day to tease and bait her. Understood?"

Diane's eyes widened with injured innocence. "Of course. I can be sensitive."

Agnes patted Diane's arm. "Today you can prove it."

They climbed out of the car just as Jeremy and Anna pulled up in Jeremy's weather-beaten compact. Anna was weaving her long, dark brown hair into a single braid, and as she wrapped a band around the end, she said something that made Jeremy toss his head and laugh. Instinctively, Agnes clutched her purse to her side and pressed herself against Diane's car. Jeremy was a smart young man, but at the moment, he wasn't watching where he was going.

The car stopped inches away from Diane's. Anna hopped out, breathlessly smothering her laughter when she noticed Agnes and Diane. "Sorry, that was my fault. I shouldn't distract him when he's driving, but he just said the funniest—well, it's not important. Has anyone heard from Gwen?"

"Anna said she never showed last night," Jeremy said, his brow furrowing as he locked the car. Tall and slender, he wasn't handsome in the conventional sense, but he had a cheerful look about him that Agnes found charming, and when he was enjoying himself, his crooked grin lit up his face so that Agnes couldn't help smiling, too. She had also never heard him say an unkind word about anyone, revealing a generosity of spirit that Agnes much admired.

"I spoke with her this morning," Agnes said, and as they crossed the parking lot, she repeated their brief exchange—so brief, in fact, that she finished before they reached the kitchen.

"I hope she made it to Judy's house in time." Anna tied on an apron and put on a fresh pot of coffee. "It would be so sad for both of them if they didn't get to say a last good-bye."

"That's what I said on the drive over and Agnes almost took my head off," Diane grumbled as she searched the cupboards for her favorite mug.

Jeremy and Anna both stared at Agnes in astonishment, then looked at each other and burst into laugher. "I'm afraid they don't believe you, dear," said Agnes, smiling.

"That's because they don't know you as well as I do."

Agnes folded her hands on the table. She supposed she could give someone a proper scolding when they deserved one, but she had been gentle with Diane. "All I meant was that Gwen surely didn't mean to slight Judy, and we shouldn't judge her without knowing what happened."

"We could go ask her," said Jeremy, but he didn't seem in any hurry to do so.

"I'm under strict orders not to say anything," said Diane, with a pointed look Agnes's way.

"I didn't mean you shouldn't speak to her at all," Agnes protested. "Just be sensitive. Empathetic."

"You might as well ask me to wear a muzzle." Diane slammed a cupboard door. "This never would have happened if she had just stuck around after the farewell breakfast instead of running off to the library. It's just like last spring when Bonnie didn't show up for her classes and we had no idea what had happened to her. I don't know why you people can't let people know where you're going to be or at the very least keep your phones turned on. Where is that stupid mug?"

Looking slightly alarmed, Anna took a large pink cappuccino mug from the dishwasher and handed it to Diane. "We have lots of other mugs."

"This is my favorite," said Diane, slightly calmer. "I can get the perfect coffee-to-milk ratio if I fill it to that little crack on the inside."

"No wonder you've been unusually grumpy this morning," said Agnes. "You were genuinely worried about Gwen. You thought we'd have a repeat of that terrible incident at Bonnie's quilt shop."

"Only at first," said Diane, reaching into the refrigerator for a carton of non-fat milk. "Last night after I dropped you off, I drove past Gwen's house and saw the light on in her office window. She was there working blissfully away, so I knew she was fine." Diane sloshed milk into her coffee mug. "Once I knew she wasn't passed out in an alley somewhere, I started to get mad."

"Her office faces the back yard," said Agnes. "You snuck around back and peeked in her window?"

"What else could I do? She wouldn't pick up the phone!" When Jeremy laughed, Diane glared at him. "Tell me you wouldn't have done the same thing if Summer wouldn't answer your calls."

"I wouldn't have to," said Jeremy. "You'd beat me to it."

"For the sake of my peace of mind, I wish all of you who live alone would move into the manor." Diane sounded as if she was only half joking. "Especially Bonnie, since she's essentially homeless. But why not Gwen, too? She's been living alone for years now, ever since Summer moved out. What's there to hold her back once Summer leaves for Chicago?"

"Summer will visit so often we'll hardly know she's left," Agnes interjected, casting a sympathetic look Jeremy's way. He was frowning and studying the floor. Surely he would miss

Summer as much as Gwen did, perhaps more, in the way of young lovers.

"She'll flunk out of school if she does that," Diane scoffed. "And why not you, Agnes? You must want the company, or you wouldn't have asked Bonnie to move in with you."

"I love my little house and garden, and I need my own place for when my grandchildren visit," said Agnes. It wasn't loneliness that had compelled her to invite Bonnie to move in with her, but compassion. "What about you? You'll be an empty nester soon. Why don't you and Tim take a suite upstairs? He'll have plenty of Elm Creek husbands around for company."

"After he retires, we might do just that," said Diane, who knew when she was being teased. "For now, he likes to be close enough to campus to walk to work. What about you, Anna? You don't need to be close to campus anymore, now that you've resigned from College Food Services."

"Me? Move in here?" Anna let out a small laugh and disappeared into the pantry. "Oh, I don't know. My apartment's a shoebox compared to the manor, but I like it."

"Think of the money you'd save on rent," Diane persisted. "And the time you'd save on your commute. Plus the bus fare. Jeremy surely won't be able to drive you every day."

"It's no trouble," said Jeremy.

Diane shook her head. "Maybe not now, but after Summer leaves, you won't have any reason to come out this way."

"Really, it's not a problem," said Jeremy, directing his reply to Anna.

"Living here would save me a commute to Elm Creek Manor, but what about my other job?" Anna emerged from the pantry carrying a sack of flour. "I'd still have to get to campus several days a week, and sometimes the special events I direct for the provost run later than the last bus out this way."

A cry of dismay went up from Agnes and Diane. "Haven't you resigned from College Food Services?" asked Agnes, wondering if Sylvia and Sarah knew.

"You mean we're in a trial period?"

asked Diane. "You're keeping both jobs until you decide which you like best?"

"Of course not," said Jeremy.

"That's not it," Anna assured them. "You don't need me when camp isn't in session, right? I'm taking vacation days from College Food Services for the rest of August so I can work here. After Labor Day, I'll go back to full-time at Waterford College, but I'll come around often to supervise the kitchen remodeling. When camp resumes in March, I'll be all yours, full-time."

"Thank goodness for that," declared Diane. "It would be cruel to tease us all month with fine cuisine and then disappear as soon as we become spoiled for anything else. You know what would prove your commitment to your new job? Moving into the manor."

"Don't mind her," Agnes told Anna, who appeared increasingly distressed. "Diane just wants you here first thing in the morning so you can have her coffee waiting for her when she arrives."

"So I have selfish motives," Diane retorted. "Everything I said is still true."

"I don't know." Anna took out mixing

bowls and a rolling pin. "Elm Creek Manor is beautiful, but I like living downtown, and sometimes it's good to be able to leave work at work."

Diane shook her head and feigned bafflement. "I have no idea what you mean."

"Leave the newbie alone," said Jeremy. "You'll scare her off. You can't all move into the manor. You won't have any rooms left over for campers."

Diane looked ready to debate the point, but she was distracted by the coffeemaker's beep signaling that a fresh pot was ready. As she rushed forward, mug in hand, Agnes regarded her young companions with a fond smile, enjoying their customary banter. It would not be so bad to give up her own home and garden to share the manor with friends such as these, and if she did not like her own little house so much, she might consider it, though it would be a strange and wistful homecoming. What Diane had apparently forgotten, and what Anna and Jeremy probably did not know, was that Agnes had once called Elm Creek Manor home. Long ago, when she was little more than a girl, newly wed and far from her soldier husband, she passed many lonely days as an interloper among her husband's family.

When she met Richard Bergstrom she was fifteen, the daughter of a wealthy Philadelphia businessman, a granddaughter of a senator, and a popular student at Miss Sebastian's Academy for Young Ladies. The Wednesday before Thanksgiving was a traditional day of service for Miss Sebastian's girls and the young men from their brother school, Warrington Prep. More than half a century earlier, the schools' progressive-minded founders had made service to the poor a voluntary but strongly encouraged part of the curriculum. They wanted the children of privilege to learn compassion for the less fortunate and gratitude for their own blessings, which had come to them by accident of birth rather than merit. While acts of charity were encouraged throughout the year, the schools made a concerted effort at Thanksgiving, when their students collected canned goods for food pantries, cleaned up parks, or sorted donated clothing to distribute to the poor. Afterward, Miss Sebastian's girls hosted a social for the Warrington men, where the students' hard work was rewarded with dining and dancing late into the night. Every year, a few of the more progressive young ladies pointed out that the women had to work twice as hard as their male counterparts since they performed community service all day and played hostesses to the men in the evening, and that the community would be better served if they canceled the party and donated the money they would have spent on food, music, and decorations to the poor instead. But most of the other girls were eager for any excuse to mingle with the Warrington men, so the dissenters never won out.

Over time, the social became the highlight of the day and giving thanks to the people of Philadelphia a necessary hurdle to surmount before the fun could begin. Many of the wealthier students took to hiring workers to fulfill their community service commitments or making large donations to charity instead. With a pragmatism that would have deeply offended both Miss Sebastian and Mr. Warrington, the administrations permitted it, noting that the less fortunate were being provided for, and that was what mattered.

Agnes's parents, like many others, did not concur that this was all that mattered, so they never offered to pay for her or her siblings' exemptions. They wanted their children to be mindful of their blessings so that they would work hard to keep them, and it didn't hurt her grandfather's standing in the polls for voters to see the Chevalier children serving meals at soup kitchens or planting vegetables in a community garden. As for Agnes, she seized any chance to experience some of the "real life" her parents endeavored to shelter her from, and she was glad that almost all of her classmates honored Miss Sebastian's principles too much to buy their way out of the day's work. Among the men of Warrington Prep, the ratio skewed in the opposite direction. The young men claimed to be unable to sacrifice a day of study so close to the end of the term, and by hiring workers to fill in for them, they were making an additional contribution to the community by providing a day's wages to otherwise unemployed men.

"You'll have a fine career in politics with that gift for rationalization," Agnes declared when a Warrington Prep senior offered her that excuse at a meeting of the two schools' committees planning the event. To her disgust, he took such a remark from a senator's granddaughter as high praise and asked her to save the first dance at the social for him. She made him no promises, but smiled sweetly and returned to the task at hand—examining requests for helpers from community groups and deciding whom to assist. It galled her that on the eve of Thanksgiving, the young men of Warrington would toast themselves for a job well done and accept congratulations from the leaders of the civic organizations the service day benefited, all without lifting a finger themselves.

"You never said yes when he asked you to save the first dance for him, but that's what he heard," one of Agnes's friends teased her as they walked to class after the meeting.

"I couldn't refuse him in front of his friends," said Agnes. "He might be lazy and ridiculous and completely oblivious to the point of community service, but I don't need to shame him."

"You should have promised to dance with him if he did his own work on service day. He would have been first in line to stock shelves at the food pantry."

"I should have," Agnes replied. "We all should have. It's too late now."

Or perhaps it wasn't. There was always the next year's service day to consider.

Thus began Agnes's campaign to goad the men of Warrington Prep into serving their community themselves instead of through proxies.

She met a great deal of resistance at first, especially among the girls who had steady boyfriends among the Warrington men. How could they refuse to dance with their boyfriends simply because they had taken the gentleman's way out? "A true gentleman doesn't shirk his duty to his community," Agnes replied. But wasn't it cruel not to warn the men ahead of time that only those who worked that day would be dancing that night? "Of course you should encourage your boyfriends to participate," Agnes answered, wishing that her sister students had done so regardless through the years, in which case her rebellion might not have been necessary. "But appeal to their sense of civic virtue; don't tell them it's a quid pro quo. Only the element of surprise will guarantee full participation in next year's service day. I promise it will, as long as we hold together. We all have to do it, or it won't work, and things will never change."

Naturally Miss Sebastian's girls wanted the Warrington men to do their share of the work instead of merely enjoying the fruits of the young women's labor, so with a bit of peer pressure and promises that the girls would still dance the night away, only with a smaller selection of partners, Agnes and her friends swore their sister students to fidelity and secrecy.

On that fateful Wednesday, Agnes and her best friend, Marjorie, joined eight other girls and ten young men from Warrington Prep at a group of row houses in one of Philadelphia's most impoverished neighborhoods to do yard work, make repairs, and prepare the homes for the coming winter. Agnes and Marjorie cleaned the home of an elderly couple and their son, a marine veteran of the Great War who had lost both legs in the battle of the Belleau Wood, while two young men cut down a dead oak in the back yard, repaired a broken fence, and hauled trash from the house to the curb. The girls, watchful for any signs that their plans had been leaked, observed the young men as they worked and concluded that their rough clothes and industriousness marked them as laborers hired by lazy, indifferent Warrington men.

"What a shame," Marjorie whispered as the two young men passed, hauling a broken armchair down from the attic and outside to the curb. "I'd like to dance with the sandy-haired one."

Agnes agreed it was a pity, though she preferred the blond with the green eyes and ready smile. He seemed to be enjoying himself as he worked, and while he was friendly to Agnes and Marjorie, he was equally attentive to the elderly residents and their son. He admired the man's war medals proudly displayed on the mantel—Agnes had not even noticed them—and mentioned that his father had served in France and two uncles had perished there. After that, the veteran joined the younger men outside and talked with them about his experiences while they tore out broken fence posts and hammered new boards in place.

"No one ever remembers my son's service to this country except on Memorial Day," the elderly woman said, tearing up. "I haven't seen him so happy in months. Your friends are kind to listen to his war stories."

Agnes did not correct the woman's mistake, for she wished the hardworking young men were their friends. They were worth a dozen Warrington men who cleared their consciences with cash payments and never looked the less fortunate in the eye or listened to their stories. And they were supposed to be the future leaders of business and government! How could they understand the plight of the working man when all they knew were wealthy sons of privilege like themselves? It was unfair that the two young men outside would never have the opportunities that the students who had hired them took for granted. Her grandfather made ringing speeches about the equality of all Americans and how every man had a chance to better himself, but even Agnes knew that the wealthy students of Warrington enjoyed a head start that mere hard work could rarely overtake.

It wasn't fair.

At noon the young people took a break from their labors and ate sack lunches on the front stoop, bundled in coats against the autumn chill. They talked and chatted, and Marjorie flirted with the shy one named Andrew. "I hear your father was in the service," Agnes said to Richard. She had never really conversed with a day laborer before and she wasn't quite sure what to say.

Richard grinned. "You heard that, did you?"

Agnes rushed ahead, embarrassed. "I overheard a little. My father says that the army is a good place for a young man with ambition. You can learn a trade and get ahead in life, and everyone's so sick of war that you needn't fear being sent to fight."

"Eventually folks always forget that they're sick of war," said Richard, unwrapping a second sandwich.

"I suppose you're right," said Agnes. "But for a man of limited options, it's something to consider, don't you agree?"

"I've considered it myself," said Richard. "But I'll probably end up working for the family business."

"Of course," said Agnes apologetically. It was probably difficult for Richard to imagine doing anything but what his father and grandfather before him had done. To call day labor a family business seemed a bit much, though. Perhaps she had damaged his pride.

"I wouldn't mind working for your family business," Andrew spoke up. "Ever consider hiring outside of the family?"

"I think we could make an exception for you," Richard said, grinning.

Their joking manner warned Agnes that she had spoken imprudently. After lunch, she held Richard back and waved Marjorie to go ahead without her. "I'm sorry," she told him. "I didn't mean to sound so patronizing."

Richard's easy smile warmed her. "Think nothing of it."

"But I still think you could do anything you put your mind to."

He knit his brows in puzzled amusement. "You've only known me for a few hours."

"But I know you." Impulsively she reached for his hand. "I want you to know that the young men who hired you aren't going to take credit for your labors anymore. There's a social tonight, but they won't be having any fun at it. If there was any justice in the world, you and Andrew could come to the dance in their place, too."

For a moment Richard merely stared at her, but she could tell that he was carefully mulling over what she had said. "So . . . you girls have something planned for the Warrington fellows, is that right?"

She felt her cheeks flush, both from the touch of his hand upon hers and from her embarrassment at so impulsively divulging the secret she had made others vow to keep. "Yes, but please don't ask me to say anything more."

"I guess you're going to make them sorry they didn't do their own community service."

"I don't mean that they shouldn't have hired you." She was making things worse and worse! "I'm sure you appreciated the wages, but don't you think you'd be better off in the long run if the future leaders of business and government understood the great need in this community?"

"Yes," he said, without a moment's hesitation. "Yes, I do."

"That's why they should be here." A strange warmth seemed to travel from his hand to hers, and Agnes could not let go of it. "I can't tell you what's going to happen, but next year, those Warrington men won't shirk their duty."

"Not all of them do."

"I know that." Two of her brothers were picking up trash at a public park on the Delaware at that very moment. "But some of them need to learn a lesson."

"Agnes—" He glanced across the yard to where Marjorie was watching Andrew hammer nails. "You haven't asked me not to tell anyone, but I promise I won't. Okay? You have my word."

He released her hand and joined Andrew by the fence. Strangely unsettled, Agnes hurried back inside to her work and tried to regain her composure before Marjorie returned inside. They finished their work before Andrew and Richard did, but that gave them little time for anything more than a quick farewell before they had to hurry back to school to prepare for the social. Agnes wished she were bold enough to ask for Richard's address. Perhaps her father could have done something for him, found him steady work, anything. But Richard might have looked upon that as a handout, and she could not bear to insult him—even if it meant losing her last chance to see him again.

Back at Miss Sebastian's, after transforming the dining hall into a festive ballroom, Agnes and her coconspirators hastened to compile a list of which young men had performed their own community service and which had simply enjoyed a day off of school. The names of the "workers" fit on one side of a single sheet, while the "shirkers" took up three whole sheets. They distributed the lists to the other young ladies with emphatic reminders that they must all hold the line, and only then did they race off to the dressing rooms backstage of the school theater to freshen up and dress for the dance.

Because of the last-minute details, the social had already begun by the time Agnes and Marjorie raced back, breathless and excited. Students and faculty from both schools were mingling and enjoying refreshments, and it seemed so like the previous year's gathering that Agnes's courage faltered for a moment. All it would take for her plan to fail was for one girl to give in to infatuation or pity and accept a shirker's invitation to dance.

Her plan had to succeed. It must.

The directors of both schools came to the podium to commend the students on their hard work that day—Agnes was heartened by the indignant frowns that appeared on many girls' faces—and speeches of thanks from charity directors followed. After a long round of applause that not all of them had earned, everyone awaited the first notes of music from the bandstand.

Faculty members and their spouses took to the floor first, and then one by one, young men summoned their courage and asked young ladies to dance. Agnes held her breath as a young couple stepped out onto the dance floor, then exhaled in relief as she recognized her eldest brother with the prettiest girl in Miss Sebastian's senior class. A few others followed, all of whom were on the "workers" list. Then, right beside her, a handsome "shirker" asked one of the most popular girls at Miss Sebastian's if she would care to dance. "I'm so sorry," she said, and she looked as if she meant it. "Since it's the Service Day Social, I'm only dancing with young men who did their share of the work today."

Agnes was to hear many versions of this refrain echoed around the room as young ladies—often sweetly, sometimes sternly, occasionally with great regret—demurred when invited onto the dance floor. Certain young men were never without a partner and, as if the rules of popularity had been entirely discarded, some of the handsomest, wealthiest young men were relegated to glowering on the sidelines while scholarship students and chess club champions enjoyed the attention of one charming girl after another. Agnes was so preoccupied with maintaining the resistance that she forgot she had come to dance, too, until a touch on her elbow reminded her.

She turned around, preparing herself to let a shirker down gently, only to find Richard smiling at her.

"How did you get in?" she exclaimed, but then she noticed his fine suit and polished shoes and realized she had made a dreadful mistake.

He frowned thoughtfully and patted

his pockets. "Sorry, I must have lost my ticket stub."

Agnes sank into the nearest chair. "You're a Warrington student."

"You said you'd dance with me if I came," he reminded her. "I intend to hold you to that."

Wordlessly she nodded, and as he held her in his arms on the dance floor, she wanted to rejoice and she wanted to die of embarrassment. She was furious that he had let her believe that he was a hired worker, and mortified that she had leaped to conclusions based upon his attire and his facility with a hammer. Of course he had worn work clothes to service day; so had she! And not all Warrington men were afraid to get their hands dirty. In her own way, she was as much of a snob as the students who had bought their way out of service.

Next year, she was certain, there would be very few of those.

The girls held fast, and the young men learned that the way to a Miss Sebastian's girls' heart was to show compassion for the less fortunate. Or at the very least, the less empathetic young men realized that they had to tolerate a bit of work first if they wanted to enjoy the dance later. Perhaps many of the young people from both schools would never pick up trash or wield a ladle in a soup kitchen on any other occasion, but Agnes hoped that some of the lessons Miss Sebastian intended the day of service to teach would linger with the students and inform the choices they made later in life.

True to his word, Richard never divulged that Agnes had organized the dancing strike, even when some Warrington men tried to organize their own counterstrike wherein they would shun the ringleaders at all school mixers thereafter. "I almost gave up your name when I heard that," Richard teased Agnes when they met for lunch a week later. "I wouldn't mind having you all to myself."

Agnes was too modest to tell him he needn't worry about competition from any other young man, but she was sure he knew.

Richard fascinated her. She knew

from the first day they met that he was nothing like the young men her parents considered suitable, the boys she met at dancing school or the endless society functions her parents forced her to attend. He had a careless roughness refreshingly free of all the practiced mannerisms and studied indifference of the sons of her parents' friends. Over time she learned that although Richard had been raised in the countryside, he was near the top of his class, admired by even the most sophisticated and urbane of his fellow students, and a natural leader. She assumed her parents would adore him as much as she did, especially since he embodied so many of the values extolled by her mother's father, the wealthy but populist senator. But when she told her parents about Richard, they heard only that he was the son of a horse farmer, of all things, probably on scholarship, with no family connections that mattered. They forbade her to see him, but she was in love and she was not under her parents' constant scrutiny. Agnes and Richard met at cafés and school functions, and her parents were none the wiser.

Then war came. To prove his patriotism in the face of anti-German sentiment, Richard left Warrington to enlist, and emboldened by his actions, Andrew did, too. Richard proposed, as so many young men did before they went off to fight, but Agnes was too young to marry without her parents' consent. She spoke to her mother first, and won her consent only after she vowed to become Richard's lover rather than wife if they forbade the marriage.

Her father was even more furious and resistant than her mother had been. "If you marry that man," he roared, "you leave this house forever. You will be dead to us!"

His words shocked her into silence. She could only stare at him, the man she had always admired and loved so deeply. He thought she had betrayed him, that she would willfully destroy the Chevalier family's good name. She knew he was wrong, but she had no time to waste, no time for him to come to know Richard, to accept him. Her darling Richard might not return from the war. She might have only those two weeks with him before he reported to basic training, two weeks in exchange for a lifetime with her family.

She was her father's favorite daughter, and yet he could cut her out of his life with a word.

"I will miss you all very much," she told him, her heart breaking. Then she hurried off to tell Richard she would be his wife.

They had a simple civil ceremony, with Andrew and Marjorie serving as witnesses. Agnes had wanted her brothers and sisters present, but she could not ask them to defy their parents and share her banishment. Later that day, Richard's brother-in-law, James, and Richard's eldest sister's beau, Harold, arrived, having learned too late of Richard and Andrew's plans. James decided to enlist so that he would be in the same unit as his brother-in-law, and Harold did as well.

Agnes was not comforted by the knowledge that James and Harold would be looking after Richard on the battlefield. Their selflessness and courage would not stop a bullet. They should have tried to free Richard from his enlistment, not join him in it. It was utter madness, and she alone seemed able to see it.

They returned to Elm Creek Manor together, for a few bleak days of grievous good-byes. The men's last days before they were due to report for basic training flew by swiftly. Harold asked Richard's eldest sister, Claudia, to marry him, and she accepted, but they did not rush off and marry as Agnes and Richard had done, as so many other young couples had done. Agnes marveled at their certainty that they would be granted the chance, later, to have a proper wedding celebration. She wished she shared their confidence, and she hid her fear as best she could. She could not bear to send Richard off to war believing anything but that he would return, safe and sound, to raise a family with her, to grow old with her. Believing anything else might bring the worst down upon them.

All too soon, the men departed. Agnes settled into a strange new life, a

bride without an adoring husband by
her side, disowned by her family, an un-
welcome stranger in an unfamiliar
home, caught between two bickering
sisters, all of them fearing for the men
they loved. In time she won over all of
the Bergstroms except Sylvia, who was
jealous that Agnes had captured her beloved baby brother's heart. Sylvia had
concluded early on that Agnes was a
flighty, spoiled, pampered child, and
nothing Agnes said or did could persuade her otherwise. Agnes resolved to
win over her reluctant sister-in-law with
time and patience, for Richard's sake.

Knowing how proud Sylvia was of her
quilts, Agnes asked for lessons, thinking
that a shared interest might draw them
together and that quilting would help
distract her during the lonely weeks between letters from the men. Flattered,
Sylvia agreed and suggested that Agnes
choose a simple pattern or a sampler as
her first project. As Agnes paged
through patterns, selecting a variety of
blocks she thought she could manage
with Sylvia's guidance, Claudia took her
aside and told her she would master the

skills more quickly and thoroughly if she chose a more challenging pattern. With no reason to question the advice of the sister who actually liked her, Agnes chose to make a Double Wedding Ring quilt, for the name seemed to promise that she and Richard would have many happy years together. Sylvia tried to convince her to stick to the sampler, a suggestion Agnes later wished she had followed. The bias edges and curved seams of the Double Wedding Ring proved too difficult for her inexpert stitches, and her first half ring buckled in the middle and gapped in the seams. She might have done better on a second attempt, but before she could cut another piece or sew another seam of her wedding quilt, the news came that Richard and James had been killed, victims of friendly fire in the South Pacific. In shock and grief, Sylvia lost James's unborn child and kindly Mr. Bergstrom was felled by a stroke.

So much loss, so much pain, so much grieving. Agnes would not have survived it except for Claudia, who forced her to keep going, who gave her work to do caring for Sylvia as she recovered. Gradually Sylvia grew stronger, but she was never the same. None of them could be, but Sylvia had lost a child. In compassion for her, Agnes found the strength to keep going.

If only she could return to Philadelphia, resume her studies at Miss Sebastian's Academy—but she had closed the door to that life, and at Elm Creek Manor she must remain.

The war ended. Harold came home, and Claudia threw herself into preparing for their wedding as if to deny all the loss, all the suffering the family had endured. She expected Sylvia to help, but Sylvia seemed unable to summon any interest and had difficulty remembering the tasks Claudia assigned to her. Exasperated, Claudia turned to Agnes, and in a futile attempt to keep peace between the sisters, Agnes took over Sylvia's duties, thinking to relieve her of an unwanted burden.

One day a few weeks before the wedding, Andrew paid an unexpected visit on his way from Philadelphia to a new job in Detroit. Agnes was pleased to see her old friend, though the sight of him brought tears to her eyes as she remembered happier times when they were carefree students in Philadelphia. He walked with a new limp caused by the wound he had suffered trying to rescue Richard, and although he treated Agnes the same as always, he coldly shunned Harold. Agnes did not ask why; something in the steely gaze Andrew fixed upon his former brother-in-arms warned her that she did not want to know what had passed between them in the war.

That evening after supper, Andrew spoke privately with Sylvia in the library. Agnes was passing in the hall when the door banged open and Sylvia stormed out, furious, tears streaking her face. Andrew had followed her as far as the library door. His face, too, was wet from tears.

"What happened?" Agnes asked him. As soon as the words left her lips, she felt a flash of panic. She did not want to know.

But Andrew had already taken her hand. "Agnes, there's something you don't know about the way Richard and James died." He hesitated. "You should know the truth."

But Agnes tore her hand from his grasp and begged him to say no more. What did it matter how Richard had died? All that mattered was that he was never coming back to her. That was burden enough. She could not bear to add to it the picture of her husband's last moments—the explosion, Richard bleeding, limbs torn off or blasted away, screams of agony ripping from his throat. She imagined too much without hearing Andrew's story.

Andrew left the next day, but before he departed, Agnes never once observed him take Claudia aside to tell her the horrific tale of the men's deaths as he had told Sylvia, as he had tried to tell her. Agnes vowed to absent herself whenever Sylvia chose to tell her sister what Andrew had said. Then, a few days before the wedding, a terrible argument erupted between the two sisters, worse than any Agnes had witnessed. Sylvia stormed from the house carrying two suitcases, and although Claudia assured Agnes she would return, Agnes knew with bleak certainty that she would never see Sylvia again.

Claudia and Harold married, although moments before walking down the aisle, Claudia had confessed to Agnes that she was not sure if she should go through with it. Even so, the couple seemed happy, so Agnes dismissed Claudia's last-minute nerves as perfectly understandable given the circumstances. Perhaps the couple was too happy. They threw lavish parties nearly every week, spending money as if to make up for all the deprivations of the war years, as if by laughing and dancing they could undo all the pain they had suffered. Agnes looked on in dismay as Harold and Claudia neglected Bergstrom Thoroughbreds, selling off horses for a fraction of their value to raise cash, which they spent as quickly as they earned it. Agnes had learned something of financial matters from her father and tried to steer the newlyweds down a more prudent course, but they laughed off her concerns. Fearful that they would lose everything, Agnes secretly invested money in stocks and bonds, but she knew the dividends could not possibly keep up with the Middens' spendthrift ways.

As Claudia and Harold's first year of marriage passed, Agnes began to detect a new tension between them, an undercurrent of hostility and accusation in Claudia's tone when she spoke to her husband, a sullen defensiveness in Harold's replies. Once, inexplicably, Claudia asked Agnes if Andrew had told her how Richard and James had died.

"No, he didn't," she said, trembling from a sudden chill of fear. "I wouldn't let him."

"Of course." Claudia gave a mirthless laugh. "Well, if it were true, if it were important, he would have insisted on telling you, right?"

Agnes could not reply, not without risking that Claudia might blurt out what she knew.

As the family business failed and the money ran out, Claudia and Harold's marriage gradually, inexorably disintegrated. The empty halls of Elm Creek Manor echoed with their mutual antipathy. Agnes had never felt more alone. She longed for her family, for her friends back in Philadelphia, and, most of all, for the love of her heart, Richard. She even missed Sylvia, who had never accepted her, never liked her. Only Sylvia could forestall the complete loss of the Bergstrom family legacy. Agnes prayed for the strength to preserve what she could until Sylvia came home.

Agnes never thought to pick up a needle again after her failed first attempt, but in desperate need of something to fill the empty hours, she asked Claudia to continue her quilting lessons. Agnes had read a newspaper article about a woman who had made memorial quilts for her two sons killed on the beaches of Normandy, and she asked Claudia to help her create such a quilt for Sylvia.

"She may never see it," Claudia replied.

Agnes would not acknowledge that possibility. "Of course she will. We should try to finish it before she returns. Think of what it would mean to her."

The memorial quilt would be a peace

offering, she thought. It was an act of hope when all hope had fled. If they made a quilt for Sylvia, they must believe that she would one day wrap it around herself in a warm embrace of reconciliation and forgiveness. Agnes had to believe that or she could not get through the days.

Eventually Agnes won Claudia's consent, and together the sisters-in-law searched James's closet for shirts and trousers and ties they knew Sylvia would recognize. From the cloth they cut diamonds and triangles and squares and sewed them into the pattern whose name conveyed all that the founders of Elm Creek Manor had wanted their descendants to find within its walls: safety, sanctuary, family, home.

"Castle Wall," Claudia murmured as she taught Agnes the pattern. Claudia had chosen it for its symbolism and not because it was an easy block for a beginner to master. But Agnes was determined to learn, and although at first she picked out almost as many seams as she put in, eventually her hands grew accustomed to the motions of the running stitch, to finger-pressing seams, to setting in pieces, to squaring up blocks that were not quite true. As they sewed, Claudia shared stories of the Bergstrom family, wistful tales of the mother-in-law Agnes had never met, stories from Richard's childhood that alternately made her smile and wrenched her heart. But even as the quilting lessons brought Agnes and Claudia closer in their shared mourning, the crevasse between Claudia and Harold widened.

Despite Agnes's efforts, the Middens steadily drained their resources throughout the second, miserable year of their marriage. All too soon the stable was empty, the last remaining stable hands sent away. Agnes begged Harold and Claudia to make some provision for the future, but the couple only brooded and offered vague assurances that things would work out somehow. Frustrated and desperate, Agnes sold off antique furniture chosen at random from the unoccupied rooms, refusing to wonder about their sentimental value to the Bergstrom family.

On one of her all-too-frequent visits to

the Waterford antique shop, Agnes met Joe, a history professor at Waterford College who occasionally appraised items for the store's owner. One day, curious how she found so many remarkable pieces, he invited her to lunch. Agnes had been so long without a confidante that the whole unhappy story spilled from her. With almost unbearable kindness, Joe offered to put her in touch with colleagues in New York who would secure higher profits for her than she could obtain in Waterford. Overwhelmed with gratitude, Agnes threw her arms around him, and he laughed in surprise and held her.

Agnes again turned to Joe for help when Claudia and Harold began selling off Bergstrom land. Agnes fought for every acre, but each time a tract came up for auction, Claudia and Harold reminded her that they had no other source of income. "Sell one last parcel and invest the cash," she begged them. "Live off the dividends. Economize."

They ignored her.

Agnes knew she had to act or there would be nothing left of Richard's beloved childhood home. Joe helped her find a savvy lawyer who managed to put most of the estate in Sylvia's name. As long as Sylvia lived, no one but she could sell those protected acres. Thwarted, but unaware that Agnes was responsible for the obstruction, the Middens brought their lavish spending to an abrupt halt—and began to lash out at each other with renewed fury. Perhaps because in her misery she wanted others to suffer, too, Claudia blindsided Agnes with Andrew's secret, that Harold had been responsible for Richard's and James's deaths.

Agnes knew Andrew never could have invented such a nightmarish tale. At last she understood why Sylvia had left, and she desperately wished to follow. As Claudia's marriage crumbled under the strain of grief and guilty secrets, Claudia withdrew into solitary bitterness. She abandoned the memorial quilt just as she had surely abandoned all hope of happiness. Agnes pretended she had not learned enough to continue on her own, but Claudia was unmoved. "Leave it, then," she muttered. "Put the blocks in the scrap bag and let someone else worry about it."

But Agnes knew there would be no one else. Alone in the west sitting room that had once been the Bergstrom women's favorite place to quilt together, Agnes sewed the blocks into rows and joined the rows into a top. She found a quilt frame in the ballroom and, drawing upon memories of Sylvia's quilting, she layered top, batting, and backing and set herself to the task. With no one to teach her the rocking, fluid stitches she had seen the Bergstrom women make, Agnes invented her own method, stabbing the needle through the top of the quilt with one hand, grasping the tip with her other hand as it emerged on the underside, stabbing it back up through to the top. The repetitive task was her only solace—that, and occasional trips to Waterford to meet Joe.

When Joe asked her to marry him, she hardly dared believe that a lifeline had been thrown to her and she had caught it. Joe's profession of love and promise of fidelity was the only glimmer of hope she had seen in three years.

He was too good a man for Agnes to deceive him. She had to tell him the truth of her heart, though it might make him pull the lifeline from her grasp. "I care for you, very much," she told him, tears falling freely, "but I will never love you the way I loved Richard. I'm sorry."

Joe looked pained, but he managed a crooked smile. "That's all right. I know you like me, and that's a start. You never know. I might grow on you."

And he did. Oh, how he did. She married Joe, and not a day went by that she didn't thank God for bringing him into her life. She did indeed come to love him with all her heart, and she knew Richard did not begrudge her the happiness she and Joe shared.

The next two quilts Agnes sewed were made in joyful anticipation of the births of her two daughters. When they were a little older, she joined the Waterford Quilt Guild and forged enduring friendships with lovely women who never could have imagined her privileged childhood in Philadelphia or her heartbreak as a young war widow. Those friendships and the love of her daughters and grandchildren sustained her years later when her loving husband of more than thirty-five years passed on.

When she thought of Richard—and she did, from time to time—she remembered him in Philadelphia, where they had met, where they had been so happy together. Her memories rarely placed him within the gray stone walls of Elm Creek Manor, where she had longed for him and mourned. She assumed she would never return to the Bergstrom estate, for she and Claudia had parted on bad terms and her former sister-in-law had lived out her years in bitterness. But although Agnes's ties to the Bergstrom family had stretched transparently thin, they yet remained, and Claudia's newspaper obituary struck her with all the force of new, raw grief. At the sparsely attended funeral, Agnes overheard a woman whisper to a friend that it was curious that Claudia had asked to be buried in the Bergstrom family plot in the small cemetery on Church Street, rather than in the larger, new cemetery on the outskirts of town, where she had laid her husband to rest. Agnes, who had seen anger and hatred divide the couple in life, was not surprised that Claudia wanted to remain apart from her husband in death.

Then, one late autumn day, she heard a rumor that Sylvia had returned to Elm Creek Manor. Only Agnes's closest quilting friends and her daughters knew of her unhappy years in the manor and of Sylvia's dislike for her, but every scrap of news about the long-lost Bergstrom heir eventually found its way to Agnes, and the rumor was soon confirmed. Sylvia had been spotted at the market buying groceries. She had met with Claudia's banker for an hour behind closed doors. She had gone to lunch with an agent from University Realtors. When Sylvia began selling her quilts on commission through Bonnie's quilt shop, Agnes resigned herself to their eventual meeting but hoped, at last, to be able to sate her curiosity. Where had Sylvia been all those long years? Was she all right? Did she have a family—a husband, children, grandchildren? And were the rumors true? Did she intend to sell Elm Creek Manor?

That summer, a newcomer to town, Sarah McClure, brought about the reunion Agnes had simultaneously longed for and dreaded. When Agnes met Sylvia in the newly restored north gardens after fifty years apart, she scarcely recognized her sister-in-law. Sylvia was as tall and slender as ever, but her lush waves of chestnut hair had gone silver-gray and were blunt cut a few inches below her chin. The girlish softness of her features had fled, and time and worry had etched feathery lines around her eyes and mouth. A pair of glasses dangled from a silver chain around her neck, but as she slipped them on and spoke, all the years fell away and the same determined, domineering Sylvia stood before her.

Never in her wildest imaginings would Agnes have thought that the path of life she followed would circle around and bring her back to Elm Creek Manor. And yet there she stood in the garden welcoming Sylvia home and offering her friendship, for they were the only ones left who remembered those long-ago days, and there was no longer any reason for enmity between them. In truth, there never had been.

In the days that followed, Agnes joined Sylvia, Sarah, and their other friends in an ambitious venture: the founding of Elm Creek Quilts. As the new Elm Creek Quilters worked to transform the manor into a quilters' retreat, the formerly estranged women shared histories and confidences about their time apart. Upon her return to the manor, Sylvia had discovered the Castle Wall memorial quilt sagging unfinished in the quilt frame, and as the bonds of friendship that had failed to form in their younger days at last were forged, Sylvia and Agnes finished the quilt together.

"Your quilting skills have come a long way since we last sewed together," Sylvia remarked as they fashioned a hanging sleeve from leftover backing fabric. Her words implied more than they said, evoking Agnes's first imperfect efforts, her unwise choice to follow Claudia's advice instead of Sylvia's, and the tragedy that had ended the lessons.

"So have yours," replied Agnes saucily, so that Sylvia would know she was not the same guileless girl Richard had brought home so many years before.

The finished Castle Wall quilt hung in the library, to one side of the fireplace on the north wall. Sometimes Agnes caught Sylvia gazing upon it, lost in thought, and she would slip her arm around her sister-in-law's waist and stand with her, so that she would know she was not alone.

Agnes came to the manor nearly every day on Elm Creek Quilts business or to visit with Sylvia, and at last she could say she felt at home there. But to live there once more? She loved her own little house—where she had lived so contentedly with Joe and where they had raised their daughters—too much to leave it, even for a place as grand as Elm Creek Manor.

She was sure Gwen, Bonnie, and Anna had reasons of their own.

"Moving every Elm Creek Quilter into the manor isn't the answer," said Agnes. "Sometimes people living under the same roof communicate least of all."

"It would solve *some* of our problems," Diane insisted, sipping from her mug.

Agnes thought of Bonnie's perpetual tardiness and Gwen's inexplicable absence from the party, and she could not disagree.

Anna remained behind in the kitchen while the others went to the foyer, where they found Sarah and Summer arranging the registration tables while Gretchen unfolded chairs. Sylvia and Gwen sat on the bottom step of the oak staircase, Sylvia's arm around Gwen's slumped shoulders. Agnes knew then that Gwen had arrived too late to bid Judy goodbye.

"The moving van had already left." Gwen's face contorted in disbelief as she told them what had happened. "As soon as I hung up the phone with Agnes, I ran all the way to her house, but they were gone."

"Did you call Judy's cell?" asked Jeremy.

Gwen spread her hands and shook her head. "No." The gesture conveyed helplessness, as if saying farewell by phone was beside the point.

"Sometimes saying a last good-bye is simply too painful to bear," Sylvia consoled her. "Judy understands."

"I don't," Gwen shot back. "How could I have forgotten her party? When I saw my car parked on Main Street, why didn't I remember why I had driven to the library? Something must be seriously wrong with me."

"I've been saying that for years," Diane remarked.

"Diane," Agnes admonished gently, then she joined Gwen and Sylvia on the step. "You're right, Gwen. No one simply forgets a farewell party. You either didn't want to come, or you couldn't. Perhaps even you don't know for certain. It's possible that Judy's leave-taking was so difficult for you to think about that you grew accustomed to putting it out of your mind. In the end it doesn't matter. A true friend would forgive you, whatever the reason."

"I hope Judy thinks so," Gwen muttered. Abruptly she rose and began helping Gretchen set up chairs next to the registration tables.

Agnes and Sylvia exchanged a knowing look. The hurt would pass, the friendship heal. They understood better than their younger friends that this misunderstanding was only one slender thread in the fabric of their friendship. The whole would not unravel even if that one brittle thread snapped under the strain.

Agnes's words lingered in Sylvia's thoughts as they welcomed a new group of campers to Elm Creek Manor. A true friend does not demand perfection; a true friend forgives. For that to happen, however, a friend who has given offense must put love before pride and apologize. Sylvia hoped Gwen would not allow the misunderstanding to fester, worsening the injury and prolonging its healing.

Agnes had an instinctive gift for forgiveness for which Sylvia would be eternally grateful. Her petite frame and sweet demeanor concealed a core of resolute strength and courage that often caught Sylvia by surprise. Sylvia doubted she would have been brave enough to approach Agnes, seeking reconciliation and risking rejection. Yet Agnes had waited for her in the garden, still willing to try to make peace long after most people would have given up all hope. "Oh, Sylvia," she had said, her eyes filling with tears, "is there any chance we could ever be friends? I know I wasn't the sister-in-law you hoped for, but now that everyone else is gone—"

At that Sylvia had reached out to her sister-in-law and begged her not to cry. Agnes had done nothing to deserve Sylvia's ill treatment all those many years ago, and Sylvia was truly sorry. She could not believe her good fortune that Agnes was willing to give her a second chance. Agnes was right—there was no one else left who shared the memories of Elm Creek Manor before its decline, of the Bergstrom family before tragedy shattered it, of Richard. They owed it to each other and to their departed loved ones to make amends. What a blessing it would be to say, "Remember when?" and have someone smile fondly and answer, "Yes."

The paths of their lives had diverged, but Sarah had brought them back together, and they would never again let such a great distance separate them. If she and Agnes could traverse the expanses that had divided them, Gwen and Judy certainly could, and Sylvia doubted they would need fifty years to figure out how to do it.

Sylvia had chosen the softest cottons for Agnes's section of her secret work-in-progress, warm tones for her sunny outlook on the present, pastel hues for her optimistic approach to the future, floral prints for the garden where she had staged their reunion and mended the breaches of the past. For all their pretty softness, the fabrics were as closely woven and colorfast as any of the others, and Sylvia was glad she had not learned too late to appreciate the texture they added to her quilt.

Summer

Summer was wrapping up her iPhoto slide show on the Amish quilts of Lancaster County when Sylvia slipped into the classroom, her pink seeksucker suit a cheerful splash of color against the white partition that subdivided the manor's ballroom. Summer smiled and beckoned, assuming that Sylvia had come to contribute to the discussion, but Sylvia quickly shook her head, motioned for Summer to continue, and seated herself in the back row. Summer went on with her presentation, hiding her amusement at the sight of Sylvia Compson, Master Quilter, hands folded on the table and eyes fixed on Summer in rapt attention, as if there were anything Summer could say about quilting that Sylvia didn't already know.

Summer's students lingered after class to ask questions and solicit help for some of their more challenging quilting projects, so it wasn't until ten minutes into her lunch break that Summer found out what had prompted Sylvia to pay an unexpected visit to her classroom.

"I hope I didn't distract you, dear, popping in like that," said Sylvia, rising as the last student left and Summer joined her in the back of the room. Sylvia was nearly as tall as Summer, thin, with silver-gray hair and an imperious expression she could never quite shake even in her most affable moments. "I wanted a word before you dash off to lunch."

"Sure. What can I do for you?"

"We have to talk. Would you have time to meet me in the library after your last class?"

Summer tucked a long strand of auburn hair behind her ear and shifted her laptop so that it rested on her hip. "You came to talk to me to see if you can talk to me?"

"I didn't expect you to have time for a lengthy conversation now. I suppose I'm asking for an appointment." Sylvia peered at her over the rims of her glasses. "Pencil me in?"

"For you, I'll put it in ink."

After Sylvia left, Summer stayed behind to pack up her things, mulling over Sylvia's request with growing trepidation. Nothing good ever came of a conversation prefaced by "We have to talk." Summer had uttered the phrase earlier that year when she told her mother she had moved in with Jeremy. She said it again a few months later before telling Jeremy she was moving out. The more time that elapsed between the foreboding line and the actual revelation, the worse things tended to be.

She suspected Jeremy was planning his own "we have to talk" moment, and she had prepared herself to listen without an emotional outburst, without anger, without tears. She had been preparing herself so long that it would be a relief when he finally got it over with.

Summer considered the possibilities as she crossed the manor's grand, three-story-high foyer, her sandals whisper-quiet on the black marble floor. The smell of fried chicken hung faintly in the air as she passed the banquet hall, and through the open doorway she saw campers lining up on the far side of the room while Anna bustled about, arranging stainless-steel trays on the buffet table with the help of two of the chain gang members. Summer didn't doubt for a minute that the young men were counting the days until the end of the camp season, just as the other Elm Creek Quilters had counted the days until Anna took control of the kitchen. All summer long, after their original chef retired, the Elm Creek Quilters had taken turns with kitchen duty. Summer had used her shifts to introduce her friends and students to a delicious variety of vegetarian cuisine, but the other Elm Creek Quilters insisted upon serving meat at every meal. Summer made a mental note to encourage Anna to offer more meatless options. She hated to think that all vegetarian dishes might fall off the menu once she was no longer there to promote them.

Because she was leaving Elm Creek Quilts, no matter what.

Surely Sylvia wouldn't try to talk her out of her plan. Everyone, even her mother, accepted that it was time for Summer to move on. She had passed the point of second thoughts months ago. The Elm Creek Quilters had hired her replacement, just as they had hired Gretchen to take over for Judy. Summer had registered for her autumn-quarter classes at the University of Chicago, putting down a nonrefundable deposit not covered by her fellowship. She would miss her friends and Elm Creek Manor, but she couldn't wait to throw herself headlong into academic life. She had backed out of her graduate school plans once, years before, but she was a different person now, surer of what she wanted.

Sylvia would be the first person to understand that, Summer reminded herself as she turned down the west wing of the manor on her way to the kitchen. Out of all the Elm Creek Quilters, there was perhaps no one more than Sylvia who had celebrated her decision to pursue her doctorate in history—

Summer stopped short in the kitchen doorway, where the odor of olive oil and roasted corn lingered in the air. Celebrate. That had to be it. A surprise going-away party, even though she wouldn't be leaving until the end of September, almost six weeks away. "I guess that just adds to the surprise," she murmured, hiding her dismay behind a friendly smile as a group of campers passed on their way from the back door to the banquet hall. A party was a thoughtful gesture, but the Elm Creek Quilters had already given her an appropriate send-off three years before, after her college graduation. They had expected her to go off to Penn to study philosophy. That was what her mother had wanted, so Summer had dutifully applied, even though she longed to stay in Waterford and nurture their fledgling business until she was confident Elm Creek Quilt Camp could survive without her. How could she have spoken up when pride rang in her mother's voice whenever she told her college-professor colleagues that her daughter was following in her footsteps? How could she have confided in any of the other Elm Creek Quilters, even Sarah, after they presented her with a beautiful Mariner's Compass signature quilt upon which each had written congratulatory messages wishing her good luck in her studies? When she had finally summoned up the courage to tell her mother she wasn't going, Gwen had burst into tears. As for the other Elm Creek Quilters, they had been happy to learn that she wasn't leaving—and taking her Internet expertise with her—but they did not approve of how she had handled things and how she had upset her mother. It was a wonder they hadn't asked her to return the quilt.

They wouldn't make that mistake again, Summer decided, reaching deep into the refrigerator for the soy milk and vegan sushi box she had hidden behind the gallon jug of orange juice. The Elm Creek Quilters had thrown her a going-away party once and she had made fools of them by refusing to go. For all they knew, Summer had no intention of going through with her graduate school plans this time, either; she just hadn't confessed the truth yet. A going-away party in the library after classes? Hardly. It was far more likely that the Elm Creek Quilters planned to sit her down in one of the leather armchairs and emphasize that they really didn't need her anymore and that she must, absolutely must, move to Chicago at the end of September. They would never forgive her if she didn't.

Summer almost would have preferred a party.

She allowed herself a leisurely lunch, enjoying the quiet of the kitchen, with only the hum of the ancient refrigerator and the distant buzz of quilters' voices breaking the silence. Usually she preferred to eat in the banquet hall with the other Elm Creek Quilters and their guests—even a vegetarian could fill up on all the meatless side dishes and salads Anna put together—but that day she wanted time alone to read through the history department's course catalog and the graduate school handbook. She had absorbed most of the information in her first fifty perusals, but she loved to gaze upon the pictures of the stately Gothic buildings, the leafy quads, and the quirky Hyde Park neighborhoods, imagining herself among them.

"They get a lot of snow in Chicago," remarked Sarah, carrying an empty stainless-steel tray into the kitchen and grimacing at the sight of Summer's familiar reading material. The tail of her light blue pinstriped Oxford cloth shirt hung loosely over her drawstring capris, and a long strand of reddish brown hair had come loose from her barrette. "It's frigid when those gusts come off Lake Michigan, too. That's why they call it the Windy City."

"That's not why they call it the Windy City, and how would you know that winters are any worse in Chicago than they are here?" said Summer. "You've never lived there."

Sarah set the tray in the kitchen sink with a clatter of dishes and silverware. "It's common knowledge."

"I won't be outside much anyway." Summer finished the last bite of her California roll and made a show of savoring every meatless morsel. "I'll be wandering blissfully through libraries and attending fascinating lectures by Nobel laureates. Winter, spring—it's all the same when you're living the life of the mind."

Sarah shrugged and poured herself a cup of organic ginger tea. Summer was tempted to tell her that not even a dozen cups would give her the boost of a single shot of espresso, but she didn't want to counteract whatever placebo effect Sarah extracted from the brew.

"Unless there's an underground tunnel connecting your apartment to the library, don't forget to pack your parka and snowshoes," Sarah teased, stirring sugar into her cup. "You have found a place to live, haven't you?"

"It's on my to-do list."

Sarah leaned back against the counter, a crease of worry appearing between her brows. "You're running out of time. You can't just show up homeless on the first day of the quarter."

"When have I had time for a road trip to go apartment hunting? I've had classes to teach, and then we were interviewing applicants—"

"Summer—"

"As soon as I get a chance, I'll search for Hyde Park apartment listings on the Internet. After Labor Day, I'll drive out and see them in person."

"If you say so."

Summer muffled a sigh, knowing that nothing short of leaving Pennsylvania in a U-Haul would persuade her friend that she wasn't going to back out of graduate school this time. "I'll see you later," she told Sarah, and hurried back to the ballroom so she could set up her project samples before her next class, a workshop on color theory. If Sylvia had a party or an intervention planned, Sarah had given no sign of it, and she was notorious for her inability to keep a secret. Whatever Sylvia had planned, Sarah wasn't in on it.

At four o'clock, the quilt campers finished their classes and went their separate ways, some to relax in their rooms before supper, others to stroll through the orchards and gardens, still more to the front veranda to work on quilting projects with newfound friends. Summer dropped off her laptop and class notes in the suite on the third floor she had called her own since moving out of Jeremy's apartment, then steeled herself and descended the curved oak staircase to the second floor, where Sylvia awaited her in the library.

At Summer's touch, double doors swung open into a room spanning the entire width of the south wing, where late afternoon sunlight spilled in through tall diamond-paned windows. The large stone fireplace on the south wall smelled faintly of old smoke and ash even though the hearth had been swept meticulously clean and a fire had not burned there since the last cool evening in spring several months ago. To the left of the mantel hung the Castle Wall quilt Claudia and Agnes had pieced as a memorial to Sylvia's first husband, James. Sylvia sat in the tall leather chair behind a broad oak desk cluttered with papers and files, chin resting on her hand, gaze fixed on the quilt.

"Sylvia?" Summer greeted her, rousing her gently from her reverie. "Is everything all right?"

"Oh, yes, dear." Sylvia straightened and smiled at her. "I was wondering, though, whether your mother has called Judy yet?"

"If she has, she didn't mention it."

"I see." Sylvia rose and went to the sofa, beckoning Summer to join her. "I suppose she will in good time. Well, let's get to it, shall we? I'm sure you and Jeremy have plans this evening."

"Not really." Jeremy had offered to take her out to dinner, but Anna's cooking was so fantastic that they preferred to eat at Elm Creek Manor. Best of all, it was free, and Jeremy could give Anna a ride home afterward. "He's coming over for dinner as usual."

"We should be done here well before he arrives. I wanted to speak with you to ask for your help planning the party tomorrow."

"The party?" Summer echoed, jolted.

"Yes, of course. Surely you saw Vinnie Burkholder at registration."

Summer breathed a sigh of relief. "Right. Vinnie's party." The septuagenarian had attended Elm Creek Quilt Camp every year since its first season, scheduling her visits to coincide with her birthday. Every year the campers threw a surprise birthday party for her, although after so many years their celebrations were no longer so surprising. The Elm Creek Quilters tried to add to the suspense by varying the time and location of the party from year to year, but everyone, including Vinnie herself, knew it was coming sooner or later. It was getting harder and harder to catch the spunky quilter off guard.

"I am completely out of ideas," said Sylvia, lifting her hands in frustration. "She wasn't expecting the breakfast-in-bed party two years ago, and I know we genuinely surprised her last year with the midnight-snack party, if only because she didn't have the whole day to speculate. I can't think of anything to top that."

"Maybe we should ask her friends for suggestions." Although Vinnie was popular with all of the campers, every year she reunited with the same small group of friends with whom she shared a special bond, the Cross-Country Quilters. One of them had even married her grandson.

"I checked with Grace Daniels, and she said Vinnie would be happy with anything. We shouldn't go overboard."

"So I guess fireworks and skydivers are out."

"I would think so."

"Instead of assuming bigger is better, maybe we ought to get back to basics," mused Summer. "What did we do for her first party? I can't recall."

"That's because it was so low-key, you probably missed it," said Sylvia. "At breakfast, I served her a blueberry muffin with a birthday candle stuck in it, and the campers sang 'Happy Birthday.' It was all I could think of on the spur of the moment. I had learned only a few moments before that it would be Vinnie's first birthday as a widow and that she had chosen to spend the day with us because the alternative was to sit at home alone and mourn. I admired her attitude and wanted to mark the day, to make it a little more special if I could. I had no idea it would become an annual event, or I might have planned better."

"I'm sure Vinnie was very pleased. Hasn't she come back every year since?" Summer thought for a moment. "Tomorrow morning, why don't we give everyone a muffin with a lit candle? All of those tiny, flickering lights would be so beautiful."

"We'd have to draw the curtains," said Sylvia doubtfully. "It might get rather stuffy."

"Only for a moment. After everyone sings and blows out their candles, we'll let the fresh breezes in again."

Summer knew that Sylvia could imagine, as she did, the vast room illuminated by tiny stars of light, constellations of friendship and song celebrating another year for their most beloved camper. "It would be perfect," Sylvia declared, clasping Summer's hand. "I knew I could count on you for a stroke of inspiration. I always can. I don't know how we're going to manage when you're gone."

"Someone will step up," Summer assured her. "Anna and Gretchen will bring

in fresh ideas, too. Don't forget to consult them."

"And Maggie, too," said Sylvia, nam-
ing Summer's successor.

"Of course." Summer hadn't meant to
leave her out, just as her mother had not
meant to miss Judy's farewell party.
"Would you like me to ask Anna to put
several dozen blueberry muffins on tomorrow's breakfast menu?"

Sylvia thanked her, adding that they
might need to send someone into Waterford for several packages of birthday
candles. Summer offered to ask Jeremy
to stop on the way. "It's the least he can
do to thank you for all the free meals,"
she said, smiling.

"On the contrary, we owe him," said
Sylvia. "Doesn't he bring us our chef
every day?"

Not every day, Summer thought as
she went downstairs to the kitchen.
Sometimes Anna took the bus. She
could just as easily get a ride with Diane
and Agnes, but Anna lived in the apartment right across the hall from Jeremy,
and it was no secret that he liked having
an excuse to visit Summer. Not that an

excuse was necessary, but Jeremy was busy with his dissertation, and Summer with Elm Creek Quilts and graduate school plans. If he didn't go out of his way to see her mornings and evenings at the manor, they might not see each other for days at a time. It was almost as if they were gradually easing into a long-distance relationship to lessen the shock later, when they were finally parted.

The next morning dawned cool and drizzly. When the campers gathered for breakfast, Sylvia drew the curtains on the storm just as the summer helpers entered the banquet hall bearing trays of blueberry muffins, each alight with a single tiny candle. The guests applauded as a muffin was set before each of them, and the white-haired guest of honor beamed as their voices rose in song. "Make a wish," someone called out, so Vinnie closed her eyes and blew out her candle. All of the candles were immediately snuffed out, plunging the room into semidarkness just as a peal of thunder sounded. Someone shrieked, startled, and Summer quickly opened the curtains to the accompaniment of nervous laughter that quickly changed to true amusement. As the skies opened up and the rains descended, Summer looked around the gathering, her heart aching even as it lifted. She would miss these moments of unexpected delight. It was a comfort to know they would go on without her, that others would share in the happiness she had known within those gray stone walls. In that way, her own joy would endure.

She had always known that Elm Creek Manor would only be a temporary home to her, a sheltering haven on the wayside of a longer journey. The time had come to move on.

She made arrangements for Sarah to take over her classes on the upcoming Friday and Monday, and over dinner, she told Jeremy of her plans to travel to Chicago to find a place to live.

"I thought you were going to wait until after the camp season," he said.

"I was." Summer couldn't explain her sudden urgency in a way that didn't sound like she was eager to leave Waterford, to leave him. "The truth is, I shouldn't have put it off this long. I have so much to do before the fall quarter begins, and if I can find a place this weekend, that will be one less thing to worry about."

Jeremy considered for a moment, and then nodded. "Okay, sure. I could use a road trip. When do we leave?"

"Jeremy—" Summer hesitated. "You don't have to drop everything because I changed plans at the last minute."

"I can afford to take a weekend off. I can make up the time later."

He would have a lot of empty hours to fill after she left, was what he meant. "What would your adviser say?"

"He'd say he's relieved I'm going now instead of after classes begin." Jeremy savored another bite of Anna's chicken cordon bleu. "Besides, how else were you planning to get to Chicago? It's too late to buy an airline ticket unless you want to throw away a huge chunk of your fellowship stipend on it, and you don't have a car."

"I thought I'd borrow my mom's."

Jeremy grinned. "Summer, seriously, it's not a problem. I'd like to go. I've been looking forward to spending some time together, and—I don't know. It will be a little easier to think of you so far away if I can picture where you are—the rooms you live in, the streets you walk along."

"The library I'm going to haunt from dawn till dusk."

He nodded and looked away. They had met in a library. Summer had been researching the Bergstrom family's early years in the Elm Creek Valley and Jeremy had sought a quiet place to study undisturbed. He had noticed her that first day, he later admitted, but he had needed a few days to work up the nerve to talk to her. Summer never told him that she hadn't noticed him working away in his carrel, letting him believe that she had admired him from a distance, too. It wasn't really deceiving him. She was sure she would have admired him had she not been so intent upon finding the information Sylvia sought.

"Hey." She reached for his hand. "I'm not planning to meet some guy in the stacks of the Reg."

"I know." He squeezed her hand once before letting go.

She let the obvious hang unacknowledged in the air between them. No one ever planned to meet someone else. It just happened.

A few days later, Summer mentioned the trip to her mother and was astonished to see her face fall in disappointment. "I assumed you and I would go together."

"You did?" Summer couldn't admit that the idea had never occurred to her. "How could you get away, with camp still going on and the new semester starting next week?"

"If we flew and made a quick weekend of it, I'd miss only two days of camp and nothing at all at the college."

Summer was torn between chagrin that she had not thought to ask her mother and exasperation that everyone seemed to be making assumptions about her plans instead of asking her directly. "Airfare's too expensive at this late date, and there aren't enough teachers to cover all of our classes at camp if we take off at the same time." Summer hugged her mother. "Come out for a long visit instead, after I'm settled. By then I'll know all the best places to show you."

"You're right. That's a better plan." But her mother remained forlorn. "If I stay longer, I'll have time to research the 1933 World's Fair during my visit."

On impulse, Summer said, "Jeremy can help me find the apartment, and you can help me move in."

Gwen laughed. "Oh, great. Give me the job that requires actual work." But she looked pleased, as if she thought she had been given the more important, more intimate role.

On Friday morning, after Jeremy dropped off Anna, Summer threw her backpack into the trunk of his car and settled into the front passenger seat. "What's that?" she asked, glancing at the cooler sitting on the backseat. "Did you pack snacks for the road?"

"Anna did," said Jeremy, starting the car. "She has a moral aversion to fast-food restaurants, and she wasn't sure what vegetarian options we'd find on the toll road."

"Oh." Summer paged through the maps and directions she had downloaded from the Internet. "That was nice of her."

"I contributed the drinks, but that didn't require any skill."

"Some fast-food restaurants have salads."

"If you call wilted iceberg lettuce and a few mushy tomatoes a salad. Anything Anna makes would be better than that."

"You're right." Summer turned on the radio and fell silent as they drove through the woods surrounding the Bergstrom estate. "I hope she doesn't feel responsible for every meal an Elm Creek Quilter eats. She did this on her own time and spent her own money. I know she's new and she wants to make a good impression, but it really wasn't necessary."

Jeremy shot her an incredulous look.

"She didn't do it because she had to. She did it because she's our friend."

"Your friend," Summer corrected. "I really don't know her very well."

As the car bounded up a slight incline and emerged from the woods, Jeremy leaned forward and craned his neck, searching for oncoming cars before pulling onto the highway. "You'd like her if you knew her better."

"I like her now." Summer hadn't meant to suggest that she didn't. Hadn't she been Anna's strongest advocate during the hiring process? "We're lucky to have her."

"I'm glad you feel that way. I hope the other Elm Creek Quilters do, too."

An odd note in his voice alerted Summer. "What do you mean? Doesn't Anna feel appreciated?"

"It's not that." Jeremy weighed his words carefully before speaking. "You know how it is. You Elm Creek Quilters form a tight circle. It can be hard for someone new to break in, to really feel included."

Summer understood what he was saying, but the original Elm Creek Quilters had known one another for years and shared a bond of friendship tested by adversity. As welcoming as they had been to Anna—and Gretchen, too—they and the newcomers did not have a shared history, not yet. "It'll take time, but everyone likes the new hires. It will happen."

Jeremy nodded, his eyes on the road. "That's what I told Anna."

Summer had a sudden mental picture of Jeremy and Anna driving home from quilt camp, animatedly narrating the day's events, analyzing conversations. It was strangely unsettling to think that she might have been the subject of one of those chats. "Do you want me to say something to Sarah?"

"No," said Jeremy, emphatic. "It's not a problem. I shouldn't have mentioned it. In a few months, I'm sure all this initial awkwardness will fade and Anna will feel like she fits in. In the meantime . . . try to be understanding if she overcompensates."

He jerked his thumb over his shoulder, indicating the cooler filled with what was surely a picnic lunch fit for a two-page spread in a gourmet cooking magazine.

"Got it," replied Summer, and found herself quite unexpectedly wishing that Anna had confided in her rather than Jeremy.

They drove on, stopping for gas or to stretch their legs or switch drivers, but mostly driving straight through, digging into the cooler when they got hungry, spinning the radio dial when the signal broke up. Sometimes they talked about how to spend Summer's last few weeks in Waterford or their plans for their separate upcoming academic years, but mostly they rode along in companionable silence. Jeremy did not seem surprised when she told him her mother planned to accompany her to Chicago to help her move in, nor did he seem disappointed that Summer had not asked him. Instead, he teased, "Are you planning to take your fabric stash? I think you need a special license to drive a truck big enough."

"I hadn't thought about it," said Summer. She might pack a few works-in-progress and her sewing machine, but the rest of her fabric and all of her pattern books would probably be better off stored at her mother's house. "I don't think I'm going to have much time for quilting once the quarter begins. I've seen how grad school is for you. I might not be able to quilt except for the absolute minimum amount required to maintain my sanity."

Jeremy grinned. "I think I had hobbies before graduate school, but I've forgotten what they were."

Summer managed a smile, though she found his words jarring. Quilting was so much more than a hobby for her. Didn't he get that? Had he learned nothing from her and from his almost daily visits to quilt camp? Quilting was her means of artistic expression and a binding thread that defined her relationships with nearly all of the women in her life. It was unthinkable to brand something so potent and so full of meaning with the deprecating label of hobby.

She remembered learning to read, to write, to ride a bike, but her history with quilting stretched back even further, into the dim predawn before her conscious memories. It seemed she had always put needle to fabric, matched squares to triangles, arranged colored shapes until they suddenly fell into an unexpected and delightful pattern.

Her earliest memories of quilting blended in a colorful mist from which a handful of distinct images emerged: attending a quilt show in Kentucky with her grandmother, helping her mother select fabric at an Ithaca quilt shop, coloring quietly in the back of the room while her mother attended a meeting of the Tompkins County Quilters Guild, begging to be allowed to assemble a stash of her own. She still kept the Jack in the Pulpit quilt her grandmother had made as a gift for her third birthday, now lovingly folded and tucked away for safekeeping so that someday it might grace her own child's toddler bed.

Her first solo project was a lap quilt made in the Rail Fence pattern from bright Amish solids that had caught her eye and captivated her imagination on a research trip with her mother to St. Lawrence County in upstate New York. Summer pieced the first fifteen blocks by hand but, impatient to see her top grow, she asked her mother to let her use her sewing machine. "When you're older," her mother promised, and although this seemed an unjust and arbitrary ruling to Summer, no argument she made altered her mother's opinion that she was incapable of running a sewing machine without burning out the motor or sewing through her own finger.

Since Gwen had always told Summer she could do anything she set her mind to—and Summer had on many occasions proved it—it was annoying to have the stumbling block of her mother's worry suddenly thrown in her path. Her mother had always praised her intelligence and self-sufficiency. Wasn't she, at age ten, responsible enough to walk home from school, let herself into the apartment, fix a snack, and settle down to her homework without any prompting or supervision? Sometimes she even started supper if her mother had a late class or a meeting with her thesis adviser. Summer could do all that, and yet she couldn't be trusted to flip a switch and press a foot pedal without injuring herself or making the sewing machine burst into flames. It was stupid and unfair.

Her mother had often read to her from Henry David Thoreau and Martin Luther King Jr., so Summer understood well that when confronted with an unjust law, it was her duty to disobey. It was just a sewing machine, after all; she wasn't going to jail for refusing to pay taxes to fund an illegal war or something. So, having quelled her guilt and convinced herself that historical moral authorities would have sided with her, she began borrowing time at her mother's sewing machine while Gwen was on the Cornell campus, studying or meeting with her adviser. Summer had seen her mother sew so often that she wound the bobbin, threaded the needle, and sent the needle whirring through her first seam without a moment's hesitation. After that, she couldn't imagine ever returning to the slow, meticulous process of hand-sewing—except in the evenings when her mother was nearby, taking note of her progress.

For weeks after her homework was

done, she filled those precious few hours alone in the house before her mother's return with the cheerful, industrious whir of the sewing machine. Rail Fence blocks came together quickly, almost effortlessly. She would turn up the radio to disguise the sound from neighbors on the other side of the too-thin walls, and the time checks announced the moment when she must scramble to restore the sewing table to its prior state, sweeping bits of thread into the trash, hiding her finished blocks in her bedroom. When her mother's key turned in the lock, Summer would be setting the table in the dinette or sprawled out on the sofa reading a book.

Then came a day when she was so engrossed in piecing her last few Rail Fence blocks that she lost track of time. At the sound of a throat clearing, Summer brought the sewing machine to an abrupt halt and turned to find her mother standing in the doorway. "Your quilt's really coming along," her mother remarked drily. "Now I understand why I haven't seen you working on your blocks for a while."

"Mom—" Hastily Summer switched off the machine and scrambled to her feet. "I can explain."

"Trust me, this scene is completely self-explanatory." Gwen crossed the room, her beaded necklaces clicking softly. She picked up one of the Rail Fence blocks, flipped it over to examine the stitching, then set it down and took up another.

"I was very, very careful," Summer assured her, drawing closer. "I didn't sew over any pins." When her mother continued to study her finished blocks in silence, Summer added, "I didn't see any logical reason why I couldn't use the sewing machine."

"I told you not to. That should have been reason enough."

"But it isn't. You just told me I was too young, but these blocks prove I'm not too young. Don't they look as good as what some of the women in your quilt guild would make?"

"Not quite." Gwen showed her the underside of one of the blocks where the seam allowances were sewed down helter-skelter. "These blocks won't lie flat. You skipped an important step. You should have pressed the seams before sewing these sections together."

In a small voice, Summer said, "You told me not to use the iron."

Gwen burst out laughing. "You follow my directions regarding a ten-dollar iron, but not a two-hundred-dollar sewing machine?"

"I've burned myself on the iron before," Summer countered. She had the fading scars to prove it. "In that case, your rule made sense, so I listened."

Gwen shook her head, eyeing Summer with—could it be?—something remarkably like admiration. "I have to admit, you make a fairly good case. Your blocks *are* just as good as those some of my friends might have made."

"Then can I keep using your sewing machine?"

Gwen muffled a groan and ran a hand across her brow. "I'm tempted to say no, just because you didn't listen to me. You should have waited for me to show you how to properly use it. On the other hand, you did some fine work here, so you're obviously ready after all."

Summer waited for her mother to deliver the verdict, resisting the temptation to point out that her mother had, in fact, shown her how to use the machine, for whenever she sewed, Summer had stood nearby, watching eagerly, absorbing every unintended lesson. At last her mother granted her permission to use the machine, but with a few conditions: Summer would take care of the machine properly, oiling it as needed and keeping the bobbin case free of lint, and more important, she would promise never to sneak around behind her mother's back again. "If you're going to disregard one of my rules because you think it's foolish, tell me first," Gwen said firmly. "Give me a chance to talk you out of it. Maybe after listening to what I have to say, you might decide that my advice is sound after all. Or perhaps you'll convince me that the time has come to amend a rule. It's just the two of us, kiddo. We have to be honest with each other, even if it means one of us doesn't get to have our own way. I need to know that I can trust you."

Summer thought she would burst with delight. She could use the coveted sewing machine openly, and her mother had set before her the possibility that rules could be negotiated.

Her enthusiasm for the quilt had always been high, but it positively skyrocketed once she was able to share her work-in-progress with her mom and seek her advice. But when her quilt top was nearly complete, she overheard one of her mom's quilting friends admonish Gwen that no good would come of rewarding Summer's bad behavior. Gwen brushed off the woman's warnings and said that she knew her daughter would never give her reason to regret her decision, never give her cause to mistrust.

Buoyed by her mother's trust, Summer hadn't—until she decided not to enroll in the PhD program at Penn and told her mother only after turning down their very generous fellowship. Even that seemed minor in comparison to the lies she had spewed a few months earlier as she tried to conceal that she had moved in with Jeremy. Her mother forgave her, would forgive her anything, but for the first time in her life, Summer detected a flicker of doubt in her mother's eyes when they spoke of important matters. Until then, Summer had known that she could tell her mother anything, anything, and be believed. She had not realized how much she valued that assumption of truth until it was gone.

Summer had hand-quilted the Rail Fence top in a lap hoop, thimble on her right forefinger, left hand beneath the three layers to push the needle tip back up to the top. The needle pricks stung until a callus formed, after which she could quilt for hours without tiring. All summer long she stitched, perfecting the rocking motion of the needle, adjusting the hoop when she completed a section. Sometimes she would spread the quilt out on the living room floor and stand back to admire it, delighting in the evident improvement of the size and uniformity of her stitches with practice. Her mother praised her efforts and assured her that she was a fine quilter—and not merely a fine quilter for her age, which every ten-year-old knew was the consolation prize of compliments.

August waned and the start of a new school year loomed. Summer spent the last few days of her summer vacation sewing the binding on her quilt, and on the Saturday before Labor Day, she spread it proudly over her bed, gloriously complete. She was eager to begin a new project, but before she could choose a pattern, schoolwork and friends and clubs drew her away from her mother's sewing table. Worried that she might lose the skills she had worked so hard to master, Summer occasionally helped her mother finish one of her quilts or sewed a block for a Tompkins County Quilters Guild charity project. She intended her next quilt to be a gift for her grandparents, and although she doubted she would be able to begin until summer vacation, she resolved to be prepared.

Then, in January, her fifth-grade class began a unit on pioneer life. They read the Little House books by Laura Ingalls

Wilder, built model Conestoga wagons, and took a field trip to the Bement-Billings Farmstead in the Newark Valley to observe demonstrations of hearth cooking, spinning, weaving, soap making, and blacksmithing. At the end of the unit, the students in Summer's class wrote five-page "diaries" of what their lives would have been like if they had set out from Ithaca for the West in the mid-nineteenth century. For their final project, they were also instructed to create a special project illustrating some aspect of pioneer life. Handicrafts, food products, and dioramas were acceptable choices, and since their finished work would be displayed in the classroom during the Spring Open House, their absolute best effort was expected.

For Summer, there was no question but that she would make a patchwork quilt. Since their teacher had emphasized that they were not permitted to have any parental assistance aside from the absolute necessities of driving and shopping for supplies, Summer didn't consult her mother about possible pattern selections and shushed her when she hovered nearby, suggestions on the tip of her tongue. After leafing through her mother's collection of pattern books, Summer decided upon the Dove in the Window block, since a quilt by that name appeared in Laura Ingalls Wilder's novel *These Happy Golden Years.* Library books advised her which tools, fabrics, and colors would be most appropriate for a pioneer quilt, although she did have to make an occasional compromise, such as using stainless-steel pins and needles instead of tin-plated brass. Since Laura had sewed by hand, Summer did, too, although she would have gladly attempted a seam or two on a treadle sewing machine just to see how it compared to her mother's electric version.

With only a month to complete her quilt, Summer reluctantly settled upon a six-block crib quilt rather than a full-size quilt that would have been more authentic. Knowing that all of her classmates and their parents would be inspecting her handiwork—and that the quilt counted for half of her unit grade—Summer stitched with meticulous care.

She put the last stitch in the binding at breakfast the morning the quilt was due and barely had time to admire it or look it over for stray pins or mistakes before she had to tuck it carefully into a pillow-case, snatch up her backpack, and hurry off to school.

After the last recess, Mrs. Shepley asked each student to present an oral report on his or her project. Summer's best friend had made tomato preserves; her other best friend had braided an oval rug from wool scraps. Four students had made dioramas depicting scenes from pioneer life, while one girl showed photographs of a garden she had planted of vegetables common to the frontier diet. A Popsicle-stick log cabin received mixed reviews from the class; it was well constructed and made to scale, but the builder should have used twigs since everyone knew pioneers didn't have Popsicles. Summer's Dove in the Window quilt received a smattering of applause even before she began her report. Mrs. Shepley listened, expressionless, as Summer explained why she had chosen that particular pattern and how she had sewn the quilt. Afterward, the girls crowded around her for a closer look and her two best friends begged her to give them lessons until Mrs. Shepley clapped her hands for attention and sent everyone scurrying back to their desks. She praised the class for their efforts without singling out anyone, and for the last few minutes before the dismissal bell rang, the students tidied up the room and arranged their projects on bookshelves and tables lining the walls for their parents to admire later.

At seven o'clock, Summer and her mother walked to school. Summer was so excited that she hardly took a breath between describing the other students' projects. Privately she thought hers was the best, but she knew better than to say so to anyone but her mother. After the principal's assembly in the gym, they made their way down the hall to Mrs. Shepley's classroom, where the students chattered excitedly with one another, thrilled with the novelty of seeing their friends dressed up in the evening when they would usually be at home in pajamas. Their parents wandered the room, reading class assignments posted on the bulletin board and inspecting the Pioneer Life projects. Summer almost burst with pride listening in on the admiring compliments paid to her quilt. Later, over punch and cookies in the cafeteria, Summer repeated the best remarks to her mother and wondered aloud whether she ought to enter a quilt in the next Tompkins County Quilters Guild show.

At that, her mother's cheerful demeanor clouded. "Oh, kiddo," she said tentatively, reaching for Summer's hand. "You know we might not be here then. I have my dissertation defense in June, and if I get that job at Waterford College, we'll move to Pennsylvania before autumn."

Summer's stomach flip-flopped. She had known forever that it was unlikely they would remain at Cornell University after her mother finished school, but it seemed so weird to think about living somewhere else and starting the sixth grade in another school while she sat in the familiar cafeteria of the only elementary school she had ever attended on Spring Open House night.

"Can we not talk about that right now?" she said faintly. Her mother nodded and quickly shifted the subject back to Summer's quilt and the possibility that she might enter it in a quilt show. They probably had quilt shows in Pennsylvania, Summer reminded herself, and it was possible that her mother wouldn't get that job after all.

Her oral report and the Spring Open House display had been such exciting successes that Summer almost forgot that their Pioneer Life projects would be graded. A week after the quilt's lauded unveiling, Summer received her quilt back with a slip of paper listing the criteria used to evaluate the students' projects. Most of the boxes next to phrases such as "Quality of Work" and "Period Authenticity of Work" were checked, but the box beside "Originality" was conspicuously empty. Summer barely noticed because her eye was immediately drawn to the notation written in blue marker at the bottom of the page: C.

A grade of C. Summer swallowed a

lump in her throat and quickly blinked away tears. She glanced at Mrs. Shepley, who was writing the day's homework assignment on the blackboard. Summer had never received such a low mark, not even for the book reports dashed off at breakfast, not even on the grammar tests she didn't bother to study for because the material came so easily. But to receive a C on a project she had worked so hard on for so long—it was unthinkable.

What would her mother say?

The hours between the end of the school day and her mother's return home dragged on endlessly. Numbly Summer put water on to boil for spaghetti and emptied a jar of pasta sauce into a saucepan. Then she flung herself onto the sofa and stared up at the ceiling, unable to muster up interest in any of her library books. She had supper nearly finished when her mother rushed in, breathless, book bag slung over her shoulder. "Smells wonderful, kiddo," she sang out, but she knit her brows and shut the apartment door softly at the sight of her daughter's mournful expression. "What's up? Are you okay?"

Without a word, Summer dug the grading sheet from her backpack and handed it over. Eyes on the paper, Gwen slowly pulled out a chair at the dinette table and sat down. Summer remembered dinner and although she had no appetite, drained the spaghetti in the colander and set the pasta and sauce on the table before her bewildered mother.

"I don't get it," her mother said as Summer seated herself, planted her elbows on the table, and rested her chin in her hands. "Is your teacher insane, or merely stupid?"

In spite of how awful she felt, Summer managed a wisp of a smile. "Maybe a little bit of both?"

"This doesn't make any sense." Gwen brought the page closer to her eyes and then held it out again as if perspective would change the handwritten markings. "Quality, period authenticity, neatness, promptness, oral repot, and so on and so forth—it looks like you've met every requirement. She didn't check

'Originality.' Did she mark you down because you used a traditional block instead of inventing a design of your own? But you were supposed to re-create something from the pioneer era. Did you tell your teacher why you chose the Dove in the Window block?"

"It was in my oral report," Summer said. "Maybe she missed that part."

"She definitely missed something." Gwen stretched out to set the grading sheet on the counter, dusted her hands of its distasteful residue, and forked long threads of spaghetti onto Summer's plate. "We'll get to the bottom of this," she promised, spooning red sauce onto the pasta. "Mrs. Shepley obviously made some sort of mistake. Don't worry about it."

Summer tried not to, but her stomach had a knot in it, leaving no room for supper. Her friends had received A's and "Well done!" for their tomato preserves and braided wool rug. Even the Popsicle-stick log cabin had earned a B–. She honestly thought that her quilt was as good as their projects, but maybe she was wrong. Maybe she had sewed a block in upside down, or maybe she had left a pin in the binding and Mrs. Shepley had pricked her finger. It couldn't be because she had made a crib quilt instead of something larger, since projects even smaller than hers had earned top grades. She was too heartsick to ask Mrs. Shepley herself, so she was relieved when her mother promised to call in the morning and arrange for a conference after school.

If Mrs. Shepley was as apprehensive about the upcoming conference as Summer, she gave no sign of it throughout the long school day. Summer had never felt herself at odds with a teacher before, and she wanted to shrink back into her seat and become invisible. She didn't raise her hand even when she knew the answers, but Mrs. Shepley called on her from time to time anyway, mostly when no one else volunteered. Teachers knew they could count on Summer for the right answer—at least that was how it had always been until the Pioneer Life project.

At three o'clock, as her classmates raced for the door, Summer packed up her folders and books and waited at her desk for her mother to appear. Gwen showed up right on time, knocking on the open door and smiling with perfect, confident cordiality. "Mrs. Shepley?" she said, striding to the teacher's desk and offering her hand. "Thank you for meeting with us on such short notice."

"It's my pleasure," Mrs. Shepley responded, gesturing to the only other adult-size chair in the room. She folded her hands on the desktop, unfolded them, and gave Gwen a tight smile.

Gwen nodded graciously and sat down. "I'm sure you've guessed why I requested this conference. As you know, Summer sets very high standards for herself, so she was troubled by the grade she received for her Pioneer Life project. Frankly, I am, too. After reading over your criteria, it's not clear to me exactly where Summer's quilt fell short. I was hoping you could give us more insight into your evaluation so that Summer knows what she needs to work on to do better next time."

Summer shot her mother a curious look. *That's* what this conference was about? She'd assumed her mother had come to demand a higher grade! It wasn't a question of what Summer had done wrong. Her mother knew she had done her very best.

"I'll tell you what she can do better next time," said Mrs. Shepley crisply. "She can do her own work."

Gwen blinked at her. "Excuse me?"

Mrs. Shepley's expression was a conflicted blend of condemnation and understanding. "Miss Sullivan, I'm a parent, too. I understand the temptation to offer our children all the help we can. In your circumstances, with no father at home, I'm sure the urge to ease your child's way is even more compelling. However, in the long run, you aren't helping Summer by doing her work for her. Although she might earn a better grade on a particular assignment, that's a short-term gain leading to long-term trouble."

"Hold on just a second." Gwen held up a hand, brow furrowed. "You believe I made that quilt?"

"It's rather obvious, Miss Sullivan. I'm well aware that you're a quilter yourself.

My mother quilts, also, and I know with absolute certainty that no child of eleven is capable of such painstaking work. They simply don't have the fine motor skills at that age."

Summer recognized the stormy expression clouding her mother's features and almost wanted to warn Mrs. Shepley to back off. "So," said Gwen, drawing the word out, "you think my daughter cheated."

"The evidence is in the quilt itself, but I don't place all the blame on Summer. I've been teaching a long time, and I know how difficult it can be for a child to discourage an overbearing parent from taking over a project."

Gwen choked out a laugh. "Oh, now I get it. She's not only dishonest, she's also spineless." Suddenly she stood. "You don't know my daughter at all. Summer, kiddo, stay put. I'll be right back."

Mortified, Summer clutched the seat of her chair and watched her mother storm away, longing to race after her. "My mom didn't make the quilt for me," Summer told Mrs. Shepley, her voice barely above a whisper. "She drove me to the fabric store, but that's all. I did everything else myself."

"Oh, Summer." Mrs. Shepley regarded her with the same knowing, judgmental look she had turned on Gwen. "You're such a good student. You didn't need to resort to this. If you needed more time, you could have come to me. We could have worked something out."

"She didn't help me," Summer repeated, just as her mother stormed back into the classroom carrying the tote bag of hand-piecing projects she kept in the car for those occasions when she found herself stuck in a waiting room at the doctor's office or DMV.

"Let's conduct an experiment, shall we?" Gwen emptied the contents of the tote bag on Mrs. Shepley's desk and beckoned Summer forward. "Kiddo, show us what you can do with this."

Summer took a deep breath and approached the desk.

Mrs. Shepley shook her head. "This really isn't necessary—"

"On the contrary, it is." A hard glint lit

Gwen's eyes. "You've accused my daughter of cheating, and she's entitled to an opportunity to defend herself."

As Mrs. Shepley sighed and sat back in her chair, Summer chose two diamonds and a square from her mother's scraps. Threading a needle, she estimated the quarter-inch seam allowances and joined the two diamonds along one side, doing her best to make small, even stitches with trembling hands. Then she finger-pressed the seam and set the square into the angle between two adjacent points of the diamond pair, sewing one side down, pivoting the pieces, and stitching the other side into place.

"I could have done better if I had pins," Summer said anxiously, smoothing the finished quarter-star between her hands before placing it on the desk. "And if I had marked the seam allowances."

"It's fine as it is," Gwen declared. "It lies flat, the points meet, the stitches are secure. Given the circumstances, this is excellent work." She fixed her gaze on Mrs. Shepley, daring her to disagree. "I don't have any batting or finished tops in my bag. Should I have Summer bring her lap hoop to school tomorrow to prove to you that she quilts as well as she pieces?"

"That won't be necessary." Mrs. Shepley rose, her mouth in a hard line. "Your demonstration has told me quite enough."

"Then Summer can expect an amended grade?" When Mrs. Shepley gave a curt nod, Gwen returned a grim smile and began to pack her tote bag with the scattered quilt pieces and notions. "Thank you. Also, as much as I regret taking a confrontational stance, I must add that I'll be watching carefully for any hint of retaliation against my daughter. I'd hate to have to take my concerns to the principal."

With that, Gwen shouldered her tote bag, seized Summer's hand, and marched from the room. Summer had to jog to keep up with her.

"I don't know what bothers me more," Gwen muttered as they left, their footsteps echoing off the lockers in the empty hallway. "That she thinks you're a cheater, or that she thinks you're a lousy quilter."

Summer knew her mother was only attempting a dark joke. It was much, much worse to be a cheater. A poor quilter could improve her skills with practice, but a liar was always a liar.

A few days later, Mrs. Shepley gave Summer a new grading sheet as she passed back spelling quizzes. She had raised Summer's grade to a B–. Her mother was outraged and threatened to call the principal, but Summer convinced her to let it go. She had so much extra credit saved up that even a B– wouldn't affect her final mark in social studies. She didn't want to make any more trouble.

"If your final grade is anything less than it should be," her mother glowered, slipping back into her Kentucky accent as she always did when particularly outraged, "you better believe I'll make trouble."

She didn't need to. For the rest of the semester, Mrs. Shepley was careful to give Summer exactly the marks any objective observer would say she deserved. Though Mrs. Shepley rarely called on her unless she was the only student to raise her hand, and while her replies to Summer's comments lacked any warmth or friendliness, Summer considered that a small sacrifice for her vindication. If Gwen regretted coming so swiftly and so adamantly to her daughter's defense, she never admitted it, although once, as they talked regretfully about Mrs. Shepley's chilly turn, Gwen apologized for putting Summer in an uncomfortable situation.

"You didn't do anything wrong," Summer exclaimed. "You know what's uncomfortable? Having my teacher think I'm a cheater. Why didn't she ask about the quilt on the day of the oral reports? Why did she give me a bad grade with no reason? If you hadn't come for that conference, we still wouldn't know that I got a C because she thought I cheated. I would just have a bad grade and a teacher who secretly thinks I'm a cheater, and who probably tells all the other teachers to watch out for me."

"Let's hope for a modicum of teacher-student confidentiality," said Gwen, but they both knew there was nothing they could do to counter gossip in the teachers' lounge. Surely all of Summer's previous teachers would know better than to believe any disparaging remarks Mrs. Shepley might utter, but what about teachers who didn't know her?

It came as a relief, then, when Gwen burst through the apartment door one afternoon, swept Summer up in a hug, and announced that she had been offered a position as an assistant professor of American Studies at Waterford College. Summer would miss her friends, but she was eager to set upon a path that would lead to a fresh start—especially since the winding way to the rural Elm Creek Valley in central Pennsylvania would bring her two hundred miles closer to her grandparents' house in Brown Deer, Kentucky.

Gwen had known Summer had made the Dove in the Window quilt entirely on her own because she had witnessed Summer's progress from choosing the pattern to putting the last stitch into the binding, but even if she had not, she would have taken Summer's word for it.

Now, too often, Summer knew her mother wanted corroborating evidence, even though she wouldn't ask for it. It was wrong to lie, but daughters did not always—could not always—tell their mothers the whole truth of their lives and risk hurting them, disappointing them. Gwen would argue that she and Summer were so close that the ordinary rules did not apply to them, but Summer had come to believe that even though she *could* tell her mother anything, it was not always the wisest or the kindest choice.

From I-80 west Summer and Jeremy followed I-90, which fed directly into the city. They reached the Stony Island Avenue exit at a few minutes after six o'clock in the evening, slowed by rush hour traffic. They drove north, making their way through the south side of Chicago, checking the street signs carefully as they drew closer to their destination. With every block, Summer sensed

Jeremy's rising tension at the sight of graffiti, boarded-up shopwindows, and litter in the median strips. "Urban blight," he muttered. "This doesn't look anything like the photos in the school catalogs."

"We're not there yet."

"We're close enough for it to matter. Don't ever walk around at night alone, understand?"

Summer eyed him, not exactly sure how to interpret his tone. They were both too road-weary to discuss safety issues without arguing, so she merely replied, "I won't take any unnecessary chances."

He relaxed somewhat as they reached the campus and recognized the grassy midway and stately Gothic architecture so familiar from photos on the University of Chicago website. "This is more like it," he said, turning north onto Woodlawn Avenue.

"It's no worse than New Haven," Summer said, more defensively than she intended.

"Maybe you should get a dog. A big dog, like a rottweiler."

Summer let the remark pass unacknowledged, instead reading aloud from
her printouts and directing Jeremy to an
apartment building near Kenwood and
56th. A friend from high school had put
her in touch with a cousin who was
studying for a PhD in Comparative Reli-
gions at the Divinity School. Her name,
appropriately enough, was Julianne Ab-
bot, and she had offered the couple a
place to stay during their visit. In a witty
e-mail, Julianne had warned Summer
that the accommodations would be
nothing fancy, but they were free and
the residents were friendly. Summer accepted her offer gratefully and hoped to
coax Julianne away from her studies
long enough to question her about the
best places to search for an apartment
of her own.

A young woman who looked to be in
her late twenties answered Summer's
knock and introduced herself as Julianne. "You're just in time for dinner,"
she said, beckoning them inside. She
wore her straight brown hair short, her
bangs pulled to the side by a small,
white plastic barrette. Her two room-

mates, Maricela and Shane, called out greetings from the galley kitchen, where Maricela was stirring something fragrant and spicy in a large stock pot while Shane set the table with mismatched plates and glassware.

"Set two more places," Julianne sang out, hooking her arms through her guests' and escorting them into the living room. "Have a seat."

"Thanks," Jeremy said, and sat down on a futon with a blue denim cover. Summer was tired of sitting and stood instead, taking in her surroundings. The apartment had one large common area with half walls separating the living room, kitchen, and dining area, and at opposite ends of the room were two doors that likely led to bedrooms. Since Summer would be on her own, she wouldn't need a place as large as this one. She hoped they wouldn't think it rude if she asked how much they paid in rent.

Over a delicious Moroccan vegetable stew—Summer's friend must have warned them about her preferences—the three roommates offered Summer

an animated overview of grad school
life, Hyde Park's restaurants and shops,
and the wonderful cultural amenities to
be found in Chicago. "Most museums
and theaters offer student discounts in
the unlikely event you find some free
time," said Shane with an ironic grin.
"They're still expensive for anyone sub-
sisting on a graduate student stipend,
though."

"Once you move in, we'll show you
around Hyde Park," Julianne promised.
"We know all the best happy hours
within walking distance. You can buy
one drink and fill up on tapas."

"Don't forget bookstores," said
Maricela, adding in a confidential tone,
"Seminary Co-op. Best academic book-
store ever."

"I've heard of it," said Summer. "My
mom sent along a shopping list."

The subject shifted to Summer's
housing options, and she soon realized
that she should have begun her search
much earlier. Sensing her dismay, Julianne assured her not to worry. "Someone's always looking for a new roommate or someone to sublet," she said.

"Take a walk around campus tomorrow and check the kiosks for posted flyers. Don't bother with newspapers. Most students aren't willing to pay for an ad anyway."

"You can always stay with us for a while, if you're desperate," said Shane, and his roommates chimed in their assent.

Despite her fatigue from the long drive, Summer was too excited to sleep. Maricela opened a bottle of wine and they stayed up late, talking about politics, music, books—the conversation flew and darted from one topic to another and back. When they finally bade one another good night, Summer lay down upon the futon while Jeremy flopped, exhausted, onto the air mattress Shane had set up on the living room floor.

"I think I'm going to like it here," said Summer, still feeling Jeremy's goodnight kiss on her lips. He mumbled a sleepy reply, and soon the rhythm of his breathing told her he had fallen asleep.

In the morning, Summer and Jeremy studied a campus map over a breakfast of bagels and coffee. Before heading out to the Div School, Julianne highlighted blocks and street corners where they were most likely to find decent apartments. "Take their paperwork with you and think it over," she advised. "Don't feel pressured into signing a lease until you've had a chance to see what's out there."

Forewarned, Summer and Jeremy set out. Summer was just as eager to see the campus as she was to find a place to live. The leafy quads were verdant with late summer foliage, an oasis of green in the midst of the city. Gargoyles glared down from the rooftops at a few students tossing Frisbees back and forth or listening to iPods on shaded benches. "They're thinking, 'Get back to work, slackers,'" Jeremy said, and Summer laughed.

When they came to the Social Sciences Research Building on 59th Street, Summer tested the doors and, given that it was a Saturday morning in August, she was not surprised to find them locked. "Pity," she remarked. "I was hoping to look around the history department, maybe meet some professors or other grad students."

"You'll get your chance at orientation. Hey, look." Jeremy indicated a kiosk at the intersection of two sidewalks on the other side of the quad, a stocky may-pole of fluttering leaflets. Just as Ju-lianne had promised, the posted flyers included advertisements for available sublets and requests for roommates. The bottom edges of the pages were cut into a fringe of contact information, and on most of them, at least half of the paper rectangles had been torn off.

"I don't know if we should bother with the ones that so many other people have already looked into," Summer said uncertainly. "Surely someone must have taken those by now."

Just in case, they weeded out the list-ings that exceeded Summer's budget, divided the remaining numbers, and settled down on the grass with their cell phones. An hour later, they had a list of four likely prospects, which were fortu-nately close enough to campus for them to visit on foot. The first two were habit-able but expensive, the third reeked of cabbage and had unidentifiable garbage in the stairwell, and the fourth seemed tolerable except that it was in a basement, with bar-covered slits for windows high against the ceiling and peeling paint on the walls.

"Lead-based, I'll bet," Jeremy said in an undertone, eyeing the paint chips suspiciously as the landlord showed them around. In the kitchen, Summer tested the stovetop and found only one functioning burner.

"Best of all," the landlord declared triumphantly, "no cockroaches! The mice eat them all."

"Well, that's just swell, honey," Jeremy said to Summer in a perfect parody of a suburban husband from a 1950s sitcom. "You've always wanted pets."

The landlord thrust a sheaf of documents at them. "This place will go fast. I'm showing it to three other students this afternoon. I can't hold it for you unless you sign and put down a deposit."

"We'll let you know," said Summer, taking Jeremy's arm and nearly dragging him to the door. "Unbelievable. What if I can't find anything in Hyde

Park? I don't want to have to worry about transportation. I should have checked Craigslist ahead of time. We could have had pages of places to see."

"Do mice really eat roaches?" Jeremy inquired as they hurried up the basement steps. "Because maybe spiders are taking care of the roaches."

Summer shuddered. "I really don't need to know."

Outside, she propelled him down the block until they came to another kiosk, but most of the postings were identical to those they had found on the main quad. "Maybe I don't have to find my own place," she said, fingering some of the flyers. "I could answer some of these requests for roommates instead."

Jeremy looked pained. "Do you really want a roommate, though?"

"Why not? I could end up with someone like Julianne and those guys. It might be fun."

"Yes, but—" Jeremy ran a hand through his unruly curls, a habit she knew meant he was carefully choosing the words that would follow. "You didn't even like living with me. Three people in a small apartment is already crowded. Wouldn't that be a little . . . awkward when I come to visit?"

Summer grinned. "I'm sure we can be discreet."

"That's not what I meant," said Jeremy. "It would be easier if you didn't have roommates that I would have to worry about inconveniencing. Even houseguests as charming as I am can wear out a welcome."

"How often were you planning to visit?"

He shrugged. "As often as I can, of course. Since I'm ABD and have a car, it'll be easier for me to visit you than the other way around."

"Jeremy—" Summer did not know quite what to say. "I don't want you to fall behind on your dissertation because you're driving back and forth to Chicago every weekend."

"I wasn't thinking every weekend. Maybe once a month."

Even that was more than Summer had expected. "I won't hold you to that, but okay, let's not give up on apartments just yet." She searched the nearest kiosk with renewed resolve. The postings were several layers deep, and as she took down an announcement for a concert that had occurred the week before, she found a flyer advertising a one-bedroom garden apartment near 58th and Blackstone for five hundred dollars a month.

"Either the location sucks or that price is missing a digit," said Jeremy.

Summer quickly checked the map. "Fifty-eighth and Blackstone is right here in Hyde Park."

"Then that price definitely has a typo."

Summer convinced him that it was still worth checking out, so they made their way back toward campus, turned east on 58th, and followed Blackstone south until they reached their destination: a four-story red-brick building with a small garden in front and a narrow driveway running through the alley along the north side of the building.

"If the apartment looks as good as the building it's in . . ." Summer shook her head, unable to believe her good fortune. "How could a place this perfect still be available?"

"It probably isn't, unless there's something seriously wrong with it," Jeremy warned as Summer pulled open the glass door to the front enclosure, spotted an intercom, and scanned the names for the correct buzzer. There was no button for the first floor, oddly enough, and the contact name on the flyer belonged to the fourth-floor resident. The landlord, she guessed, and pressed the button.

After a lengthy pause, the intercom crackled. "Yes?"

"Hi. Is this Dr. Mayer?"

"Yes, 'tis."

The man sounded elderly and British, but maybe that was just the static from the old speaker, which looked to be original to the building. "I saw your flyer and I was wondering if the first-floor apartment is still available?"

"It's occupied at the moment but it will be free at the end of the month."

"Perfect timing," Summer said. "Do you mind if I take a look around?"

"I'll be down shortly," Dr. Mayer said, and the intercom went silent.

Jeremy had followed her into the glass enclosure, about the size of two telephone booths. "Summer," he said, "if something seems too good to be true—"

"I know." She heard slow footsteps descending wooden stairs on the other side of the front door, along with a solid thumping sound she couldn't place. Then the door opened and a stout man who looked to be in his sixties joined them outside, wheezing slightly and supporting himself on two canes.

"I'm Summer Sullivan," she introduced herself. "I hope this isn't a bad time."

"Not at all." Dr. Mayer offered his hand and a pleasant, red-faced smile. "I rang the current occupant, but he didn't answer, so he must be on campus. He won't mind if we pop in." He gestured with one of his canes, indicating that Summer and Jeremy should precede him outside. "Your entrance is on the other side, down the alley."

As they made their slow progress

around the building, Dr. Mayer explained that the building had three flats, with one condo on each floor starting with the second story. Most of the first floor was a large storage area for the upstairs residents, with one long corridor linking the garages at the rear of the building to the side entry. "Which is your only entry," he remarked, unlocking a single door that opened into a tiny foyer. To the left was a tight, narrow staircase, with only four steps up to the first landing. Pointing with his right cane, Dr. Mayer noted a door directly opposite the entrance, which led to the storage area and corridor, and to a door on the right, the apartment. "Originally this was the super's residence," he said, finding the appropriate key from among many on a large ring and unlocking the door. "My wife and I bought it many years ago, and as a bit of university service, we keep the rent down so that a student might afford it." Just as Summer and Jeremy were about to follow Dr. Mayer into the apartment, he stopped short, blocking the doorway. "You are affiliated with the university, I presume?"

"I'm entering the graduate program in history this quarter," Summer said.

"Very good." Dr. Mayer beckoned them inside, into a surprisingly spacious kitchen with linoleum and appliances that looked as if they had not been updated in decades. "I'm a professor at the Pritzker School of Medicine and a cardiologist at the university hospital. Usually I offer the apartment to a medical student first, but I suppose a young lady from the humanities will do. Those bars on the outside of the windows are very secure, my dear, very secure, but you should always lock your door nonetheless."

"Of course," Summer replied, ignoring Jeremy's pointed look. As far as her safety was concerned, he seemed to have found an ally in Dr. Mayer.

The apartment ran half the length of the building, with the kitchen doorway opening into a living room. On the opposite side of the room, a small hallway led past a full bath and ended at the bedroom door. The place was functional, with worn hardwood floors and pipes along the ceiling, painted radiators, and an ancient tub. The current occupant was from overseas and would probably sell Summer his furniture for a reasonable price, since he would not want to take it with him. The rent included all utilities, except for cable, as only the upper stories were wired for it.

"Speaking of the rent," said Jeremy, "is this place seriously five hundred dollars a month?"

"My wife and I don't believe in gouging students." Dr. Mayer briefly indicated the direction of and distance to the nearest coin laundry, bank, and grocery store, then turned a beatific smile on Summer and Jeremy. "Shall I run upstairs for a copy of the lease? You'll need time to read it over and think on it; it won't do to have you sign anything this moment. If you do decide to take the flat, I'll need to collect some financial information, you understand, but we shan't worry about that today."

"I'd appreciate the lease, thanks," said Summer, quickly adding, "take your time."

They followed Dr. Mayer to the foyer, then went outside to wait in the alley while he returned upstairs for the lease. "I hope he understood there's no rush," Summer said. "When he said 'run upstairs,' I had this horrible vision of him tripping over a cane and breaking his neck."

Jeremy braced his foot against the red-brick building and yanked on each set of bars in turn. "No one's getting in through these windows," he said. "I think you should take it."

"It will mean a long way to haul a laundry basket, especially in winter."

"Maybe you can befriend one of the upstairs neighbors and use their washer and dryer."

Summer couldn't count on that. "There's no cable hookup, and that means no high-speed Internet access. I'm having withdrawal pains just thinking about it."

"Maybe one of the neighbors has a wi-fi network you can tap into, or you can check your e-mail on campus."

"That's another maybe," Summer countered, "but I can't beat the location or the price."

She wished they had another day to

search. She hated feeling pressured to rush into a decision without giving herself ample time to see what else was out there. Still, what if that meant losing a perfectly decent apartment out of longing for a perfect apartment that might not exist?

She might be better off to play it safe and forget about the possibilities that might—or might not—be waiting around the next bend in the road.

When Dr. Mayer returned with the documents, Summer promised to review them promptly and give him her decision as soon as possible. When he replied, regretfully, that he couldn't promise to hold it for her, she assured him she understood. She and Jeremy thanked him for his time and bade him good-bye.

"We can look over the lease at Julianne's tonight," Jeremy said as they headed north on Blackstone in search of an early dinner, since they had missed lunch. "If everything looks good, we could sign it and bring it back to Dr. Mayer tomorrow."

"We could sign it?" Summer teased.

"I meant you."

"I know." She laced her fingers through his. So far, the former super's flat was the uncontested front-runner in the apartment campaign. It might be a very bad mistake to leave Chicago without signing Dr. Mayer's lease.

She could always wash her clothes by hand in the sink.

Near the corner of Blackstone and 57th, Jeremy pointed out an Italian restaurant called Caffe Florian and easily convinced Summer to give it a try, since she knew he had been craving a slice of real Chicago-style pizza ever since they had left Pennsylvania. Inside, where the exposed red-brick walls were adorned with framed posters of Impressionist art in pastel hues, they sat in mismatched chairs at a rather dilapidated table and shared the best spinach and artichoke heart deep-dish pizza with whole-wheat crust that Summer had ever tasted.

It did not, however, seem to be what Jeremy had had in mind. "You know what would make this even better?" he asked, helping himself to a second slice. "Pepperoni."

Summer made a face. "You're deliberately provoking me, aren't you? I bet
Anna could make a tofu stir-fry even you
would enjoy."

"No doubt, but not everyone can
cook like Anna."

Summer finished her pizza and asked
the waiter for a refill of iced tea. "I think
I'm going to sign the lease."

"Really?" Jeremy looked as pleased
as if he were the one who had made the
lucky find. "You will read it first, though,
right?"

Summer assured him she would, later
that evening at Julianne's.

They continued to explore Hyde Park,
searching rental office windows in vain
for vacancy notices until by unspoken
agreement they shifted into mere sight-
seeing. They stopped by the Seminary
Co-op Bookstore, where Summer found
several books on Gwen's shopping list
and a biography and political analysis of
Abraham Lincoln to read on the way
home. At the university bookstore, Summer bought herself a T-shirt in the official school color, maroon, and chose

two tiny University of Chicago onesies for Sarah and Matt's twins.

Then they made their way back to Julianne's apartment building, where they read Dr. Mayer's lease carefully as they waited on the stoop for her or one of her roommates to return and let them in.

Maricela was the first to come home. Apologizing profusely, she berated herself for not giving them the extra key. "We thought you'd be gone all afternoon," she explained, preceding them upstairs to the third floor. "Does this mean you've had good luck? Did you find a place?"

Summer described the apartment and how they had come to find it, a story she repeated when Shane returned, and again for Julianne. "What a marvelous discovery," Julianne said. "I'm almost jealous."

"I'm in the med school," mused Maricela, smiling. "Maybe Dr. Mayer would let me have it instead."

"No," exclaimed Julianne, seizing her forearm. "You're staying. Don't you dare make me find yet another roommate.

One never knows what horrors may ensue."

Everyone chuckled, even Jeremy, who raised his eyebrows at Summer as if to say that he was not alone in recognizing the hazards of taking on a roommate.

"Didn't I say that letting her look for a place might backfire?" Julianne asked her roommates, her tone suddenly losing its merriment.

"You can still ask her," said Shane. "It gives her another option. She can always say no."

"Ask me what?" said Summer.

After exchanging a look with her roommates, Julianne said, "Here's the thing: Shane graduates in December and he's moving out. We were going to start looking for someone to take his room, or maybe two someones, but by that time, everyone will have their housing arranged for the year."

"The only students looking for new places in December are the most antisocial who can't get along with their current roommates," Shane said. "I can't in good conscience foist someone like that on these wonderful, considerate women."

They rolled their eyes. "You're still not getting out of the ten bucks you owe us for groceries," Julianne teased. "We're immune to your charms by now."

Summer pretended not to notice Jeremy's deepening frown. "It sounds great, but I need a place for the end of September."

"The futon wasn't that bad, was it?" said Maricela. "Wouldn't it do for one quarter, considering that you'll be at the university for at least six years?"

Julianne smiled, encouraging and hopeful. "I know we just met, and I know we might seem a little crazy, but my cousin says you're cool and from what I've seen, we'd get along great. Won't you think about it?"

"The rent's three hundred a month, plus one-third of the utilities," Shane added. "There's a coin laundry in the basement open to residents only and you can pay extra for a parking space, but there's a waiting list a mile long."

"That doesn't matter. I don't have a

car." Summer felt her heart lifting. "It sounds great. Really, it does."

"You don't have to decide tonight," Julianne said, but her expression told Summer she hoped she would. "We're not going to start advertising until October because otherwise we'll be having people wanting to move in at the start of the quarter."

"We don't offer our futon to just anyone," said Shane.

"I'll definitely think it over," said Summer. She was so glad they had asked her, so relieved to have an option to weigh against Dr. Mayer's apartment. "Thanks. Thank you so much."

Early Sunday morning, Shane brought back pastries from a bakery called Medici on 57th. Julianne made coffee, and after breakfast, she gave Summer a copy of the lease. "Think about it, and if you're interested, sign it and send it back," she said. "But send me an e-mail as soon as you decide, so I can stop stressing."

Summer promised she would.

By nine o'clock, Summer and Jeremy were driving through Hyde Park, past the Museum of Science and Industry, along the western shore of Lake Michigan, following their maps and Julianne's handwritten directions to I-90 east.

They spoke little as they left Illinois except to note exit ramps and lane changes. Summer scanned the two leases, comparing clauses, and imagining herself in one apartment versus the other. When they crossed the Indiana border, Summer slipped the leases into her backpack, knowing she had already learned as much as she would from them, and she could not choose her course based upon objective facts alone.

"I keep thinking," she said, as Jeremy's car sped east along the interstate past rolling farmland, "that I might be less homesick if I started graduate school with three friends already."

Jeremy was silent for a moment. "They'll still be your friends even if you don't live with them."

"I know, but it wouldn't be the same."

"Dr. Mayer's apartment is closer to campus, and it would give you more privacy."

She imagined trudging home from the library, backpack full of books and study notes, and unlocking a door that opened into a quiet kitchen with a single chair pulled up to a table, or alternatively, a room alight with cheerful banter and the fragrances of spicy Moroccan stew. "Maybe too much privacy."

Jeremy drew in a breath and slowly let it out. "I know you're leaning toward Julianne's place, and obviously it's your decision because you're the one who's going to live there. But Summer—" Jeremy hesitated. "I'm going to finish my dissertation in a few months. I'll be leaving Waterford, but I can't guarantee that I'll find a job in Chicago."

"I wasn't expecting you to," said Summer, startled. "You should take the best job you can find, no matter where it is."

"I'm just saying that we might not be in the same town for years." Jeremy flexed his hands around the steering wheel, and if he weren't driving, Summer knew he would absently run his fingers through his curly dark hair, framing his next words carefully. "If you had your own place, it would be *our* place, at least when I visit. And it will probably be a long time until we can have more than just visits, until we can work things out so that our paths lead us to the same city." He gave her a rueful half smile. "I'd settle for the same state."

An ache filled Summer's chest, and she lay her hand on his leg. "There are so many colleges and universities around Chicago. One of them is bound to need a new assistant professor of history within the next year."

He closed his right hand around hers, eyes on the road ahead. "Or a postdoc. That could hold me over until you get your degree, and then we could plan our job searches together."

"That would work," Summer agreed, resting her head on his shoulder.

They drove along in silence, neither of them mentioning how unfair it was to ask Jeremy to delay his own career while he waited for Summer to complete her education, or how unlikely it was that when that day came, they would find a single history department with two available tenure-track faculty positions for newly minted PhDs.

The candle had traveled halfway around the circle when the door to the manor swung silently open and Summer stepped out into the twilight of the cornerstone patio. Sylvia watched as she made her way around the periphery of the circle of quilters—who were unaware of the newcomer, rapt by the sharing of confidences and hopeful expectations for the week ahead—to her mother. The mother and daughter shared a long embrace and a few inaudible whispers before Summer broke away and went to murmur something in Anna's ear. When their new chef nodded, Sylvia guessed that Summer had told her that Jeremy was waiting in the kitchen to take her home after the Candlelight welcoming ceremony. Sylvia was surprised, but pleasantly so, when Summer took a seat beside her mother instead of racing back to her boyfriend.

Then again, they had just spent many hours together in a very small car. Perhaps it was no surprise that for the moment, Summer preferred to enjoy the open air, the night sky, and the company of friends. The Elm Creek Quilters had missed her more than her short absence warranted because it had offered a bittersweet taste of what was to come.

If only pursuing her goals would not lead Summer so far away from them.

Choosing fabrics for Summer's section of the Winding Ways quilt had been a simple task of pairing contrasting shades of the young woman's beloved Amish solids. Summer's blocks were the first Sylvia had completed, for she had anticipated Summer's departure long before the young woman announced her intention to return to school. She had assumed that Summer might leave with Jeremy after he completed his degree at Waterford College, but Sylvia was no longer certain that they would walk side by side through life. Now she suspected that their paths would diverge, though they might try to prevent it or to pretend, for a time, that they still followed a single road together. Sylvia knew they loved each other and she hoped for their sakes that she had misread the signs. Perhaps all would be well. Perhaps Jeremy and Summer would find their relationship strengthened by the tests of time and distance.

Sylvia knew that if they were meant to be, the winding ways they followed would meet again, somewhere near the horizon.

Diane

Diane backed out of her garage, noting with some surprise the two newspapers lying at the end of the neighbors' driveway. Usually Mary Beth was up at dawn to walk her yappy little Pomeranian and she picked up the paper on her way back. When the Callahans went on vacation, the fastidious Mary Beth never forgot to stop newspaper and mail delivery until the morning of their return. Mary Beth had many faults—and Diane was capable of listing them in great detail—but forgetfulness was not one of them.

Then again, Mary Beth had been distracted lately. She believed that her son, Brent, was the victim of a great injustice, and Diane's cheerful wave as she drove past on her way to Elm Creek Manor renewed the insult each and every morning. All summer long, Mary Beth's perfect son had worked for Diane's former troublemaker, a reversal of fortune neither of them could have imagined a few years before. Brent's official employer was Elm Creek Quilts, but Michael had been placed in charge of the young vandals working off their sentences. If Brent put in only a half-hearted effort, it was Michael who ordered him to do the work over. If Brent showed up late, it was Michael who met him in the back parking lot and informed him that he could skip his lunch hour or stay after, but he would make up the time.

How it must be *killing* Mary Beth to know that Michael was Brent's boss— and would be every summer until the debt to Bonnie was paid. Diane almost felt sorry for her, but then she remembered the look of pure devastation on Bonnie's face as she waded through the wreckage of Grandma's Attic, and her heart hardened. No punishment would suffice for the young men who had shattered her friend's dream. Diane only wished that their parents could have been sentenced, too.

Mary Beth, most of all, would be well served by a lesson in humility. When Diane reflected upon the long history of their mutual antipathy, a clear trend emerged: Believing herself superior to all around her, Mary Beth always got her own way through intimidation and bullying. That was why, Diane concluded, though she and Mary Beth were long-time neighbors, they could never be friends.

Diane's roots in the Elm Creek Valley stretched far deeper than Mary Beth's, for she was born and raised in Waterford, the daughter of a chemistry professor and a homemaker. She could have attended Waterford College for free thanks to the tuition waiver for the children of faculty, but at eighteen she was restless for change and she begged her parents to let her apply elsewhere. It was no less of a journey for all that she chose the University of Pittsburgh, little more than 150 miles from home. She thrived in the city, on the friendships she formed with other girls in her sorority, and, if she'd had her way, she would have stayed in college forever. Since the university frowned on that and her parents would pay for only the standard four years, Diane did enough to pass her classes and earn her teaching degree. She hadn't planned to return to her small hometown after graduation, but on a weekend visit home, two factors conspired to make the path back to Waterford very attractive: She heard a rumor that the middle school needed a new sixth-grade teacher, and her father brought home to dinner the newest member of the chemistry department faculty, a cute assistant professor named Tim Sonnenberg.

Shortly after their second anniversary, Diane and Tim bought a charming home a few blocks south of campus in a neighborhood populated by Waterford College professors and administrators. The gray stone house with a sloped roof and Tudor woodwork backed up to the Waterford College arboretum, insuring lots of shade and privacy. It was only after Mary Beth's family moved in four years later that their domestic tranquility was shattered.

Diane had tried to be friendly to her new neighbors and took over a plate of lemon squares after the Callahans moved in. She understood that Mary Beth was busy unpacking and wasn't miffed when her new neighbor didn't invite her in to chat. But the very next week, Diane returned from the grocery store to discover to her horror that Mary Beth had dug up a row of forsythia bushes Diane had planted the previous spring. Mary Beth claimed that according to the lot survey the former owners had shown them, the bushes were actually on the Callahans' side of the property line. "I had no idea they were yours," Mary Beth exclaimed, her eyes wide with innocence. "What were they doing in our yard, I wonder?"

Even after Diane called the county and paid for a new survey that confirmed the property line was precisely where the Sonnenbergs had always thought it to be, the damage was done. Worse yet, Mary Beth planted some sort of berry bush in place of Diane's forsythia, and the birds who feasted on the tiny blue fruit dropped obnoxious thank-you cards all over the Sonnenbergs' red-brick patio. For two months Diane grimly hosed off the splotches every morning until realization smacked her in the face: Mary Beth's berry bushes were on Diane's property. Berating herself for her oversight, Diane pruned back the bushes, dug up the stumps, and raked the whole mess onto the Callahans' lawn. The next day, Mary Beth left a terse letter in Diane's mailbox demanding reimbursement for the berry bushes. Diane responded with an invoice for new forsythia bushes and soil mix. Mary Beth never paid.

Even so, Diane felt victorious, never suspecting that she had won only the first battle of an interminable war.

When Diane's son and Mary Beth's became best friends in the second grade, the women's husbands, who got along just fine, fervently hoped that their wives would seize the opportunity to resolve their differences. Instead, they exercised their dislike in subtler ways, and Diane, at least, tried to keep their sons out of it. Diane almost didn't join the Waterford Quilting Guild when she overheard at Grandma's Attic that Mary Beth had been elected president, but since that would have been exactly what Mary Beth wanted, Diane joined anyway. They avoided each other within the larger group, and Diane befriended other guild members who, like her, stayed well outside the periphery of Mary Beth's inner circle. After a few years of feeling like an outsider in her own guild—and hearing that others felt the same—Diane decided to run for guild president.

If she had known she was trampling on nearly a hundred years of tradition, she might have kept her mouth shut. Or maybe not, because under Mary Beth's leadership, the guild had become cliquish and moribund, inviting back the same handful of local speakers every year, running the same block swaps, and hanging the same quilters' works at quilt shows, showing little variation from one year to the next. The guild's creativity had so stagnated that Diane could predict with unfailing accuracy which guild members would bring what dishes to the holiday socials and potluck picnics.

The guild desperately needed change, so perhaps even if Diane had known that incumbents and popular nominees were always allowed to run uncontested, she might still have asked Gwen to nominate her. Mary Beth would have struck back with the same ferocity either way. Diane had refused to be intimidated, even when Mary Beth unfairly used her time at the microphone during guild meetings to promote her own campaign. When Diane protested and asked to be granted equal time, the guild voted to allow each candidate to make a campaign speech on the evening of the election. Diane used her time onstage to emphasize that new leadership would bring a change of pace and fresh ideas, and that if she were elected, she would invite better speakers, direct new workshops, and spend members' dues more frugally and with more accountability. When it was her turn to speak, Mary Beth kept her remarks unexpectedly brief. She described the accomplishments of her previous terms and then, "for the benefit of my opponent, who may not be aware of what is required of the president," she read the president's official duties from the bylaws, punctuating each line with a gesture or facial expression meant to show how unqualified Diane was for that particular task.

"The president shall prepare the agenda for and preside at quilt guild meetings and shall direct such meetings in a pleasant and professional manner." A tentative bite of the lower lip, for everyone knew Diane was the reigning queen of sarcasm.

"The president shall appoint committee chairpersons and coordinate the activities of all the committees." A worried intake of breath, for Diane could barely keep her purse organized.

"The president shall be authorized to cosign checks on behalf of the guild." Eyebrows arched warily, for Diane rarely managed to pay even her own member dues on time.

"The president shall appoint an ad hoc committee to help coordinate all necessary activities for producing a quilt show." A helpless shake of the head. "Oh, honestly, ladies, need I go on? Would any of us feel comfortable entrusting our beloved Waterford Summer Quilt Festival to someone who has never won a ribbon?"

A murmur of dismay swept through the crowd, breaking on the island of motionless calm that was Diane's friends. One of them squeezed her shoulder, a brief gesture of encouragement, but Diane knew she had lost before the first ballot was cast. She realized then that the guild would never change, and that it would never fulfill its potential to be a fun, energetic, and meaningful group, enriching its members and benefiting the community. So she dropped out of the guild, and her friends left with her. Mary Beth and her cohorts quickly spread rumors that Diane had blackmailed her friends into leaving, and in the frenzied speculation about what dirt Diane might have had on them, everyone forgot the legitimate points Diane's campaign had raised about problems that threatened the guild's long-term survival.

Mary Beth never forgave Diane for stirring up so much conflict and threatening her position. Diane didn't care. As the years passed, she found more pleasure with the Elm Creek Quilters than she ever had known with the Waterford Quilting Guild—and fresh, new reasons to dislike her next-door neighbor. Once Mary Beth hung wind chimes outside her kitchen window that rang and clanked and banged with the slightest breeze so loudly that Diane and Tim couldn't sleep at night unless they shut every window facing the backyard. When Mary Beth refused to take them down, Diane researched city noise ordinances, discovered that Mary Beth was risking a fine, and threatened to turn her in. Mary Beth took her revenge two years later when the Sonnenbergs built a skateboard ramp in their backyard, unaware of codes restricting recreational construction in their historic neighborhood. Mary Beth was not content to merely threaten Diane; she filed a complaint with the city, who ordered the Sonnenbergs to dismantle the ramp.

Their most recent spat occurred when

Mary Beth refused to announce the Elm Creek Quilters' request for help with Sylvia's bridal quilt, even though many members of the guild knew Sylvia personally and would have gladly contributed a block. Indignant, Diane snuck into a guild meeting, lured Mary Beth away from the podium with a fake cell phone call, and made the announcement herself. The guild members were so upset that Mary Beth had refused the invitation without consulting them that she was eventually forced to resign. Mary Beth's youngest son, Brent, became so enraged that he stole Diane's keys to Grandma's Attic and destroyed the shop in a misplaced act of revenge, a twisted act of defending his mother's honor.

Brent had aimed for Diane, but he had struck Bonnie. It was so unfair, so wrong, that Diane wished her friends were sterner taskmasters. Working at Elm Creek Manor was hardly punishment enough; the vandals performed the same duties as Diane's own two sons, only less competently and without pay. If it had been up to her, she would have sentenced them to hard time.

How could anyone take their punishment seriously if it went on hiatus at the end of the summer? Already it was the last week of camp, with only one more week until the juvenile delinquents who destroyed Grandma's Attic would be temporarily released from their commitment. One more week for Brent, Will, and Greg to learn a valuable lesson, if they let themselves, and one more week for Diane's own sons to earn spending money for the upcoming school year. One more week—Diane choked back a tearful sigh—until Diane and Tim would load up the car and drive their youngest son to Princeton.

It seemed only five minutes ago that Todd had been running through the sprinkler, learning how to ride a bike without training wheels, reading comic books under the covers with a flash-light—and now, before she could catch her breath, he was leaving for his first year of college. She was so proud of him she thought her heart couldn't con-tain all she felt, but it pained her to think of his empty room, his empty chair pulled close to the breakfast table. She liked to joke about how their grocery bill would plummet, how she would no longer have to do laundry three times a week; in truth, she would gladly fill her hours with the tedious chores she had spent the last twenty years decrying if it meant her boys were home again, and that everything was still ahead of her.

How was she supposed to fill the hours once the boys were out of the house, after quilt camp ended for the summer and she had no place to go each morning? Once she would have asked Bonnie for extra shifts at Grandma's Attic, but with the quilt shop gone, Diane faced a long, cheerless, empty winter, counting the days between Todd's visits home. At least Michael, a junior at Waterford College sharing a rented house downtown with a few other students, would continue his weekly visits home to do his laundry and have supper with his parents, so she would not feel entirely abandoned. But what of the other six days of the week?

"Get a life," Diane muttered aloud as she pulled into Agnes's driveway. Suddenly it occurred to her that that was exactly what she needed to do. It wasn't her sons' responsibility to give her meaning and purpose. That was *her* job. She could sit around and mope, or she could plot a new route for herself, following one of the shaded footpaths she had glimpsed in passing as she faithfully trod the well-traveled road of motherhood. Now she would have more time for herself and for Tim, for Elm Creek Quilts and for her friends. Wasn't that what she had always said she wanted?

Why didn't the prospect of so much freedom cheer her?

Agnes emerged from the house and waved, her blue eyes cheerful behind her pink-tinted glasses. "Last week of camp," she declared, smiling, as she settled into her seat and buckled herself in. "What a summer it's been. So much change, so much upheaval."

"So many good-byes," Diane grumbled, setting out for Elm Creek Manor. "With more to come."

"Oh, Diane," said Agnes sympathetically. "I know you're going to miss Todd."

"That's the understatement of the month." Yes, he would come home for school breaks, but she would not pretend things would be the same. Todd was setting forth upon a one-way journey from home into the greater world, and she doubted he would be content to settle down in Waterford afterward as she had done. He would soon come to think of his childhood home as his parents' home, and himself a welcome visitor within it as he built a wonderful life for himself elsewhere.

And this was what she wanted for him, although it meant a loss to herself.

"You and Gwen should talk," Agnes said. "You're both sending children off to school, and I imagine you're both feeling a sense of loss. You could help each other through it."

"Gwen doesn't really know what I'm going through," said Diane. "She had Summer around a lot longer than I had Todd."

"I suppose you're right. You're suffering much more than Gwen is." Agnes's voice carried a trace of amusement. "Even so. You have Tim at home, and Michael is still in Waterford, for now. Gwen is on her own."

"Gwen isn't on her own," said Diane. "She has the Elm Creek Quilters."

And so did Diane.

The Elm Creek Quilters who lived in the manor joined the campers for breakfast, but those who lived elsewhere usually arrived after the meal was finished, just in time to prepare for their first classes of the day. Diane had time to stop by the kitchen to fill her favorite mug with coffee before meeting her Beginning Piecing students in the apple orchard. When the weather was fair, Diane couldn't stand to be shut up within four walls, so she and her students would spread old blankets on the ground and hold their class in the shade of the leafy boughs. Her students reveled in the relaxed, casual atmosphere of her outdoor classroom. At this time of the year, crisp, ripe apples dangled temptingly overhead as they practiced their running stitches or learned how to sew curves. Sylvia allowed her guests to eat as many apples as they liked, and after class, most of Diane's students returned to the manor with an apple in hand and an extra tucked inside a tote bag for a friend.

Diane enjoyed teaching beginning quilters—but not, as her friends teased, because they were the only campers whose skills did not surpass her own. She enjoyed encouraging them to take their first tentative stitches and shared their glow of accomplishment when they competed their first hand-pieced blocks. She knew she had a way of teasing the fear out of them when they were reluctant to try something that seemed too difficult. She found respite in the slower pace, the attention to fundamental skills, the wisdom that came in being absorbed by the process of the craft, rather than seeking the quickest route to the end product. Gathering novices around her in a circle in the shade of the apple trees, Diane felt connected to generations of women before her who had passed along their knowledge and wisdom, affection and encouragement. This, she believed, was the essence of Elm Creek Quilts, the fostering of community the heart of their mission.

Her own initiation into the quilting world had embraced these principles, for she had been fortunate to find a patient teacher with a gift for clear explanations and gentle critiques. If her virtuous teacher had known why Diane had suddenly become so determined to learn, however, she might have given her stubborn pupil a scolding along with her lessons.

Her mother had quilted, and her mother before her; Diane could only guess how many other quilters claimed even higher branches on her family tree. Even the kindly lady who babysat her, Agnes Emberly, knew how to create soft, snuggly quilts with the most beautiful appliquéd flowers Diane had ever seen. Yet somehow, growing up surrounded by quilts and the women who made them, Diane had not had the slightest inclination to learn to sew. Why should she invest months or years into making a single quilt when so many other people were happy to make quilts for her?

She was grown, married, and the mother of two before the urge to quilt seized her. One summer day, Agnes, who had become a trusted friend, invited Diane to accompany her to the Waterford Summer Quilt Festival. Diane's sons, nine and eleven at the time, were off at day camp, so she gladly accepted.

In the sunny library atrium, quilts of all descriptions hung in neat rows from tall wooden stands. Quilters and quilt lovers alike strolled through the rows, admiring patchwork and appliquéd pieces both large and small, in every attractive color combination imaginable, and a few that Diane thought should have been left to the imagination. She and Agnes viewed each quilt in turn, reading the program for the artists' names and their thoughts on their work. Quilt guild members wearing white gloves mingled through the crowd, ready to turn over an edge so onlookers could examine a quilt's backing, where the fine quilting stitches appeared more distinctly than on the patterned top.

Although Agnes was too modest to consider herself a master quilter, she had built up an impressive store of knowledge over the years, and whenever Diane lingered before an especially remarkable work, Agnes murmured an analysis of its pattern, design elements, and construction techniques. With Agnes's help, even Diane's inexpert eye could distinguish between a truly challenging pattern that tested the maker's skills and one that merely appeared difficult, but could be assembled rather easily if one knew the technique. Diane learned how subtle variations in color and contrast added intriguing complexity to relatively basic patterns, and how uninspired fabric choices detracted from otherwise technically masterful quilts.

Some of the quilts were just plain bizarre. "I could have made that," Diane said, loudly enough for Agnes to hush her. "Look at all those threads she forgot to trim. Your flowers are always perfectly smooth."

"I do needle-turn. This is raw-edge appliqué," murmured Agnes. "It's a particular technique."

"I get it," said Diane. "Do something badly and fend off criticism by calling it a technique."

Agnes took her by the elbow and steered her away from the quilt. "The artist or her best friend or her mother might have been standing right behind you."

Before Diane could protest that if the quilter didn't want feedback she shouldn't have entered her quilt in a show, she stopped short, captivated by a stunning quilt at the end of the aisle. It was a simple arrangement of twenty-four blocks in six rows of four, with a narrow blue inner border framed by a scrappy pieced outer border. She did not recognize the pattern, which resembled a star with a square in the center overlying a cross. The horizontal and vertical crossbars seemed to create a woven net that captured the sparkling stars. But it was the quilt's colors that charmed her the most. What at first glance appeared to be simply reds, blues, and greens actually ranged in each color from a soft pastel to the true, clear hue. The colors were restful to look upon, contented and happy, as if the quilt knew a reassuring secret that it meant to share.

"It's simply gorgeous," said Diane, soaking in the peaceful feelings the quilt inspired.

"It certainly deserves that ribbon," Agnes remarked.

Diane tore her gaze from the quilt and spotted the purple "Viewer's Choice" ribbon affixed to the tall post supporting the quilt stand. Above it was the placard announcing the title of the quilt, "Springtime in Waterford," and the quilt-maker's name.

Diane's heart flip-flopped. "You've got to be kidding me."

"What? What's the matter?" asked Agnes.

Diane couldn't speak. It couldn't be true. It was inconceivable that her mean-spirited troll of a next-door neighbor could have created such a delightful quilt. "Someone mixed up the names," she managed to say.

"Don't be ridiculous," said Agnes. "They take good care to make sure mistakes like that don't happen. Even if they had, someone would have noticed well before now and corrected the sign."

Diane stared at Mary Beth Callahan's name for a moment in utter disbelief before stalking off down the next aisle. "She only won that ribbon because she's popular," she muttered, even though she knew it wasn't true. "Notice how the quilt didn't win any technical awards?"

Agnes would have none of it, and in a voice barely above a whisper, she insisted that Diane sweeten her sour temperament or they were going home. Diane was tempted to remind Agnes that she wasn't her babysitter anymore, but she hated to see the older woman so distressed, so she promised to cheer up and keep her editorial comments to herself.

A few days later, Diane was in her backyard moving the sprinklers when Mary Beth stepped out onto her deck to refill her bird feeders. "Hello," Diane called after a moment. Her neighbor eyed her warily before offering a nod in reply.

Diane stepped clear of the hose and drew closer to the row of forsythia bushes that marked the boundary between their yards. "I saw your quilt at the show in the college library," she said. "It was beautiful. Congratulations on winning a ribbon."

"Thanks," said Mary Beth warily, as if waiting for the punch line of a nasty joke.

"It must have taken you a long time to make."

"Naturally you assume I'd have to struggle to make a prizewinning quilt."

"That's not what I meant. It just looked like a difficult pattern."

Mary Beth set down the bag of birdseed and tied off the opening. "It's not that hard if you know what you're doing."

"What's that block called, anyway?" asked Diane. "I never saw my mom or her friends make anything like it. I wish I could."

"You?" Mary Beth burst out laughing. "Oh, Diane. I knew you were up to something, but I still didn't see that zinger coming. Go ahead, get all your quilting jokes out of your system. I can take it. Oh wait, let me guess the first one. 'Where's your rocking chair, Grandma?' That was it, right?" Mary Beth shook her head and slung the burlap bag over her shoulder.

"I don't have any quilting jokes," said Diane, irritated. "I mean it. I'd love to be able to make something as beautiful as that quilt."

Mary Beth studied her, eyebrows lifted in skepticism. "Jeez Louise, Diane. I thought you said your mother was a quilter."

"She was."

"Then you ought to know you aren't cut out to be a quilter, no pun intended."

Diane tried to tamp down her rising ire. "And why is that?"

"It takes patience to be a quilter. Patience and perseverance. Attention to detail—and let's face it, you're practically allergic to details. But it's more than just that. Those things can be learned with practice and willpower. You also need—" Mary Beth gazed speculatively somewhere past Diane's shoulder before fixing her with a patronizing, sorrowful smile. "You need the soul of an artist."

"And you think I don't have one," said Diane. "That soul-of-an-artist thing."

"Exactly." Mary Beth made her way around the side of her house to the garage, the heavy bag on her shoulder giving her the appearance of an overdressed thief making off with stolen goods.

Diane stood watching her go, fuming, until a gust of wind dashed her with cold spray from the sprinkler. Storming back into the house, she kicked off her wet shoes in the foyer and padded to the phone. She dialed Agnes's number, and before her old friend could begin the usual exchange of pleasantries, Diane begged her to teach her to quilt.

She'd show Mary Beth who had the soul of an artist. She'd learn to sew circles around that wretched woman, and one day she'd wave a handful of Best of Show ribbons beneath her nose and watch gleefully as Mary Beth melted into a puddle of envy. Diane used to teach middle school, for crying out loud. If she didn't know patience and perseverance, she never would have made it through student teaching.

That was her plan, but it didn't quite work out that way.

Agnes was so delighted that Diane had finally "caught the quiltpox" that she didn't ask why Diane suddenly, urgently needed to learn to quilt. Agnes probably assumed that Diane had been inspired by the glorious display at the quilt show, and it wouldn't have been completely dishonest to claim that was so. Diane didn't dare reveal her true purpose. Agnes strongly disapproved of the ongoing battle of wills between the two neighbors, and she might have ended the lessons rather than contribute to the tension.

But Diane soon discovered that anger could only sustain her so long. Under Agnes's gentle but unyielding tutelage, Diane's hunger to prove herself better than Mary Beth disappeared, to be replaced by a genuine love for the traditional art form. The infinite diversity of possible combinations of color, pattern, and arrangement appealed to her desire for variety, and Agnes charmed her with folk tales of block patterns and their curious names. Once Diane had gained a passing facility with piecing and quilting by hand, Agnes offered to show her how to transfer those skills to the sewing machine so that she could assemble her blocks and tops more quickly. Recalling Mary Beth's accusations that she lacked patience, Diane flatly refused. "True quilts are made entirely by hand," she declared, threading a needle.

"Why on earth would you say that?" asked Agnes, genuinely baffled. "Women have been making quilts by machine for as long as there have been sewing machines."

"True quilters don't cut corners. They enjoy every stage of the process and don't want to rush through it."

Agnes shook her head, exasperated. "You've become very opinionated where quilting is concerned. You're almost as bad as—"

"Who?" demanded Diane, fearful that she would name Mary Beth.

"Someone who tried to teach me to quilt, many years ago. Never mind. You don't know her."

Only years later, after Sylvia returned to Elm Creek Manor and reconciled with her formerly estranged sister-in-law, did Diane learn enough about their shared history to conclude that Diane had reminded Agnes of Sylvia. Diane found the comparison rather flattering. Sylvia was a strong-willed Master Quilter with exacting standards, someone Diane would do well to emulate. Why had Agnes phrased the comparison as criticism?

At the end of class, Diane and her students gathered their things and returned to the manor for lunch, greeting Gretchen's husband, Joe, as they passed the barn. He was sanding an old chair Matt had brought down from the attic. Back in Ambridge, Joe had run his own small business, restoring old furniture and designing custom pieces. Diane thought the Hartleys' move to Elm Creek Manor had signaled Joe's retirement, but apparently Sylvia's attic held enough worn but reparable antiques to keep him busy for years to come. With any luck, his search for bureaus and bedsteads would uncover more of the Bergstrom family's heirloom quilts, or perhaps a journal or two.

Inside the banquet hall, mingling with friends and students as she made her way from the buffet to her usual table, Diane gathered scraps of news and bits of gossip she had missed by spending the morning outside. Gwen was nowhere to be found, and after asking around a bit Diane remembered that it was the last week of August, classes had resumed at Waterford College, and Gretchen had cut back her camp schedule to two evening programs and a Friday afternoon seminar on color theory. Sarah's morning sickness had subsided and she looked much better for it, but she was upset about her mother's reaction to the news about the twins and brooding over some disagreement from years before, something about a cherished quilt lost in childhood. Judy had called the office that morning to announce that their Internet connection was working at last and that she was planning to buy a webcam so they could have video chats. In Chicago, Summer had found two great apartments and faced the difficult task of choosing between them. Anna had offered to cater a housewarming party at Bonnie's new apartment, but when asked to suggest a date, Bonnie offered only vague replies. Agnes was querying everyone about cell phones and service plans, because, she said, she was sick of wondering what important phone calls she might be missing while away from home.

"That's why you have an answering machine," Diane pointed out.

"Yes, but then I have to hurry home to check it," Agnes said, impatience creeping into her voice. "What if it's urgent?"

Diane couldn't imagine what urgent calls Agnes might receive. Elm Creek Quilt Camp was only days away from wrapping up for the season, so there wouldn't be any work emergencies demanding her immediate attention. News from her daughters and grandchildren, though important, probably couldn't be classified as urgent. Still, to humor her friend, Diane answered her questions and offered to help her choose an affordable plan if Agnes decided to go through with it.

"Do you need a ride home?" Diane asked Agnes as they cleared away their lunch dishes. Diane usually went home after her last class to have supper with her family and returned to Elm Creek Manor later for the evening program. Agnes often preferred to remain behind to dine with the campers and rode home with Gwen after the evening's events concluded.

"I think I'll stay," Agnes said. "Are you coming back for the talent show?"

Diane hated to miss it, but Todd had few evenings home left, and they had a million things to do before his departure for Princeton. "I have too much to do at home," she said. "I'm not even sure if I'll make it to the Farewell Breakfast on Saturday."

"But it's the last one of the season," Agnes protested. "You shouldn't miss saying good-bye to your students—and to Summer. Saturday's her last day. We might not see her again for months."

Diane shook her head. "Judy's farewell party was hard enough. I don't know if I can say any more good-byes."

"Oh, Diane." Agnes gave her a fond embrace. "For you, every silver lining has a cloud, doesn't it? None of these good-byes are forever. Come to the Farewell Breakfast. If it makes you feel better, instead of 'good-bye,' say 'until we meet again.' You'll see Judy again, and Summer, and of course you'll see Todd often. All of us will follow different paths for a time, but we'll reunite somewhere down the road, probably sooner than you realize."

"I hope you're right."

"I'm certain I am." Agnes held Diane at arm's length, smiling. "In the meantime, to make the separation easier, don't dwell on tearful good-byes. Think about the fortuitous meetings and all the joyful times that followed. That is what really matters, not how you said good-bye."

"As long as you say good-bye some-how," said Diane, disguising wistfulness with a quip. "You've convinced me. I won't miss the Farewell Breakfast. I wouldn't want to repeat Gwen's mistake."

Agnes glanced worriedly across the banquet hall, where Gwen and Summer sat engrossed in conversation at an empty table. They seemed oblivious to the time, to the room emptying around them. "I know Gwen regrets how she and Judy parted," Agnes said, "but I hope she knows that one mistake can't tarnish their friendship. One forgotten good-bye doesn't make the day they met any less memorable."

"Well, that would be impossible, wouldn't it?" retorted Diane, and Agnes laughingly agreed. None of the Elm Creek Quilters would ever forget the day Gwen and Judy met.

It was a Saturday, Diane recalled as she drove home later, alone. It was a cool, sunny day like so many others, crisp with the first hints of autumn, only a few splashes of yellow and red lighting up the forested mountains sheltering the Elm Creek Valley. Agnes had volunteered to coordinate the Waterford Quilting Guild's annual charity raffle quilt, and Diane had agreed to help her select fabrics. They strolled downtown to the quilt shop on Main Street, enjoying the sunshine and the respite from the summer humidity, window shopping, and discussing Agnes's plans for the quilt.

The quilt shop was only minutes away, on a busy block right across the street from the Waterford College campus. The red-and-gold GRANDMA'S ATTIC sign hung above the door next to a large front window with an enticing display of quilts, fabric, books, and notions. A bell on the door tinkled merrily overhead as they entered, and the owner, Bonnie Markham, called out a greeting from the cutting table in the center of the room. Music played softly over hidden speakers—hammered dulcimer, guitar, violin, and flute—and somewhere Diane smelled coffee brewing. She recognized the stout auburn-haired woman setting bolts of wild geometric prints on the table for Bonnie to cut; her name was Ginny or Gwen or something, and she was a professor at the college. Diane sometimes overheard her at guild meetings offering interesting historical anecdotes about some aspect of the quilting arts or making fairly astute observations about the work of their invited speakers, but she invariably spoiled her remarks with some liberal claptrap that set Diane's teeth on edge. If not for that, Diane might have spoken to her, maybe even asked her for some advice about color selection because she certainly had a distinctive style. The woman's daughter, a very pretty teenager who often accompanied her mother to guild events, waited for her turn at the cutting table, two bolts of vivid Amish fabric in her arms, one deep black and one bright blue. Her name was a warm-weather month—June or April or May, or something. If it were something weird like October or January, Diane would have remembered. She seemed bright and friendly, confident and fun, the kind of girl Diane sought out for babysitting. It was unfortunate that she would very likely grow up to be a hippie like her mom.

Diane followed Agnes as she wandered through the aisles, comparing different bolts of fabric to a floral swatch she had brought from home. When Agnes found a fabric she liked, she pulled the bolt from the shelf and gave it to Diane to carry. Twice—once in the pastel solids aisle and once in children's novelty prints—they passed the only other customer in the shop, an extremely pregnant woman of Asian heritage carrying a patchwork crib-size quilt top draped over her left arm. She was so slender everywhere but around the middle that Diane marveled how she managed to stay upright. Every so often she winced and rubbed her tummy, but whether the baby had given her an especially hard kick or if she could not find the perfect backing fabric for her top, Diane could not say. Either reason would have justified that pained expression, especially since the woman seemed to be running out of time if she meant to finish that quilt before her baby arrived.

Soon Diane's arms were loaded with bolts of bright, cheerful, warm colors with a few darks thrown in for contrast. The mother and daughter had moved on to the cash register, where they paged through magazines and chatted while waiting for Bonnie to finish cutting fabric for the expectant mother. "I couldn't decide," the woman confessed after asking Bonnie to cut two yards each from the three different bolts of primary color prints. "It would be so much easier if I knew what my baby will like. Balloons or safari animals? Trucks or dolls? I want her to snuggle up with this quilt for many years to come, so it can't be anything she'll tire of quickly."

"Babies love bright colors," said Agnes, as she and Diane lined up behind her with their bolts. The expectant mother turned around, eager to hear more. "Any of these fabrics you have here will do nicely."

"Go with the animals," Diane advised. "All kids love animals."

"Do you think so— Ouch," the woman

interrupted herself with a gasp, and after a long moment in which the others watched her with alarm, she took a deep breath and smiled, embarrassed. "I know one thing this kid doesn't like: the cranberry scones at the Daily Grind. She's been active all morning."

"You must have a future soccer star in there if her kicks hurt that much," said Bonnie, unrolling the second bolt.

The woman shook her head and placed a hand on her lower back, setting her purse and quilt top on the cutting table. "It's not the kicks; it's those Braxton-Hicks contractions. They've never been this bad, and they've been getting worse all day."

Diane and Agnes exchanged a worried look. "Do you mean worse in intensity or worse in frequency?" Diane asked.

"Both—" She drew in another sharp breath and steadied herself against the cutting table. When she could finally speak, she gazed down at her abdomen and panted. "All right. I get the message. No more cranberry scones."

"That was five minutes apart," said

Bonnie, answering Diane's unspoken question. "Four minutes, tops."

Agnes took the expectant mother gently by the arm. "Why don't you sit down, dear? May we call someone for you?"

The woman shook her head, her obsidian black hair slipping gracefully over her shoulder. "Really, I'm fine," she said, just as her water broke. Diane jumped out of the way, too late to save her shoes.

Bonnie snatched up the phone. "I'll call nine-one-one."

"That's not necessary," the woman said through clenched teeth. "I'm fine."

"You're in labor," said Diane, incredulous, pointing to the pool of evidence slowly spreading on the floor.

"Is everything all right?" said the hippie mom, joining them at the cutting table.

"Everything's fine," said Agnes soothingly, leading the panting pregnant quilter to a chair. "This young lady is about to have a baby."

"Here?" asked the hippie's daughter, eyes widening. "Now?"

"Looks that way." Diane dumped Agnes's fabric bolts on the cutting table and hurried over to help Agnes ease the pregnant woman into the seat. Diane recognized the look of apprehensive disbelief in her eyes and did not envy her, even knowing the joy that would follow the pain. She said a silent prayer for a safe delivery—and the world's fastest ambulance driver.

"I can't be in labor." The woman clutched the armrests so tightly that her knuckles went white. "My baby isn't due for three more days."

Diane snorted, but the hippie quilter knelt on the floor beside the woman's chair. "This is your first baby, isn't it?" she asked.

The woman nodded.

"You've taken a prenatal class or two?"

Another nod.

"Then you know a baby is full term at thirty-seven weeks." The hippie quilter smoothed the woman's silky hair away from her face and took her hand. "Your baby's coming."

The woman shook her head, tearful. "But I haven't finished her quilt yet."

"The ambulance is on the way," said Bonnie, hanging up the phone. "Judy, is there anyone else you'd like me to call?"

"My husband." Judy recited the digits between gasps. "That's his cell phone number. He's in Harrisburg covering the state senate hearings. Labor takes longer for first babies, right? He'll make it in time?"

"Traffic should be light at this time of day," the hippie quilter replied.

Diane exchanged a glance with Agnes and saw that she, too, realized the hippie quilter had not really answered Judy's question. She strongly suspected that Judy had been in labor—and in denial—for hours already.

"I left a message on your husband's voicemail," said Bonnie, hanging up the phone. "I gave him the shop's number, too, in case you can't answer your cell."

"He probably had to turn it off in the capitol building," Judy said, her voice breaking. "I can't believe this. The one day I really need him—"

"Is there anyone else?" asked the hippie's daughter. "Your mom, maybe?"

Judy shook her head. "She's in Philadelphia. Steve and I moved to Waterford only a few months ago. It's just the two of us for hundreds of miles. If he misses the birth, I—I'll—I don't know—"

"He'll get the message," the hippie mom said. "Just relax. Everything's going to be fine."

Together they kept Judy as calm and as comfortable as possible until the ambulance pulled up to the front of the shop in a frenzy of flashing lights and pealing sirens. The two paramedics cheerfully and reassuringly took Judy's vital signs, radioed ahead to the Elm Creek Valley General Hospital, and escorted her outside.

"Wait." Judy threw a desperate look over her shoulder to the hippie quilter. "Come with me. Please? In case Steve doesn't get back in time."

"Me?" The hippie quilter glanced at her daughter. "I don't—"

"Go ahead, Mom." April (May? June? Diane couldn't recall) scooped up Judy's purse and passed it to her mother. "I'll walk home. Let me know what happens."

"Let us all know," Bonnie urged. "Call me at the shop as soon as you have any news, okay, Gwen? Judy, if your husband returns my message, I'll send him straight to the hospital."

Judy and Gwen departed with the paramedics, and for a moment, the others stood watching in stunned silence.

Then Bonnie sighed. "I'll get the mop. Please watch your step."

"Too late," Diane muttered under her breath, frowning at her ruined shoes.

As Bonnie disappeared into a utility room at the back of the shop, Agnes shook her head worriedly. "I do hope she'll be all right. The poor dear seemed so frightened. I hope her husband arrives before the baby does."

"My mom will take good care of her," the auburn-haired teen said.

Suddenly the phone rang, but only muffled clatters and thumps came from the back of the store. Diane shrugged, reached over the counter, and snatched up the phone. "Grandma's Attic," she said. It wasn't Judy's husband, just a customer inquiring about the brands of sewing machine needles the shop carried. Diane checked the shelves and read off the names, and she was just hanging up when Bonnie returned with a mop and a wheeled bucket of soapy water. "Sorry about that," said Diane, indicating the phone. "I thought it might have been the father-to-be returning your call."

"No need to apologize," said Bonnie. "You handled that like a pro. I should hire you."

Everyone chuckled except for Bonnie. "You're not serious," said Diane, stepping out of the way of the mop. "Are you really offering me a job?"

"I could use some part-time help around here, and you're one of my best customers."

"Would I get an employee discount?"

Bonnie smiled, stuck the mop head into the wringer, and yanked the lever. "I think we could work something out."

"Let me think about that." Diane would need to work around the boys' schedules, but why not? It might be fun. She imagined Mary Beth's reaction on her next shopping trip when she discovered Diane behind the cutting table, wielding the rotary cutter deftly, dispensing sage advice to novice quilters and experts alike. Yes, she thought, working at Grandma's Attic sounded like a wonderful idea.

"She's waiting until you finish cleaning up that mess before she signs on," said Agnes.

"I am not," Diane retorted over the others' laughter. "I was just mulling it over. Besides, Bonnie's almost done."

"At least Judy hit the linoleum instead of the carpet," said Bonnie with a sigh, wheeling mop and bucket back to the utility room.

"Oh my gosh, you guys, look," said the hippie girl, pointing to a forlorn bundle of fabric on the floor beside the cutting table. "She forgot her quilt."

Agnes gingerly reached for it, pinching two adjacent corners with thumbs and forefingers and holding the crib-size top out at arm's length. Diane recognized the pattern, for Agnes had made one of her granddaughters a Baby Bunting quilt several years earlier. It reminded Diane of the Grandmother's Fan block, with a quarter-circle wedge in one corner and four fan blades radiating outward, but the blocks were arranged so that one fan curved into the next, creating a winding design over the entire surface of the quilt. The clear, bright colors reminded Diane of a bowl of fresh berries—reds, purples, greens, blues, and golden yellows. The curved pieces made it a more complex pattern than any Diane had ever attempted, so Judy obviously knew her way around a needle. Then Diane spotted the soiled blocks along the bottom edge, and she groaned.

Agnes looked as dismayed as Diane felt. "Do you suppose this will come out in the wash?"

"I doubt it," said Bonnie, returning to the cutting table, where she folded Judy's cut yardage, set the pieces aside, and placed the bolts on a cart for reshelving. "What a shame to see such lovely handiwork ruined."

"It looks salvageable to me," said Agnes. "Only those three blocks in the lower corner and those little sections of the border are stained. I'm sure Judy's skilled enough to manage the repairs."

The hippie girl brightened, but Diane shook her head. "It's not a question of skill. She's a new mother. It would have been difficult enough for her to finish a perfect quilt top with a newborn baby to care for. Trust me, picking out stitches and redoing blocks will fall to the bottom of her list of priorities."

"We could do it for her," the hippie girl said. When the older quilters exchanged dubious looks, she persisted, "Why not? If you each make one block, I can do the border, and if my mom were here, I know she'd volunteer to machine quilt it."

"Heirloom baby quilts should be quilted by hand," said Diane, without thinking that it might commit her to the project.

"If you insist." The hippie girl smiled and jerked her thumb in the direction of the classroom at the back of the store. "We can use the store's standing frame instead. Right, Bonnie? It's a small quilt. We could finish it in an afternoon."

"I suppose so," said Bonnie. "Judy

bought the fabric for the top from Grandma's Attic, and I know I have some yardage left over I'd be happy to donate."

"And I can donate the batting," Agnes declared. "Count me in for a block, and save me a seat at the quilting bee."

"Better make that two," said Diane. "One for you and one for me. There's no way I'm going to spoil this quilt with my first attempt at this pattern. I've had a lot of practice picking out stitches. That'll be my job."

And so it began.

Bonnie rinsed the lower half of the quilt top in the utility room sink, and while it dried, Agnes, Diane, and Summer—for that was her name, not a month but a whole season—searched the aisle for the fabrics Judy had used. While Diane carefully picked out the stitches with a new seam ripper Bonnie donated to the cause, Agnes created templates by placing tracing paper over one of Judy's finished blocks and transferring the penciled outlines to sturdy card stock. They worked in the classroom at the back of the shop, chatting and sharing quilting tips, with Bonnie occasionally bounding from her seat to assist a customer. Once, when she was busy ringing up purchases at the cash register, Diane smoothly stepped in to cut yardage for another customer. "You're hired," Bonnie said as they both returned to the classroom. Diane accepted, figuring they could sort out the details about wages and work schedules after the crisis had passed.

Judy's husband never returned Bonnie's message, but Gwen called shortly before the shop closed to report that Judy was dilated to ten centimeters and Steve was by her side, holding her hand. "That's wonderful," said Bonnie, quickly repeating the news to the others. "Please tell Judy our thoughts are with her. Do you want to speak to Summer?"

Everyone heard Gwen's exclamation of surprise upon learning that her daughter was still hanging out at the quilt shop. Summer quickly got on the line and told Gwen about their aspirations to finish the Baby Bunting quilt before Judy left the hospital. "You're assembling the top, Mom," she told her mother cheerfully. "I'll meet you at home with the blocks and the borders."

"I'll send you home with some spare fabric, just in case," Bonnie called out.

Summer's eyebrows rose. "Seriously? If you keep giving everything away, you're going to go bankrupt."

Everyone laughed—even Summer's mother on the other end of the line—because it was unfathomable that Grandma's Attic would not always be a haven for quilters throughout the Elm Creek Valley.

Working on Judy's project had kept Bonnie from her usual duties, so Diane, Agnes, and Summer helped her tidy up and race through her closing tasks. She flipped the sign in the window to CLOSED and locked the door only ten minutes late, and then she bade them good-bye, inviting them to meet her back at the shop at noon the following day. Bonnie and Agnes had finished their blocks, so Summer tucked them carefully into a Grandma's Attic shopping bag with the border section she had pieced and the undamaged section of the quilt top. "My mom and I will put the top together to-night," she called over her shoulder as she hurried off down Main Street. "See you tomorrow."

The next day, Diane and Agnes re-turned to Grandma's Attic to find the quilt frame set up in the back of the store, backing fabric and batting already in place. Soon Gwen and Sum-mer arrived with the finished quilt top—the repairs indistinguishable from Judy's handiwork—and the happy news that Judy had given birth to a beautiful, healthy baby girl. The joyful announce-ment lifted their hearts and invigorated their hands, so their needles swiftly flew over the Baby Bunting quilt, silver flashes darting swiftly in and out of the soft cotton, threads drawing the lay-ers together, giving depth and dimen-sion to the meandering patchwork paths. Their conversation, too, darted from one topic to another as shared in-terests emerged, the distances between strangers bridged. Diane was pleasantly surprised to discover how much she had in common with each of the other women—even Gwen, who turned out to be fairly reasonable for a left-wing wacko, and an exceptional quilter who graciously shared her knowledge. She imagined Gwen was mulling over similar revisions to presumptions about her.

Several hours later, after the last quilting stitch was tied off and the quilted top removed from the frame, the quilters broke for supper at the Bistro, a popular restaurant a few blocks down Main Street, to rest their hands before binding the quilt. As they ate, they debated how to deliver the finished quilt to Judy. Summer and Gwen wanted to take it to her at the hospital, so Judy could cuddle the newborn in its soft folds on the trip home. Bonnie pointed out that the baby would probably not be bundled up in a quilt, but rather buckled into a car seat, and Agnes thought they ought to wait a week and deliver the quilt to Judy's home after she and the baby had settled in. Diane recommended wrapping up the quilt and leaving it anonymously on Judy's doorstep, in case she didn't like what they had done to her quilt. "That way she won't know whom to blame."

Everyone laughed, and Gwen in-
toned, "Oh, what a tangled web we
weave, when first we practice how to reveal that we took over another quilter's
project without her permission." They all
laughed again, but the cheerful sound
quickly faded. None of them had considered that perhaps Judy would have
preferred to finish her first child's crib
quilt entirely on her own, regardless of
how long it took.

"Maybe we should have stopped with
taking out the ruined parts," said Summer.

"It's too late now," said Diane, sipping
her iced tea. "Anyone want to second
my motion that we leave it on her doorstep at night when no one's watching?"

Gwen, who knew Judy better than
any of them thanks to their bonding moments in the hospital, assured them that
Judy didn't seem the type to rage because they had violated her artistic in-
tegrity. The quilters eventually decided
to deliver the quilt to her in person the
following afternoon and accept whatever thanks or blame they deserved.

Sitting in a rocking chair near the window, her precious daughter slumbering in her arms, Judy looked up in astonishment when the quilters she had scarcely known two days before rapped softly on the open door. She beckoned them inside and, in whispers, introduced them to her husband, sleeping on the sofa, and her daughter, Emily, a beautiful girl with delicate features and a shock of silky black hair. Gwen eagerly offered to hold Emily while Judy opened her gift— and to Diane's eternal relief, Judy gasped with delight, her eyes filling with tears, as she unfolded the lovely quilt. "It's beautiful," she murmured, embracing each of them in turn. "It's the most wonderful gift I've ever received. I don't know how to thank you—for this, for everything."

If Diane had known that she was surrounded by the women who would become her most cherished friends, she would have kept a souvenir of the occasion: her hospital visitor name tag, perhaps, or a group photograph. But none of them suspected that they would greet one another like long-lost friends at the next quilt guild meeting, or that Summer would join Bonnie and Diane on the staff of Grandma's Attic, or that they would form a quilting bee called the Tangled Web Quilters inspired by Gwen's remark over dinner at the Bistro, or that a few years later, they would quit the Waterford Quilting Guild as a show of support for Diane, one of their own. How could they have known they were living one of the most important days of their lives, that they had just met the women whose friendships would help shape the women they would become?

Sometimes Diane wondered where she would be if Agnes had not invited her fabric shopping that morning, or if Gwen and Summer had left Grandma's Attic before their arrival, or if Judy had gone into labor any other day. She would be bereft of the most important friendships of her life, and she would never know it. Elm Creek Quilts might still have been created, but Diane would not have been a part of it. What if she had never learned to quilt? What if she had missed the aisle where Mary Beth's quilt proudly hung at the Waterford Summer Quilt Festival, or what if she

and Mary Beth had been cordial neighbors instead of bitter enemies? Diane
might have admired the lovely quilt, paid
her neighbor a few friendly compliments
over the forsythia bushes, and forgotten
it a few days later. She certainly would
not have been driven to learn to quilt, in
which case she would not have asked
Agnes for lessons, would not have
joined the guild, and would not have
been in Grandma's Attic that day helping Agnes choose fabric for the charity
raffle quilt.

In a sense so true it pained Diane to
consider it, she owed Mary Beth a deep
debt of gratitude for all the good that
had ever come to her through quilting.

The undeniable truth of her debt
nagged her all the way home. She
passed the two desiccated newspapers
at the end of Mary Beth's driveway on
the way into her own garage. She collected the mail, went inside, checked
the answering machine, put dinner on.
Soon Todd came home from shooting
hoops with a friend, Tim from his lab in
the Nadelfrau Hall of Science. Over
chicken cacciatore, they discussed their

upcoming road trip to Princeton, why Todd was only halfway finished with his packing, and what Diane still needed to rush out and buy before they loaded up the car. It was a conversation like so many others, written in the family short-hand of wisecracks and inside jokes, and Diane blinked away tears even as she teased and laughed, knowing it would never be this way, exactly like this, ever again.

After supper, she cleared the table and loaded the dishwasher, then went outside to pull weeds from the beds in the front yard and water the hostas. The sun was setting as a car pulled into the Callahans' driveway and disappeared into the garage. A few moments later, Mary Beth walked slowly down the driveway, platinum pageboy haircut windblown, legs stiff from hours in the car. Diane watched from the corner of her eye as her neighbor retrieved a few envelopes from the mailbox and stooped to pick up the newspapers.

"Back from vacation?" Diane called, twisting the nozzle of the garden hose to adjust the spray to a fine mist.

Mary Beth halted, arms full of sun-yellowed paper, her expression wan. "No, from taking Brent to school."

"Oh, that's right." Diane had wondered why she hadn't seen him and Will serving lunch earlier that day. "Penn State follows the same schedule as Waterford College."

Mary Beth slowly flipped through her mail. "Actually, Waterford College follows the same schedule as Penn State."

"Oh." It wasn't worth an argument. "Is Brent excited about the first week of college?"

"Not really." Mary Beth fixed her with a baleful look. "You know very well that he graduated in the top one percent of his class. He's convinced that his classes won't challenge him."

"I'm sure that won't be the case, especially once he gets all those freshman requirements out of the way."

"He won't have many of those, thanks to his AP credits. No one can take those away from him." Mary Beth tucked the bundle of paper under one arm and sighed. "I told him to seek out other ways to enrich his curriculum—research projects, independent study. After graduation, he'll be up against kids with degrees from Ivy League schools. He's going to have to work ten times harder just to compete."

"You know, Penn State is an excellent university," said Diane. "Tim does a lot of joint projects with professors in their chemistry department, and he's had nothing but praise for their facilities and faculty and the students he's met. In fact, I think he's a little jealous. And everyone knows Happy Valley is a great place to be a student. I know Penn State wasn't Brent's first choice—"

"It was his last choice." Fatigue took the edge off Mary Beth's retort. "It was his safety school. He's had his heart set on Yale since the ninth grade. I'm sure your son told you that Yale revoked Brent's acceptance because of his legal troubles."

As far as Diane knew, Brent and Todd barely spoke anymore, and only then when forced to work together at Elm Creek Manor. "Todd didn't give me any details."

"Well, now you know, so let the gloating commence."

Diane didn't have the heart for even the least offensive one-liner. "Brent's going to be fine," she said. "He'll get a great education. None of this will hold him back, not in the long run."

Mary Beth looked away, and even in the twilight Diane could see her chin trembling as she fought back tears. "I hope you're right." Suddenly she fixed Diane with a look of smoldering, helpless anger. "I want to blame you for this, but I can't. I know I can't. For weeks after it happened, at the shop—" She inhaled sharply, still incapable of admitting aloud what her son had done. "I kept thinking that if only you hadn't humiliated me at the quilt guild meeting, Brent wouldn't have lashed out. But then I have to trace the events back to an earlier source: If only I hadn't forced you to take down that skateboard ramp, you wouldn't have humiliated me at the quilt guild meeting. Then further back: the wind chimes. And before that, the guild elections. No matter how far back I search for the place where I can lay the blame at your feet, there's always some earlier cause, something I did to you to provoke it." She raised her hands in helpless frustration, scattering newspapers and mail. "It comes back to those stupid forsythia bushes. You brought over lemon squares, and I uprooted your plants. That's the source. That was the first conflict. You know what keeps me up at night?"

Diane shook her head, speechless.

"Knowing that if not for what I did in those few minutes all those years ago, Brent might be settling into a residential college at Yale right now, instead of a dorm at Penn State. My bitterness for you poisoned my child. What he did in that quilt shop he learned from me."

"You're judging yourself too harshly," said Diane, unsettled by the venomous self-loathing in Mary Beth's voice. "You talk as if Brent has no future. He has to finish his community service and he'll attend Penn State instead of Yale. Granted, that's not what he wanted and it's not what you wanted for him, but it's not the end of the road, either. He still has the whole world open to him. He could take any path, go anywhere."

"That's easy for you to say," Mary Beth snapped. "Your son's going to Princeton."

"My son didn't wantonly destroy a woman's livelihood," Diane retorted.

"Right." Mary Beth lowered her head. "It's hard to break the habit of blaming you."

Diane decided to accept that as an apology. "Brent's going to be all right. It might be hard to see that from where we stand, but he'll be all right."

"I didn't know he had that in him." Mary Beth's eyes glistened with tears. "I didn't know he could be so cruel, so destructive. But now—" She took a deep, shaky breath. "But now we know, and maybe it's not too late to root out what I planted there, every time I was vindictive to you."

"I can't let you take all the blame," said Diane, thinking, as she had only a few hours before, that if not for the fight that had led to Brent's undoing, she wouldn't be an Elm Creek Quilter. "I chose to retaliate each time. That was my decision, and it was wrong. I could have ignored you. I could have responded like an adult. I didn't. Maybe you started the conflict, but I let it escalate, and I never tried to make peace."

"It would have been pointless. I wouldn't have agreed to make peace."

"You don't know that. You might have."

Mary Beth shook her head. "I've hated you for so long I don't know how to relate to you any other way but with anger."

Somehow, although she knew how Mary Beth felt, hearing it stated so bluntly still hurt. "We don't have to be friends. All we have to do is stop being so stupid."

Mary Beth stared at her, and suddenly started to laugh. "At least ten bitingly sarcastic remarks come to mind, and yet, I can't bring myself to say them."

"I'll use my imagination," said Diane drily.

Mary Beth managed a smile, and for a moment Diane glimpsed the woman she might have known if she had not been so quick to anger, so slow to forgive.

"Just for the record, I honestly did think those forsythia bushes were on my property."

Diane sighed. "Considering the way those evergreens are aligned, I can see why you might have assumed that."

They stood in the driveway watching each other, each waiting for the other to make the next move. Suddenly Diane realized that Mary Beth had shaped the woman she was as much as the Elm Creek Quilters had. She had allowed her worst enemy to define her for far too long.

She was tired of having an enemy.

"I honestly did love your quilt," Diane said.

Mary Beth's brow furrowed. "Which one?"

"The one that earned the Viewer's Choice ribbon at the Waterford Summer Quilt Festival a few years ago. I know it had 'Spring' in the title."

"Oh, right. 'Springtime in Waterford.'"

"That's the one. That's the quilt that inspired me to become a quilter."

Mary Beth looked skeptical. "Is that so?"

"Really." Diane hesitated. "I asked you the name of the block, but you never told me."

"Providence." Mary Beth bent down to pick up another newspaper. "It's called Providence."

"Let me help you with that," said Diane, crossing the grassy strip between her driveway and Mary Beth's, bending over to pick up an envelope that had blown her way.

What fabrics to choose for Diane, Sylvia mused, a woman who defied easy and narrow categorization? She loved short-cuts and quick fixes but made all her quilts by hand. She was an impatient student but a generous teacher. She was unfailingly loyal to friends with whom she disagreed on every conceivable political issue, and she had made a sworn enemy of a woman with whom she had much in common.

She was, perhaps, the most difficult Elm Creek Quilter to like, and Sylvia was certain no one cherished her friends more.

That was why when Sylvia made Diane's portion of the Winding Ways quilt, she chose fabrics she had used when making the other Elm Creek Quilters' blocks: silken reds with golden cranes and tortoises, whimsical children's prints in deep roses and clear blues, homespun barn reds and forest greens, tie-dyed cottons in a rainbow of hues, rich Amish solids, and a few purples, Sylvia's own favorite color. Thus all the Elm Creek Quilters came together in Diane's nine patchwork blocks, just as Diane held her friends fast and close to her heart.

Sylvia put the last stitch into her quilt, tied the knot, and snipped the thread.

Sylvia

The last week of camp always caught Sylvia by surprise, leaving her breathless with the suddenness of its approach. A few days more and Elm Creek Manor would become quiet and still, the industrious buzz of sewing machines and the ringing laughter of friends only a memory. Sylvia held off melancholy by reminding herself how busy she and Sarah would be the following week, cleaning the manor from top to bottom, preparing it for its winter slumbers. And although Judy had left and Summer was soon to depart, there were new friends to celebrate; Gretchen and Joe were settling into the manor nicely and they would provide welcome companionship in the months ahead. In January, their other new teacher, Maggie, would move into the manor, and their preparations for the next camp season would begin in earnest. In February, the manor's youngest residents would arrive on the scene in what was sure to be a whirlwind of happiness, excitement, and every blessing that new babies promised.

Sylvia would keep a light in the window and a fire on the hearth for her journeying friends, for she knew in her heart that one day the winding ways they followed would lead them back to Elm Creek Manor. She would be waiting to welcome them home.

On Thursday afternoon, Sylvia was walking past the open door of the library when she glanced inside and spotted Sarah seated at the antique oak desk, staring into an open box sitting atop a mound of crumpled brown paper wrapping.

Sarah sat so wide-eyed and still that Sylvia grew worried. "What is it, dear?" she asked, entering the library. "Not bad news in the mail, I hope."

"No," said Sarah distantly, barely moving. "Not at all."

Sylvia hastened to her side and peered into the box. Within a cloud of white tissue paper lay folded a lovely pink-and-white Sawtooth Star quilt. Beneath it, Sylvia glimpsed the edge of a second quilt, a Sawtooth Star pieced from blue-and-white prints.

Something about the quilts prodded Sylvia's memory. "Why do these quilts seem so familiar?"

Sarah withdrew both quilts from the box and draped them over the desk. "My grandmother made this quilt for my eighth birthday," she said, running her hand over the pink-and-white stars. "This one— I think this is the quilt my mother began when she came to quilt camp a few years ago."

Thinking back, Sylvia remembered Carol holding up a blue-and-white Sawtooth Star block at the Farewell Breakfast show-and-tell. Eliciting laughter from the campers and scowls from Sarah, she declared that she would like it to be the first block of a baby quilt, if only Sarah would cooperate by providing the baby. "It is the same pattern," Sylvia said carefully, uncertain of Sarah's mood. "I assume this pink quilt is the one you told me about during our quilting lessons, the one your mother kept hidden away and only let you use when your grandmother visited?"

Sarah nodded, her gaze shifting back and forth between the two quilts. "My mother used the same number of blocks as my grandmother, the same layout, everything. Well, not everything. The level of skill is obviously very different, but even so—" Sarah drew in a deep breath, her hand absently coming to rest on her abdomen. "My mom clearly took my grandmother's quilt as her model."

"There's a note," said Sylvia, indicating a white envelope tucked into the tissue paper.

Sarah opened it and withdrew a small card with Noah's ark on the front, smiling animals gathered two-by-two. She opened it, read silently first, and then spoke aloud. "Dear Sarah. Congratulations to you and Matt on this blessed news! I'm so happy for you both. I'm sure you remember the pink-and-white quilt your grandmother made. I can't remember why I insisted upon keeping it for special occasions, but at least it's still as good as new. The quilt I made is new, but not as good, but I'm hoping the babies won't mind. Please don't make my mistake and hide the quilts away like precious artifacts destined for a museum. These quilts—even my imperfect imitation of your grandmother's—were made with love and should be loved. I hope that your children will be as miraculous and wonderful to you as you were to me. I'd like to come visit soon and kiss your tummy. Please don't tell me you're too busy, because I know camp is almost over for the season. Don't be surprised if I show up unannounced anyway! I've done it before and I know you have plenty of guest rooms. Love, Mom."

Sylvia watched as Sarah studied the note in silence, then closed the card and returned it to the envelope. "When I called her to tell her I was pregnant—" Sarah paused to clear her throat. "When I gave her the news, she said that she hoped my children would be just like me. I thought she meant difficult, ungrateful, never quite good enough." Gently, Sarah stroked the quilts, first the pink and then the blue. "All these years, I've felt like a burden. Apparently I was also a blessing."

Sylvia's throat tightened, her heart aching for her young friend who should not have had to wait so long to learn how deeply she was cherished. Carol should have done so much more through the years to show Sarah how much she was loved, but Carol had her own hidden griefs and secret heartbreaks, and perhaps she had done the best she could.

Looking into her young friend's face, interpreting her tears, Sylvia knew that the quilts conveyed messages only mother and daughter fully understood, words that should have been spoken years before.

It was enough that they were spoken now.

Later that evening, as a quartet of musicians from the Waterford College music department took their seats on the ballroom dais to an enthusiastic round of applause, Sylvia saw the door open and one last latecomer dart into the room—Gwen, returning to Elm Creek Manor for the evening program later than promised. When her eyes met Sylvia's, Gwen offered an apologetic shrug and a sheepish grin, and Sylvia waved a hand and shook her head to show that it didn't matter. Gwen had promised to run the evening program, and indeed she had done the more difficult work of scheduling the musicians' appearance. All Sylvia had done was welcome them—which she would have done anyway—and read the introduction Summer patched together from information posted on the quartet's website.

After the last note faded away and the musicians bowed to the cheers of their grateful audience, Gwen made her way to Sylvia's side. "I'm so sorry I was late."

"No apologies are necessary. I didn't mind filling in. I'm sure you would have done the same for me."

"Except that you're so reliable, I'll never need to." Gwen smiled and waved to campers who greeted her in passing as they filed from the ballroom. "I meant to be here. I lost track of time."

"Research is going well, I take it?"

"Yes." Gwen brightened. "Actually, it's going very well."

"So your department chair has come around, then?"

"Oh, no. He still hates that I write about quilts and quilters, and he still thinks I'm wasting my time and talent on subjects of little or no consequence." Gwen grinned. "Thank the goddess, I have tenure. Bill can fume, but he can't fire me."

Sylvia shook her head, torn between admiration for her friend and bemusement. "And yet you press on."

Gwen's amusement vanished. "What choice do I have? If I don't ask these questions about women's history, if I don't tell these women's stories, who will? I refuse to be intimidated into re- searching topics that will make me more popular with my colleagues or bring the department more money. I have to study what intrigues me and hope that, in time, everyone else will come around."

"And if they don't?"

"I'll still know that I followed the right path." Gwen waved as Summer called out a greeting from across the ballroom. "I'm having a blast. My daughter's proud of me. Who cares what anyone else thinks?"

Summer wasn't the only one, Sylvia thought, smiling to herself as she watched Gwen hurry off to embrace her daughter.

On Friday morning, Sylvia rose early to meet Matt in the apple orchard before breakfast to discuss the upcoming harvest of the early fall varieties. They strolled through the neat rows of trees, the fragrance of apples sweet and heavy in the warm summer air, and Matt updated her on his experiments with organic farming and his plans for expansion the next season. Sylvia congratulated him on a job well done and told him to proceed as he wished. Matt had nurtured the orchard from near ruin to abundance, and Sylvia had no intention of interfering in what was obviously working well.

As Sylvia returned to the manor for breakfast, she overheard an impassioned discussion in an adjacent row of trees. "I *did* think about what you said." It was Summer, her voice strained with barely contained exasperation. "If you were able to visit more often, I wouldn't need roommates. I'm sorry, but I can't choose an apartment based upon your needs during your rare visits."

"They don't have to be rare visits." Jeremy's voice, low and earnest. "I can come more often."

"No, you can't, Jeremy, not enough to justify the isolation."

At that moment, Sylvia came upon the row of trees where the young couple argued. She tried to steal quietly past, but her arm rustled a low branch and they both looked her way. Sylvia greeted them pleasantly, pretending she had not overheard their disagreement.

"I have to go," said Jeremy, managing a halfhearted smile for Sylvia in passing. His back to her, Summer lifted her hands and let them fall, shaking her head in frustration. Clearly, from her point of view, the discussion was far from over.

"Is everything all right?" Sylvia asked when Jeremy was out of earshot.

"How much did you hear?"

"Enough to gather that you've chosen an apartment, and that Jeremy isn't terribly pleased with your choice."

"It's not up to him. He doesn't have to live there." Summer clasped a hand to her brow and smoothed her long auburn hair away from her face. "I can't choose an apartment based upon what's best for us as a couple when we're going to be together so rarely. I have to choose what's best for me, and what's best for me is to have roommates. How can I go from living among friends at Elm Creek Manor to living alone? I'd feel like a monk in a cell."

Sylvia nodded. "I'm surprised Jeremy doesn't understand that."

"He does understand, but he's reading so much more into it. I don't consider us less of a couple just because I'm making this decision alone. I mean, what about when it's his turn to decide? After he finishes his dissertation and graduates, I wouldn't ask him to choose a faculty position based upon me."

"Perhaps he wishes you would."

Summer started to speak, but then she looked past Sylvia in the direction Jeremy had taken and shook her head, frowning. "I hope he doesn't."

Sylvia put her arm around the younger woman, thinking that one of the young people was bound to be disappointed. Perhaps Jeremy was not reading into Summer's decision after all. Perhaps he was only seeing clearly

what Summer was determined to ignore.

After breakfast, Sylvia met Sarah in the
library to go over the last invoices of the
season. They were nearly finished when
Agnes bustled in and asked to use the
phone. Sylvia couldn't help noticing that
Agnes never spoke a word throughout
the call, but only listened and occasionally pressed buttons on the keypad.

"That was a rather one-sided conversation," Sarah remarked after Agnes
hung up, apparently less concerned
than Sylvia about the impropriety of
eavesdropping.

"It was only my answering machine,"
said Agnes. "Diane taught me how to
check my messages when I'm not at
home. Did you know all you have to do
is type in a code?"

"The wonders of modern technology,"
said Sarah with a straight face.

"And by that you mean I'm several
decades behind the times," said Agnes,

smiling. "Yes, dear, I know. You needn't tease. Just for that, I'm not going to tell you my big news."

"Wait," Sarah called after Agnes as she darted from the library. "What big news?"

"You'll have to ask Bonnie later," Agnes sang, waving her fingers at them over her shoulder.

"Bonnie." Sarah gasped. "That furniture sale. It was this morning, wasn't it? Agnes has been waiting to hear the final amount from her guy in New York."

For a moment, Sylvia and Sarah stared at each other, calculating what grand total would be sufficient to put that spring in Agnes's step. Then they bolted from their chairs and hurried after her.

From the top of the grand oak staircase, Sylvia spotted Agnes speaking with Bonnie near the entrance to the banquet hall. Bonnie stepped backward, stunned and wide-eyed, and raised a hand to her forehead. As Sylvia hurried down-stairs, Sarah at her heels, Agnes took Bonnie by the arm and guided her into the banquet hall. By the time Sylvia and Sarah caught up with them, Bonnie was seated in a chair, eyes fixed straight ahead but unseeing. Agnes was pouring ice water from a pitcher into a glass.

"With the money from the insurance," Bonnie murmured, "that's almost eight hundred thousand dollars."

Agnes closed her fingers around the glass. "Have a drink, honey."

"Did she say what I think she just said?" said Sarah. "Eight hundred thou-sand?"

Agnes beamed at her and Sylvia, pat-ting Bonnie comfortingly on the shoul-der. "You heard right. I'm afraid the news was a little shocking for our friend."

"There's a proper order to these things," Sylvia remarked. "You should have asked her to sit first, and then an-nounced the news."

"I'm all right." Bonnie gulped water. "Really. My knees just went a bit wobbly for a moment." She gasped and glanced at her watch. "My workshop starts in five minutes."

"Take a moment," Sylvia ordered. Bonnie shouldn't stand in front of a classroom, or anywhere else for that matter, in her dazed condition. "Your students will be patient."

"I can't believe this." Bonnie shook her head slowly. "Craig was hiding a fortune from me. All those vacations we skipped because he said we couldn't afford it. We could have bought a reliable car. We could have— He could have saved Grandma's Attic."

"You can save it yourself, now," said Sylvia. "Whether you hang your sign here in the manor or someplace downtown, you can have your own quilt shop again, if that's what you want."

"That's the question, though, isn't it?" Bonnie sipped her water, lost in thought. "I loved Grandma's Attic, but it's gone. I can't save it, only resurrect it, and a new shop couldn't duplicate all that Grandma's Attic meant to me." Bonnie rose and smiled wistfully at her friends.

"I think I need to move forward, not back, but I'll need some time to decide. I need to get away and clear my head. I can't make the decisions I need to make so close to everything I've lost."

With a sudden pang of worry, Sylvia said, "You aren't thinking of following Summer or Judy's example, are you?"

Bonnie shook her head. "I can't imagine leaving Elm Creek Quilts for good. It's all I have."

"Not all," said Agnes. "You have your children and grandchildren. And you have us."

"Believe me, I wouldn't have made it through the past year if not for that." Bonnie gestured to the door. "I have a classroom full of students waiting. I have to go."

Bonnie left the ballroom, head held high. For a moment Sylvia glimpsed in her proud carriage the woman from the sepia-toned photograph Bonnie had once displayed so proudly on her desk in the office of the quilt shop.

Saturday morning found Sylvia and Sarah in the kitchen helping Anna prepare the last Farewell Breakfast of the season. The departure of Brent and Will for college had left them short staffed, but Sylvia had not expected to feel the loss of their reluctant conscripts so sharply. Apparently they had worked harder than any of the Elm Creek Quilters had realized, which Sylvia found encouraging. Perhaps in their own way, the young men had learned a lesson and had sincerely tried to pay their debt to Bonnie. She had been kinder to the young men than any other member of the staff. If the young men had any sense of shame, the worst part of their punishment would not have been bussing tables or scrubbing out trash cans, but getting to know the very real woman they had harmed. They might have felt the pangs of conscience less had she been angry or vengeful, but instead they would be forced to face what their actions had cost a good woman.

Just as Anna directed Sylvia and Sarah to carry the serving dishes outside, Diane appeared in the doorway and beckoned to Sylvia. "Can we talk?"

"Just for a moment." Sylvia started to remove her apron, but on second thought, she snatched another one from the hook beside the pantry and tossed it to Diane. "We can chat while we work."

Quickly Diane tied it on, and as Sylvia picked up two baskets of croissants, Diane pulled on two oven mitts and hefted a stainless-steel tray full of miniature Denver omelets. "I invited a few guests to breakfast," she said, following Sylvia down the hall to the cornerstone patio exit. "Was that all right?"

"That's fine, as long as we have enough food to feed everyone. When you say you invited a few guests, do you mean three or thirty?"

"Two, actually."

"That's no trouble at all, then." Sylvia thanked a camper who held the door open so they could step outside onto the cornerstone patio. Insects droned in warm, heavy air that promised a humid day to come, but their guests, soon to depart, would miss the worst of it. Matt, Andrew, and Joe had set up the tables and chairs on the gray stone patio, and with the help of a few campers, Summer was draping each table with a tablecloth. "What's the occasion?" Sylvia asked Diane. "Family visiting from out of town?"

"No, it's more like a summit meeting kind of thing."

Sylvia set the croissants on the buffet table and gave the scene a nod of approval before turning a wary eye upon Diane. "And that inscrutable description, when translated into plain English, would mean . . . ?"

Diane hesitated, grimaced, and set down her tray. "Maybe I should just introduce you."

"We don't have time for games," Sylvia protested as Diane yanked off the oven mitts, linked her arm through Sylvia's, and led her around the north side of the manor to the parking lot out back. On the back steps, conversing in hushed voices, stood three women: Agnes; Diane's troublesome neighbor, Mary Beth; and Nancy, the new president of the Waterford Quilting Guild, whom Sylvia recognized from her stay at quilt camp a few weeks earlier. Surreptitiously, Agnes shot Sylvia a look clearly conveying that although she had carpooled with Diane, she'd had no part in arranging this unexpected gathering of adversaries.

"Welcome to Elm Creek Manor," Sylvia greeted them, thrilled to find them chatting pleasantly rather than tearing one another's hair out. "Breakfast is almost ready on the cornerstone patio, if you'd like to follow me."

"Sylvia?" said Mary Beth when Sylvia started to lead them back the way she had come. "If you don't mind, could we go through the manor? I've never seen it and I'm dying of curiosity."

"It's shorter to go around the side yard," objected Diane, but as if determined to be agreeable, she quickly added, "but we have time for the scenic route. Why not?"

"Very well, then." Sylvia gestured up the stairs to the back door. "Please, go right inside. You can say hello to our new chef, Anna, in the kitchen to the left. We'll pass through the original wing of the building, built by my great-grand-

parents in 1858. The exit to the cornerstone patio was once the front door, but
when my grandfather added the new
wing, he changed the front entrance to
the eastern exposure to take advantage
of the morning light."

As the most unlikely tour group in the
history of Elm Creek Manor followed her
down the hallway, Sylvia promised Mary
Beth a longer tour another day.

Her heart rejoiced when both Mary
Beth and Nancy nodded, as if they too
expected this to be the first of many visits to Elm Creek Manor.

Before long, all of the campers had
gathered on the cornerstone patio for
breakfast, their mood subdued and nos-
talgic. Sylvia could read the thoughts on
their faces: They missed their families
back home, but Elm Creek Quilt Camp
had fulfilled their fondest wishes and exceeded every expectation, and they
couldn't bear to see the week end. They
were surely wondering whether they

would ever enjoy another time such as this, another week full of perfect moments. Sylvia hoped they understood that they could return next year, and every year thereafter, to find inspiration and respite within the strong, gray stone walls of Elm Creek Manor.

After another of Anna's sublimely delicious breakfasts, the campers gathered in a circle for show-and-tell. Each quilter displayed something she had made that week and shared her favorite memory of Elm Creek Manor, often referring to the hopes expressed at the Candlelight welcoming ceremony and how they had been fulfilled, or not. Even the newest quilters proudly displayed their simple pieced blocks or partially assembled tops and received ample praise and encouragement. But it was the stories each quilter shared of the moments she would cherish when the summer sunshine was but a memory that sent the campers into gales of laughter and sometimes made them blink away tears. The Elm Creek Quilters, founders and newcomers alike, looked on proudly from outside the circle, honored by the guiding roles they had played in each quilter's journey.

To Sylvia's surprise and delight, Mary Beth spoke up after the last camper showed off a beautiful Rosebud quilt top. "I haven't shared this week with you, but I can see in your eyes that you had a wonderful, glorious time," she said, then she smiled and wagged a finger at them. "My son has been cleaning up after quilters just like you all summer long, and oh, the stories he could tell the folks back home about what you've been up to." Everyone laughed. "The folks back home wouldn't believe you, though, would they? They wouldn't understand how restful it is to be among people who understand your passion for quilting, who understand that the bonds that unite us are so much stronger than the dozens of petty differences that divide us." She glanced at Diane and Nancy before looking around the circle. "I hope someday to learn what you've learned."

Everyone murmured gentle encouragement, though they were unaware of the long story of Mary Beth and Diane's feud and her more recent estrangement from the Waterford Quilting Guild, and thus they had no idea what had prompted Mary Beth to speak. Then a hush fell over the circle, and someone sighed. Every quilter had taken her turn to share her handiwork and her memories. The week of camp was over. Another season had come to a close.

As the Elm Creek Quilters cleared away the dishes and tidied the cornerstone patio, the campers returned to their suites to finish packing and bid their newfound friends sad good-byes. They carried suitcases and tote bags downstairs, Sarah collected room keys, and Matt loaded luggage into the Elm Creek Quilts minivan for the first shuttle ride to the bus station and airport. Mary Beth and Nancy departed together, after promising to call Sylvia soon to arrange a guided tour of the manor. Gradually the upstairs halls fell silent, the back parking lot emptied. The Elm Creek Quilters collected linens, emptied trash, discovered forgotten items under beds or in drawers. They broke for a simple lunch of salads and sandwiches, which they enjoyed in the shade of the veranda, reminiscing about the season past, sharing odd or amusing stories about their favorite campers and unexpected classroom mishaps. Afterward, they resumed their work for another two hours until Sylvia decided that they had accomplished the most necessary tasks. Since they did not need to prepare for a new group of campers right away, the rest of the work could wait until Monday.

The other Elm Creek Quilters agreed, and so they returned cleaning supplies to storage closets, washed the dust and sweat from their hands and faces, and congratulated one another on another successful year. One by one they made their way downstairs to the kitchen for lemonade and iced tea, where they lingered, reluctant to part.

"Before you go," Sylvia said, "I have something to show you upstairs in the library." When Summer let out an involuntary groan, she added, "Never fear, Summer. I've obeyed your wishes. I promise you, there's no surprise farewell party waiting for you upstairs."

Summer sighed, obviously relieved. "You had your party a few years ago, remember, kiddo?" Gwen teased.

Gretchen, who had not been among them in those days, said, "A few years ago? Wasn't that a bit premature?"

The others laughed, and as Gwen and Summer talked over each other in their urgency to explain, Sylvia thought of all the Elm Creek Quilts history Gretchen and Anna—and Maggie, come January—would need to learn over time.

Then, suddenly, her heart cinched.

She had forgotten the newcomers. As she had pieced and pinned and sewed all summer long, she had thought only of the founding Elm Creek Quilters and not of the newest members of their circle.

It was too late to take back her cryptic announcement that a surprise awaited them upstairs, and her friends were too curious to forget. What could Sylvia do but lead them upstairs to the library? There she urged them to seat themselves, hoping they wouldn't notice the nine hanging quilt rods Andrew had installed in three rows of three on the southern wall to the right of the fire-place, or her own section of the quilt, hidden beneath the desk.

"I'll be right back," she promised, and hurried off to her suite for the seven gift bags tied with raffia bows she had pre-pared earlier that day for her friends. What could she do? She couldn't bear the thought of Gretchen and Anna look-ing on politely, excluded while the oth-ers were honored.

Quickly she put the eighth section into an extra gift bag and hoped that her explanation would be enough to spare her new friends' feelings.

Her friends' animated speculation broke off as Sylvia returned to the li-brary, her arms through the loops of the gift bags. They exclaimed in wonder as she distributed the bags and admon-ished them not to peek until everyone had theirs. To Anna and Gretchen, she explained, "This is for both of you, and for Maggie, and for anyone else who fol-lows." They nodded in puzzlement but seemed as pleased by the unexpected gift as the others.

At last, Sylvia announced that they

could open their bags, and the library rang with exclamations of surprise and delight as each of her friends discovered a nine-block Winding Ways quilt, identical in arrangement and size, differing only in the fabrics chosen to reflect their individual styles or interests or personalities.

"Winding Ways," mused Gretchen, admiring her tie-dye and floral quilt. "An appropriate and evocative choice, Sylvia, considering the block name and the secondary pattern of overlapping circles it creates. When I think of all the different paths I could have followed in my life, all the twists and turns that could have led me anywhere, it's something of a miracle that I ended up here, surrounded by loving friends."

"It's a miracle for all of us," said Bonnie. "I only wish I knew where my winding way is going to lead me."

"If you knew your destination, you might be tempted to take a shortcut, and then you'd miss all the beautiful scenery on the way," Diane pointed out.

Bonnie smiled, admiring her quilt top, racing a circle created by homespun wedges and arcs and curves. "I suppose you're right."

"There's more," Sylvia said, taking her own nine-block section from its hiding place and beckoning her friends to join her at the southern end of the library. In the center was the fireplace; to the left hung the Castle Wall memorial quilt Agnes and Claudia had begun so many years before; Sylvia's newest creation would have a place of honor on the right. Demonstrating with her own quilt, which favored jewel-toned purples, greens, and golds, Sylvia instructed her friends to hang their quilts from one of the rods, placing her own in the upper left corner and Gretchen and Anna's in the center. The lower right corner remained empty, a place for Judy's quilt, still in its gift bag.

When eight sections of the quilt were at last properly aligned on the wall, the Elm Creek Quilters stepped back to take in the display. An electric murmur passed through them as they admired the mosaic of overlapping circles and intertwining curves, the careful balance of dark and light hues, the unexpected harmony of the disparate fabrics and colors. Together the separate quilts created a wondrous design, many winding paths meeting, intersecting, parting; concentric circles like ripples from a stone cast into a pond, overlapping, including, uniting. Sylvia had ingeniously quilted the different sections so that the meticulous stitches seemed to flow from one section into the next, drawing them together, creating the illusion that they composed a single quilt. Gazing upon Sylvia's creation, each woman could now see that her individual section was beautiful in and of itself—but was also part of a larger, more magnificent whole, a single quilt harmonizing their differences, embracing all that made each of them uniquely themselves.

Only the lower right corner remained empty. When her friends looked to her for understanding, Sylvia gestured to a single gift bag that remained on the floor beside her desk.

Judy's quilt.

"The Winding Ways quilt will remind us of friends who have left our circle to journey far away." Slipping the hanging rod from the sleeve, Sylvia removed Summer's portion from the wall and returned it to her. "When one of our circle must leave us, she'll take her section of the quilt with her as a reminder of the loving friends awaiting her return. The empty places on the wall will remind those of us left behind that the beauty of our friendship endures, even if great distances separate us. When the absent friend returns to Elm Creek Manor, she will hang her quilt in its proper space, and the loveliness of the whole will be restored."

Summer held her quilt lovingly, her eyes bright with unshed tears. "I'm not leaving for a few more weeks. Can't I leave my quilt on the wall until then?"

Laughing, Sylvia assured her that she could, and as Summer returned her quilt to its proper place, Sylvia turned to Anna and Gretchen. "I have a confession to make. When I envisioned this quilt, I thought only of the founding members and not of those who would join our circle later."

"That's perfectly understandable,"

Gretchen said, and Anna nodded. "This quilt honors the founders of Elm Creek Quilts. We're Elm Creek Quilters now, but we'll never be founding members. That's all right."

"And yet you shouldn't be excluded." Sylvia nodded to their gift, the section in the center of the large quilt. "This section is for you, and for Maggie, and for every new Elm Creek Quilter that may join us. This way, as long as Elm Creek Quilts endures, no matter what becomes of the founding members, this section at the heart of the quilt will remain."

Anna blinked away tears. "Thank you, Sylvia."

As the others chimed in their gratitude, embracing her, Bonnie bit her lip and gazed at the lone gift bag by the desk. "I wish Judy could have been here for this."

"Someone will just have to explain it to her," said Diane with a shrug. "Summer's a good writer. She can type up what Sylvia said and include it in the package when you send her her section of the quilt."

"No," said Gwen. "I have a better idea."

A shriek of laughter outside distracted Judy's attention from unpacking a box of cookware. She glanced out the kitchen window and spied Emily and Hannah riding their bikes in the long, tree-lined driveway, trying to balance on the wavy, winding chalk line Caroline had drawn. The three girls had been inseparable ever since the family had moved into the three-story Queen Anne home, and Judy had promised Emily she could invite her new friends to spend the night the following Friday to celebrate the first week of school. Emily and Caroline would be in the same third-grade class, thanks to an understanding principal who agreed that Emily would make a smoother transition to her new school if she shared a classroom with a familiar friend.

Judy had felt the same way on her first day at Penn. Rick was eccentric but they had been friends since graduate school, and walking into the lab that first day had been easier knowing he waited inside to show her around and introduce her to her new colleagues. Steve, who had never known a moment's shyness, spent his morning on the job meeting everyone in the *Philadelphia Inquirer* newsroom and had already signed up for the company soccer league. Judy smiled to herself as she bent down to shove a pair of muffin tins to the back of a low cupboard. Every day brought a fresh confirmation that they had made the right choice. Gradually but surely, they were beginning to feel at home.

"Car," Judy heard one of the girls call out to the others, followed by squeals of excitement and exaggerated danger as they scrambled out of the way. Over the tinny clanks of cookware, Judy heard a car slowly pulling up the driveway, an engine shutting down, a door opening and slamming shut. Rising, she tucked a loose strand of hair into her ponytail, dusted off her hands, and glanced out the window. At the sight of Gwen coming up the front walk carrying a bag with a raffia bow, she gasped and hurried to the front door.

She yanked it open before Gwen had a chance to ring the bell. "What are you doing here?" she cried, stepping out onto the front porch and flinging her arms around her friend without waiting for a reply.

Gwen's eyes shone with unshed tears. "Would you believe I came to help you unpack your fabric stash?"

"Sure," said Judy, smiling, "and I bet my best batiks will somehow end up in your car instead of my sewing room."

"Special delivery." Gwen's smile trembled as she handed Judy the gift bag. "This is from Sylvia. She said to tell you she's sorry she didn't finish it before your farewell party. There's also a story behind it, which I'll share after you open it."

"Sylvia's gifts always have stories behind them," said Judy, sneaking a peek into the folds of the tissue paper. "This must be quite a story to warrant such a long drive."

"That's not the only reason I came,"

said Gwen. "I'm sorry I missed your party. I should have been there to say good-bye and to tell you how much I'm going to miss you."

Judy's voice caught in her throat. "I'm going to miss you, too."

"Good-bye, Judy."

"Good-bye, Gwen."

The three little girls looked on curiously as Gwen and Judy embraced each other, laughing, wiping away tears. "Are they happy or sad?" Caroline asked.

"Both," said Emily. She hopped on her bike and led her new best friends on a winding way down the shady driveway, following the twists and turns and zigzags of a chalk line that would disappear with the next rain.

Dove in the Window

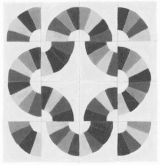

Baby Bunting

Rail Fence

Winding Ways

Providence

Pineapple